A not quite Perfect Family

Claire Sandy

PAN BOOKS

First published 2017 by Pan Books
an imprint of Pan Macmillan
20 New Wharf Road, London N1 9RR
Associated companies throughout the world
www.panmacmillan.com

ISBN 978-1-5098-3128-9

1 3 5 7 9 8 6 4 2

A CIP catalogue record for this book is available from the British Library.

Typeset in Sabon LT Std 10.75/14.5 pt by
Palimpsest Book Production Limited, Falkirk, Stirlingshire

Printed and bound by CPI Group (UK) Ltd, Croydon, CR0 4YY

Visit www.panmacmillan.com to read more about all our books
and to buy them. You will also find features, author interviews and
news of any author events, and you can sign up for e-newsletters
so that you're always first to hear about our new releases.

A not quite Perfect Family

Claire Sandy lives in Surrey with her husband, her daughter and their dogs. Before she wrote books, she made radio jingles and sold wool (not at the same time). Now she has her dream job as a novelist, having already written *What Would Mary Berry Do?*, *A Very Big House in the Country* and *Snowed in for Christmas*.

Also by Claire Sandy

What Would Mary Berry Do?
A Very Big House in the Country
Snowed in for Christmas

This book is for Michael and Alison Anderson

We went here for
me & Adam's anniversary!!!

La Boite Rouge:

fine dining since 1926

delicious nibbles

1. Hors d'oeuvres

amazing soup → 2. Potage

3. Poisson ← *fish*

meat ↘ 4. Entrée

5. Sorbet ← *to cleanse the palate!*

pièce de résistance! ↘ 6. Relevé

7. Salade   *just salad . . .*

vegetables but not
as we know them ↘ 8. Légumes

dessert -
9. Entremet *chocolatey & divine*

cheese, 10. Savoureux *savoury toast (?!)*

LOTS of cheese ↘ 11. Fromage

12. Café
coffee

CHAPTER ONE

June: Hors d'oeuvres

Fern Carlile was a woman who lived from meal to meal, already fantasizing about dinner as she washed up her lunch plate, but the annual Midsummer supper in the garden was her favourite meal of the whole year. Lanterns in the trees, a blushing dusk supplying the flattering light a lady needs, and the soft *boom*, *crash* of next door's nightly vicious argument. A lifetime Londoner, Fern knew better than to expect birdsong; her summer soundtrack was fox orgies and bin lorries.

Her family's raised eyebrows couldn't dent the simple happiness Fern felt laying out nibbles on pretty mismatched plates.

'Quails' eggs? Seriously?' Adam looked askance at the tiny ovals. 'What happened to the usual breadsticks and own-brand hummus?' He looked deflated; he was highly attached to own-brand hummus.

'I'm recreating our meal at La Boite Rouge.' It had been a high point of her year, so Fern pouted when he looked vacant. 'You can't have forgotten! We had that incredible dinner for our anniversary?'

1

'Oh. Yeah. All those weird courses.' Adam patted his tummy, as if it was a skittish pet. 'I had raging squits all the next day.'

Fern, not for the first time, wondered why she bothered. She'd been blown away by the attention to detail at the famous old-style French restaurant as plate after plate of delicious grub was brought to their table. When the waiter heard that they were celebrating their anniversary, he'd brought them a glass of scented, sweet dessert wine 'on the 'ouse'; he wasn't to know it wasn't their wedding anniversary, but a celebration of the night Fern and Adam had first made love.

She paused for a moment, a dish of stuffed figs in mid-air, and remembered the single bed in Adam's digs. It squeaked. *And so did I!* Fern watched Adam lug chairs over the pot-holed lawn. If she squinted she could still see the lean, keen young stud inside the outline of the forty-three-year-old dad.

'Where's that pretty platter with the gold rim?' she asked him.

'Do I look like the kind of person who could answer that question?' Adam was out of breath; the chairs Fern insisted on for this feast were cast iron, and took some lugging.

'I s'pose not.' Fern let him off the hook. 'Sometimes I forget you're not a girl.' She left him frowning at her receding back as she hurried back to the house, taking off her shoes as she did so. Lawns and heels don't mix.

Down in the cellar, the platter sat alongside piles of similar charity-shop crockery which was either dead people's junk or bargainous treasure, depending on whether you agreed with Adam or Fern. Moving items to get at the platter, Fern put her hand on a dusty box, patterned with faded flowers and tied with mouldering ribbon.

Recognition made her pause. 'Bloody hell,' she whispered to it. 'Fancy meeting you here.'

Outside once again, she placed the platter just so on the table, which sat happily in their shambles of a garden as if it had grown there. Everything that Fern owned was slightly wonky – she included Adam in this analysis. The lawn sloped. The ancient conservatory leaned. The roof of the rambling, vaguely Gothic house undulated as if it was breathing. *Roof next*, she promised herself. The house was a never-ending project, a mountain of DIY.

Inheriting the multi-windowed, red brick Homestead House in her twenties had transformed Fern's life. She'd been as round as a small planet, pregnant with their son, when she and Adam first looked round the big old house. The creaky floorboards and the resolutely unmodernized bathrooms and the cracked stained glass had saved their bacon, allowing them to move out of their dismal rented room. From then on, the young couple lived mortgage-free while their friends sold their souls for a toehold on the bonkers London property ladder. Homestead House had enfolded them in its warm Edwardian embrace of brick and tile, offering them more rooms than they could fill, and a garden like a green bowl of sunshine.

Standing back to appraise her handiwork, Fern accepted that the table setting didn't look much like the picture in the magazine, but it was pretty and she was starving, so it was time to yell, 'Kids! C'mon!'

'Are there chips?' shouted Tallulah hopefully as she vaulted down the crumbling steps, Boudicca their rescue whippet at her heels. She was never far from Tallulah; eight-year-olds tend to spill food, and food spillers are dogs' favourite people. 'Please God let there be chips.'

'There are chips,' said Fern gravely. Michelin star pretensions were all very well, but nobody in their right mind would get between Tallulah and a hot chip. 'And before you ask, there's ketchup too.'

'Where *is* everybody?' Ollie turned a slatted chair the wrong way round and sat astride it. It seemed to be a teenage badge of honour never to just *sit* on a chair. 'There's usually a big crowd for Midsummer Night.'

'I thought it'd be nice to have just us this year.' Fern avoided Adam's eye. Infamously ready to throw a party for the lamest of reasons – the dog not weeing in the utility room, or a month with a vowel in it – Fern had kept this Midsummer a strictly family affair. Today was the day they'd tell the kids their news. 'So we can, you know, really talk for a change.'

'We're always talking, Mummy,' said Tallulah.

'*You're* always talking, you mean,' said Ollie.

'Hey, now, be nice.' Adam waved a stick of celery as he took his seat. 'Mum's gone to a lot of trouble over this meal.' He winked at Fern.

Fern winked back.

'Urgh!' said Tallulah, who cringed at any proof that her parents might own functioning genitals.

4

'Quiche?' Ollie's lip curled as he peered from beneath the black quiff of hair that hovered over his brow like a glossy bird's wing. 'For real?'

'I'm not sure about posh food,' murmured Tallulah.

'Ollie, you like quiche.' Fern knew it was ridiculous to tell people what they liked, but Ollie *did* like quiche. Just recently, he'd eaten his own weight in it.

'Ollie,' said Adam in a warning way. 'There's plenty of other food. Just choose something else. I can't stand quails' eggs but you don't hear me saying so.'

'Except you just did,' said Fern.

'Oops,' said Adam.

'Mmm, the quiche is *yummy*,' said Tallulah with a sideways look at her brother, who failed to rise to the bait.

Skirmishes between the seventeen-year-old and his little sister had tapered off over the summer. Ollie had shrunk, retreating into himself. Adam put it down to the rigours of sixth-form mock exams, but Fern knew how much Ollie missed Donna.

His first girlfriend worthy of the title, Donna had been a constant at their dinner table until a couple of months ago when she'd inexplicably stopped appearing. According to Tallulah, there was another chap in the mix, somebody called Maz. Solid, clever Ollie, a boy who managed to combine common sense and cool, had confided in nobody, but Fern knew tears had been shed up in his turret bedroom.

'I propose a toast!' Adam stood up, brandishing his glass. For a moment, Fern thought he was pre-empting her with their news, but instead he shouted 'To *Roomies*!'

'*Roomies*!' echoed the others, raising their squash, Coke,

and the wine Fern had chosen for the label but which tasted like meths.

'My dad's the coolest dad in the class 'cos of *Roomies*,' said Tallulah complacently, helping herself to some char-grilled halloumi, a cheese she'd never met before.

'I like to think I was *always* the coolest dad.' Adam pulled a mournful face.

'Just 'cos you like to think it doesn't make it true, Dad.' Ollie crammed his face urgently with carbs and protein as if he had a train to catch.

'Oi, you! When I was in my twenties my band was the bee's knees.' Adam squared his broad shoulders, tossed the thick brown hair peppered with grey that always needed a cut, and sat up straighter, presenting his profile with mock vanity. 'The first time Mum ever laid eyes on me I was setting the stage on fire at a nightclub.'

Tallulah looked concerned and Fern knew she'd have to explain later about metaphors; *Daddy's not an actual arsonist, darling.*

'Yeah, yeah, we know.' Ollie made sure Adam knew just how unimpressed he was. 'You could've been a pop star, et cetera et cetera.'

'You're better than a pop star.' Tallulah was a veteran daddy-pleaser.

Fern guessed at the scenes spooling in Adam's head, snapshots of the far-off summer when he and the rest of Kinky Mimi had clubbed together to buy a knackered Ford Transit for their European tour. She recalled his face when she'd shown him the little stick with its life-changing blue stripe. Pregnancies, especially accidental ones, have a way of speeding life up; in a trice, the van was sold, Kinky Mimi were history, and magically, providentially, Fern inherited this house. She saw Adam's eyes linger on Ollie and supplied the subtitles: *eighteen years ago you were the cluster of cells who put paid to my career and now you're sitting there, all five foot ten, eleven stone of you, laughing at me.*

'When does the new series of *Roomies* start?' Fern knew, but wanted to give Adam his moment. The transition from rock god to writing advertising jingles had been hard; he deserved this late burst of glamour.

'Fourth of September.' Adam burst into song, and Tallulah joined in.

> *Sometimes stuff just seems to get you down*
> *Feelin' like there's no one else around*
> *You wish you could reach out and find a friend*
> *Who'll be here today, tomorrow, until the bitter end*

Written twenty years ago, Adam's cheerful melody had lain in a drawer until he dug it out and filmed himself singing it at the piano. Meant as a bit of fun for commercial producers browsing his jingle website, the song had somehow reached the ears of a Hollywood creative. One phone call later and the song was re-recorded as the theme song for a hot new project: *Roomies*. Like *Friends* – which it shamelessly ripped off – *Roomies* took over the known world, breaking viewing records and making superstars of its cast.

As the writer of the theme, Adam was famous. Sort of. In a not-really-famous-unless-you-bother-to-read-the-credits-right-through-to-the-end way. He tried to pretend it was no biggie, but Fern knew it was a hugie.

Fern joined in with the spirited, jangling chorus.

> *Roomies – we're always there*
> *Roomies – we always care*
> *Your mates are here to stay*
> *And your life's a holiday*
> *With Rooooooooomies!*

They sat back, exhausted from the big finish; Tallie always stretched out that last 'Roomies' as long as she could. It was a sunny song that never failed to uplift them; now millions of people around the world hummed it and felt uplifted too.

'Did you hear about Lincoln Speed's latest?' scoffed Ollie.

The star of *Roomies*, Lincoln Speed was a film actor who'd found a second wind on TV. 'Clean' at last from various bad habits, he wasn't yet over the hill but was dangerously near the summit; to his fans that made him all the more sexy and glamorous.

'What's he done now?' Adam was agog.

'He bought a monkey,' said Ollie.

'I want a monkey!' said Tallulah.

'You don't want a monkey,' said Fern, who'd overseen the lonely deaths of hamsters and fish and stick insects abandoned by their fickle owner. 'Even Lincoln Speed doesn't really want a monkey.'

'I'd like a *small* monkey,' insisted Tallulah, setting down a stuffed fig with a mixture of shock and sadness that such a thing could exist. 'What's that box in the kitchen? The really old one.'

'It's a box of letters.' Fern's eyes whisked towards Adam, who was pulling a morsel of something out of his back teeth. 'From Daddy to me.'

'Love letters?' Tallulah asked, as Ollie mimed hanging himself.

Elbows on the table, Fern leaned over to Adam, her face amused in the candlelight. 'They're from the Great Rift of '93. Remember?'

'Christ, yes.' Adam pushed a hand through his hair, half laughing, half in awe. 'I was nineteen and you were eighteen. Hard to believe we were ever that young.'

'Speak for yourself,' said Fern, even though she felt as if she'd been born aged forty-two with two children and a stupid dog. 'Daddy and I had been going out for a year,' she explained to Tallulah, who was listening avidly. Even Ollie was earwigging, although he took pains to look uninterested. 'And we had a row. A big one.'

'You have one of those every couple of days,' murmured Ollie.

'No we don't. Do we?'

'Go on, Mummy!' Tallulah rapped the table impatiently.

'Sorry. Yes. So, big big row. I told him he was chucked. He told me I was chucked.'

Tallulah swallowed, possibly imagining an alternative reality where she didn't exist. 'Then what?'

'Then Daddy wrote to me. Every day for eleven days.'

'I had no idea you'd kept them.' Adam played with a spoon, turning it over, smiling to himself.

'And you took him back?'

'Well, duh,' said Ollie.

'I was teaching him a lesson for looking at my best mate's legs for a millisecond too long.' Fern could feel Adam listening, his eyes on the spoon. 'There was never any doubt in my mind.'

'Muggins here didn't know that.' Adam threw his crumpled paper napkin at Fern. 'I was writing for my life.'

'It's hardly the greatest love story ever told, Dad.' Ollie shifted even lower on his chair. 'You only split up for eleven days.'

Fern thought of Donna, and longed to hug her man-shaped but still juvenile son. That wasn't allowed, so she poured him some more of the lemonade she made once or twice a year and everybody pretended to like. 'I could probably quote those letters,' she said.

'Show me! Read them out!' Tallulah, a child with very few of the traditional girly notions, who wore combat trousers and had made her mother sign a document banning pink from her bedroom, was nevertheless riveted by this evidence of her boring old parents' romantic past.

'Not now, darling. Dad and me have something to tell you.'

Adam interrupted, looking into the middle distance. 'I wrote two songs during the Rift of '93. Good songs. Music poured out of me back then.'

'I remember them,' said Fern, her tone soft to match his.

'One was called, oh, what was it?' Adam clicked his fingers. '"Love of my Life"!'

'Aww!' trilled Tallulah.

'Pass the sick bucket,' said Ollie.

'The other one,' said Fern, 'was "Psycho Bitch", if I remember rightly.'

'Oh yeah.' Adam looked sheepish. And, she thought, secretly pleased with his younger self.

'Kids, like I said, me and Dad have something to—'

Ollie flourished a piece of paper. 'Reasons Why Fern Martindale is the Best Girlfriend in the World.' He whooped and slapped the page. 'Go, Dad!'

'That's from the box!' Fern was suddenly possessive of the letter that her nosy son had pilfered. 'Give it back, Ollie. Don't muck about.'

'Reason number one.' Ollie was on his feet, twirling. 'She has the best bum in the United Kingdom.'

'Daddy!' Tallulah was shocked.

Fern was chuffed.

'Two. She listens to my rubbish.'

'Ollie!' Adam couldn't quite do stern when his mouth twitched with the need to laugh.

'Three.' Ollie jumped onto the trampoline and bounced as he shouted, 'She kisses brilliantly.'

'No!' Tallulah went scarlet.

Fern took a bow. 'What can I say?' she laughed. 'When you gottit, you gottit.'

'Four, she knows me better than anybody else.'

'That's a silly reason!' giggled Tallulah.

Fern was quiet. Adam was quiet. When she looked over at him, he was looking away. Fern suddenly remembered what number five was. 'Give me that paper, Oliver Carlile,' she said. '*Now.*'

11

Ignoring the use of his full name, Ollie's eyes widened. 'Five, she knows just how to—'

Leaping onto the trampoline, Adam rugby-tackled the boy. The list was folded up and stashed safely away. With pointed looks in Tallulah's direction, Adam said, 'Let's get back to the table, yeah?'

'I need to bleach my eyes,' muttered Ollie as he took his seat.

When the atmosphere had calmed a little, when Tallulah had stopped whining *Tell me what number five is!*, Fern said, 'Maybe now Daddy and I can make our announcement.'

The phone bleated from indoors.

'I'll get it!' Tallulah was off her seat.

'No, darling, I'll go.' Fern was firm. Tallulah was apt to answer the phone with *Good afternoon the Carlile residence how can I help you thank you please?* Galloping through the French windows, Fern located the landline beneath a dam of cushions on the sofa. 'Hello?'

The caller's identity took a moment to register. Fern's face dropped. 'Hi, Auntie Nora,' she said, scrutinizing her reflection in the mirror over the mantelpiece and wondering why none of her family had bothered to mention that her mascara had pooled, raccoon-style, beneath her eyes. Fern tried to be groomed but her body defied her; expensive dresses hung like shower curtains and make-up rearranged itself on her broad face, with its merry brown eyes and straight brush-stroke brows. Adam used to say she looked like a little girl in a storybook, with her shiny bobbed hair and her solid snub nose. *Now I'm more of an old bat in a storybook*, she thought, as Auntie Nora began the conversation with her usual niceties.

'You took your time. I almost hung up. Where were you? Timbuctoo? I thought something had happened. Not that anybody would think to tell me. You could all be dead and nobody'd bother to let me know.'

'We're all alive, I promise.' Fern kept her tone light. The quickest, simplest way to deal with her aunt was to ignore the jibes. Nora was eternally spoiling for a fight and Fern refused to give her one. 'How are you, Auntie? We must come and visit.'

This white lie – the family would rather holiday in hell than knock on Nora's front door – was pounced on with relish. 'You can't, dear. Not any more. They're knocking me house down.'

'Who are "they"?' asked Fern, alarmed.

'The government. There's one of them compulsory purchase doodahs on Mother's beautiful house. It's being knocked down to build a new road.'

The 'beautiful house' was a dimly lit bungalow, full of flammable upholstery and a very old, very farty cat, all of which Nora had shared with Fern's terrifying Nana since the dawn of time. With Nana long dead, Nora looked after the house as if it was a museum dedicated to her memory.

'Oh dear,' said Fern, adding 'That's awful.' Nora displayed so few human traits it was hard to know how to sympathize, even for somebody like Fern, who felt everybody's pain. 'Isn't there anything you can do to stop them?'

'Like what?' Nora was scornful. She was good at scorn; she and Nana had practised daily and it paid off. 'Lie down in front of the bulldozers? I'm ringing to say you can expect me on Sunday. I require an electric blanket and don't offer me decaffeinated tea, please. It does terrible things to me innards.'

'Sorry? What?' Fern felt as if she'd fallen asleep and missed the body of the dialogue. 'I don't under—'

'I've been cast out of my home, Fern. I'm homeless. I have nowhere to go. Are you saying you won't take me in?'

'I'm just saying—' Fern said very little, because Nora butted in once more.

'Is it money? Do you want money? I've only got pennies but have them, have them! If my giving up all dreams of happiness in order to look after your beloved Nana means nothing to you, then take it all.'

'Auntie! Of course I don't want your—'

'I'll go to a hotel. And get beaten to death.'

Yes, because that's how hotels work. Fern sighed. Conversations with Nora always went along these lines. The woman was a runaway shopping trolley hurtling down a hill, and it was all Fern could do to keep up. She ascertained what time to expect her wrinkled relative, made promise after promise about control of the TV remote during *Emmerdale*, silence during nap times, and fresh prawns for her antique cat. By the time Fern hung up, she had a lodger.

'Mummy!' Tallulah's shout sounded outraged as Fern trailed back to the table. 'Daddy's being sexy!'

'Really?' said Fern, incredulously.

'The word,' said Adam, 'is *sexist*. And I wasn't.'

'You were. You said I look pretty in my new T-shirt. That's sexist.' Tallulah banged the table. Passionately idealistic, she fought the good fight against the isms: racism; ageism; eight-year-old-girl-ism. Her core cause was sexism; she was the smallest, most vehement feminist in her postcode. 'You should say I look clever.'

Ollie saw his cue. 'But you don't. You look like a dork.'

'Nobody looks like a dork,' said Fern firmly, taking her seat, reaching for the salad bowl, thinking better of it, snaffling a chip. 'And aren't you a little old to trade insults with an eight-year-old?' She eyed Ollie, or tried to; it was easy for him to retreat under that overhanging hair.

'Which mocks did you have this week, Ollster?' Adam, baffled by his son's brains, was also proud of them. 'Maths, wasn't it?'

'Another "A", I suspect,' laughed Fern. 'It's so *boring* having a genius for a son.'

'I won't get an "A",' mumbled Ollie, with a 'please change the subject or I'll die of parent-based embarrassment' tone.

'I'm not saying anything,' said Tallulah. 'Nothing at all. Don't try and get it out of me, Mum.'

'All right, darling, I won't,' said Fern, amused. Then she paused. Something in Ollie's demeanour, a still watchfulness, made her ask, 'What mustn't I try and get out of you, Tallulah?'

'Stop it! I'm no snitch.' Tallulah, cheeks hot, glared at the tablecloth.

'Tallie?' Adam was gentle.

'Thanks, Tallulah,' spat Ollie. 'Thanks a million.'

Tallulah burst into tears. Not big on crying, when it happened it was spectacular. With those abrupt about-turns

15

typical of her age group, she morphed from militant to clingy. Scrambling onto Fern's lap, she burrowed into her mum's chest, reciting a muffled mantra of 'Sorry sorry sorry.'

'Ollie.' Fern dusted off her special calm-yet-stern voice. 'What's going on?'

'Look, God, shut up.' Ollie flailed around, trying hard to be affronted, before giving in and saying, all on one breath, 'I've left sixth form, OK?'

Fern and Adam gawped at each other. It took a few seconds for the words to sink in, then Adam was on his feet, Fern was reaching for the wine, and Tallulah was shrieking, 'You told them! I didn't! S'not my fault!'

'That's impossible.' Adam loomed over his son, his face contorted with the effort of understanding. 'You leave the house every morning in that horrible drip-dry suit and—'

'And I don't go to sixth form, OK? Jesus,' shrugged Ollie.

'That's it? That's all we get, a shrug?'

Fern flashed a warning at Adam. Anger would make Ollie retreat, turtle-like, back into his shell. 'Ollie, darling, we need an explanation. You see that, surely?'

'Don't do the whole *tolerant mum* bit.' Ollie didn't have to look at his mother to know his comment had stung. 'Why's it such a big deal? It's my life. I have a plan. Calm down.'

No amount of coaxing could prise this 'plan' from Ollie. 'I know what I'm doing,' he repeated. 'Don't hassle me. I'm not a child.'

He had never looked more like a child, but his parents beat a tactical retreat.

'Pavlova!' Fern stood up with a flourish, drawing a meringue line under the problem. For now.

'What sort?' Tallulah reserved judgement until she heard the answer and then flipped out, kissing the dog's narrow snout with joy. 'Strawberries, Boudicca! Strawberries!'

Over the gory red and white remains of the once-majestic pav, Fern sat back, her stomach groaning, the waistband of her jeans begging for mercy. This was the point at every midsummer meal when she and Adam would open a bottle of something halfway decent beneath the lanterns. They'd watch the children mooch away: Ollie to his room and his Spotify account, Tallulah to her small army of soft toys. And they'd move closer together, get a little drunk, get a little soppy.

Tonight, though, she had an announcement to make.

'Dad and I,' she began. She stalled, sending a silent plea to Adam.

'Mum and me,' said Adam. 'We . . .'

'You what?' Ollie, who'd been the most charming little boy Fern had ever known, was showing them only his hardest face tonight. It was standard teen behaviour, Fern reminded herself. 'I'm going out in a minute, Dad. Spit it out.'

'Your mum, well, me, I've, we've . . .' Adam, who wrote lyrics every day, who could come up with impromptu rhymes for toilet cleaner, was stammering.

'Your dad's moving out.' Fern hated how bald that

sounded but however she put it, the reality was unchangeable. Her children were struck dumb, as if somebody had pushed that elusive 'mute' button all parents dream of. She rushed forward into the silence, knowing it wouldn't last long. 'We're not separating. Not really.' Fern watched the colour rise in her daughter's little face and pushed on. 'Dad's going to stay with Granny and Granddad for a while.'

Tallulah sucked her lips until they were just a thin, pale line, while Ollie looked from one of his parents to the other, as if watching a slow and horrible tennis match.

His voice low and hesitant, Adam said, 'Mum and I need to sort out some stuff.'

Fern couldn't look him in the eye. They both heard the hollow clanging of their weasel words; they'd already tried to work things out. 'Everything,' she said, trying to believe it, 'will be fine.'

'I promise,' added Adam, and now Fern did look directly at him, astonished by such rashness.

'Other people's mummies and daddies break up, not mine!' wailed Tallulah, head back, as Boudicca looked on in alarm, her slender tail thwacking the floor anxiously. 'Don't go, Daddy!'

Hearing the agony in Tallulah's voice was like nails being scratched down a blackboard. Fern put her hand over her mouth, sick that she and Adam had brought this upon their own little girl.

Adam, his eyes unhappy, reached out for Tallulah and took her small damp hand. 'We don't have to live together to be a family,' he whispered. 'We don't have to live together to love each other.'

When they'd agreed on that line, it had sounded brave and warm. It had sounded as if it would help. Now it hung stale on the night air.

It was so short, the gap between telling the children and Adam not being there any more. His packed bags were stowed in a wardrobe, so all he had to do was pick them up, pat his jacket for his wallet and phone, and leave. He closed the door gently, but it echoed through the house as if he'd slammed it.

'So,' said Ollie, in a strangled voice as Fern loaded the dishwasher like a sleepwalker. 'You never really loved each other, yeah?'

'Don't say that, Ollie.' Fern struggled to keep control of her voice. 'Grown-ups' lives are complicated.'

'And mine isn't?' Ollie sounded insulted. 'You and Dad are important, but me and Tallie don't matter?'

'Did I say that?' Fern heard the exhaustion in her voice, and knew it would sound like irritation to Ollie. 'You matter more than anything.'

'That's crap, Mum, and you know it.'

'I'm not sure what I know any more.' Fern stood, checking her son's expression. That had slipped out; she couldn't bear him knowing how lost she felt. The children needed something strong to lean on, a still point in the chaos. As Adam had been the one to leave, the job fell to

Fern. It was a woman's lot, she supposed. 'Actually, that's wrong. I do know how Dad and I feel about you. You're the best thing that ever happened to us.' *Don't cry. Don't tear up. Do. Not.* 'It's amazing that two idiots like us managed to make something as wonderful as you out of thin air.'

'Bit late for soppiness, Mum.'

Ollie had pulled up the drawbridge.

'See you later, darling!' called Fern as he left the house. At the kitchen table, alone, she shunned the come-hither looks from the half-finished wine bottle. 'I know what you're up to,' she told the Viognier as she screwed its lid back on. 'You're trying to get me tipsy and make me cry.'

Maybe I should have told Adam that I know, she thought, looking out into the dark garden. It didn't look romantic any more, now that the lanterns were switched off and the table was cleared. It looked overgrown, untended. A bit of a mess. Fern pushed her hair back, confronted her hollow-eyed reflection in the blank, black window. She was glad she hadn't confronted him. *I kept my dignity*, she congratulated herself.

The woman in the glass didn't look dignified. She looked sad. She looked just like you'd expect a woman to look who'd just squabbled her way into a break-up without ever once letting on that she knew about the other woman.

CHAPTER TWO

July: Potage

Kryptonite green, the home-made, super-healthy soup sat smug in the fridge, as if to say *I know you hate me but you can't bring yourself to throw me away, can you?* Fern had given her all to this soup – chopping, sauteeing, processing – and it still tasted like the bottom of a garden pond.

Upending it into a pot, Fern stirred the wholesome sludge as she stared out of the window at Adam's recording studio. A narrow wooden cabin, it had been quiet for six weeks, and she missed the reassuring *tish-tish-tish* that usually leaked from it.

The studio was Adam's domain. He'd built it himself, then slowly kitted it out, adding new equipment as their budget allowed. Many times late at night Fern had appeared at his shoulder while he surfed the net, only for him to slam his laptop shut. The thumbnails he lusted over weren't 'slutty singles in your area' but cheeky little microphone preamplifliers and seductive ATC monitors. With the first *Roomies* money Adam had bought every piece of equipment on his wish list, and now it all lay idle.

The studio door opened, and Fern was jolted by a lightning flash of *déjà vu*. Every day at this time, Adam used to emerge, sniffing the air hopefully, mouthing *Soup?* through the window. They'd sit down, slurp the soup, comment on it – 'not one of your best, love!' or 'I'd happily drown in this soup' – and discuss the countless trivialities that mattered that day.

Today, though, the figure emerging was small and hunched. Tallulah cradled a shoebox, which could mean only one thing; another patient had died in the night. Crammed with hi-tech hardware, the studio was now an insect hospital. Tallulah had converted her unhappiness into yet more concern for the suffering. Fern blew a kiss to her self-consciously woebegone daughter, and braced herself for officiating at yet another bee funeral.

One of the last things Adam had said was *I'll be back to work every day in the studio, if that's OK.* Fern had said 'Of course,' awkward that he should ask. She'd been relieved that some things wouldn't change, that Adam's lamp would still shine from the cabin window, as he composed mini epics for cat-food commercials.

But Adam hadn't set foot in his studio. He'd come to the house, whisking the kids off for 'treats', occasionally staying to dinner or playing a round or two of Uno with Tallulah. One evening he'd fallen asleep in 'his' chair before waking up, embarrassed, and letting himself out.

A gentle pressure on Fern's thigh alerted her to Boudicca. The sensitive pooch had laid her head along the crackling whiteness of Fern's overall. 'You don't like this new set-up, do you, Boudi?' Fern fondled the dog's soft ears. 'It'll be fine,' she promised in a whisper, pulling a face at the soup.

The iPad sat on the worktop. 'Shall I?' Fern asked the dog. The dog didn't answer – Boudicca's grasp of English didn't stretch beyond 'din dins' and 'walkies' – so Fern took matters into her own hands.

'Just a little look . . .' She stroked the screen, surprising the icons to life, and bent over the iPad as if it was a good book.

There was nothing good about this reading matter.

Adam was a whizz with his recording gear, but verged on incompetent with other technical equipment. He'd never caught on that his online calendar was visible to Fern. She'd almost come clean the time she'd read, a week before her birthday, *Meeting @ pub re: F's surprise party*. Hating to burst his bubble, she'd simply rehearsed a look of pure amazement for when forty people yelled *Surprise!* as she walked into the White Horse.

Despite their physical separation, the iPad told Fern exactly what Adam was up to today. Scrolling past *9 a.m. – dentist* and *10.40 – bank meeting*, she found what she was looking for. *1 p.m. – lunch P.W. @ The Wellness Shack*.

Yesterday he'd lunched with P.W. at some other worthy-sounding establishment, and the evening before that they'd gone to see a play. This mysterious P.W. dotted his days, a string of pearls whose ghostly glimmer caught Fern's eye.

She remembered the first time she'd seen those initials. Fern hadn't been probing back then, she'd simply been looking for the date of the parents' evening at Tallulah's school when she'd read *4 p.m. – P.W. @ Starbucks*. It had intrigued her, but not unduly. *Probably some client*, she'd thought, before noticing the initials again one week later. *Lunch P.W.* The day after that: *3.30 p.m. – P.W. @ White Horse.*

When, oh so very casually, she'd asked Adam where he'd been on the day of his 3.30 rendezvous, he'd answered, 'The gym.'

That's when it had started. The rot. The cold, damp tentacles of distrust. Fern had always boasted that she and Adam never lied to one another, but now he was covering his tracks.

Why? That question had dogged her, tripping her up on the stairs, prodding her awake at dawn, insinuating itself into her quiet moments. When Fern was upbeat, she answered *Who cares?* But when Fern was vulnerable, when she and Adam had argued, she would answer, *Oh come on, why does any man lie about where he's been?*

Hating herself, Fern had delved further. Going through paperwork that Adam had 'filed' (i.e. thrown in a folder and forgotten), she married up the date of P.W.'s lunch and a receipt from a tapas place in W1. She knew what this P.W. had eaten but she knew nothing else, except that once or twice a week P.W. met A.C. at a variety of upmarket bars and restaurants. Champagne cocktails were drunk; Dover sole was eaten; hefty tips were left.

Whatever else went on was beyond the power of the receipts and the calendar to reveal. That didn't stop Fern from gazing at them, addicted to the pain they caused. She and Adam had managed to break up their happy home without mention of the mysterious P.W.

It wasn't cut and dried. P.W. could be a guy, some time-consuming producer. It wasn't necessarily a Patricia or a Paula; it could just as easily be a Paul. Or a Peregrine. *OK, that's unlikely.* Adam would tell her eventually, and oh, how they'd laugh. She could already hear herself hooting *And there was me thinking you were having an affair!* and Adam would giggle, *You loony! What do you take me for?*

Truthfulness was a habit they fed, a muscle they kept warm. Fern had never doubted Adam, until the day she'd asked, offhand, if they knew anybody with the initials P.W.

Without asking why she wanted to know – which, to newly neurotic Fern, had been suspicious in itself – Adam thought hard. He thought so hard it was as if he was acting a part in a play: 'middle-aged man thinking hard'. 'Aha!' he'd said finally. 'We do, Fernie. You remember. Percy, um, Waddingsworth . . . ington.'

'Percy.' Fern had repeated slowly. 'Waddingsworthington.'

The name had squatted between them like a toad. Fern knew there was no living human named Percy Waddings-worthington. She'd given Adam ample time to break, to open up, to be honest about P.W.

You used to tell me everything. Part of Fern had to believe that Adam would come clean. That they would reclaim that sunlit stretch of land where they used to live, where there was trust.

The soup burped, bubbling like lava, calling Fern back to the present. She switched off the iPad and took up her ladle.

Other soups, other times; Fern recalled the excellent broccoli and Stilton they'd been sharing when the first

Roomies royalty bank transfer had landed with a *ping!* in their account. Stunned by the noughts, they'd immediately booked a holiday; Tallulah had been unamused that their annual fortnight in a Welsh caravan had been traded in for a boring old Caribbean spa resort.

It had been pea and mint the day Adam suggested, 'Why not send Ollie and Tallulah to better schools?'

'You mean fee-paying ones? Why?'

'Because we can. I bet Lincoln Speed sends his kids to private schools.'

'Lincoln Speed can do what he likes with his tribe.' Each year brought the firebrand actor another child by a stripper or a reality star; they looked just like him, all seven of them. 'He's not my first choice to consult on family matters. There's a Vine of him snorting coke off a cat.'

'OK, OK, forget Lincoln.' Adam had taken to referring to the actor by his first name; Fern had taken to pretending not to notice. 'But doesn't it stand to reason they'd get a higher standard of education in a private school?'

Fern had conjured up Ollie's glistening new sixth-form block, Tallulah's sprawling low-build academy. 'They're happy at school, Adam. They have friends and they're doing well. Why get them beaten up by a better class of bully?'

She'd won that round – all marriages are more or less boxing matches – but Adam came in with a killer punch that put her on the ropes.

'At least let me get you a cleaner,' he said.

Biting her tongue at that 'get *you* a cleaner' (was she

really the only one of the family who liked to live in a clean home?), Fern let him rattle on.

'This house is too much for you. You're looking knackered lately.'

More biting of tongue; at this rate her tongue would be lace by the time they finished their soup.

'Fern, this is a big place for one person to manage. Admit it. You could do with some help.'

'What's stopping *you* helping?' Fern had noticed a subtle change in Adam since the money started rolling in. He did less about the place, his attitude suggesting that such a breadwinner shouldn't have to worry about trivialities like clearing the table. *Or am I imagining that?* She certainly wasn't imagining the fact that Adam called a workman in to cope with every little odd job that cropped up in their ageing house. Seeing Adam up a ladder, in his oldest jeans, paint in his hair, had always given her a discreet thrill – *you man, me woman*. As if he'd speared a mammoth just for her.

'*You're* stopping me.'

'Me?'

'Forget it.' Adam had waved his spoon. When he realized that wasn't going to happen, he'd said, with a sigh, 'If I wipe down a worktop you tell me I'm using the wrong cloth. If I pour out Coco Pops for Tallie you tell me they make her hyper. If I make the bed, the pillow arrangement offends you.'

There was no credible defence. 'You win. We'll get a cleaner.'

Evka interviewed well (although Adam may have been

27

as impressed by her less-is-more approach to clothing as he was by her references), and she'd turned up on time twice a week for the last three months. As yet, no cleaning had been done. A statuesque Slovak, Evka was prone to many ailments, all of which prevented her from lifting a can of Mr Sheen. They didn't seem to stop her trying out Fern's face creams, however.

The minestrone had been a disaster. Fern remembered stroking her new marble worktop and grumbling to Adam that the recently bought range hadn't improved her soup-making skills.

'I like the funny little pasta bits,' Adam had said loyally.

'There's no pasta in it,' Fern had said anxiously.

'Oh.' They'd giggled in unison as they seated themselves at the new table by the new dresser. The kitchen had been transformed and Fern still pinched herself every morning, as if fairies had come in and pulled down the gloomy Ikea cupboards Adam had put up, badly, twenty years earlier. These tasteful, efficient fairies had installed cream-painted bespoke carpentry. Artfully lit, it was like the kitchens Fern drooled over in interiors magazines, but thanks to the cookbooks and dented wooden spoons and homework strewn all around, it was homely as well as magnificent.

Fern had warned, 'I've only got ten minutes or so before my next client.'

'Anyone I know?' Adam could see his wife's customers tramp around the side of the house from his studio window. He'd painted the sign – 'FERN'S BEAUTY ROOM' – and installed the glazed door below it.

'Old Mrs Allen. Massage.'

'And will old Mrs Allen actually pay?'

'She's lonely, Ads. She doesn't feel a human touch from one week to the next, except for mine.' Fern worried about her customer, who seemed thin to her. Sometimes the massage ended with a bowl of leftover soup.

'We could eat a leisurely lunch together every day if you gave up your job.'

Fern wasn't sure she'd heard him properly. 'Eh?'

'It's not as if we need your income any more.'

Fern put down her spoon, pondering the differing definitions of 'need'. She needed her clients; didn't they *need* her? The measured response that she meant to make to Adam's casual insult to fifteen years of hard graft came out, well, *not* measured. 'Haven't you been listening all these years? Or are those impressive ears of yours full of wax?'

Adam had tugged at his hair, his eyes telling Fern that this was a low blow; he was self-conscious about his ears, and that comment undid two decades of sterling work along the lines of *Nobody notices them except you, silly!* 'I do listen,' he'd said, matching her intensity. 'But maybe I stopped round about the eight hundredth anecdote about some pensioner's aromatherapy.'

When he'd roared off in their new, sleek car, Fern had shouted from the porch, 'Do you *need* that car, Adam?' and he'd honked the horn in reply. Two short, rude, easy-to-decipher notes.

Possibly the first couple to chart the decline of their relationship via the medium of soup, they'd started disagreeing about small things, then bigger things, then fundamental things. The butternut soup hit the wall before they'd even tasted it. Something snapped in Fern when Adam produced a pile of estate-agent brochures.

'But you love Homestead House!' she'd said, instantly regretting throwing her lunch at the new paintwork.

'But it's . . .' Adam had shrugged, wiping soup out of his hair.

'It's what?' Fern's volume control knob was broken; everything came out as if she was standing on an opposite river bank. 'Go on! What is it?' Surely the man could understand that this house was a metaphor for *them*? 'Adam, we had our babies here. Homestead House has sheltered us. When my dad died it was quiet around us, and when your brother needed to recuperate he came *here* because we had space. Not having a mortgage meant you didn't have to take a soul-destroying office job when Ollie came along. It meant you could build up your jingle business and—'

Adam had cut her off, his hand slicing air as he made his points. 'Every time I mend a hole another appears. Damp. Rot. Subsidence. When I sleep I dream of B&Q. I've watched our friends buy sensible semis while we've been shackled to this . . . this hungry mouth! And by the way,' he'd said, coming in close, the snarl on his face making him almost unrecognizable, 'haven't *you* been listening to *me* all these years? Writing jingles *is* a soul-destroying job. I used to write songs about you. Now I write about toilet roll.'

Fern had shut her mouth abruptly. She'd never seen Adam's career in that light before. *Perhaps I haven't been listening.* A ravine opened up in the new limestone flooring. Their intimacy, something she'd taken for granted, seemed paper-thin. 'Is every part of your life so terrible that you have to fix it or change it or whitewash it?' she'd whispered.

'Don't twist my words,' he'd said. 'You always—'

'Nobody *always* does anything,' she'd shouted, that faulty volume knob cranked up again.

'You stole that line from *Sex and the City*.'

'No I didn't,' said Fern, twice as annoyed to be rumbled. 'Should I have liposuction?'

'You what?' Adam had looked at her blankly but warily, the way he looked when she mentioned periods.

'Or a bum lift? Why not just replace me with a more up-to-date model?'

'One that didn't shout so much might be nice.'

'Charming.'

'One that didn't fit me into her life after the kids and her job and feeding Boudicca.' Adam was on a roll; not a roll that Fern particularly liked. 'Sorry. That was a bit . . .'

'It was very,' she'd corrected him.

Unaccustomed to arguing, they were amateurs. They went too far, too fast. The day Fern made chicken soup, Adam irritated her by mentioning, yet again, how Ollie's accidental conception had derailed his rock-star ambitions.

'Oh for God's sake, Adam!' she'd snapped. 'You weren't Mick Jagger!' Fern was tired of Adam revising the past so he was his generation's lost icon. 'You minced about in shiny trousers. Some nights the band outnumbered the audience.'

'We got a four-star review!'

'In the local free paper. Written by the drummer's dad.'

'He said we had potential.'

'He got your names wrong. Even his son's.'

'The truth is, you don't know how far we could have gone!' Adam had paced, roused by this alternative biography. 'We might have ended up colossal! I could have been Sting!'

'Well, *Sting* is Sting,' Fern had pointed out. 'Being Sting is kind of taken.'

'Don't be so bloody flippant. You know what I mean. You loved our gigs!'

'Yes, I did. I really did.' That was true; the dizzy glamour of nights long gone flared in her mind. 'But then it was time to stop doing that, to live differently. We weren't kids any more. It was time to think about a family.'

'I had years ahead to think about that!'

You were twenty-five, she'd wanted to shout. *Hardly an adolescent.* Instead she'd murmured, 'Are you saying you regret Ollie?'

'How could I ever say that?' Adam's eyebrows had done a jig. 'It's just that he wasn't planned, he was an accident, so—'

Something that had been stretched and taut inside Fern for eighteen years finally snapped with a resounding twang. 'For Christ's sake, Adam, haven't you worked it out yet?'

'Worked what out?'

It was too late to backtrack, to grab her words from the air between them. Until she'd blurted it out, Fern hadn't realized how corrosive her secret had been to keep. 'Ollie was no accident.'

Adam had gone white, his boyish sun-kissed face suddenly old.

They hadn't shared lunch that day.

Fern would have given a great deal – certainly the cursed *Roomies* cash – to take back her outburst. She tried to broach the subject, but Adam cut her off each time by the simple tactic of leaving the room.

Fern had known within half an hour of meeting Adam (in a tower-block lift, en route to a party, both of them skinny in *de rigueur* Nineties black) that they would make babies. And not just any old babies; these babies would be top-quality little humans.

After seven years together, years in which she'd studied and worked two jobs at a time while Adam had strummed and gigged and arsed about in rehearsal rooms, Fern had begun to dwell on these potential, theoretical babies. Queasily, she'd intuited that they could remain theoretical for a decade or more if Adam kept chasing rainbows. She knew – *knew* – that Kinky Mimi wouldn't hit the big time. At their best, they were so-so, a bit of fun. Even the other Mimis saw the band for what it was: a hobby. Only Adam had stars in his lovely brown eyes, uncreased in those days, and sparkling with love and lust for Fern.

So she'd given baby-making a gentle push. A helping hand. Fern had looked the other way, whistling, and let clever old Mother Nature do her thang. Egged on by girlfriends who assured her that women did this 'all the time', Fern swore herself to secrecy. Adam must believe it was fate that threw little Ollie into the mix, not the blister pack of pills that Fern threw away.

One lunchtime, cock-a-leekie cooling between them,

Adam had torn apart a bread roll and said, 'We have to talk.'

'Uh-oh.' Fern's jokey reaction was replaced with panic. *He's serious*. 'About what?'

'What do you think? This. You and me.'

'Right,' said Fern, slowly. They'd never had a 'state of the nation' summit. No problem had ever threatened their comfortable status quo. 'Why not start by telling me why you barely talk these days?'

'It takes two to make a silence.'

Dead air had lain between them for weeks, broken only by banal necessities such as 'What time will you be back?' or 'Let the dog in.'

Fern said, 'I've been afraid to open my mouth. You're so aloof.' This was the moment to introduce the mysterious P.W., but Fern held back. *I'm not sure I can take the truth*. 'Like you're pissed off, simmering about something.'

'And why's that, d'you think?'

'I never answer sarcastic questions, Adam.'

'If you found out that your family life was based on a lie, if you discovered that the person you trust more than anybody had deceived you for years, would that make you feel chatty?'

'Are we talking about Ollie?'

'Yes.'

Taking in Adam's grim mouth and tense shoulders, Fern could have regrouped, could have imagined herself in his shoes for a moment. Instead, worn down by the sullen atmospheres and tired of his disenchantment with the house and their life, Fern picked up her weapons and went on the defensive. 'It was a long time ago!'

'What difference does that make? How many other lies have you told?'

'None. I don't lie to you.' That was a lie in itself; all partners lie to each other. Without the occasional 'You look great in those jeans', the divorce rate would be one hundred per cent. 'Something had to give, Adam. We were coasting. You were messing about with Kinky Mimi and—'

'Messing about?' bristled Adam.

'Yes,' said Fern, adamant. 'Messing. About. Ollie isn't the reason you're not playing the O2, Adam.'

'Thanks.'

Balling her fists, Fern counted to a number somewhere north of ten. Adam's tendency to retreat into a schoolmarmy, insulted persona provoked her into saying too much. 'Look, in the grand scheme of things, our family life is surely more important than anything else. Wouldn't you rather have Ollie than a gold disc?'

'There you go again. Putting it like that. That's not the point. You robbed me – yes, *robbed*, Fern, stop making that face – of my ambitions. You tied me down. I had no say.'

'Just like it takes two to make a silence, it takes two to make a baby, Adam.' Fern sagged; the picture Adam drew of her was unappealing. She'd be furious if a girl schemed Ollie into fatherhood. 'I was wrong, maybe, I don't know, I was a different person back then, young, a twit, but I didn't want to tie you down. We wanted the same thing, ultimately. Or so I thought. I didn't realize that having children with me was so unappealing.'

'Christ, do you have a master's degree in twisting people's words?' Adam made a visible effort to calm down. 'This isn't working, is it?'

'No, it's not. We're terrible at arguing.' Relieved, Fern held out her hand to cup his face, but she'd misunderstood.

'How could it work when it started with a lie?'

It was the marriage that wasn't working, apparently. Fern was grateful that Adam turned away; it took a moment to wipe the shock from her face. Even this pointed at the truth of Adam's pessimism; *when did I start arranging my face for my husband?* Without thinking, she blurted, 'So. What now? Maybe we should separate.' The S-word was a nuclear deterrent. A suggestion so absurd that the mere mention of it would bring Adam back to his senses. *Please love me again* was the contradictory subtext.

'Do you really mean that?' Adam was unreadable, defiant, fearful, but somehow triumphant.

Chilled that he hadn't shot her down, what could Fern say but a haughty *Yes*? In that moment she meant it; *you made me push the button, you coward*. Adam laid a bear trap and Fern ambled into it; the separation was officially her suggestion, despite it being her greatest fear.

'If we're going to do it,' he'd said, 'we should do it quickly. Cleanly.'

Feeling like an embarrassing knick-knack that had to be swept out of sight before visitors arrived, Fern had nodded. 'Can't be quick enough for me.'

They'd stared at each other then. In retrospect, Fern would pinpoint this as the juncture when it was still possible to stand down, to dismantle the grinding gears of the separation.

'So,' Adam had said. The word seemed deliberately ambiguous. He quivered with something intense that might have been anger, but could have been terror.

'So.' Fern felt boxed in. Accustomed to being naked in front of Adam, all her flaws and delights on show, she was now unable to bare her soul. *He has to be the one to say this is a mistake.* Adam had, after all, engineered the showdown in the first place.

Neither stood down. Both were angry, dissatisfied, heartily sick of the other's behaviour.

Breaking the spell, Adam was brisk. 'Let's keep things normal for the kids. This'll be tough on them, no need to make it any worse.'

'Why not keep things normal for the sake of, ooh, let me think, being together for twenty-five years?' Fern had been sharp. Was Adam insinuating that without the kids for an audience he'd simply ignore her? Instead of softening, instead of asking to rewind, she pushed forward. 'Let's tell them on Midsummer Eve. We'll all be together, out in the garden, relaxed. Then you can, I suppose, what? Go to your mother's.' *Or to P.W.*

'Yeah.' Adam had seemed hesitant. She noticed him gulp. The denouement had unfolded at ninety miles per hour; pushed buttons are tricky to un-push.

Now, seeking out bowls for today's alarmingly green soup, Fern admitted there were benefits to separation. No constant fretting about what was happening to her relationship, like bad muzak in a lift. *At least I know where*

I stand. If Adam could walk away from all they'd built, then it was best he did just that.

'Auntie Nora!' she hollered.

'All right, all right.' Lumbering into the kitchen, her white perm as stiff and unyielding as her moral code, Nora took a seat with many an *oof*! An archetypal old lady, from her polyester twinset to her wide-fit shoes, Auntie Nora had looked that way ever since Fern could remember. Black and white snaps of a teenaged Nora showed a pensioner-in-waiting, the scowl and frumpy dresses needing only a pull-along shopping bag to complete the look. 'Soup? Again?'

'Soup's nice,' said Fern lightly.

'Not every day.' Nora glared around the well-appointed kitchen. The zig-zag stain left by the thrown bowl of soup had been painted over; in what Fern thought of as the olden days, pre-*Roomies* royalties, any stain would have stayed for years, gradually fading. 'That loft's very draughty, Fern.'

Fern looked up at the ceiling, as if she could see through the floorboards and timbers and gaze at the loft. It was, without question, the nicest room in the house. Full of intriguing angles, yet large enough for a new king-size bed, it was painted sparkling white with the beams picked out in a powdery grey. The final touches to the hotel-style en suite had been made just days before Nora arrived. 'Draughty?' she queried.

'Where's my Binkie?'

'Probably playing with Boudicca.' The cantankerous fuzz-ball had chased the whippet out into the garden. Although half the dog's size, Binkie had the confidence of a mafia don.

'If that beast bites my pussy . . .' said Nora darkly.

That beast was far more likely to be wetting itself in fear. 'Bread, Auntie?' Fern held out a baguette.

'With these teeth?' Nora seemed outraged by such a suggestion. 'No Adam again today?'

'Not yet. He's taking Ollie and Tallulah out for a burger later.'

'A burger,' repeated Nora, as if Fern had said Adam was taking them out for an orgy. 'What on earth did you do to a lovely man like that to make him abandon his family?'

'He didn't aban—' Fern took a deep breath, changed the subject. She couldn't win against Nora. 'So, Auntie, how long are we going to have you here with us?' She asked this every day, and every day Nora managed not to answer.

'Oh, well, I—'

The doorbell rang. Apparently the gods were on Nora's side.

'I'll get it!' Tallulah flew in from the garden. 'It's Donna!' she yelled from the front door. 'And she's wearing jeggings!'

Donna was the little girl's idol. Her hair, her shoes, her lip gloss were all obsessed over. Fern was a fan too; since Donna had come back on the scene, Ollie had relaxed a little. She released Donna from Tallulah's iron grip by calling the little girl into the kitchen.

'What?' Tallulah's face was granite.

'Fancy joining me and Auntie for lunch?'

'Urgh, no.' Tallulah's rudeness was a new accessory, to go with the hairbands and bangles and pricey trainers Adam showered her with each time he took her out.

'*No thank you*,' chanted Fern gently.

'Oh god, Mummy, no thank you! There! Is that all right? Can I go?'

Fern looked at the little jaw so defiantly stuck out, the blue eyes sparkling and hard. 'Yup,' she said, knowing she must absorb this behaviour, that it was to be expected from a child with a walk-on part in a separation. 'Off you pop.'

'Fancy a sweet?' Nora, who liked very little in life, liked Tallulah. She either didn't notice or excused the child's glowering moods.

'Yes please!' Anybody's for a sweet, Tallulah's good manners flooded back, her face pink again. 'Oh.' Her face fell. 'They're liquorice allsorts. No thanks, Auntie.'

Off she went, smashing the patriarchy one bee at a time.

'I see your Ollie's been fighting again,' said Nora, with a magnificent side-eye.

'Ollie never fights.'

'Where'd he get that bruise over his eye, then?'

For a woman who needed a magnifying glass to do the crossword, Nora had laser-beam vision when it came to ferreting out sin.

'It's a good thing,' she went on, between slurps of soup, 'that me brother's dead, because this divorce nonsense would have killed him.'

'Dad would have understood,' said Fern, quietly. 'Dad always understood.' She screwed up her mouth; an old tactic to stem tears.

'Hmm.' Nora pulled in her chin. 'He spoiled you.'

Fern said nothing, not trusting her voice. Memories of her father were too precious to be manhandled by Nora.

'What does your mum have to say about it?'

'Not much,' said Fern. 'I haven't told her yet.'

Nora clucked at such daughterly neglect. 'When she finds out she'll be on the first plane from Cor, Cru, Crof . . .'

'Corfu.' Nora had never been able to get her dentures around the exotic word. 'I doubt that very much.'

With half an hour before the Beauty Room's next client, Fern nipped out to the park with Boudicca. She was, she realized, escaping her own home, running away from Ollie's clenched anger, Tallulah's confused grumpiness and Nora's relentless criticism.

At least there was a guarantee of a welcome from her fellow dog walkers. Now that she walked the whippet without Adam, Fern had become a member of a pack. Dog owners were a methodical bunch, sticking to their routines for the sake of their beloved pooches, and Fern was in the loose 'gang' of sorts that met by the southern gate each afternoon. No names were exchanged; Fern thought of them by their dogs' names. Pongo was an older woman in pristine gym gear, who treated her haughty Chihuahua like a child. Maggie was small and bald, constantly sucking mints as his golden Labrador padded alongside him. Tinkerbell was younger, and nice-looking with a soft look about his eyes. His Cockapoo was a nitwit, but it was a happy nitwit and Tinkerbell obviously extravagantly loved the little chap.

Off the leash, Boudicca sprang ahead, longs legs loping,

taking huge joy in her own speed. A rescue dog, Boudicca had been through God knows what horrors before she rocked up at the Carliles'. The family took care to treat her gently; even Tallulah, who was prone to loving soft toys to death, stroked Boudicca carefully with her childish hands.

None of them could save the dog from being bullied by Binkie. The cat ruled the roost, moving in on the wicker basket in the kitchen, the fleecy mat in the utility room, even the sweet spot under the piano where Boudicca retired when she was nervous. (The list of things that made Boudicca nervous was long, and included sudden loud noise, hedgehogs, the Queen.) Nowhere was safe from Binkie's Napoleonic need to invade. The fluffy grey moggy roamed the house like a flat-faced raincloud.

There, in a knot by the gate, was Fern's doggy crowd, singing out hellos and expressing the ritualistic British amazement at the weather as the dogs wove in and out of their legs, pressing noses to proffered bums.

Fern chanced a weak joke about how 'It's a good thing we don't greet each other like that!' She was rewarded with appalled looks from Pongo and Maggie, and was grateful when Tinkerbell gufffawed.

'We missed you yesterday,' said Pongo, carefully setting down her Chihuahua as if its little paws might shatter.

Tinkerbell winked at her. 'We thought you'd forgotten us!'

The wink knocked Fern off balance for a moment. 'I could never do that,' she smiled, recovering. Tinkerbell was handsome, if you liked that sort of thing. If you liked tilted green eyes, a ripely curling mouth wide enough to suggest all sorts of fun, and a body that boasted – quietly – about how well it knew the gym. Fifteen years ago, when Fern was about Tinkerbell's age, she would have stammered and blushed, possibly even blown off, at being this close to him but nowadays she coped, knowing that her middle-aged force-field of wrinkles and mum-tum protected her. 'This is the highlight of my day, God help me.'

'And mine!' Tinkerbell had a guileless smile. He glowed with positivity, like a sexy Disney character.

'Yeah, right!' Maggie laughed. An accountant, he seemed keen to live vicariously through Tinkerbell, choosing to believe that every minute the younger guy spent away from the park was spent whooping it up with scantily clad lovelies, a beer in each hand.

'Off we go!' said Pongo, and the little group set off for the mild slope they'd dubbed 'the mountain'.

'Yo, bitch!'

'Yo, er, um, ho!'

Fern missed Layla. Their weekly Skype didn't make up for the countless suppers and coffees and stream-of-consciousness text trails.

'Do da kidz even say *yo* any more, Fern?'

'No idea. My own kidz barely speak to me. I'm the wicked witch of the south-east. The one who wrecks marriages and throws lovely daddies out into the snow.'

'There's no snow in July, not even in that godforsaken country.'

Layla's defection to the Île de Ré, a sun-baked comma off the western coast of France, meant she got to gloat about the weather she'd left behind.

'Shush, you garlic-breathing Brie eater.' Fern leaned forward as her computer screen went fuzzy. 'Oh no, where've you gone?' She relaxed, relieved, when Layla's familiar face rearranged itself. 'I wish you were here,' she said, wondering if the giggle would lighten the weight of feeling behind the simple declaration.

Evidently, it didn't. 'Don't sound so sad!' Layla's wide, Bambi eyes creased in concern. 'It's going to be fine, Fernie.'

Hearing her own corny promise on Layla's lips exposed its flimsiness. 'Why'd you have to marry that Luc person? What'd you see in him?'

This was a running joke. 'Hmm, let me see. Was it his French good looks? The way his black hair flops? His fit bod? Was it because he's a vet and selflessly saves fluffy lambs' lives every day? Was it because he offered me a home in the medieval barn he refurbished with his own bare, very sexy, hands? Dunno. Can't put my finger on it.'

'How's the lingo going?'

'I can now say *good morning* and *goodnight* and order a croque monsieur with confidence. How's my goddaughter?'

'Still hates me.'

'Don't say that.' Layla was stern against the backdrop of pale stone. 'She's acting up because she *can*, because she trusts and loves you. This is bewildering for Tallulah. You and Adam tell her you still love each other yet you don't live in the same house any more. That's a lot for an eight-year-old to compute. She's still your little Tallie.'

'It all sounds so simple when you talk about it.'

'That's because it *is* simple.'

'How's the job-hunting going?' Time to wrench the spotlight back to Layla. Fern knew her friend didn't like talking about herself; her ability to stand back and let others shine was what had made her such a good actors' agent.

'Without the language, it's tricky. Something'll come up.'

It was odd to think of Layla being unemployable. In London she'd been a name to conjure with in show business; the Carliles had lapped up her tales of celebrity misbehaviour. A self-anointed 'second mum' to Ollie and Tallulah, she'd been a staple at Fern's table, happy to babysit at the drop of a hat. Single for ever, she'd found love on a French cycling holiday. Two years in, Fern was still getting used to having a long-distance bezzie, and working hard not to let her resentment of Luc show.

Handsome, certainly, and decent, but was the monosyllabic man really good enough for vibrant, shimmering Layla? 'Can't you work at Luc's veterinary surgery? Bandaging kittens or something?'

'You have a very basic idea of what vets do. He spends most of his time getting to first base with cows.' Layla closed her eyes, as if dizzy, then shook her head.

'You OK?' Fern frowned. 'Is it the Skype or are you looking tired, Layla?'

'Must be the Skype. How's my Ollie? Still not . . . ?'

'Back at school? I wish. No, he's doing endless small-time

jobs. Handing out flyers for a pizza place. Labouring on a building site. Doing Saturdays in a sportswear shop.'

'I thought Donna might encourage him to be sensible.'

'Me too, but what the hell do I know? Tallulah said she's actually been back for a few weeks longer than I thought. She was in on this stupid decision to ditch his exams.'

'For somebody who doesn't want to be a snitch, that child's doing a great job. You're being hands-off, like you promised me?' Layla looked sideways at the frigid little camera on her laptop. 'Are you?'

'I'm trying.' Fern protested over Layla's sighs. 'I'm not a hands-off person! I don't do standing back, I do wading in!'

Before they signed off and Layla's smile disappeared, leaving only a grainy darkness in its place, Layla said, 'This isn't the end, you know. The Fern'n'Adam show can't just stop dead in its tracks after all this time.'

'Hmm.'

'If you want it to carry on, I mean.' Layla looked as if something had just occurred to her. 'You do *want* Adam to come home, don't you?'

Layla's question sent Fern to the box of letters, looking around furtively as if she was snooping.

In a way, she *was*. This was another life she was peeking at. When a boy called Adam was nuts about a girl called Fern. *Just one*, she told herself, like a junkie, picking a leaf at random.

With her hand over her mouth she read.

WHY I'M THE BEST BOYFRIEND FOR YOU

I'm not saying I'm the best boyfriend ever.
Just the best for you. E.g. who else would laugh
at your impressions if I wasn't there? Seriously
Fern, you sound nothing like Audrey Hepburn.

Who told you your skirt was tucked into your
knickers on New Year's Eve? ME.

Who held your hair back when you were sick
after your sister's engagement party?
ME.

Who gets you? Who loves you?
ME ME ME ME
Adam x
P.S. And you love me you idiot.

Clichés were clichés for a reason. Adam had only half believed that separated dads take their kids to burger joints, but he'd become such a McDonald's/Wimpy/Burger King connoisseur in the past six weeks that he associated his children with condiment sachets and laminated menus.

'And I don't even like burgers all that much,' he thought to himself as he passed the closed sitting-room door. Behind the door, his parents were watching *Midsomer Murders* as if their lives depended on it.

Taking off his jacket in his room, he hung it on the handlebars of his mother's exercise bike. Adam's childhood room had morphed into his mum's hobbies room. He fell asleep each night surrounded by discarded half-sewn quilts, papier mâché models of London landmarks and dumb-bells that lay in wait on the fitted carpet like mantraps.

The filing cabinet in the corner held what remained of Adam's teenage tenancy; some exercise books, a well-thumbed lingerie catalogue and a stack of Kinky Mimi publicity photos for the European tour that never was. Adam hadn't known whether to laugh or cry at the naive optimism in the young men's eyes. He barely recognized the skinny bloke claiming to be Adz Carlile, cringing at that forgotten 'z'.

The mark on Ollie's eye bothered him. A purplish bruise, it was an honour wound, apparently. Some joker called Maz had challenged him in the street, shouting 'stuff' about Donna. According to Ollie, this Maz had come off worse. 'Don't tell Mum, please, Dad.' Ollie had bent in two like a paperclip at the thought of the fuss Fern would make.

The telly roared through the floorboards. Adam lay on the single bed, nylon sheets crackling beneath him. He sniffed the air; Mum had done her famous hotpot again. *Why is it famous?* wondered Adam; because it was horrible enough to put any sane person off diced meat?

He yawned. Fiddled with his collar. Turned onto his right side, then his left. The feeling of having nothing to do was peculiar. He remembered the very same sensation as a teenager in this very bed. No responsibilities. Hours stretching ahead.

Naming this state of mind 'loneliness' was something Adam stoutly refused to do. He scrolled through 'favourites' on his phone, and was just pressing 'Penny' when he heard a shout from downstairs.

'Ad-am!' called his dad's familiar sing-song. Adam clattered down the stairs, aware that they'd turned down *Midsomer Murders*; something was up. They *never* turned down John Nettles for anything less than a death in the family.

'What's wrong?' Adam stood on the orange rug, its tuftiness Hoovered flat long ago.

'We need to talk, son.' Dad looked shifty, unable to meet Adam's eye.

'Yeah?' Adam bit his lip, taking a nervous inventory of his parents and deciding they both looked healthy. Never better, in fact; they were busy-busy-busy retirees who whizzed through life on their bikes, forever visiting castles or 'taking in' a show.

'Son, you know we love you. We're devastated by what's happened to you and Fern. We'll do anything we can to help.'

'Ye-es.' Adam wondered where this was going.

Mum cut in, her fingers impatient on the remote control. 'What Dad's trying to say, dear, is you've got to sod off. I want my sewing room back.'

And with that, John Nettles was turned back up.

'This one's amazeballs.' Adam tapped the leaflet. 'Two terraces!'

'Yeah, amazeballs,' murmured Fern, who was folding

laundry, waiting for a client, and keeping her eye on a spider in a matchbox who wasn't expected to last the night. 'Christ, Adam, the price!' She'd just noticed the figure at the top of the page.

'It's OK, we can afford it.'

'But *we're* not buying it,' said Fern. '*You* are.' The stack of estate-agent details dismayed her. As long as Adam was in his parents' spare room he was on a piece of elastic that kept bouncing him back to Homestead House. Transplanting Adam to one of these chrome and glass bachelor pads would change things yet again, place him further away. She'd had enough of change for a little while. 'Why not rent for a bit?'

'Doesn't make economic sense.' Adam, who didn't know the price of a pint of milk, was suddenly a financial expert. 'Besides, just *look* at them!'

Flipping through the bland photos of arctic open-plan new builds, Adam wore the expression that Fern reserved for looking at cake. 'Very swish.' She managed not to add *but they're not you*, because, apparently, they *were*. 'When are you getting back into the studio, Adam? What about that deodorant jingle? Did you finish it?'

'Yeah. No.' Adam, uninterested, refused to be sidetracked.

'You'd better reclaim the shed from Tallie. There are recuperating worms all over your speakers.' Fern checked on the spider in his cotton-wool hospital bed; he seemed comfortable. Or dead. Hard to know with spiders.

'I might turn a corner of the new pad into a recording space. That set-up out there,' Adam waved a hand vaguely at the kitchen window, 'is all a bit awkward. Good enough for the old me, you know?'

Sadly, Fern *did* know. *I prefer the old you*, she thought as she went to the fridge.

'I'm a very wealthy man, Fern. It's not a sin. I can't just ignore it. Fact is, I don't have to make do any more.' Adam turned the pages of the brochure, as rapt as a monk with a Bible. 'I feel so liberated, you know? So free.'

Liberated from your family home. Free of your responsibilities. 'Fancy some soup? Gazpacho. Nice and summery to suit the weather.' Fern was proud of the gazpacho, which, for once, looked like the picture in the book.

'Nah.' Adam was engrossed in the images of glossy flooring and free-standing baths.

'Tallulah should be ready in a minute.' Fern was aware of making conversation. With *Adam*. Weird. 'I sent her upstairs to wash her hands. She's drawn all over them. And Ollie's supposed to be back by now.' She checked the time on the large railway clock; she'd always wanted one, and when the *Roomies* money came in she'd stopped wanting one and bid for one on eBay. 'He's only got an hour before the evening shift at the White Horse.'

'Did I tell you?' Adam looked up, the enthusiasm on his face doing more for it than a face lift ever could. 'About the band?'

'What band?'

'Fern!' Adam was taken aback at such ignorance. '*The* band. Kinky Mimi.'

'What about it?'

'I've got the boys back together!'

'But they're all in their forties by now.' Fern pulled a

face. 'Aren't they too old to qualify as boys, never mind be in a band?'

'The Rolling Stones do OK.'

'You laughed your head off at Duran Duran's comeback tour. You said they looked like Lady Gaga's nan.'

'Kinky Mimi aren't Duran Duran.'

And they're not the Rolling Stones, either, thought Fern disloyally. 'Didn't your drummer move to Ireland?' Fern reached out and turned off the radio. For the third time that day, the *Roomies* theme was spilling out of it.

'Lemmy's back in the UK, now. Making rabbit hutches.'

'That's a thing?'

'Not really. He's broke, so he's up for it. Keith's not keen, but I'm talking him round.'

'Keith . . .' Fern went into a short reverie. Keith had been tall, lean, a golden boy with wild blond hair. 'When he used to shake his hair during a guitar solo . . .'

'He's gone bald.'

'Oh.' The reverie fizzled out. *Pfft.*

'Plus he'll need to shift a few pounds.'

'Hmm. Satin trousers are *so* unforgiving.' Fern relented, seeing how Adam's face fell. 'Sorry, love.' They both tensed at that word, as if such easy fondness was forbidden now, a form of adultery. 'It's a brilliant idea. You'll have a giggle.'

'Giggle? We're going to be famous, Fern.'

In retrospect, it had been wrong to laugh quite so loudly.

CHAPTER THREE

August: Poisson

'No, no, honestly, please don't get up.' Fern vacuumed around Nora and Evka as they sat on the sofa, offering each other Mr Kipling fondant fancies and criticizing her leggings.

'We weren't going to get up.' Sarcasm sailed over Evka's choppily boyish haircut. She'd watched Fern dust and polish, her self-confidence almost visible, like a stole she wore around her shoulders. Evka was slender and leaf-like; her fingers tapered, her nose was long, her features wolfish, as if a Slovak woodland creature had morphed into a woman. A woodland creature with an aversion to human clothing; Evka's peach-coloured camisole was scanty, her nipples protruding like thumbs.

Her seductive, sleepy drawl, as if awakening from a drugged sleep, corroborated Nora's theories. 'Yes, Nora, perhaps Adam left Fern because she dresses like cowboy.'

Fern glanced down at her chequered shirt. Now that she came to think of it, it was a little *Brokeback Mountain*. 'Adam didn't leave me,' she interrupted. 'It was a mutual decision.'

As they lifted their legs for the Hoover, the two women on the sofa shared a giggle. 'If she showed bit of boob now and again,' said Evka, her mouth full of fondant fancy, 'he might stay. Men like boob, Nora.'

Nora nodded wisely, and once more Fern marvelled. If Fern were to use the word 'boob' within a twenty-mile radius of her aunt, Nora would spontaneously combust. When Evka let rip – as she frequently did – with a heavily-accented expletive, Nora simply raised a finger and said fondly, 'Now, now, missy!' With Nora, it would seem, you were 'in' or you were 'out'; Evka, despite the slutty outfits and the laziness and the bad language, was 'in'.

'I'll make a start on the bathrooms now, shall I?' said Fern loudly, unplugging the vacuum cleaner.

'Yes. Whatever,' said Evka grandly.

'You could help, if you like. Or even, gosh, let me think, *actually clean the bloody bathrooms*. Like I pay you to do.'

'Language!' Nora was horrified, her mouth pursed into a perfect hen's bum.

'Please, Fern,' said Evka sadly. 'Your aunt fucking hates it when you swear.'

'Poor Evka has tennis elbow,' said Nora, glaring at Fern as if she was a slave trader.

'Last week she had housemaid's knee.' Fern was curious to hear what next week would bring. The plague? Shingles? 'Surely she can lift a J-cloth?'

'Leave Evka alone, Mummy.' Tallulah appeared from the garden, trailing mud over the carpet Fern had just de-mudded. 'She helps me feed the patients.'

A cooing and a clucking began from the sofa as both Evka and Nora reached out for Tallulah, brushing back her fringe, tucking in her T-shirt, chucking her cheeks.

'You are so prrritt-ee.' Evka spun out the word luxuriously in her Slovakian accent. 'My little Tallulah.'

'The child needs a good broth inside her.' Nora looked Fern up and down.

'She's full of Pop Tarts,' said Fern, who remembered Nora's broths and would never wish them on her own children. 'Tallulah's perfectly fine, Nora.'

'She's ailing, poor wee abandoned mite.'

'She's not ailing, nobody abandoned her, and she's far from a mite.' Fern disliked the picture Nora painted of them all huddled in an attic waiting for Adam to come back. 'She saw her dad just yesterday, didn't you, love?'

'Yes. I had two Big Macs. I was sick in his glove compartment.'

'Clever girl,' said Nora indulgently.

'Mum,' said Tallulah, twirling her dark plait. 'Will you and Daddy sort out custard of me?'

'What is custard?' asked Evka, her heavy-lidded eyes on Fern.

'It's a yellowy sauce, a top-notch item. But,' smiled Fern, reaching to fold Tallulah to her, 'I think she means custody.'

Tallulah resisted, stepped away. 'It's when mummies and daddies ask a judge who gets to keep them.' The brow was lowered, the lips were thin; Tallulah was scared of the answer.

'We don't need to ask any silly old judge,' said Fern, wondering why she copped all the sticky questions whereas

Adam oversaw the Big Mac binges. 'Mummy and Daddy would never argue about you. Your home is here and always will be. Nothing will change, sweetie.'

Using the special mournful voice she saved for talking about 'poor Adam', Nora sighed, 'When I think of that sad, brave man all alone in a miserable bedsit.'

'But Daddy's flat is gorgeous!' Tallulah's custard worries were all forgotten. 'Maybe I'll live *there*.'

Such casually thrown daggers came thick and fast some days. The Mumsnet forums Fern cruised late into the night assured her this was just 'acting out'.

'Any more tea?' Evka held up her cup.

'You've got some nerve,' said Fern.

'What is nerve?' asked Evka.

Later, polishing taps while Evka played table tennis in the garden, Fern tried to rub away her frustration along with the limescale. What had possessed Adam to buy a flat in the pretentious riverside development that they'd both cheerfully ridiculed? Day in, day out, walking Boudicca, they'd watched the ark-shaped block rise and rise beside the park. They'd sniggered in unison at the advertising hoardings outside the show home, scoffing at the computer-generated people enjoying computer-generated cappuccinos. Adam had read out the motto: 'Live at Canbury Tower and nothing will spoil your view.' Shaking Boudicca's frisbee in anger at the modernistic monstrosity, he'd shouted 'That's because you've built in front of all the lovely old houses that have been here for years, you pillocks!'

That had been the original Adam, the one Fern knew

as well as she knew herself. The new Adam, the one who revered Lincoln Speed as a lifestyle guru, was a mystery.

At that moment, the new Adam was on his terrace, ignoring his view of the river in favour of reading his blog on www. KinkyMimiTheComeback.com. Dressed all in white, he fitted right into his new habitat.

The sitting room was metres long, its pale floorboards giving way to white carpet in the sunken entertainment area. The recessed lighting had fourteen different settings – 'candlelight' to 'operating theatre' – and could be controlled from anywhere in the world if only Adam could work out the app.

The bath in his en suite filled in less than a minute. The oven cleaned itself. Adam had landed in the arms of all the twenty-first century had to offer. No dark corners here, no sinister stains on the ceiling that needed his attention. This flat asked nothing of him.

Fern's face swam suddenly in front of him, wearing the new expression he suspected she'd created just for him. A mish-mash of scorn, disappointment and sadness, it aged her. Sometimes she embellished it with an eye-roll; she'd done a grandiose one when he'd tried to show her the marble samples for his splashback. *I deserve marble*, he thought, aggrieved.

Lying back on a leather L-shaped sofa the colour of a geisha's bottom, Adam contemplated his own face peering back at him from his blog. *Ol' Brown Eyes is back!* shouted the headline. 'Doesn't that make it sound like I'm comparing myself to Sinatra?'

'Yes!' Penny paced the room, her heels rapping on the wood before falling silent on the shag pile, only to *click-clack* again as she continued her circuit. 'Sinatra's one of the greats and so are you.'

'I'm great at cheese and pickle sandwiches, true, but surely . . .' Penny wheeled round, her thin frame in its sleek black sheath turning like a spoke. 'When did you have a cheese sandwich, Adam? Come on, champ, we talked about this. Your bod is public property now.'

'Is it?' Adam's voice went high-pitched when he was alarmed; he was alarmed three or four times a day since moving out of Homestead House. 'Don't panic. I'm a no-cheese area. I'm sticking to the diet.' He felt rather than saw the repressive glance. 'Nutritional manifesto, I mean.'

When Adam had arranged to meet Penny Warnes in Starbucks back in March, he'd been impressed with her vitality, her air of barely suppressed energy. She'd shamed him into pretending that no, he never drank coffee either; that day he'd tasted his first wheatgrass and goji berry smoothie, when she'd marched him across the road to a hipster joint where a beardy chap with a man bun handed him a beaker of slime.

The aim had been to find a manager for the reformed band; *I found so much more than that*, thought Adam, with fond ruefulness. Penny had been the only woman on the shortlist. She'd torn up her CV in front of him, saying, 'I'll be frank with you. I don't have the qualifications for this. I've only ever been a P.A. in the music biz. I'll tell you why you need me.' Her red lips mesmeric, Penny was the most groomed woman Adam had ever seen close up. Her hair was a shade of blonde that seemed almost transparent, and her skin sang as if fairies massaged it in the night with tiny magic fingers. 'You need me because *this* changed my life.' She'd reached into one of those massive handbags that women inexplicably love and brought out the CD he'd sent her of Kinky Mimi's raggedy demos from 1995 – the Bad Old Days, as his son referred to Adam's youth.

'*That* changed your life?' Adam had wondered briefly what on earth Penny's life had been like before.

'You. Changed. My. Life.' Penny brandished the CD like a weapon. 'The track called "Beans"! Masterly! Seemingly just a silly ditty about baked beans, but actually a no holds-barred journey through one man's mental breakdown. It's genius!'

When Adam had said, 'Actually it really is about baked beans,' Penny hadn't seemed to hear. She'd repeated, 'You need me, Adam, because I share your vision. I know this thing can go global. But.' She'd folded her arms, and Adam had sat back, because he knew from long years of being with Fern that when a woman folds her arms like that something not particularly nice is about to happen. 'You'll pay me twice what you're offering. You'll give me total control over your image, your material, your social media. I want *you*, Adam. Not just the music. I want the man.'

This woman made Adam's absurd dreams sound

feasible. He had no option but to offer her the job. 'You're a whirlwind! I feel as if my hair is blowing back.'

Shaking his hand, Penny had said, 'The hair will have to go, by the way.'

Proximity to a whirlwind was exhilarating after decades spent in the gentle weather of life with Fern. He'd never had a bona fide fan before and was happy to let Penny call the shots, even though his new hipster haircut took him by surprise whenever he passed a reflective surface. Ollie approved of the shaved sides and walnut-whip top, an event so unusual that Adam had been struck dumb until they finished their respective BBQ Whoppers.

'As my name's on the blog,' he said to Penny, 'shouldn't I write it?'

'God, no!' Penny pulled a face. 'This is a tool, Adam. If you want the world to buy you, we can't let them know the real you.'

'I see.' Adam *didn't* see; what was so wrong with the real him that the world mustn't be allowed even a glimpse? Perhaps, he thought sadly, the world didn't like fart jokes.

Joining him on the sofa, sitting close, Penny fanned out the new publicity shots on the glass coffee table. She'd taken charge of styling, overriding the expensive professional she'd insisted on hiring. 'Sateen!' she'd barked. 'Feathers!'

'Doesn't Lemmy look great?' Penny tapped a burgundy nail on a shot of Lemmy in paisley dungarees, his jowls airbrushed.

'Keith really didn't like the hat.' Adam picked up the photograph, remembering Keith bellowing, *I don't see you*

*for nearly twenty years and in ten minutes flat you've got
me wearing a purple fedora.*

'You and the guys have to get with the programme.
This is your look. Kinky Mimi is retro grunge meets glam
soul. You look knockout in that suit.'

Adam tried not to look smug. He'd almost burst into
tears when confronted by the cornflower-blue satin three-
piece. But the camera doesn't lie. 'I *have* lost a few pounds,
haven't I?'

'We photoshopped the lumps and bumps.' Penny flashed
him the un-retouched shot and Adam recoiled. He looked
as if he was smuggling a family of hamsters in his waistband. 'Tosh is a bit of a problem.'

Once the wildman bassist, Tosh was now a geography
teacher, who seemed to be praying for death as he stared
out of the shots in a leopardskin trench.

'Tosh'll come round.' Adam had spent days persuading
his old mate to give Kinky Mimi a second chance, and
that damn coat had nearly undone all his good work.

'Does . . .' Penny paused. It was unusual for her to
pause and Adam braced himself. 'Does Fern know? About
me? Have you told her yet?'

'No.' Adam put up his hands defensively as she breathed
out heavily through her nose. 'Strictly speaking, you're not
really any of Fern's business.'

Fern had always pooh-poohed those magazine articles that
list 'Seasonal fashion must-haves!', with their thumbnails

of bags and boots and scarves. Flicking past them, she'd wonder, *who has the money to rush out and buy an item of clothing just because they saw it in a magazine?*

The answer to that question, it would seem, was 'Fern Carlile'. Gripped by jacket-lust when she saw a tiny picture of a linen kimono in impractical mint green, she'd rushed out and bought it. Just because she wanted a new jacket.

Accustomed to her new role as the anti-Adam, the keeper of feet on the ground, Fern saw how he'd been seduced by flamboyant, 'just because' spending. The novel feeling was fun.

Her dog walkers didn't comment on her new designer item. Pongo was a Lycra and leggings devotee, Maggie not the sort of man to get into conversation about ladies' jackets. When Fern caught up with them, nodding hello to timid newcomer Sabre (German Shepherd/overweight/covered in odd sores – the dog, that is), she looked around for Tinkerbell.

'He's late.' Pongo read her mind. 'Let's get going.'

'Can't we wait? Seems a bit harsh.' Fern examined her kind impulse and decided that yes, of course she'd do the same for Maggie or Sabre. *Almost definitely.* As she uncrossed her fingers, she saw a figure over the road on the other side. 'There he is!'

'Wait for me!' called Tinkerbell, one hand in the air as he watched the traffic trundle past. His face split by his smile, tall untidy Tinkerbell was made for pleasure, his eyes constantly ready to crease in laughter, his pace always just above slow, as if he had all the time in the world to get where he was going. The type of man everybody was happy to see, his bulky presence lifted the dog walkers' collective mood.

But especially mine. Fern dissected herself with the cool interest of a scientist in a laboratory studying a particularly dim white mouse. A white mouse who seemed to fancy the pants off a much younger and therefore uninterested white mouse.

'Come *on*!' roared Pongo, making Sabre jump.

As Tinkerbell chose his moment and stepped off the kerb, a sports car gunned past him, forcing man and dog to leap backwards.

'Jerk!' roared Tinkerbell. The car sounded its horn in response, a boorish two-note tune which made Fern's ears prick up.

Jogging to catch up with the dog walkers, Tinkerbell was still fizzing. 'Did you see that? Talk about a midlife crisis on wheels.'

Tell me about it, thought Fern, who'd recognized Adam's number plate.

'Hello beautiful!' Tinkerbell leaned down to greet Boudicca, who looked up at him with the demented devotion she showed everybody. Then he was on his knees amongst the dogs, ruffling ears, offering his chin for canine kisses.

'Careful, you don't know where they've been.' This banal politeness was the language of the group; it calmed Fern to have half an hour of daft chatter.

'Oh, but I do.' Tinkerbell straightened up. There was a lot of him to straighten up. He was tall enough to make Fern feel dainty; another novel feeling, another one she liked. 'They've been sniffing each other's behinds, remember?'

So it was *their* joke. Fern was pleased, then annoyed at feeling pleased, then annoyed at feeling annoyed – *this could go on forever*.

As the group moved on, Tinkerbell surveyed Fern. 'Nice jacket. Nicole Farhi?'

'Yes.' A man who recognized labels? *Is Tinkerbell gay?* Fern tried to ignore the disappointment she'd feel if Tinkerbell was what Tallulah called a homosexyman. 'How'd you know that?'

'I'm a metrosexual.' Tinkerbell shrugged. 'You can't grow up with three sisters without learning a bit about clothes. I can talk credibly for forty-five minutes about skirt lengths.' He took in Fern's sudden roguish look. 'But don't test me, please.'

'Come on!' Pongo, some way ahead, could be imperious, just like her little pooch. 'Let's do two laps this morning!'

'She's keen.' Tinkerbell's merry eyes turned down, like a child trying to look sad. 'I had a bit of a night last night.'

'Me too.' Fern's 'bit of a night' had involved staying up until after eleven to finish a *CSI* marathon. 'Feeling rough?'

'There are tiny men in my head, all of them clog-dancing or moving wardrobes or dropping anvils. What I really need is a sausage sandwich.'

'I always really need one of those.'

'My sisters give me a lecture about healthy eating when I suggest anything fried or anything involving carbohydrates.'

'Frying carbohydrates is one of life's main pleasures.'

'You're not a *my body's a temple* bird, then?'

Bird? Fern wanted to squawk like a cockatoo. Half of her was in Tallulah-style consternation. The other half was thrilled to be still in the 'bird' sector of the Venn diagram; by now she should have graduated into the part labelled *Sexually off limits – only useful for housework*. 'I've never been able to turn down a sausage.' Fern closed her eyes briefly. 'That came out wrong.'

'Did it, though?'

'Stop it,' said Fern, swatting him.

Tinkerbell – the dog, not the man – suddenly broke free from the freewheeling pack and hurtled across the grass. 'Shit,' said Tinkerbell – the man, not the dog – and set off in pursuit.

'Very flighty chap,' said Maggie.

'Mmm.' *Nice bum, though.* Fern cottoned on; Maggie meant the Cockapoo. 'Not much more than a pup, really.'

'You know his owner's a millionaire?'

Pongo chipped in. 'Billionaire, more like.'

'Really?' Fern frowned at the figure in jeans chasing his dog *à la* Benny Hill. 'You wouldn't think it to look at him.'

'That's what billionaires look like nowadays.' Pongo seemed sure of her facts. 'Look at Steve Jobsworth,' she said, not noticing the smile shared by the others. 'Or that Richard Branston.'

'Always getting himself in a pickle,' murmured Sabre.

'Take my word for it, that man's loaded. He sold his internet company for a fortune.'

'He bought and sold domain names.' Maggie sniffed approvingly. 'You know, he snapped up, for example, all the wedding-related names, such as weddings.com and gettingmarried.com and what have you, then sold them to companies that were called that but hadn't bought the domain.'

'Sounds a bit . . .' Fern was going to say *sneaky.com*, but Pongo got there before her.

'Clever? The man's a genius.'

'A genius who just tripped over his own dog,' said Fern, watching both Tinkerbells roll in the mud. Suddenly her world was riddled with millionaires, like Jackie Collins' lost suburbia novel.

'Damn!' Fern tossed down her phone. 'I rush back for my three o'clock and she cancels at the last minute.'

'So what?' Evka was pulling on her rucksack after two gruelling hours of tea-drinking. 'You have cancellation policy, yes? She pays you.'

'She's been coming to me for years. Poor thing's got two kids and she's going through a divorce, so . . .'

'Poor thing sounds just like you.' Evka dropped her bag with a thud. 'If you have free hour and you don't need paying, why not wax me?'

Before Fern could come up with any of the very good reasons why not, Evka had hopped up onto the adjustable treatment couch. 'Knicks on or off?' she asked, workman-like.

'The appointment was for the upper lip, so *on*.'

'I want rude bits waxed.' *Rood beets.*

'OK,' sighed Fern, who hadn't expected to see quite so much of her so-called employee. Pottering about, heating the wax, Fern was perfectly at home as the musky smells floated around her and the wavering pan pipes tooted their endless wispy tunes. The room was compact, but designed so carefully that it was perfectly comfortable. She relished the calm, and knew her clients did too.

The shelves, drawn on the back of an envelope by Fern, had been put together by Adam over one long, very sweary weekend. They housed all the tools of her gentle trade: creams, lotions, tissues, tweezers, plastic gloves, spatulas, cotton-wool balls, pristine fluffy towels, mysterious electrical kit. They were all snug in designated cubby holes, the edges stencilled with a pattern of ferns Adam had added as a surprise. 'Because you're a Fern.'

As Evka drawled on – 'I used to have Brazilian but now I prefer smooth fanny like Barbie' – Fern recalled how she and Adam had dithered about the tiled floor. They'd compared prices, trawled the internet for sales, until finally driving out to some remote industrial estate to nab a bargain. How times had changed; Adam had bought a property without blinking.

'Ready?' Fern smiled reassuringly at Evka.

'Ready! I have big plans for much sex at weekend, so make me pretty down there please.'

'I didn't know you had a boyfriend.'

'I don't. I'm going to *aaaaargh*!' Evka yowled as hot wax met her softest parts. Made of stern stuff, she kept talking as Fern worked speedily, deftly. 'I go tomorrow to bowls tournament, and there I find sexual partner.'

'Bowls? As in . . . bowls? Aren't you a bit young for that?'

'I try out British pastimes, one by one. I already do afternoon tea and car sale boot.'

'I'm not sure you'll find a sexual partner at a bowls tournament.'

'I find one if I want one. Man I met at car sale boot was filthy beast.'

'Nice,' said Fern, uncertainly. 'Don't tell me you met a man among the Victoria sponges at afternoon tea!' She'd had more than one afternoon tea, and it was nobody's idea of an X-rated activity.

'No. But the waitress covered me in cream and we—'

'You're done!' Fern snapped off her gloves. 'You'd better not tell Nora those stories.'

'Why not? Nora is my friend.' Gingerly pulling on her thong, Evka said, 'I come to this country for adventure. I say to myself, Evka, I say, you are young, do not waste life doing same stupid thing over and over.' No drawling now, she sounded urgent, as if it was vital that Fern understood. 'Do you know what I mean?' She grabbed Fern's arm. 'I make own rules. I do not ask what people think of me. I am heroine of my story. And my story is adventure story!'

Fern asked, 'Am I boring, Layla?'

'You? No! Well. Hardly ever. When you go on about *Downton* I tune out a bit. And when you talk me through the many, many new massage oils on the market I tend to have a little snooze.' Layla, her sun-kissed shoulders hunched as she leaned in, said, 'Hold on, you're being serious.'

'Maybe Adam got bored of me. And this house. And our life.' Fern looked around the study, a small triangular room off the hall which had been repainted a rich red post-*Roomies*. It all looked so static – the books, the framed family photos, the cushions she'd made when she was pregnant with Tallic. 'Our life *has* been pretty samey for the past few years.' Possibly Percy Waddingsworthington could talk about Russian literature, or liked to dance naked in the dawn dew. 'It's so easy to get bogged down in domesticity, Layla. This house takes a lot of looking after. So do these kids.'

'Every woman feels like that.'

'But I became the Band-Aid holding everything together. I haven't thought of myself as a lover in a long time.'

'Don't tell me about your sex life. Jesus, I hate it when people talk about bonking.'

'Don't panic, you're safe.' Sex with Adam had been good, no, *great*. When it happened. 'Maybe we turned into friends who shared responsibilities.'

'Listen, chum, you're not boring. Why would I have come to your house every single Sunday for lunch if you were dull? Trust me, your Yorkshires aren't *that* good. I came for the conversation and the mad stories and wondering when you'd get drunk enough to miss your chair and land on the floor.'

'*Once* I did that!' Fern defended herself. 'Once!' She let out a fluttering sigh. 'I miss our Sundays.' She missed their Mondays too, and the rest of their weeks. The Layla on the screen wasn't substantial enough to grab and hustle off to the nearest wine bar.

'Oh, yes, I forgot – you're at your most boring when you moan about me moving to France.'

'Maybe *I* should move to France.' Fern shook her head. 'Nope. Even just saying it makes me start worrying about Tallulah's schooling and how many pairs of pants I should pack for Ollie. I *am* boring. I'm rooted here like that yew tree on our drive.'

'No, you're a mum.' Layla took a deep breath, and was silent for so long that Fern wondered if the internet connection had sputtered out. Suddenly she said, with her usual animation, 'What's brought on all this navel-gazing?'

Fern told her about Evka. 'That girl left behind everything familiar, and now she lives for adventure.' The word glowed, a gilded pebble in the dust. 'She has more sex than I have Cadbury's Mini Rolls, and we both know that's an unfeasibly high number.'

'You have adventures.'

'Like what?'

Layla put on a comical 'thinking face' and seemed pleased when she came up with 'That time you rode an elephant in Thailand! *I've* never ridden an elephant.'

'So that's it? One slightly pissed elephant ride is the sum total of my life's exploits?'

'You're talking as if everybody else lives in an episode of *24*. The high point of my day is strolling down to the boulangerie by the harbour to buy a baguette.'

'But you adore that boulangerie. The baguette is a mini-adventure, because you were brave enough to uproot yourself and go to live in a land brimming with wine, cheese and nice arses.'

'You've summed up my life nicely. But this mad cleaner of yours . . . if she really did run away from home, hungry for experience, then she's probably running away from some sort of pain.'

'Believe me, Evka's more likely to cause pain than feel it.'

It was easy to rationalize her addiction.

By taking another letter from the dusty box, by reliving the Great Rift of '93, Fern was reconnecting with the real Adam, the authentic model rather than the bizarre clone currently trundling around town in tight, tight, tight trousers. Only that morning he'd told her over the phone that all she had to do was snap her fingers and he'd install her and the kids in a brand new house. *As if we're dolls to move around.* 'It's about time,' he'd said, 'we sold that dump.'

It was important to remind herself that no matter what was happening now, they had once shared passion and commitment. And terrible handwriting.

HOW I KNOW YOU LOVE ME

You love me, Fern. You know you do. Otherwise you wouldn't be asking my mates how I am. How do you think I am!!!! I MISS YOU. That's how I am.

Also you used to hang about waiting for me after you finished beauty college so we could get the bus together. You hate being cold so that proves something.

Also you let me nick chips off you. OK so I'd never dare sneak a bite of your saveloy, but all the same.

You look at me the way girls look at boys when they love them.

So give in, Fernie, and take me back.

Please.

'Fish and chips?' Nora said it again, more slowly, with scandalized emphasis. 'Fish. And. Chips.'

'Yes, yes, Auntie, fish and chips,' said Fern. 'The national dish, beloved by everybody.'

'Actually, Mum, you're wrong.' Tearing open the greasy paper, releasing the sacred scents of vinegar and batter, Ollie never missed a chance to correct his elders and betters. 'Chicken tikka masala is the national dish now.'

The smell, the clatter of plates, the sourcing of ketchup, the skirmishes over portion size, the pro/con pickled onion debate all delighted Fern and convinced her that she was right to down tools in the kitchen and declare it takeaway night. Her cod was the size of a whale; Adam always used to say 'Look, it's Moby Dick!' Tonight, she said it instead, but it fell flat.

Tallulah lurked under the table, sharing with Boudicca, and Ollie took his chips up to his room, where Donna sat waiting.

'I bet you Adam's not eating chips,' said Nora, with so much acidity she had no need for the vinegar bottle.

Except she said *chipsh*. Fern eyeballed the blameless-looking glass of water in front of her aunt, and made a mental note to mark the level on the gin bottle that constituted the Carlile cocktail cupboard.

Nora asked, 'I expect you've visited his new place by now, dear?'

You know I haven't. 'Haven't had time.' *I haven't had an invitation either.* No longer able to imagine him in his parents' godforsaken spare room, Fern felt that Adam had inched a few squares further away on the chessboard of her life.

'How's the house-hunting, Auntie?' Fern hoped she'd said it lightly, gaily.

Apparently not. Nora was on to her. Tipsy or not, her iron curls shuddered with outrage as she spat, 'I can move out tonight if I'm in the way.'

'No, Auntie, I just—'

'Is that what you want? Should I drag meself all the way up to the loft with these bad legs of mine and pack me bags?'

Bagsh.

'Auntie, I didn't mean—'

'I hope when you're old and penniless, your life isn't a living hell like mine.'

'Please, Auntie, let's forget I spoke. I'm sorry.'

Nora's life didn't seem that hellish from where Fern stood. It started with a lie-in, ended with an early night, and was crammed with meals brought to her on a tray, all her favourite television programmes, cosy chats with Evka, and the endless fun of telling the only relative with whom she was still on speaking terms how bad she was at everything. Not to mention access to gin.

Creeping out from under the table, tomato sauce on her chin, Tallulah said, 'Mummy, please don't throw Auntie out.'

'Nobody's throwing anybody out!' Fern felt tears prickling, as they often had since Midsummer Night. It was a sort of hell to try and try and not get anywhere, to feel misunderstood, to wonder where she'd gone wrong. Unaccustomed to self-pity, Fern pushed it away, but those tears were persistent little buggers.

'Mummy?' Tallulah peered closer.

'Something in my stupid eye!' Fern had promised herself never to let her little girl witness proof of her falling apart. It might scar her forever, on top of whatever scars the child had already accrued from the separation.

'You're crying!' Tallulah looked astonished. 'Aw, Mummy, it's all right to cry. Let me squeeze you.' Closing her eyes, Tallulah closed her short arms around her mother as tight as they would go. 'Is that better?'

'It is.' So much for scarring; Tallulah could teach her a thing or two about emotional intelligence.

'After all I've done for this family.' Nora was working her way through her repertoire. 'Looking after Mother, throwing away any chance of my own happiness.'

'Auntie, let's not discuss it again. You're welcome to stay as long as you like.'

Nora's mouth closed, her face a vision of surprise.

Perhaps, thought Fern, *I've stumbled on the way to control her. Just say 'yes'.* The old girl was so accustomed to battle that she seemed unable to cope when her opponent just rolled over. 'Oll-*ie*!' Fern knew that if she didn't shout up for the smeared plate she'd find it under his bed at some point, crusty and supporting its own miniature ecosystem.

As Ollie clattered into the kitchen, Donna at his heels like a cat, Fern asked, 'Fancy some ice cream?' She'd always had a fond and jokey relationship with her son's girlfriend, but since the rapprochement Donna had clung to Ollie's side, padding in and out of the house on silent feet.

'No thanks, Fern.' Donna's eyes were on the floor. A self-possessed young woman, the same height as her beau, she had slender limbs the colour of wet sand and wore her exuberant afro pulled back. There was an austerity to Donna that belied her age, and she ignored her own beauty as if it was insignificant. Preferring to lead with her brains, she was a superb role model for Tallulah, who could sometimes be heard saying she wanted to be a lawyer 'like Donna's going to be'.

'No ice cream? I don't understand you young people.'

Fern laughed as she bent over the new dishwasher, a plate in each hand. She loved that dishwasher; she loved it *hard*. 'Kids, standing there like that, you look as if you're about to sing.' Fern waved a dirty spoon like a baton, and sang, in the cod-operatic voice she knew her children hated.

> *Sometimes stuff just seems to get you down*
> *Feelin' like there's no one else around*
> *You wish you could reach out and find a friend*
> *Who'll be here today, tomorrow, until the bitter end*

'Oh, come on,' she begged. 'Worth some applause, surely?'

'Mum,' said Ollie, his fingers closing over Donna's hand. 'We're having a baby.'

'Jeshush, Mary and Josheph,' whispered Nora into the silence that blossomed in the space where Fern's brain used to be.

'I'll ring your dad,' said Fern eventually, picking up her phone on automatic pilot. 'Sit down, kids. We'll sort this out. Don't worry. It'll all be fine.' Fern planted a smacker of a kiss on both Ollie and Donna's foreheads as they sank like bags of flour onto kitchen chairs.

The teenagers looked as stunned as Fern felt; perhaps it was only properly real to them now that they'd told her. Ollie's defection from sixth form fell into place. As Adam's mobile rang in her ear, Fern asked Donna, 'Do your parents know yet?'

'Are you kidding?' Donna's family could out-Puritan Nora.

'Adam!' Fern was relieved to hear his voice, the crisis

instantly downsized by a millimetre or two. This man had been Fern's first port of call when things went wrong since her late teens; at least *that* hadn't changed. 'We need you here. Something's happened. We're having a family pow-wow right now.' Fern reached out to Ollie, succumbing to a primeval need to touch her son. Leaning sideways on his chair, he bent instinctively into her, then stiffened so she was hugging a plank.

'It's a bit tricky now, as it goes.'

'Adam, I said we need you.'

'Can it wait?'

'Is somebody . . .' Fern stopped herself, ignoring the female mutters in the background. 'It's an emergency, Adam.'

'Is somebody ill?'

'Well, no.'

'Then surely it can wait. I'm not feeling great.'

'This is important, Adam.'

'I'm coming down with something.'

I bet you are. I can hear her. 'Donna's pregnant.'

The journey from penthouse to Homestead House took fifteen minutes; Adam made it in eight. 'Christ on a bike, what's going on?' he said instead of hello, joining the family in the kitchen and almost tripping over Binkie, who prided herself on winding around visitors' legs like a furry noose. Nodding sternly at Fern, he ignored the wordless question in her expression.

It was Tallulah who supplied the words. 'Daddy!' she squealed. 'What happened to your face?'

Peering through dark glasses – *another boozer's trick* – Nora said, 'You look just like Mr Spock in them *Star Trek Wars* films.'

Manfully pretending he had no idea what they were talking about, Adam shrugged off their puzzled looks, saying, 'I've washed my hair, that's all.'

'It's not the hair.' Fern missed the old shaggy shapelessness. 'Is that *gel*?' The Adam she'd lived with had been vehemently anti-hair-product.

'It might be.'

Nora put her head to one side. 'No, it's not the hair. It's definitely your face.'

Ollie laughed. 'Dad, you've totally had Botox.'

'Language!' said Nora.

'He said Botox, Auntie,' said Fern. 'Not . . . what you thought. Adam, it's not true, is it?' She squinted at his face, wondering if perhaps he'd had a stroke on the way over.

'OK. Full disclosure. I've had Botox.' Adam stood straight, nose in the air. 'What's the big deal?'

'You tell us,' said Ollie. 'You're the one who looks amazed.'

Fern studied Adam surreptitiously as she made his coffee. It came together in her hands just the way he liked it: mug not cup, not too milky, one sweetener; another skill rendered useless.

The kids' teasing was relentless. Nora was confused, asking only 'But Botox is for actresses, surely?' over and over.

Once two wickedly waggling stripes, Adam's eyebrows were now stark inverted Vs, as if two suicidal seagulls had crashed into the vast open spaces of his forehead.

'So they *inject* poison into your face?' Nora struggled to understand. 'And you pay them?'

Adam took it all in good part, nodding, accepting the insults raining down on him. Then Tallulah put her finger on it, the way eight-year-olds sometimes can.

'You don't look like my daddy any more.'

Fern handed Adam his mug and their eyes met. His were shiny and round, like a teddy's. *My eyes must look like withered raisins to him now.* This permanently startled, smooth-faced man didn't look like Tallulah's parent, nor did he look like Fern's ex. She felt something prod her already beleaguered heart as she wondered why Adam didn't respect his sweetly ageing face the way she did.

'Never mind the surgery face,' said Ollie. 'What's with the velvet pantaloons, Dad?'

All eyes went to Adam's lower half. 'They're not pantaloons, you little sod.' Tallulah wolf-whistled – a new accomplishment she was proud of – but Fern, knowing she was a party pooper, said, 'Never mind Dad's alarming trousers, we're here to discuss . . .' The word, such a soft word, felt like a rock in her mouth. 'The baby.'

'What's to discuss?' Ollie sought Donna's fingers again as if groping for a hand-hold on a cliff face. The look he attempted was 'not bovvered', but Fern, who had seventeen years' practice in translating Ollie's looks, read it as 'terrified'.

Fern glanced at Adam: *I'll go first.* This tag-match parenting was an old trick of theirs. One parent starts laying down the law; loud expostulations from child; other parent takes the reins, going in harder with their agreed strategy.

'Ollie, Donna,' said Fern, in presidential candidate tones, 'we're glad you've shared this with us. From now on, Adam and I will do everything in our power to help. You're not on your own.'

Tallulah put her hand up. 'If it's a girl can we call it Beyoncé? And if it's gay can we call it—'

'Shush, darling.' Fern pulled Tallulah to her side. Pregnancy fascinated the girl, so it was vital to close her down with a firm cuddle before she got onto her theories about how babies can see out through their mothers' belly buttons. 'The thing is, Ollie, Donna, this doesn't have to derail your lives. You have many options. You're not stuck. We'll talk them all through with you.'

When Ollie set his chin like that, he was the image of Adam. Adam in a stinking mood. 'What're you on about, Mum? Nobody's life is derailed. We don't need options.'

'Look at your girlfriend's face before you say that.'

'She's nervous, yeah. So am I. But we're doing OK. We told you 'cos it's the right thing to do, but we're not looking for advice. We're not children.'

'Says he,' said Fern. 'Standing there in clothes I bought him. You're a *sixth former*, Ollie.' She wanted to yell *You're my little Ollster* and scoop him up the way she had in the playground when the class bully nicked his champion conker.

'Not any more. I'm a DJ. Well, I will be, when I save up enough for some decent gear.' Ollie looked to Donna for endorsement. She lifted her head and nodded at him, both of them rock-solid, as if a plan to DJ at some point in the future was the time-honoured way to welcome a new life.

'What about your law studies?' Fern turned to Donna, the brightest student in her competitive girls' school, the one who'd wanted to be a barrister before other girls could spell the word.

'I can go back to it later.' Donna didn't have Ollie's fire. Her eyes slid around the room, never landing.

Your go, Adam. Fern had to signal him twice before he got the message; maybe the Botox had leaked into his brain.

'Ah. Yes.' Adam coughed, looked his son in the eye, every inch the Victorian papa, despite the lady's face and the skin-tight trews. 'Congratulations, guys!' he said. 'Why not have a baby? It'll work out.'

'But—' Fern was flummoxed, the only one holding back from the noisy group hug, disentangling herself from the arm Adam held out from the scrum. Even Nora was on her feet, and she believed that sex before marriage was right up there with genocide in the sin stakes.

If this pregnancy was planned, thought Fern, *I'd feel differently.* It was clear that it had been a mistake.

After the euphoric hugging, both Nora and Tallulah were lured away to their respective bedrooms – Tallulah to cluck over puzzled ants in a jar, Nora to tut at the ten o'clock news – so Ollie and Donna could flesh out their future.

'We've really thought about this, Mum,' said Ollie. 'We're going to live apart until the baby's born, so we can

81

save up. We're not fools, we know it costs a lot to look after a kid, so save the speech you're dying to do, yeah?'

The speech battered at the back of Fern's teeth, desperate to be free. Ollie's idea of what it cost to 'look after a kid' would be unrealistic; his perception of money related to how many pairs of trainers it could buy.

'Let him speak, Fern,' said Adam, as if she'd shouted Ollie down. Fern knew this tranquil acceptance of the youngsters' kamikaze 'plan' was part and parcel of Adam's new-found grooviness, just like his frozen face and gelled hair.

'When I can afford decks, oh, and a van actually, and I guess, printing flyers'n'shit, I'll set myself up as . . .' Ollie paused for effect. 'DJ Dirty Tequila.'

Fern stared at her son, feeling approximately a thousand and three years old.

'Kickin',' said Adam.

The hard look that said *Come OFF it* that Fern sent Adam's way simply slid off his smooth new face. '*Kickin*'?' she hissed in disbelief.

Animated now, Ollie couldn't keep up with his own thoughts. Words tumbled out, his confidence boosted by Adam's approval. 'Donna's going to, like, nanny, 'cos she can keep doing that after the baby arrives. We'll find somewhere to rent, somewhere small with a garden, and we'll move in when the baby comes.' He sat back, pleased. 'Simples!'

'We haven't heard much from Donna.' Fern felt it was time the woman who would actually grow this baby inside her had her say. 'Did you see yourself becoming a mother in your teens, Donna?'

'Not really.' Donna, usually so mouthy, the girl who out-glared hard girls on the bus on Tallulah's behalf, was cowed. She shrank against Ollie in a neat reversal of their usual roles; Fern and Adam used to giggle together about how their son was dominated by his girlfriend. 'These things happen, don't they?'

'No, they don't.' Fern was tired of tiptoeing around a basic truth. 'These things happen only if you fail to take basic precautions.' She'd gone to great lengths to educate Ollie about contraception, repeating herself no matter how much he blushed or begged her to stop, squealing, 'TMI, Mum. Way TMI!' The thought of her little boy 'doing it' was tough – no parent can look that one straight in the eye – but she'd never been naive enough to think he and Donna would be content with holding hands. Fern's sex life had been a constant source of naughty joy; she didn't want Ollie's early fumbles to result in a lifelong commitment he simply wasn't ready for.

A thought struck Fern, like a wet haddock in the face. *Is my sex life over?*

'There's no point going backwards.' Adam was the voice of tolerance, of forbearance, of making your ex want to beat you with the nearest wok. 'These two crazy kids should have been more careful but, hey, they weren't.' He coughed meaningfully, deliberately not looking at Fern. 'They wouldn't be the first couple in history to have a baby before they were ready. Let's deal with the here and now.'

Many times, Fern had been grateful for Adam's talent for

cutting the crap and getting to the heart of the matter, but tonight she felt they should linger awhile in the crap. 'Adam, you know as well as I do that these *crazy kids* are totally unprepared for the stresses and responsibilities of parenthood.' His crack about Ollie's conception was irrelevant; Fern had been a twenty-four-year-old woman, and she'd been with Adam for seven years. 'They're seventeen! When you were seventeen you chickened out of a camping trip because you didn't want to wee in a bush. Ollie here can't boil an egg without setting off the fire alarm, but suddenly he's a world-famous DJ who can raise a child on the side? Can we please talk realistically about this?' Fern hated being so combative with the people dearest to her; but that was *why* she was being fierce. She had to do her best by Ollie; parenting isn't a popularity contest. 'Our son and this lovely girl are at a crossroads, Adam. I won't let you sacrifice them on the altar of your quest to be cool.'

Hands on hips – somewhat slimmer hips, Fern noticed – Adam blew out his cheeks, puffing like a weary horse. A suspicion, hot and ugly, flared in Fern's mind. How much did that female voice she'd heard peeping in the background have to do with Adam's waxwork face and hip attitude?

Blinking rapidly, Donna jumped up, flapping her hands in front of her face. 'I'm sorry. I'm just really really sorry. Ollie, you don't have to stand by me. I understand.' She tried to bolt, but Ollie grabbed her by the waist. Donna turned her face away as if his words were blows.

'Donna, it's not your fault!'

Appalled, Fern said softly, 'Donna, love, nobody's suggesting that you do this on your own.'

'But it's all my fault.' The girl bent over, crying hard, tears rolling off the end of her nose, looking pitifully young.

'It is *not*.' Fern was firm. 'It takes two to tango.'

From the doorway, an earwigging Tallulah put her right. 'You don't make babies by tangoing, Mummy.'

'Scoot!' Fern clapped her hands at Tallulah, who darted away. 'Ollie, Donna, you share the responsibility. I know my son and he would *never* walk away at a time like this.' Fern's heart swelled with the truth of that. Her son trembled with the need to protect his girl. *You look just like your dad*, she thought, before suppressing such an observation as unhelpful. Adam didn't feel that way about her any more.

'Mum's right. Why not—'

Adam got no further. 'Will you both just back off!' yelled Ollie, as if his flesh and blood were conspiring against him instead of doing their best to help. 'Me and Donna are going to raise our little family and love our baby and each other and it's all going to work out.' His nostrils flared as he panted out the words. 'Don't you dare lecture us on something you failed at.'

Seeing Adam out to his car, Fern wrapped her arms about herself. August had turned huffily cool, and her tartan shirt was inadequate. 'Thanks for coming over.'

'What else would I do?' Adam seemed irked by her gratitude as the roof of his Mercedes peeled itself back. 'I'm the little bugger's dad.'

'I didn't mean . . .' The ground around Adam was strewn

with booby traps. Tired of negotiating them, Fern didn't try to explain. 'Just, you know, it was good to have you here. This has really thrown me.'

'Me too.' Adam looked up at her from the driving seat. The Botox couldn't disguise the strain.

Melting slightly, Fern risked a sad smile. She remembered how comforting Adam's arms were at times like this.

He said, 'You look soooo tired.'

'And you look twelve,' snapped Fern, who knew she looked tired, thank you very much. There was no way she could ask this distant, kooky-looking man the questions banging around inside her head: *is Ollie right? Did we really fail at raising a loving family?*

The car revved throatily, its headlamps painting a bright stripe on the trunk of the old yew that stood guard over Homestead House. 'Look, if Ollie and Donna can't cope, we can afford to bail them out.'

'Not everything can be cured with money.' Fern wasn't sure if he heard her over the bite of his tyres on the gravel.

'See ya, babe!' With a toot of the horn, he was off.

High above Fern's head, Nora slammed the loft window shut.

CHAPTER FOUR

October: Entrée

Up so early it qualified as night, Fern groped her way around the dark park, following the flashing light on Boudicca's collar. 'Why is it always me who walks the dog?' she muttered into her scarf. The same reason it was always her who fed the guinea pigs. When Tallulah's current obsession with the insect hospital ended, it would be Fern who'd deal with a ward full of legless beetles.

Skirting the wet black ribbon of the Thames, Fern averted her eyes from Adam's apartment block, like a devout nun confronted with a builder's bum. He was probably up there in the penthouse, snoring like a sick gnu on some absurdly costly mattress. It was odd that he lived somewhere she'd never seen. Odd, and somehow humiliating.

'Hey!' A tall figure waved from the gates, also bound up in scarves and topped with a woolly hat.

'Hey yourself.' Fern had time to regret not cleaning off yesterday's make-up as Tinkerbell approached. 'I thought I'd be the only one out this early.'

'The dog was bored, so I thought, why not take him

to the park?' The Cockapoo yawned at his feet. 'Fancy a coffee?'

'Oh. Coffee?' Fern queried the suggestion as if coffee was some mythical brew she'd heard tell of. 'At this hour? Where?' She sounded very much like somebody who didn't want to go for coffee with Tinkerbell, when the opposite was true. He loomed over her, making her bend her head back to look into his eyes. It was worth the effort.

'That caff.' Tinkerbell pointed to a lit window in the dark row of shops opposite the park. 'No pressure. Just an idea.' He took a step back.

'Coffee sounds great.' Fern took a step forward, telling herself to calm the hell down. If Maggie or Sabre had suggested coffee, she wouldn't have blushed. Nor would she have said 'yes', but there was no need to go into that now.

The coffee *wasn't* great, and, unless you were into greasy Formica, neither was the café. The atmosphere at their table, however, made up for all that. Fern sat back, glad to be there, glad to be infected by Tinkerbell's wry, playful mood. 'So, listen,' she said, relishing the contrast between the gloomy 'out there' beyond the steamy windows and this bright room. 'I have a confession. In my head I call you by your dog's name.'

'Snap!' Tinkerbell put down his 'proper' (i.e. Mother's Pride and brown sauce) bacon sarnie. 'Which is fine in your case, as Boudicca suits you.'

'It does?'

'Ya-huh! I can see you fighting the Romans in your chariot with knives sticking out of the wheels.'

'Thank you. I think. You're not really a Tinkerbell.'

'How about Hal? Does that suit me?'

'Yes. Hello, Hal. I'm Fern.'

'Hello, Fern.'

Something moved beneath the surface of their words, as if both of them were listening harder than the silly jokes deserved. As if they were laying down a memory. For Fern, this was an abrupt about-turn in her dealings with what Nora would call 'strange men', a blanket term that covered all men who weren't Adam.

Decades of being Adam's Other Half had anaesthetized her to male charms. Obviously she'd lusted after sexy celebs – if Orlando Bloom could read Fern's mind, he'd take out a restraining order – but she was a steadfast, loyal lover and had never indulged in even mild flirting. If she'd imagined a dating life after Adam, it had been a barren desert scene, with vultures circling overhead and Fern gasping on the sands. She'd never imagined a poky café where the couple at Table Four kept looking at each other's mouths.

They gossiped about the dog walkers. Both were wary of Sabre, with Hal describing him as 'murderer-y' and Fern agreeing. They were both secretly afraid of Pongo and they both suspected that Maggie was lonely.

'Poor Maggie,' said Fern.

'He lives by the station,' said Hal. 'Sometimes I see him letting himself into his house with a takeaway.'

That didn't sound so bad to Fern. Some nights she'd *kill* to let herself into an empty house with a chicken korma in her handbag.

'Where do you live?'

'Um . . .' Hal's directness took Fern by surprise.

'Am I being nosey?' He put his hands up. 'Sorry. I promise not to follow you home and murder you or anything.' He grimaced. 'Which totally makes it sound as if I plan to follow you home and murder you.'

'I live on the corner of Archer Close, three streets away.' *And you're more than welcome to follow me home.*

'That big house with the turrets and the porch?' Hal clapped with excitement. 'I love that house! It has soul.'

'It really does.' After Adam's criticisms, Hal's praise warmed Fern, as if somebody had finally appreciated a misunderstood child. 'I've lived there for years.' She didn't dare say how many. *As if not saying how old I am will make me younger.*

'You and Mr Fern, I guess.' Hal looked her in the eye.

'Not any more.' Fern wasn't accustomed to saying that. 'It's complicated.' The bubble was burst. The caff was just a caff again.

'Christ, I *am* nosey,' said Hal. 'None of my business. Sorry.'

'I don't mind talking about it,' fibbed Fern, to make him feel better, to try and glue their bubble back together. 'How about you?'

'I'm footloose and fancy-free. Or single and suicidal, depending on the time of day.'

'You don't seem suicidal to me.' He was rainbows, sunshine, unicorns. *And I'm going mad.*

'I'm just putting a brave face on my despair.' Hal flashed her one of his quick, conspiratorial smiles. 'Some of my mates go from girl to girl, but I'm in no hurry.'

'Quality rather than quantity.'

'Exactly. I'm picky.'

'Is that so?' This frothy conversation was balm after the fractious interaction with the other males in her life. Fern smiled, wishing she'd brushed her teeth before leaving the house. Her morning breath could stun toddlers. 'What are your deal-breakers?'

'They must have a pulse. I'm a stickler for that. And just the one head.'

'High standards indeed. Do they need a GSOH?'

'Obviously, so we can LOL and ROFL.'

Fern couldn't ignore the clock on the wall any longer. 'I should get going.' It was almost time to get Tallulah up for school. 'I have to . . . do stuff.' Just like that, her beloved daughter, light of her life, was transformed to 'stuff' and denied access to this roped-off area.

'Me too. So much stuff,' sighed Hal theatrically. 'Tons of stuff, all over the place.' He plonked down a note that would cover the bill.

'Thank you,' said Fern, watching him pull on his bulky khaki jacket, noting the lack of status symbols. No chunky watch, no flashy belt for Hal, despite his riches. 'My treat next time.'

'So there'll be a next time?' Hal had dimples and he knew how to use them.

As Boudicca pulled Fern along the pavements, away from Hal and towards home, she examined a thought clearly for the first time. 'I fancy that man,' she said into the dawn, as if chanting an ancient, forgotten spell.

The house came into view. Within its walls she was a mum and a woman struggling to make sense of the ruins of her relationship. Fern dawdled, hanging onto the silvery air of wonder that she'd never thought to feel again.

Along with the tingling excitement came vulnerability. Adam knew and accepted all her body's peculiarities, but if she was on the market again, Fern wasn't sure of her value.

Just as she made herself look at the gory bits in films, Fern forced herself to confront a scenario in which she unwrapped her orange-peel thighs in front of Hal. It was easy to imagine the horror in his unlined eyes.

Putting her key in the door, Fern shook off the cobweb of feeling and was back on predictable, solid ground. 'Tallulah!' she yelled. 'Time to get up!'

'I'm already up.' Tallulah called down from where she stood at the end of Ollie's bed, head on one side as she surveyed Donna, propped alone against the bed head.

'Breakfast in ten mins,' shouted Fern. 'Don't annoy Donna, please.' The rules about Donna not staying overnight had been relaxed: she and Adam used to be vehemently against it but now, well, horses/stable doors.

'You are six months pregnant,' said Tallulah with dour authority. 'The foetus is approximately twenty-eight centimetres long. About this length.' She demonstrated the wrong length with her fingers as Donna nodded, straining to look interested through sleepy eyes. 'It's definitely human.'

'That's a relief.' Donna rearranged herself in the tangled bedclothes. Fern was not allowed in this room, so the bed was never made and a faint smell of biscuit hung in the air.

'Are you taking your vitamin D?' Tallulah was stern,

tapping a list she'd made on her Etch-a-Sketch. 'Tell me about your discharge. Whatever that is.' She gasped, dropping the Etch-a-Sketch. 'OMG, Donna, what if it's twins or triplets or fourlets?'

'One's plenty, Tallie.' Donna let out an *oof*, throwing her legs over the side of the bed.

'Can I feel?' Tallulah was fascinated by the bump that had budded, so soft-looking yet so strong, beneath Donna's Topshop ensembles. She put her mouth close and whispered, 'Hello, niece or nephew. This is your aunt or uncle speaking. I already love you.'

Sauntering down to the kitchen, Tallulah picked up her mother's phone, which was chirruping on the marble. 'It's Daddy.' She handed it over. 'Be nice.'

'Yes, be nice,' said Nora from the table.

'I'm always nice.' With the phone in one hand, Fern doled out scrambled eggs with the other. 'Adam, good morning.'

Nora said, 'Scrambled eggs make me tummy go queer.'

'Can you talk?' said Adam.

'Yes.' Fern buttered toast: not too much on Ollie's, not too little on Tallulah's, margarine for Nora.

'Can I put you on the guest list for Saturday?'

The question took her back to their beginnings, when Fern would roll up to some grotty nightspot chewing gum, a bottle of illicit voddy in her handbag, and tell the bouncer 'I'm with the band.' 'Which guest list?'

'My gig. I told you. I think. Did I? Well, anyway, it's Kinky Mimi's comeback, our first live show in–' *mumble mumble* '–years. We're playing the King's Arms.'

The King's Arms was all tacky carpet and loos that only

the truly desperate would consider. 'It's Halloween on Saturday. Tallulah will want to go trick-or-treating.'

'Take her first, then come down. We don't go on until nine. Please, Fern. Please come.'

It felt so good, so *unusual* to be necessary to Adam. 'I wouldn't miss it for the world.'

'Excellent. We need as many bums on seats as we can get.'

Maybe not as necessary as all that. Fern wondered if P.W. would be there, eating Dover sole and being mysterious. 'Hang on, don't go. We need to talk.' Fern wedged the phone beneath her ear as she leaned down to feed Boudicca and toe Binkie out of the way. The table bayed for more toast. 'About the hall.'

'The hall?' Adam sounded above such things, like a duchess.

'Yes, the hall,' said Fern with ironic patience. 'Remember? I pointed out the damp patch by the coat stand and you said get a man in, so I got a man in.'

'So far, so fascinating.'

'The damp patch is gone, but now the hall needs repainting.'

'So get another man in, one with a paintbrush this time.' Adam said something else, but it was muffled, underwater-sounding, as if he'd covered the phone with his hand.

'Is someone there?' *Early for visitors.*

'Nope. It's nobody.'

Fern let a long pause unfurl, during which this nobody made a number of peeved noises. Evidently Nobody didn't like her new name one little bit.

'Anyway, back to the hall.' Fern put Adam out of his misery as Donna appeared in the doorway, making the international sign for *Can I have some scrambled eggs please*? Fern nodded and pulled out a chair for her. 'Should we go for off-white again? Or risk a colour? A nice sunny yellow might work.'

'It's your wall, Fern. Paint it whatever colour you like.'

As Fern put down her mobile, cracking eggs and ignoring Nora's advice on how to crack eggs *properly*, she checked the gin bottle on its shelf. The clear liquid had inched further and further down.

This evidence of Nora's secret boozing didn't concern Fern at that moment. She was busy digesting 'It's your hall, Fern,' and diagnosing the hard lump that had swelled in her throat.

The hands of the clock turned. Personnel at the table changed. The younger generation trailed out and Evka took their place, cosying up to Nora.

'How was Buckingham Palace?' Fern had managed to cajole Evka into wiping the microwave last week; progress was being made. 'Did you see the throne?' She enjoyed seeing familiar British things through Evka's knock-off designer shades. Sometimes these stories turned X-rated, and Fern would try and look as if she heard such tales every day. She'd been quite proud of how calmly she'd listened to Evka's tale of oral sex under the buffet table at the bowls tournament.

'Throne is flashy. Bit common.' Evka screwed up her full mouth. 'Queen was not there. Is scam.' Her hair had grown, and was piled up anyhow, her eyeliner flicked like a modern-day Nefertiti. 'Did not even see bloody corgi.'

'What's next on the list?' asked Nora.

'I think I like to see traditional British punch-up in pub,' said Evka. 'Proper big one with smashed window and crying barmaid.'

'I,' said Nora, lifting her nose high in the air, 'have never set foot in a public house. Nor have I allowed alcohol to pass my lips.'

Evka was admiring. 'You are good woman, Nora.'

You are liar, liar, pants on fire woman, Nora.

'Me,' continued Evka happily, 'I am not good woman. I prefer to be slut.' She and Nora laughed heartily together. 'Should we . . .' Evka cocked her head towards Fern. 'Tell her?'

'Tell me what?' Fern was on immediate red alert.

'Ah. Yes.' Nora toyed with a button on the latest of her inexhaustible supply of inoffensive M&S cardis. 'Poor Evka's been turfed out of her flatshare.'

Guessing what was coming, Fern tensed herself for a scrap.

'My flatmates are evil wanker people,' shuddered Evka. 'Never do they clean loo. They steal my Peperami. They complain when I borrow shoe.'

'I'll help you find nicer people to share with,' said Fern.

'She already has,' said Nora. 'Us!' She flung a podgy arm around Evka's narrow shoulders. 'I've told her she can stay here as long as she likes.'

'Auntie,' began Fern, 'with respect—'

'I see.' Nora stood abruptly, Binkie rolling off her lap and landing on Boudicca with a thud. 'Typical.' She leaned her knuckles on the table. 'Take no notice of me, as per usual. Perhaps I should go off and die quietly under a hedge.'

'What?' Fern was always blindsided by her aunt's sudden leaps.

'Yes, yes, I see it in your eyes.' Nora looked heroically into the middle distance. 'I'm old and useless. Throw me on the scrapheap! No, don't bother. I'll throw myself on it.'

'Is all right, Nora.' Evka's hands fluttered at her chest. She seemed to be taking Nora's diva strop seriously. 'Do not upset self, please. I find other flat.' Her eyes glistened.

Does Evka cry? The girl was so hard-faced, so grabby, but yes, she was crying, over Nora. 'I give in!' said Fern, literally throwing in the (tea) towel. 'Evka, you can have the spare room. Auntie, please stop talking about the scrapheap. At this rate, I'll beat you to it.' She waited for them to compose themselves. 'What shall I charge for rent, Evka? Something nominal.'

'Rent?' Nora banged the table. 'You'd charge this little lost lamb *rent*?'

Little lost lambs rarely wear Wonderbras (Fern suspected Evka of wearing two at once; nothing else could account for the contents of her jumpers) but Fern couldn't bear another scene. She'd lost control of her little Queendom. 'Fine, fine, Evka, just babysit instead.'

'I am happy to babysit the lovely Tallulah,' said Evka graciously. 'Rate is fifteen pounds per hour.'

'Mum. It's me.'

'Fern! Is everything all right? Everybody OK?'

'Yes, everybody's alive and well.'

'When I heard your voice I thought . . . Good. Good. The kids? How's my Ollie?'

'He's, well, he's, I'll tell you his news another time. How's your husband?'

'He does have a name, dear. Dave's very busy, retiling the pool. We're trying to attract a better class of tourist, so we're doing the place up a bit. When are you going to come and visit? You could all stay in our new family suite.'

'There's been some changes, Mum. Adam and I, we've kind of, we're not living together any more.'

'What? No!'

'There's no drama, Mum. It's just a decision we came to. Together.'

'Is there somebody else? Are you playing away? You and Adam can't split up!'

'Well, we can . . .'

'The children. What about the children? They say youngsters go off the rails when this happens.'

'Everybody's still talking to each other. They see Adam all the time. Honestly, it's going as well as can be expected.'

'You better pray Nora doesn't get wind of this.'

'Nora's living here.'

'Are you mad? Did *she* break you and Adam up?'

'No, no. She had to move out and she's here temporarily. I hope.'

'Don't be so sure. Be careful, dear. Nora likes to ruin

things. It beggars belief that she and a lovely man like your dad were siblings . . . Fern? You still there?'

'Yes. Yes, Mum. It's just that . . . I think that's the first time you've mentioned Dad in years.'

'Not this again, Fern.'

'It's like he ran off or something, not died. As if we mustn't—'

'How long has this been going on, this separation?'

'He left in June.'

'Oh.'

'I would have rung, but I didn't want to worry you.'

'Sure. Sure, love. It doesn't matter, not a bit. Would you like me to . . .'

'Come over? That's up to you, but yeah, if you like . . .'

'Although you've got a full house by the sounds of it.'

'Mmm.'

'And I shouldn't really leave Dave with all the work.'

'No. Look Mum, somebody's at the door, so . . .'

'Bye, dear. Look after yourself.'

'Bye, Mum.'

Fern put down her mobile. 'I love you,' she said, almost to herself.

Another day, another dark walk in the park, but this time it was in the evening. Hal had been missing from Fern's morning circuit with the usual mob. 'Probably busy!' Pongo had said.

Or regretting being so friendly. Fern's inner dialogue had turned on her since the split, as if she needed Adam's bulk around the house to bolster up her self-esteem. This was an unwelcome thought, not the mindset of the mother of a rampant feminist. *Hal's opinion of me is neither here nor there*, she told herself.

Boudicca's flashing light leapt in graceful arcs around the grass, like a mini fireworks display. 'Here, girl!' called Fern, waving the lead.

In the darkness a bush moved, grew legs. Fern tensed, her fight or flight impulse stirring. But then the bush with legs said, 'Evening,' and she realized it was Hal.

'You scared the life out of me!'

'God, sorry.' Hal took a step back. 'I didn't mean to.' He folded his arms around himself. 'Sometimes blokes forget how it is for women out on the streets at night. I should have called out.' He looked sad, his large features drooping. 'Should I, you know, sod off?'

'No, silly.' Fern was glad to see him, his Cockapoo romping giddily at his heels. 'I thought I'd be the only dog walker out this late.'

'You said you sometimes walk Boudicca about this time, so . . .' Hal was smiling, a little uncertainly.

Glad of the darkness, Fern bent to snap on Boudicca's lead. She felt the warm surge of a forgotten power.

'How about another coffee? A slightly more salubrious place this time.'

'Bored of coffee,' said Fern.

'Oh, well, OK.' Hal looked at the ground.

'But if you were to suggest a glass of wine . . .'

By the time they'd taken their seats at the back of a poshed-up pub, Fern had discovered some pertinent details about Hal. He walked a little too fast, making her skip; he put his hand on the small of her back when they crossed the road, making her flutter; his favourite TV show was *Roomies*, making her wilt.

'*Roomies* is reliably funny,' he said as he set down their glasses. 'Nothing else touches it. I watched the whole first season just the other night, with a giant pizza for company. That Lincoln Speed is brilliant.'

'Quite a character, according to the papers. Bit of a bad boy.' Fern neglected to spill her one interesting bean, her *Roomies* connection. 'Bad boy used to mean a little kid with a stink bomb. Now it means a bed with your name on it in rehab and a sideline in punching hookers.'

Hal barked a short, merry laugh. 'Apparently he's denying an affair with his *Roomies* co-star, the blonde one, even though he was papped leaving her mansion at three a.m. He reckoned they were discussing politics.'

Fern knew every move Lincoln Speed made. Adam kept her informed. Her ex's specialist subject on *Mastermind* would be 'Lincoln Speed's Stupid Behaviour 1998 – Present Day'.

'Do you like bad boys, Fern? Don't all women secretly yearn for a bastard?'

'Are you a bad boy?' Under the table, Boudicca stirred, as if taken aback by her mistress.

Hal's eyebrows shot up, as surprised as Boudicca by the flirtatious question. 'Me? I'm not bad. I'm not saying

I'm good. No man in their right mind describes themselves as good.'

'Conjures up a comedy vicar.'

'Like most people, I'm somewhere in the middle. Not so good that I'd bore you to death, but I wouldn't say I'm dangerous.'

Oh, yes, you bloody are.

Twirling his glass on the table top, his eyes on it, Hal said, 'And you? Where do you stand, Fern, on the good/bad spectrum?'

'I am extremely good.'

'I believe you.'

'What do you do with yourself all day?' Fern felt the need to move the subject away from the subtext, although as soon as she left it behind, she missed it. 'Now that you've sold your business.' She clocked his confusion. 'Your internet company.'

'I'm a potter,' said Hal.

The misunderstanding took seconds to unravel. The dot-com mogul was Hal's cousin. 'I walk his dog.'

'Tinkerbell's not even yours!' That was the most shocking revelation for Fern.

'My cousin bought Tinks 'cos Cockapoos are fashionable, but he doesn't see her as a living, breathing thing. He neglects her, so I trot around the park with her as a break from the studio.'

'What sort of pots do you, um, pot?' Fern was reassembling the jigsaw. Now Hal's low-key wardrobe made sense.

'Big pieces. Platters, mainly. Quirky one-offs. Too arty

for my own good, though. At some point I'll have to give in and get commercial. When I'm sick of being broke. But I'm not doing so bad only three years out of uni.'

Three years out of uni. Three years ago Fern had been wondering if she could squeeze out one last baby; Adam had been against the idea. 'I'd like to see your work.'

'I'd like to show you.' Hal shook his head, sighing with amusement. 'Can't believe you mixed me up with my cuz. He's an arsehole. You know the type, over-rewarded, a ton of money for doing very little. It ruins people.'

Fern didn't trust herself to comment on that.

Walking home, walking away from Hal, Fern was equal parts attracted and repelled. The man was undeniably to her taste; as if some diligent Cupid had created him just for her.

But he's in his twenties. Fern had bras older than Hal. There were fewer years between Hal and Ollie than there were between Hal and Fern. *I'm no cougar.*

The real impediment, rearing up between them like the Berlin Wall, was Adam.

'From my window in Bratislava I see ninth-century castle.' Evka pulled down the spare-room blind. 'Here I see lady next door shaving legs.'

'What's it like,' asked Fern, putting clean towels on the freshly-made bed, tweaking the duvet, 'in Bratislava?'

'Is small.' Evka took a stone apple from a shelf and

rolled it in her hands, a Slovak Eve. Her voice dropped. 'Is long way away.'

'Are you happy here? In the UK?' Such a personal question was risky. Despite Evka's chumminess with Nora, she bristled with *Keep Out* signs for Fern; but when Evka was low-key like this, Fern felt she was more authentic. And approachable.

'I am busy here,' said Evka, putting down the apple. 'I have much sex.'

'Not what I asked.'

'I like being busy and I like sex so I am happy,' said Evka. 'By the way –' she was proud of this new phrase, and said it slowly and lovingly – 'you need more gin. I finish last night.'

'That was you?'

'This room . . .' said Evka.

'Yes?' Fern braced herself.

'I like.'

'Ouch.' Nora pulled her hand away. 'You clipped me skin.'

'Please hold still.' Fern would rather have given Boudicca a manicure. The old woman was a fidget. 'I need to tidy your cuticles.'

'I didn't even know I had cuticles,' grumbled Nora. 'Will you be late tonight?'

'I'm not sure. All I know is that Adam's band goes on at nine. You don't have to wait up. Tallie will be in bed.'

'If you're not back at midnight I'll bolt the door, young lady.'

Wielding her file, Fern let her aunt ramble. She was grateful for Nora's offer to babysit; Evka had a 'hot date' at a bingo hall, but was taking Tallulah trick-or-treating before she went out. Without being asked.

'I've told Evka,' said Nora, who made a habit of telling people, 'not to let Tallie out of her sight.'

'She'll be safe with Evka.' No ghoul in its right mind would take on Fern's lodger.

'Nobody's safe,' said Nora with great satisfaction. 'There are murderers on every corner.'

'Perhaps every second corner.'

'It's not funny, Fern. You're as bad as me brother. He never took anything seriously. You're just like him.'

'Good.' Fern's dad had taken *her* seriously. She unscrewed a bottle of base coat.

'It was a noble thing to do, taking in Evka.'

'I didn't have much choice.'

'She's had a hard life.'

Living rent-free with more sex than you can shake a stick at? 'Evka will always get by.'

'Has she told you why she left Slovakia?'

Mildly interested, determined not to show it, Fern held up two bottles of almost identical pale pink varnish for her aunt. When Nora favoured one, Fern began to stroke the colour across her nails. 'No. What happened?'

'That's just it. She won't say. Her boyfriend did something *unspeakable*.' Nora loved that word. 'She won't reveal exactly what, but it was bad enough for her to jump on the first plane out of there.'

'Did he hurt her?'

'Maybe he beat her.'

'Or he was unfaithful.' Fern bent lower over Nora's hand. 'That certainly hits a woman where it hurts.'

'You look nice,' said Layla, from her French kitchen. 'Green suits you.'

'Shut up.' Fern stuck out her tongue, a vivid red against her green face paint. 'Do you like my stick-on warts?'

'Very much,' said Layla earnestly. 'You've really gone for it.'

'Is it over the top?' Fern pulled at the black wig and regretted the stick-on nose. 'Actually, you look a wee bit green yourself. Are you feeling peaky?'

'I love that expression. Where does it come from? I'm good, thanks, hun. How are things with you and Adam?'

'It's like *Alice in Wonderland*. Everything upside down and topsy-turvy.'

'He still loves you, Fern. I'd put money on that.'

'He loves me so much, he lives in a different building.'

'You started that ball rolling.'

'You know, it would be easier if Adam and I didn't have to talk to each other. You should hear the way we communicate. Like CEOs of a small failing company.' Fern considered telling Layla about P.W., about the twittering voice in the background when she called the penthouse.

Instead, because she didn't want tear tracks down her green face paint, she said, 'And my children hate me, so that's nice.'

'Tallulah still blames you?' Layla knew the little girl inside out.

'How come Adam leaves and I stay, I tuck her in every night, I bathe her, feed her, read to her, but *I'm* the villain of the piece?'

'Maybe 'cos she's eight, and this is tough even at our age.'

'You're saying *suck it up, bitch*, aren't you?'

'I am.'

'There's just so much to suck up. She and Nora get on like a house on fire. I feel shut out.'

'Little girls and old ladies are natural allies. They have a nose for trouble, no responsibilities and plenty of free time to tease the ones they love the best.'

'It's not love I see in Nora's eyes.'

'It was *you* she came to when she needed somebody.'

''Cos I'm a mug.'

''Cos you're *kind*. Tallulah and Ollie aren't some perfect family from a TV commercial. They love you and Adam. They'll come round.'

'If you say so. You are their Other Mother, after all.'

'I miss them.' Layla sounded raw, as if she'd opened a door she hadn't meant to.

'They miss you.'

Both rooms, separated by a mass of land and a strip of sea, were silent for a while. It was an electric silence, fizzing with the women's need for one another, by the friend-shaped void in their day-to-day lives. Through the wonders of technology – and love – Fern and Layla had a vibrant moment of togetherness.

'This'll make you laugh.' Fern changed the mood. 'I think I've got the hots for somebody.'

Layla's face was a perfect illustration of 'gobsmacked'. 'You?'

'Yes, million-year-old, about-to-be-a-Grandma me.' Fern screwed up her nose. 'I feel a bit of a perv.'

'Why?' Layla sat back.

'He's young.'

'Not one of Ollie's mates?'

'Dear God, no.' Fern thought of Ollie's posse, a constellation of pimples held together with self-consciousness and Lynx. She described Hal.

'Sounds bloody gorgeous. *I* fancy him. Go for it.'

'Go for it? What sort of advice is that?' Fern realized she'd wanted Layla to throw cold water on her. 'You know my situation.'

'What's the worst that could happen?'

'Apart from utter humiliation? How about Adam finding out?'

'You asked Adam to leave, remember? If you want him back, you should tell him so.'

It sounded so simple. Like a Ladybird book. 'There's no guarantee he'd want to come back. If he did, the rows would begin again. We lost our footing.'

'It wasn't always like this. Sometimes there's a route back.'

Fern hesitated. Just out of the camera's reach was the battered box. Today's slice of handwritten nostalgia was so loving, so daftly affectionate, that it had made her weep. Partly because of its loveliness, but partly because she couldn't imagine Adam ever writing anything like it again. As soon as she and Layla said their goodbyes, she picked up the letter and sat back.

The heading was 'MY FAVE PICS OF YOU'. Adam had glued snapshots onto the page. There was Pritt Stick over her face in the square image of a fresh-faced Fern sunbathing in a black bikini. *Didn't we wear any colour at all in the nineties?* One hand shading her eyes from the sun, she glowered at the camera. Or at the person wielding it, presumably Adam. Beneath it he'd scribbled:

Portugal with your family. Our first holiday. My first trip abroad.
  You were telling me not to take this but I thought 'oh God she's so pretty, I'll take a few snaps in case she dumps me' and now you have!!!

Next up was a photo-booth strip. Close together, cheek to cheek, above the sheepskin collar of a jacket Fern had forgotten, but which brought back a visceral memory of its feel and smell. The pair pulled faces, their eyes wide and their tongues out. The last little square was, inevitably, a full-on snog.

Your freckles really show up in these. I love your freckles. They spill onto your shoulders. I remember kissing you so I could show the picture off to my *mates, but when it came out I knew I wouldn't show it to anybody.*

Asleep between sheets so lurid they just had to be Adam's, Fern was in Adam's digs. *He was my older man*; the sophisticate at music college. The one-year age difference had made Fern feel she'd hooked Cary Grant.

I took this without you knowing. Which sounds dead creepy like I'm a ~~spycho~~ ~~pysco~~ murderer. I'm including it because it shows you trust me. You sleep like a baby in my bed. Even though my room smells of armpits (according to you). I want you back in that bed please.

Fern traced the faces in the photo-booth pictures, remembering Layla's soothing words. Could there really be a route back to a place that no longer existed?

Shouldering through the Frankensteins and vampires, wondering when sexy schoolgirls had become Halloween characters, Fern made her way to the back bar of the King's Arms. The green make-up was itchy, and one of her warts fell into her G&T as she arranged her witchy robes on a bar stool.

I'm early. Fern had forgotten that music-venue time runs differently to the rest of the world. Bands go on late. She'd dashed out of her door, her pointy hat askew, squawking instructions for Nora: *Tallie must stay in bed. Don't let her bamboozle you into letting her have fizzy drinks. If her tummyache comes back, give her Calpol.* It was hard to leave the house, as if glue seeped from the hall parquet. She'd almost turned back to reiterate the microwave instructions for Nora's supper.

An air of expectancy hung about the handful of people, some in fancy dress, all about her age, loitering in the back bar. It was a laid-back expectancy; more like a receptionist's leaving party than a gig.

Double doors flew back, and another witch stalked in. Where Fern had gone for comic effect, this witch had gone for glamour in a tight black dress and a feathered cape. Her faultless make-up was not green.

A sixth sense, like the one that made Binkie's fur stand on end if another cat even *thought* about entering Homestead House's garden, made Fern's skin prickle. *Nice to meet you, P.W.*

'In, in!' Her glossy black wig strobing, the woman ushered in a lively, hooting mob. This solid slab of party filled the room, running into corners like mercury. Boas were waved, and air was punched.

'Chant, guys.' The witch checked her phone.

'Kink-ee Mee-mee! Kink-ee Mee-mee!' The noise was deafening.

'As we agreed,' yelled Penny. 'Free bar. Stay till the end or you don't get paid.' Swivelling on patent Louboutins, she was gone.

Crushed at the bar, Fern jumped as the room went black. Spotlights landed on the band, who'd snuck on. She gasped. Lemmy, still recognizable despite the passing years and his velour all-in-one, pounded the drums like an orang-utan. She only recognized Keith by his height; all his youthful glamour had melted, along with his hair.

Leaping at the mike, a feather in his hat and quite possibly ants in his pants, Adam belted out "Psycho Bitch".

Fern took in every lean inch of him. The cut of his trousers and the narrow shoulders of his striped jacket accentuated his weight loss as he skipped and wiggled and got down with his bad self.

The crowd went crazy – except for the green-faced woman at the bar, who watched as if turned to stone. The sense that she didn't recognize Adam was by now familiar. Her ex surprised her daily.

What rooted her to the spot was a revelation. *He's happy*. Adam was free, lost in the song, literally jumping for joy. Fern had assumed that Adam was struggling beneath the veneer of new clothes, just as she was. The man on stage wasn't struggling; he was ecstatic.

'Woo-hoo!' When the other witch cheered, the crowd followed suit, even though the band was ragged, out of step. Lemmy looked as if he'd had a home brew or two in the dressing room, and Keith had the air of a man in the grip of a cheese dream, desperate to wake up and find himself safe in his bed. It was a shambles, only saved from collapse by Adam's dogged showmanship. He was the psychedelic equivalent of a captain going down with his ship, and he cavorted until the last note of the last tune.

'Goo'night King's Head!' shouted Adam, suddenly

mockney, as Keith strode off stage as if his fluorescent bell-bottoms were on fire.

'MORE!' yelled the audience, half-heartedly.

'That's yer lot!' Adam bowed low, like a jester, and scampered off stage. Fern prophesied that those pixie boots would play merry hell with his athlete's foot.

'You're my first groupie.' Adam strode towards Fern in the now-deserted bar.

'Can I have your autograph?'

Adam threw his head back and laughed, then said, 'Oh, you meant it?'

'It's a consent slip for Tallulah's school outing.'

'Top marks for bringing me back down to earth,' murmured Adam as he took the proffered biro. 'So.' He cocked his head.

Oh God. 'So!' Fern repeated. 'So, indeed,' she said, slapping her thighs, without knowing quite why. 'So . . . so . . . stunning!'

'You think so?' Adam was so boyishly keen to believe her, he'd forgotten how to read body language. 'You didn't think we were a bit, you know, scrappy?'

'Yes, you were. Only a bit!' added Fern as his face fell. He was wearing mascara, she noticed. It made his eyes glisten naughtily. 'You're out of practice, so—'

'We've been rehearsing non-stop for a week.' Adam's gaiety was kaput. 'You hated it. I knew you would.'

'I didn't hate it.' Fern scrabbled, trying to regain lost ground. 'You, sir, were extraordinary.'

'Was I?' Adam warmed up a little. This late-night, eye-lined doppelganger was anyone's for a compliment. Luckily, he didn't stop to consider that 'extraordinary' is a double-edged sword of a word.

'You haven't mentioned my make-up,' laughed Fern.

'Are you wearing any?'

Swatting him, she relaxed. 'Git. Look, shall we grab a burger or something?' Fern recalled her nemesis witch. 'Unless you've got plans.'

'The guys and me . . .' Adam stopped, and Fern felt him weigh up the situation. She wondered if she was emanating need; she needed some little proof that she had a toehold in Adam's life. 'Burger's a good idea. Let me make a quick call.' Adam took out his phone and retreated to a distant corner.

When he'd finished what seemed like a tricky conversation, Adam marched back and took Fern's arm. 'Come on. We have to be quick.'

In the gourmet burger joint, after the obligatory scoffing by Adam – 'What's a gourmet burger? Bring me a hunk of mince to aim at my gob. End of' – their order was slow arriving. Adam fidgeted, watching the door.

'Relax,' said Fern, already made uncomfortable by the looks her green face was attracting.

'I'm hungry. The adrenalin just pumps through you on stage.'

'I noticed.'

'The next gig'll be better. Although this one sold out within twenty-four hours.'

So Adam was unaware of P.W.'s ploy. 'Who's the elegant lady in the long black dress?'

'Long black dress?' Adam writhed, looking for the waiter, playing for time.

'Yes, Adam.' Fern was calm. It felt right to ask. 'Is she Percy Waddingsworthington?' She sat back. If her feelings weren't so engaged, Fern might have relished the way Adam kept opening and closing his mouth as he rummaged desperately for an answer. She cared too much about him to enjoy his predicament. She felt sorry for him. And for herself. 'It's time we talked about her.'

'She's called Penny,' said Adam, before stopping dead, as if that was all he knew about the woman.

'And?'

'And?' Adam splayed his palms on the tablecloth. 'And what, Fern?'

'And you've known her, been seeing her, since before we separated.' Fern held back from adding *She's partly why we separated*. There was enough kindling on this particular bonfire.

'That's true.' Adam took off his hat. His new haircut looked forlorn, flattened. 'That's true,' he repeated, on a sigh that sounded self-hating to Fern.

'Your burger, sir.' The waiter, so longed-for, now appeared at the most inopportune moment. 'And yours, madam.'

'Eat,' said Fern. 'You're starving. Eat first, talk later.' She'd always enjoyed watching Adam eat. He enjoyed

115

every morsel and was that darling of the home cook, a man who asks for seconds.

'Thanks.' Adam picked up the bun, but another hand swooped like a vengeful seagull and snatched it.

Holding it high in the air, Percy Waddingsworthington said 'No!' the way Fern did to Boudicca when the dog stretched out an exploratory paw towards an unattended custard cream. 'Do you want to undo all our good work?' She turned to Fern, her smile a blade. 'We haven't been introduced. I'm Penny Warnes.'

Adam slumped, the mystery initials finally explained.

'And you are?' said Penny.

About ten years older than you. 'I'm Fern,' said Fern. Penny's age shouldn't really matter, but it really did.

'The ex!' Penny's eyes lit up. 'I've heard a lot about you. You're exactly as I imagined.'

'I'm not usually green.'

'Adam said you were funny,' deadpanned Penny.

'He didn't say anything about you at all.'

Adam stood, putting down his napkin, all a-bustle. 'Maybe we should, you know, the after-party . . .'

'I manage Adam,' said Penny, standing firm, her feathered cape gleaming black. 'All aspects of his life. All his nooks and crannies.'

'Interesting mental image,' said Fern.

'What did you think of the gig?'

'I thought it was very good,' said Fern carefully.

'It was out of this world. Kinky Mimi are on their way. You can say you used to live with a superstar this time next year.'

'Where is this after-party?' Fern stood too, disliking the way Penny was looking down at her. She'd sat on her hat, and decided to leave it where it was.

'That nice Italian place on the corner,' said Adam, obviously glad to have something to add, something neutral.

'Guest list only,' said Penny. She pulled a comically sad face. 'Soh-wy. If Adam had asked I'd have put you on the list, but it's too late now.' Penny took hold of Adam's arm. 'Come on, guest of honour. Mustn't disappoint the fans.'

'Come, Fern, please,' said Adam.

'But she's not on the list.' Penny was firm.

'That doesn't matter,' said Adam.

'I should get home.' Fern moved fast, refusing to squabble over Adam as if he were a bone.

'Thanks for coming!' called Penny as the night air swallowed Fern up.

'Adam!'

'Don't sound so surprised, Layla. Fern didn't get custody of you.'

'No, I just meant . . . Adam! It's great to see you, even on a squiggly computer screen.'

'It's late. Sorry. Did I get you up?'

'Yes, but that doesn't matter. You look well. Is that . . . eyeliner?'

'What? Oh shit, yes. I forgot. It was Kinky Mimi's first gig tonight.'

'How was it?'

'Mind-blowing.'

'That's nice.'

'You're rubbing your eyes. I shouldn't have disturbed you. I'm a bit pissed, to be honest.'

'I'm not sleeping these nights. It's fine.'

'Now you're yawning!'

'Adam, sweetheart, what do you want?'

'To say hi.'

'You've said that, and it was fascinating, but what's on your mind?'

'Just . . . how does Fern seem to you?'

'No you don't, Adam. Uh-uh. These are questions you should ask Fern, not me.'

'I can't. She's distant.'

'*She's* distant?'

'Sometimes I see her down in the park with Boudicca. And a guy.'

'Shock, horror!'

'He looks young.'

'Do you have a telescope, Adam Carlile?'

'Of course not. Well, yes.'

'You know what, Adam, if you're so bloody interested, ask Fern.'

'OK. Blimey, Layla. I'm sorry I got you up. Give Luc my—'

'Adam, it's not you, it's me.'

'Is something wrong?'

And with that, she told him.

'Layla, Layla, Layla,' whispered Adam. 'I'm so sorry.'

CHAPTER FIVE

November: Sorbet

Christmas casts a long, sparkling shadow. By mid-November, Fern was a slave to lists: presents to buy; cake to make and ice; impossible fantasies of perfection to nurture. Not on any list, yet done every day, were two dog walks. Boudicca had never been so fit and lean; her owner had never been so sexually confused.

The gang had fallen away. Maggie went to live in Leeds, Pongo was on a cruise and Sabre was – well, nobody knew where Sabre was. Morning and evening, Fern met Hal at the south gates and they wore a rut in the grass as Boudicca and Tinkerbell stole crisp packets out of bins.

Setting off one chill, starchy morning, Hal described the mugs he'd created that morning in his studio. 'The handles were tricky. They're . . .' He'd tailed off. 'You know all about me, right down to the boring stuff about handles. But what do I know about you?'

'What do you want to know?' Fern had been spy-like, only offering information when it was strictly necessary. It was one way of keeping Hal safely in his box, to be taken out, dusted down and enjoyed twice a day for forty minutes. 'I'm not very interesting.'

'Everybody's interesting,' said Hal. 'For starters, what do you do?'

'I'm a beauty therapist.'

'What's that? Do you do massages?' Hal's eyes lit up.

'What is with men and massages? Yes, I do, but there's nothing saucy about it. I use aromatherapy oils.'

'Do you wear a nice white coat? Like a sexy matron?'

'My coat is white, yes. I also wax. Ah, thought that'd make you wince.'

'I've guessed you have kids.'

'How?' Fern had been careful never to mention Tallulah or Ollie. As if they might be tainted by this flirtation of their mother's. *As if*, she thought, irritated with her puritan conscience, *this is somehow wrong, when all it is is a walk in the park*.

'Dunno. You're so capable.'

As adjectives go, it was so-so. Fern preferred being a sexy matron.

'There's a warmth about you. Tell me about them.'

Fern dithered before saying, 'My daughter's eight. She's Tallulah. She's a feminist and an activist and a big fan of Enid Blyton. Ollie is . . .' After a brief temptation to re-invent Ollie as a toddler, Fern said, 'My son's seventeen.' She eyed Hal to check if he'd gone pale or poked out his own eyes. The air quivered, as did Fern, who felt as if she was standing naked beside him. Ollie's age underlined, in black ink, the gap between Fern and Hal.

'Cool,' he said, sounding just like Ollie.

Years might take an age to pass or rush by in a flash, but in the rear-view mirror they are solid and immovable. *I'd already had my first snog when Hal was being born.*

'And your other half,' said Hal. 'Is he still around?'

'He's a good dad,' said Fern.

'But a lousy hubby?'

'Not lousy, no.' Fern cleared her throat. Her mohair scarf seemed to have tightened about her neck. 'We grew apart. He wanted more.'

'More than you?'

There was no mistaking the *he must be mad* undertone. Fern smiled, grateful, excited. 'Yes, even more than a beauty therapist who comes complete with her own whippet.' She looked around for Boudicca. 'Where's Tinkerbell?' Fern stopped dead. 'Hal, I can't see her!' Panic gripped her as she looked across the frigid early-morning grass.

'She's in Suffolk,' said Hal, unperturbed. 'With her owner.'

'So you didn't bring her,' said Fern dumbly. 'Then why . . .'

'Why did I drop the pretence of taking the poor little sod for a walk twice a day when all she wants to do is lie in her basket and chew her own bum? You tell me.'

When Fern didn't tell him, when she just went a violent shade of red, Hal helped her out. 'I work on my own in the studio all day. I love it, but sometimes I need to air myself. To talk. And I like talking to you. And our occasional coffees are good too, and our wine. It's just nice and good and you don't need to be scared.'

'I'm not scared,' said Fern.

'You look it,' smiled Hal. 'I've never come across a

121

woman so bad at taking a compliment.' He thought for a moment. 'This ex . . . didn't he pay you compliments?'

'He used to.' It was unjust to demonize Adam. 'When you're together for a long time . . .' As Fern said this she realized that she'd been with Adam nearly as long as Hal had been alive. 'Things change. You become more of a partnership. You don't notice each other as much. To me, that was sweet, the feeling we were in it together. I was too busy to notice we weren't on the same page.'

There was more; much had coalesced in Fern's mind since the separation. Adam had over-relied on her during the marriage, as if she was his mother, not his wife. More than anything, she wanted to tell Adam, 'You didn't take me along for the ride when the money arrived.' He'd taken flight, giddy, *drunk* on his new power, but he hadn't looked back at the shrinking figures he'd left at ground level. 'Shit, ignore me, Hal.' After so long saying very little, Fern had gone too far. 'You're not my shrink.'

'It's time,' said Hal, taking out his phone, 'that we exchanged numbers.'

Homestead House had a light at every window when Fern shut up the Beauty Room. Homework was (allegedly) being done upstairs. Ollie was resting between shifts in his room. Donna was reaching over her bump to stir a stew on the stove. Nora was worshipping at the altar of Alan Titchmarsh in the sitting room. Evka was doing Pilates in the newly yellow hall.

'Did you think about question I ask?' Evka tailed Fern up the stairs.

'Yes.' Fern put her hand on the handle of her bedroom. Once *their* room, it was now all hers, and she'd be very glad to see it after an afternoon of blackheads and feet. She liked this time of day, when the deepening night was kept at bay by the house's lamps. 'And the answer is no, Evka, I can't give you a rise.'

'You are slave-driver.' Evka crossed her arms. 'You pay less than going rate.'

'You work less than the going rate,' retorted Fern. 'One hundred per cent less. You've been my cleaner for seven months and you still don't know where the mop lives.'

'Yes I do!' Evka was outraged.

'Ha!' Fern was triumphant. 'Trick question. I don't own a mop.'

'Fiend.' Evka laid a hand on Fern's arm. 'I have way I could earn a rise.' She whispered her idea into Fern's ear.

'You sneak,' said Fern, admiringly. 'You've earned yourself that rise.'

Younger people can't help making older people feel old. Hal wasn't to know that his habit of using txtspk when he messaged her brought out Fern's inner schoolmarm. *How r u?* she'd repeat to herself. *What's so arduous about typing 'are' and 'you'?* Her texts – a paragraph or two long – were checked for punctuation, spelling and grammar, and Hal would reply *C U there.*

Once free and easy with her phone, Fern now kept it close. Some corners of life can't be shared with the family. Even innocent texts arranging the next dog walk were out of bounds for her children.

When Adam walked into the kitchen one morning while she was midway through smiling at Hal's latest, brief message, Fern slipped the phone into a drawer as if it was a revolver.

'God, you're thin,' she said, instantly regretting it. Evil imps lived inside Fern and Adam, goading them to make personal remarks. Knowing that Penny was behind his healthy eating had curdled it for Fern; she could never approve.

'The word you're looking for is slim.' Adam did a twirl in his overcoat. 'I've been taking those new diet pills endorsed by Lincoln Speed.'

Lincoln Speed was the cool kid at school and Adam his adoring geek disciple, the boy who tried to be like his hero but ended up with his head stuck in the railings. Fern had seen the ads; a page of hokum, making absurd claims for the pills. 'Isn't one of the side effects death?'

'Good enough for Lincoln,' said Adam. 'Good enough for me.'

'I saw pictures of the funeral online.'

'Yes. May he rest in peace.' Speed's monkey had died a hopeless alcoholic. Adam closed his eyes respectfully for the animal, who had really gone downhill after giving up smoking.

Debauched monkeys and diet pills were safe territory. They barely mentioned Penny. Refusing to be pinned down on the woman's exact role, Adam's vagueness frustrated Fern. 'She's vital to me,' he'd say. Or 'She gets it.'

'Daddy looks like a model,' said Tallulah, who was head to toe in camouflage gear, a tiny guerrilla. 'Come on.' She tugged at his hand. 'We're buying me new Uggs today, Mum.'

'Exciting!' said Fern. 'Run and get your parka, then.'

'Thank you,' said Adam, after Tallulah had clomped out. 'For Evka.'

'My plesh,' said Fern. 'Ollie mentioned your cleaner had defected, so . . .'

'She started today. Seems very thorough.'

'Hmm.' Fern closed the door carefully, and dropped her voice as Tallulah tore up the cupboard under the stairs. Her parka was somewhere amongst the dog leads and tennis balls and padded jackets. 'Listen, Adam: Christmas.'

Homestead House was big on Christmas. Fern pushed the boundaries each year, adding more tinsel and more Baileys.

'What's the plan?'

'Why do I have to come up with the plan?' Fern wasn't about to fall into that trap again; the last time he'd made her do that, he'd left her.

'Don't be so touchy,' said Adam, making Fern instantly ten times as touchy. He drooped slightly. 'With things the way they are,' he held out his hands helplessly, as if describing some terrible barren scene, 'perhaps we'd better do separate Christmases this year.'

He was right: Fern knew that. Being right doesn't help when you feel like crying, however. 'I suppose it's for the best.'

'Crazy, really. That we can't even have Christmas together.'

'Yeah.'

'But this way,' said Adam, brightening, 'there's no tension and the kids get to have two Christmas Days. Can I have them on the actual day? I'm off to Rome on the twenty-sixth.'

'With Penny?'

'And the band. A special gig in the Piazza Navona.'

'Ooh.' Fern was impressed, despite the pact she'd made with herself never to be impressed with anything that involved Penny.

'We're improving all the time. The groove is back. Keith's loving it now.'

'Good,' said Fern. She so wanted to be wholeheartedly happy for Adam, but when the things he wanted took him further away from Homestead House it was an effort for her to sound sincere. 'So that's a deal? You have everybody on Christmas Day, and I'll have them on Boxing Day.' As she said it, Fern felt Christmas slip below the horizon like the Titanic. Down, down, down it went, with just her and Nora on board, pulling a wishbone.

Evka came in as Adam, Ollie and Tallulah were leaving. Closing the door behind them, she pressed her back against it. 'I have information,' she hissed.

'Tell all!' Planting a mole in Adam's flat was a low trick, a cheap stunt, a stroke of genius. It would cost Fern an extra twenty pounds a week, and she wasn't sure she wanted to hear the 'information'.

'Adam leads you up garden path.' Evka's eyes flashed Slovak fire. '*She* lives there. With him.'

'They've moved in together?' Fern hadn't expected this calibre of revelation.

'Silly cow monograms everything. There is P.W. on towels. Dressing gown. Probably on adulterous fanny.'

'Are you sure? Maybe Penny just leaves stuff there, because she spends a lot of time, you know, working with Adam.'

'I know kind of work they do together,' sneered Evka, who could be very Nora-like when it came to other people's sex lives. 'Wardrobes are full of lady clothes. Bathroom is full of serums. There are napkins in kitchen drawer. Adam is not napkin man.'

'No, he's not.' Adam had once wiped his mouth on a bride's veil.

'There is new rug on bedroom floor. Adam is not rug man.'

Adam had once suggested they use paper plates to cut down on washing up; the domesticated touches weren't his. Fern's belly dipped; Layla had once prophesied that the hardships of day-to-day bachelor life would bring Adam running back to a warm house filled with cooking smells. 'You're sure Penny's not a lodger?'

'Penny,' said Evka darkly, 'is not lodger.'

The house ticked gently, settling down for the night, as sleepy stars pressed down on the roof. Fern had looked in on Tallulah, who lay across her bed as if flung there, various soft toys spread-eagled around her. She'd knocked on Ollie's door and received a gruff 'G'night.'

At the foot of the stairs to the loft, she called, 'Everything all right, Nora?'

There was a bump from inside the room, as if Nora had stumbled. 'Yes, yes,' answered Nora, irritable. 'Why wouldn't it be?'

Passing Evka on the landing, Fern complimented her on her black silky nightdress before realizing it was her own.

'Can I wear it for hour?' Evka asked, not even slightly ashamed at being caught out. 'I have appointment for Skype sex with man I meet at football match.'

'On second thoughts,' said Fern, 'keep the nightie.'

The house was full but Fern's bed was empty. Plumping her pillows, she lay back in the powdery lamplight and contemplated the familiar shapes in the flowery wallpaper. Old-fashioned when they'd moved in, the paper had patiently waited for trends to catch up with it, and now the room was shabby chic as opposed to just shabby.

Lying there with Adam, night after night after night, Fern had concocted various new decorating schemes. At one point she'd been mad for aubergine walls, before entering a long phase when only built-in mirrored wardrobes would do. The money had arrived and they'd found themselves stumped.

The room was as static as the relationship.

Time heals, they say. Fern had discovered that it also brings perspective. She'd never stopped to examine her life with Adam. *When would I have found the time to do that?* Their jobs, the children, the house were a treadmill that propelled them into the future. Everything around them changed – Tallulah grew, Ollie matured, bits dropped off the house – but nothing changed between Fern and Adam.

It had seemed like a plus. *We never change* was a cheering thought in a society where love seemed difficult to maintain. Many of their circle were on second marriages. One intrepid woman was on her third. At the ceremony, Adam had whispered to Fern, *till itchy feet do us part.*

We were smug, she concluded. Or perhaps it was just Fern. Adam's accusation that she didn't listen smarted, but only because it was true. Fern hadn't realized that Adam needed tending; she'd thought of him as an extension of herself, but she'd been wrong. Very wrong. As wrong as she'd been about that tankini last summer. Adam had his own needs and wishes and desires.

Time *wasn't* healing – bang goes another proverb – but the five months had gently transported Fern to a different landscape where she didn't have the same expectations of Adam. His life apart from her no longer seemed preposterous, a silly experiment. It had taken, like a grafted limb.

If Fern was her own best friend, she would counsel against scrabbling about under the bed for the box of letters. She imagined a ghostly Layla waggling a finger. *Shoo!* she said, and plucked one at random from the chest. By reading Adam's unedited splurges, Fern was reassured that although their relationship had *gone* wrong, it hadn't *been* wrong.

AN OPINION POLL

*In the interests of keeping things scientific I carried
out a survey among the general public of why you
and I should get back together. Here are some quotes.*

YOUR MATES: *'Please get back with her 'cos then
she'll ring you in the middle of the night and not
us'/'You and Fern make a great couple because you
let us put lipstick on you when you're drunk'/'Fern
should take you back 'cos some dodgy guys are chatting her up and she seems to think they're cool and
might even fancy them.'*

YOUR MUM: *'Shut up, Adam, and stop annoying
me.'*

YOUR BROTHER: *'Fern should get back with you
mate 'cos she's less of a pain when you're on the
scene.'*

YOUR SISTERS: *'You and Fernie are good for each
other'/'Fern can do better.'*

YOUR DAD: *'All I care about is my Fern being
happy. When she's with you, she's happy!'*

That had been a clever touch by the much younger Adam,
putting Fern's father last. The emotional role reversal of her
parents – Dad warm, approachable, big on cuddles, while
Mum was practical – had made a daddy's girl of Fern.

The loss of her father to a heart attack with no warning,

no notice, had hit Fern like a lorry. She had been left speechless with shock; each day had brought a new way to miss him, another tiny landmark she couldn't tell him about. Dad was such a celebrator, always making a loving fuss. The silence was deafening as the family budged up into their new positions.

Sensing how deep the pain went, Adam had taken over care of little Ollie, fed them all microwave meals, and talked long into the night about the man Fern had lost. When she'd stammered out, through tears that simply wouldn't stop, that she hadn't got to say goodbye, Adam had held her close and said, 'All the declarations that people make to their loved ones at the very end weren't necessary between you and your dad. You said those things to each other every day.'

It was true. Dad sprinkled *I love you*s like confetti. Mum's way of coping was to build a wall around his memory, bricking in the vibrant, laughing man as if he hadn't existed. She carried on valiantly, refusing to break step, as her daughters and son struggled.

Eighteen months on, as Fern resurfaced, her mother remarried. None of the siblings met Dave before the engagement party, and the consensus when they did meet him was *Eh?* He was colourless and small, like the ghost of a mouse; he'd forgotten to grow a personality. At the reception, Fern's mother's speech was mainly about the B&B she and Dave had bought.

In Corfu? Fern and her sisters exchanged looks, but their brother was nonchalant: 'It's Mum's life.'

Visits had been awkward. Watching Dave take her

father's place – *as if he could!* – set Fern's nerves on edge. Had it been Mum's intention to make Fern feel as if she and her dirty-fingered children were taking up valuable guest rooms? The rest of the family didn't seem to notice, and Adam said of course not, but Fern was too hurt to dig deeper.

Folding up the letter, Fern switched off the lamp, glad to be tired, glad that sleep would soon come.

'Adam, have you got a moment?'

'I'm with the guys, Fern. We're jamming. I was just about to turn my phone off.'

'I want to talk about these decks or whatever they're called. The ones you're buying for Ollie.'

'The software controller system? Ollie will *die*.'

'I don't think you should buy it for him.'

'Hang on, let me . . . Fellas, I'm just going out on the fire escape! . . . Christ, it's freezing out here. Fern, you've got to stop this.'

'Stop what?'

'Tying my hands.'

'How am I—'

'You behave as if it's a sin to spend money, but if some la-la land TV company wants to spaff cash at me, what should I do? Duck?'

'This isn't about money.'

'No, it's about teaching our kids to scrimp and save and wear clothes made out of curtains. They don't *need* to save!'

'They do! Ollie and Tallulah need to take control of their own destinies. What if I hadn't stopped wiping their bottoms? They'd never learn how to do it and now they wouldn't be able to leave the house.'

'Your frankly weird metaphors aren't useful, Fern.'

'And neither is you swooping in and throwing money at our son. Ollie and Donna haven't even started thinking properly about where to live and the birth is two months away. Wouldn't a modest deposit for a little flat be a better place to start with your money and *advice*, not this starry-eyed dream of being a famous DJ?'

'Penny said you'd do this.'

'Did you just say *Penny said*?'

'Yeah. She did, she said—'

'Penny said? *Penny* said? Fucking Penny fucking said?'

'She's a smart woman with a lot to offer. What does that noise mean?'

'Just clearing my throat. Look, you're busy and I've got a luxury pedi any minute. I'm just saying think before you buy, yeah?'

'And I'm just saying . . . I don't really know how to explain this . . . Fern, I always wanted to be a parent. Yes, it happened a bit too quickly, before I felt ready, but right from the start I loved that feeling of you and Ollie relying on me, depending on me. Some years, things were so tight, and I'd see you muffled up in cardigans 'cos we couldn't afford to put the heating on, or Tallulah would get an extra term out of her tatty coat, and it just killed me, you know? Inside. So this feels good. Being able to provide for my kids feels good.'

133

'I hadn't thought of it like that.'

'I know, Fern. You never do.'

In a building the size of Homestead House there's always scope to be alone, but everybody was in the kitchen. Maybe it was the sleety rain rattling the windows that brought them all to the warm beacon of the room where the good stuff happened.

'Nice hat,' said Fern to Ollie.

Ollie touched his flat cap self-consciously. 'Part of my new look,' he said.

'Marvellous.' *You're your father's son, all right.* 'Donna, sit, sweetheart.'

The girl, who looked as if she was shoplifting a space-hopper, eased herself onto a bench. 'Oomph.' Donna had a widening repertoire of variations on *ouch*.

Wearing a sparkly top that clung to her like a frightened child, Evka elbowed Fern out of the way at the hob. 'I fry egg. Go please.'

'Can I have an egg?' Tallulah was incapable of watching people eat without wanting exactly what they had.

'No, spoiled child,' said Evka, but so fondly that the spoiled child beamed.

'I could die of thirst waiting for a cup of tea in this house.' Nora heaved herself up.

'I'll make you one,' said Fern, hoping to forestall a marathon of huffing, puffing and sarcasm about Fern's choice of kettle, mugs, teabags.

'I'm just an old lady, no use to anybody. Everybody ignore me.'

'I can't ignore you, Auntie Nora,' said Tallulah as Nora lumbered past. 'Your bum's right in my face.'

'Tallie, shush,' said Fern. 'Honestly, Auntie, let me do it.'

'I'll have to use this pornographic crockery,' sighed Nora, taking down a mug bearing Pamela Anderson's (fully clothed) picture, a joke present to Adam one Christmas.

'What's pornographic?' asked Tallulah, faltering over the pointed syllables.

'Ask brother,' growled Evka, making Ollie pull his funky cap over his eyes.

The cup fell, and tiny shards of Pamela's mighty bosom scattered over the floor.

Mild uproar ensued, the sort that always accompanies a broken cup, but Nora was more agitated than anybody.

'Stupid!' she gasped. 'Stupid stupid stupid!'

'It's just a cup,' smiled Fern.

'I'll miss it,' said Ollie.

'Oh will you now?' said Donna.

It's hard to stomp in slippers, but Nora tried. Fern caught up with her in the hall and helped her into the study, closing the door behind them.

'Seriously, Auntie, it doesn't matter.' Nora was a sizeable pain in Fern's sizeable arse, but it touched her to see her aunt so upset.

'There's something you should know.' Nora subsided into Fern's office chair and was alarmed when it spun a little. 'I had a stroke.'

Fern pulled the chair back round to face her and knelt in front of it. 'When?'

'A while back. About a year. There are after-effects. Me hand.' Nora held up a plump hand, the wrinkled fingers curled. 'The strength comes and goes.'

'Is the stroke the reason for the dark glasses?'

'I like dark glasses,' said Nora, insulted.

'Did you have physical therapy?' Fern knew a little about strokes. 'Exercising your hand, for example.'

'Of course not,' snapped Nora. 'I didn't hang about in that smelly hospital one minute longer than I had to. Sitting there in a backless gown while doctors got a good look at what no man has ever seen.' Nora's mouth turned down. 'I hadn't a day's illness in my life before that stroke. I didn't want to tell you. I'm ashamed.'

'Ashamed?' Nora's mind was a dark rollercoaster, forever catapulting Fern round nasty curves. 'There's nothing to be ashamed of in illness. It happens to all of us.'

'Not me,' said Nora. 'Not Mother. We lived a good life and we had good health.' She looked at her lap. 'Don't tell anybody. I don't want them all to know.'

'This isn't a punishment from God, Auntie.' Fern chose her words carefully. It was so easy to offend Nora. 'Why don't I make an appointment with my GP?'

'You'd like that, wouldn't you?' Nora took off her dark glasses. 'Next stop a nursing home. Then the grave, next to Mother.' With difficulty, she stood, with Fern holding the revolving chair. 'I shall take my dinner in my room,' she said haughtily, as if Fern was her housekeeper. 'No red peppers in me rice.'

Later, picking out the red peppers – *the recipe's called 'Rice with Red peppers', for God's sake!* – Fern listened to Ollie trying out his new software controller system in the conservatory and wondered what to do about her aunt. She hated to think of Nora steeped in useless guilt.

As she put the plate on a tray, Fern admitted another, less noble thought. *I don't want to be lumbered with an ailing old lady who hates my guts.*

Asked what she really wanted, what would be the best possible treat after the gruelling horrors of netball club in the rain, Tallulah chose a sorbet at a pastel and chrome café on the high street.

'Are you bribing me, Mummy?'

'Nonono,' said Fern, setting a sugary lemon ball in a silver cup in front of her daughter.

'I wouldn't mind. I love bribes.'

'I noticed that you and me haven't spent much time together lately. Just the two of us.'

'So this is like a date?'

'If you like.' Fern needed to reconnect with the little soul opposite. Tallulah's hostility had tapered off. The child was, Fern supposed, adjusting to the new regime. This was for the best, but didn't make Tallulah's enforced maturity any less poignant. 'How was school? Any murders?'

'We're learning about ess ee ex,' giggled Tallulah, shoulders hunched.

'Sex?'

'Shush!' Tallulah was happily scandalized. 'Miss Shore calls it reproduction but we know what she means. Is it true? Did you and Daddy actually do all that sperm stuff?'

'Yes.' Fern had known this moment would come, but she'd expected a little notice. She braced herself to answer all questions openly and honestly, leaving out anything too graphic.

'Urgh.' Tallulah looked her mother up and down. 'I'm *never* doing it. Don't the sperms go everywhere? Up the curtains?'

'Umm . . .'

'What are the sperms' faces like?'

'Err . . .'

'Is Daddy's willy detachable? I couldn't quite work that bit out.'

'Well . . .'

'Next we're doing pregnancy but I'm already an expert because I looked it all up for Donna's baby.'

Yes, yes, please stay on pregnancy and don't veer back to detachable willies. 'Shall I test you?' Fern knew Tallulah couldn't resist a test. 'Question one: where does the baby grow inside Donna's body?'

'Too easy!' Tallulah flicked her plait. 'In her womb.'

'OK, a hard one. Question two: how long does the baby spend in the womb?'

'Right.' Tallulah thought hard, scraping the silver dish. 'Thirty-eight weeks! Which means Ollie detached his willy in . . .' Tallulah counted on her fingers. 'April!'

'No, can't be, darling.' Maths wasn't Tallulah's strong point. Whenever Adam blamed Fern's genes, he pointed out that she herself often put two and two together and got five. 'The baby's due in January, so nine months back-wards is December, November, October, September, August, July, June, May . . .'

'April!' yelled Tallulah. 'More sorbet, Mummy, pleeeease!' She widened her eyes. 'Say something, Mummy. You look as if you've been frozen by the Snow Queen.'

The steamy Beauty Room smelled of eucalyptus.

'What have you been doing in here? Massaging koalas?' Adam perched on the treatment couch before remembering how rabidly protective of it Fern could be and leaning instead against a glass cabinet.

'Epic pimple procedure, but never mind that now.' Fern was speaking in low tones, as if this dreadful development might leak through the walls. 'Adam, did you hear what I just said? That baby isn't Ollie's.'

'We don't know that for sure.' Adam looked on women's bodies as a strange land that was nice to visit but had many odd traditions. 'The baby could be premature.'

'A baby's only premature when it arrives. I've peeked at Donna's pre-natal folder and—'

'You've snooped, you mean.'

'Yes, Gandhi, I've snooped. Sorry to be such a low-life, but we need cold, hard facts. Donna's date of conception is bang in the middle of April.' When Adam's expression didn't change, Fern prompted him. 'And where was our son in April? The *whole* of April.'

It dawned, finally, on Adam. 'California. That school exchange thing.'

They'd been so proud of Ollie when he won a place on a prestigious exchange with a prominent San Francisco high school.

'So, unless he posted Donna his sperm, that baby is most definitely and definitively and certainly not his. It's Maz's.'

'Who?'

Fern often wished for a laminated card with *Keep up!* on it, but this was no time to squabble. They must pull together on this one, like oxen. Tired oxen who'd rather be watching telly. 'The bloke Donna had the fling with. He's a bit older, a player, I think. I don't really know. It's easier to break into the Kremlin and steal the nuclear code than get a straight answer from your own teenagers.'

'Does this Maz know about the baby?'

'Why are you asking me?' Adam always expected Fern to know things. *Is this cheddar off? Why does my scalp feel itchy? Do I have a pension?* 'What do we do, Ads?' The nickname slipped out. They both noticed it, and pretended they didn't. *If he mentions Penny in the next few seconds, I swear I'll . . .*

Adam didn't mention Penny. He made all the right parental noises, and when they called Ollie and Donna down to the sitting room – having turfed out a suspicious Evka and Nora, who were busy disparaging a female newsreader's hair – they were as one.

'This is difficult to talk about,' began Adam.

'Then don't talk about it,' said DJ Dirty Tequila.

'Ollie . . .' said Donna, with a squeeze of his thigh.

Fern surmised the future pattern of their relationship from that one gesture; Ollie pulling ahead, Donna guiding gently back. *If they survive the next few minutes.*

'Mum and I did some sums.'

Donna straightened, as if her spine had spasmed.

'And?' Ollie's cool fell away.

Adam had taken Fern's advice to be as straightforward as possible without being brusque. 'The baby was conceived in April. Ollie, you were in Fresno for the whole of April.' Adam faltered. Donna's face, slightly puffy from the sterling work her body was doing building a new life, was painted over with pain. 'I'm sorry, Donna, but there's no way that Ollie can be the dad, is there, love?'

Donna shook her head slowly.

Fern leaned forward on the sofa. 'We hate this, guys. But it has to be faced.'

'Why?' Ollie was on his feet.

'Sit down, son,' said Adam.

'No,' said Ollie, sitting down.

'We're not laying down the law.' Fern carried on over Ollie's ostentatious 'yeah, right'. She took in Donna, who was looking at a spot somewhere over Fern's head, quivering with the effort not to cry. 'We love you, Donna. You're one of the family.'

'Don't say but, Mum!' Ollie's voice was torn from him.

Adam said it for her. 'But this inevitably changes things.'

'Dad's right.' Fern hadn't said that for a while. 'This is heavy-duty decision making. Donna's having another man's baby. He has rights—'

'No.' Donna was fierce. 'Maz gave up his rights.'

Ollie screwed up his mouth. 'He's a bastard.'

'That's not the point,' said Adam. 'We don't have to like him. He's the father.' He left a pause before saying 'And you're not, Ollie.'

Fern looked at the bump filling out Dawn's fluffy jumper. *And it's not my grandchild*, she realized, as the point of an arrow pierced somewhere soft inside her.

'I *am*.' Ollie punched one palm with his fist. 'I am, Dad. Shut up. And you, Mum. Just shut the fuck up.'

'Listen, you,' said Adam, who was always galvanized when Ollie swore at them.

In an echo of Donna's earlier movement, Fern laid a hand on Adam's arm. 'Let's leave it there. We'll talk again, when we've all calmed down.'

Grabbing their reprieve with both hands, Ollie and Donna disappeared upstairs, to the dark and whiffy sanctuary of Ollie's room. Down the stairs came Tallulah, Evka and Nora, all eager for titbits.

'Why's Daddy sad?' Tallulah peered in at Adam, who sat with his head in his hands.

'He's not, he's just thinking.' Half-truths littered the house.

'That child,' said Nora, 'has been talking about sperm all evening.' Unable to bring herself to say *sperm*, Nora mouthed it, her eyes fluttering at warp speed.

'Sperm sperm sperm,' warbled Tallulah, as Nora blessed herself.

'Catchy,' laughed Evka, reaching for the gin bottle.

In her overall pocket, Fern's phone cheeped. Turning away from the nosey parkers, she read: *Hey! Where R U? I'm at park with T. x*

The 'x' was new. It reared up at her. *Will I have to add a kiss to my texts now?*

Another text dropped in: *Come on! It's cold! xx*

Two kisses? Practically an orgy.

The park, though cold, would be clean and simple, with none of the knotty complexities of her nearest and dearest. Fern felt the tug of Hal's artless expectancy, the cold-milk purity of just walking a dog and chatting to a man she liked who seemed to like her back.

I'll be there in five mins.

As her finger wavered over the 'x', the stairs shook. Ollie stormed past her into the sitting room. Fern deleted the message and followed him, shutting out the others, almost flattening Evka's nose with the door.

Ollie stood with his back to the fireplace, legs apart. 'Mum, Dad,' he said curtly. 'I'm only talking to you 'cos Donna said I should.'

Great start. Fern sat beside Adam, and he took the lead. 'Then at least one of you has some sense.'

'You didn't say that when I was acing my exams, Dad. Suddenly I'm an idiot? Because I'm not doing exactly what your so-called society wants me to?'

'My so-called society?' If it wasn't for the Botox Adam would have raised an eyebrow. 'You big drama queen, this isn't about society. It's about your future.'

'Giving up your education for your child is one thing,' said Fern. 'But darling, packing in sixth form for another man's child is crazy.'

'Is it crazy to love Donna?' Ollie pulsed with energy. 'Is it crazy to know I never want to be with anybody else?'

There was no answer from his parents, who'd both felt that way when they were teenagers – and been proved wrong.

'All we're asking is that you to stop and think,' said Fern. Ollie's idealism was a thing of beauty but she couldn't stand by while he shot himself in the foot. 'You can support Donna as a friend, without giving up all your opportunities.'

'This is the only opportunity I want.' Ollie crossed his arms and hung his head. 'Are you really asking me to dump my girlfriend when she's seven months pregnant? Leave her just when she needs me? Are you?'

They weren't. They couldn't.

Fern said, with immense weariness, 'We'll make the best of it, like we always do. Go back to Donna. Tell her it's lasagne later.'

'If you're worried,' said Ollie, as he left the room, 'that we'll make a mess of things like you and Dad, don't be. We're staying together.'

'Well, that told us,' said Fern as Adam shrugged on his sharp-shouldered coat.

Propelling Tallulah into the hall, her hands on the child's shoulders, Evka said, 'You might want to take off coat.' She kissed the back of Tallulah's head. 'Tell Daddy.'

'I've been excluded,' mewed Tallulah. 'For shoplifting.'

'Ding ding, round two.' Adam hung up his coat.

The text said: *Oi! Have U gone off dog walks??! xxx*

Fern switched off her phone. Some voodoo rendered her unable to message Hal while Adam was in the house.

Talking it over, being gentle with each other, Fern and Adam agreed that the shoplifting was more to do with their split than with Tallulah's possible future as a crime overlord.

'It's so out of character,' said Fern, as they slumped on opposite ends of the big old chesterfield. She had the end where the spring stuck out, but she didn't care; Fern was so tired she'd have sat on a bed of nails. In the past she would stick her feet in Adam's lap, but tonight she kept them curled beneath her.

'If anything, Tallulah's too honest.' Adam looked scrawny rather than slender, all the colour bleached from his face. 'This is about us, isn't it?'

'Yup,' sighed Fern, whose job these days seemed to be best described as Blame Taker. 'It's classic. Children go through a period of instability after their parents split.'

'This is a separation, though.'

'How does that differ from a split?'

'It doesn't,' admitted Adam, with a sorrowful shake of his head.

A moment bloomed between them. It shone with potential, a moment in which one of them could reach out and bare themselves, ask for forgiveness, plead for understanding, so they could just be Fern and Adam again.

The moment grew and grew. Fern was shackled by her knowledge of Penny. Adam was shackled by . . . Fern couldn't guess; possibly Penny stood in his way, too. The moment dissolved, and they were just two weary people on a chesterfield at the end of a day full of bad news.

'At least she confessed,' said Adam.

'She'd never lie.'

'Before today I'd have said she'd never steal.'

'Are we making a huge deal out of this?' Fern searched for a way out. 'It's practically a rite of passage for most people. Nicking a few sweets from Woolworths.'

'Tallie's not most people. And she didn't steal from a faceless high-street store. This was a little corner shop run by an old gent who knows her. If Ollie had nicked something at his age, I'd have told him off, made him return it, then early to bed. But with Tallie – it's a signal.'

'A distress signal.' Fern looked up at the ceiling, beyond which her daughter had sobbed herself to sleep beneath her camouflage duvet. 'I'm disappointed by the school's attitude.'

'Suspending a good kid the moment she does something wrong seems harsh.'

'I'll go and talk to the head,' said Fern.

'Shall I come with you?'

'I assumed you would.' Nothing could be taken for granted. 'I mean, if you want to.'

'Of course I want to.' Adam's face creased in discomfort. 'She does know we love her, doesn't she?'

'Yes.' Fern was strong; he needed that. 'Tallie is loved and cared for. She's just having a wobble.'

'I know how she feels.' Adam looked at his watch.

Penny waiting up for you? Fern was impressed with the speed she could jump to conclusions; she never moved that fast at the gym. 'Look, do you have to dash? I could open a bottle of something.'

'Um.' Adam looked undecided. 'I guess I could hang around. For a bit.' He sat up politely, as if in a waiting room. 'I don't want to keep you up.'

'I won't sleep tonight.' Fern would have to fight the impulse to go to her daughter's room and curl up round Tallie's warm body.

With the bottle opened – Fern made a palaver of it, Adam had to step in, no change there – and a glass or two downed, the atmosphere lightened enough for Fern to get out her probe. It was a clumsy instrument: 'Penny,' she said, and got no further.

'Penny,' repeated Adam.

'She's your . . . what, exactly?'

'I don't know that she's *my* anything.' Adam shifted in his seat. 'She's my manager, of course, and great at it. Plus a lot more besides. Penny's amazing.'

Great. Amazing. Fern waded through the slag heap of compliments. 'When are you going to get round to telling me you live together?' At Adam's quick look, she gabbled, 'Not my business, sure, but then again, in a way, it *is* my business, isn't it? It would've been nice to find out from you. We're not really *us* any more, but there *was* an us, so . . .' She tailed off.

'Not us any more? What're you on about?' Adam was laughing. 'Who are you now, then? Liza Minnelli? Queen Elizabeth the First? I'm still me, just thinner.'

'I preferred you before.' *That came out wrong.* 'There was nothing wrong with you that needed fixing.'

'That's not what Penny thinks. And I trust her implicitly. She's not living with me in *that* way.'

'Which way is that way?'

'The shagging-each-other-senseless way. She's in the spare room. Did you think . . . ?'

'What was I supposed to think?' Fern felt a weight disappear inside her, as if an anvil had grown wings.

'Penny's got a rat infestation at her flat. She's just staying at mine. It works well. She's a laugh.'

How about you mention Penny's name just the once without praising her? Fern no more believed in Penny's rat infestation than she believed in the tooth fairy. Clearly something was going on, but apparently it was unconsummated. 'Adam, about Christmas. What if you were to come here after all? If we have a normal-in-inverted-commas Christmas Day?'

'I was just thinking that.' Adam seemed chuffed, even though his forehead barely moved. 'For the kids.'

The bed didn't seem to be quite as wide as it was most nights. When Fern had invited Adam for Christmas she'd felt like a shy teen asking her crush out on a date. Christmas would be a glittering amnesty to round off the year. Perhaps somewhere in this mess there was an answer, an obvious answer, to the mess they'd made.

Downstairs, on its charger, Fern's mobile sang.

Where'd U go Fern?

CHAPTER SIX

December: Relevé

Pale. Flabby. Somewhat pimply. And far too large. The turkey and Fern had a lot in common as they stared each other out on Christmas morning.

This was it, the moment when all the to-do lists kicked in. When Fern proved herself against this age-old adversary. Fern and turkeys had history.

Crying into a tea towel was one tradition Fern planned to avoid this year. She'd chosen the turkey from a line-up at the butcher's, stipulating 'Organic, please,' just as the magazine articles insisted. She'd paid for it, after double-checking the price and wondering if the butcher was under the impression he was selling her a small car. She'd taken it home and weighed it. She'd wiped it inside and out, stifling a 'Yeew'. She'd stuffed it. Then she'd weighed it again. Then she'd calculated the correct cooking time with the spectre of Boxing Day salmonella at her shoulder. Fern knew that turkey better than she knew her own children, and now that it was time to put it in the oven at the correct temperature in a specially bought roasting tin, she had a sudden attack of self-doubt and re-did the sums.

Clanging chords from Tallulah's new guitar drifted down the stairs, competing with the carols on the kitchen's tinny radio. Heaving the bird into the oven, Fern ticked the list. *Only one thousand and three things left to do before lunch*. Homestead House's residents had congregated for a noisy breakfast as they opened their presents together, and now the sitting room was knee-deep in discarded wrapping paper. Boudicca patrolled in her new quilted coat, nosing out fragments of Terry's Chocolate Orange and coughing up satin bows.

'Need a hand?' Nora crossed to a cabinet and took out a vegetable peeler. 'Those parsnips won't chop themselves,' she added crossly, as if Fern had expected them to do just that.

A dab hand, Nora made short work of the Everest of Maris Pipers after she'd undressed the parsnips. Carrots were next, her bent fingers working deftly, with little sign of her stroke. Fern knew Nora had good days and bad days. On bad days she not only dropped things but barged into cupboards and missed her footing on the stairs.

One night Fern had tried to start a conversation about therapy, but it brought out Nora's imperious worst. Her aunt had frozen her out, adding a comment about Fern's bottom in those jeans just to underline how she felt about intervention.

'Mother of God.' Nora snatched the whisk out of Fern's hands. 'Let me do the bread sauce.'

Unaccustomed to help in the Christmas kitchen – Adam had always had urgent battery-putting-in to do, or a vital *It's a Wonderful Life* to watch – Fern was grateful for back-up. *Or maybe* I'm *the back-up*; Nora was a born general.

'Wash up as you go along,' said Nora, chucking the whisk into the sink.

'Yessir.'

'Tallie's come out of herself today.'

So Nora had noticed the change in the child. Tallulah's end-of-term report had been a litany of failed tests and daydreaming. 'The guitar's cheered her up.'

Nora tasted the gravy, made weeks earlier with chicken wings and defrosted last night. 'More salt,' she said.

'I don't think so.' You insult a woman's gravy, you insult her very soul.

'I wasn't asking.' Nora jiggled the salt cellar. 'I've been thinking about Tallie's shoplifting . . .'

'Can we please not talk about that today?' Fern pushed at her fringe. The steam in the kitchen was turning her hair punky. It was the only day of the year that she cooked in high heels and the strain was beginning to show.

'She stole liquorice laces, and that's queer, because Tallulah doesn't like liquorice.'

'Where's the gravy boat?' Like Christmas itself, the inherited gravy boat only appeared once a year. Fern tuned out Nora, tired of her aunt's constant harping on Tallulah's one and only fall from grace. The little girl was suffering enough with her new nickname – 'Crim' – and the cold-shouldering by snooty friends with high grades and pushy parents. It cut Fern to see her child hurting at the hands of others. Young girls were so sweet and so generous, and then suddenly so cruel; school was no longer a haven for Tallulah, but at home she was forgiven and that was that.

'Oh Jesus Christ, cranberry sauce!' she shrieked, hands to her face. 'Auntie! I forgot the cranberry sauce!'

Christmas lay in ruins at Fern's feet. Long after she was dead, her children would reminisce, 'Remember that Christmas there was *no cranberry sauce*?' The turkey in the oven laughed at her, in a gobbly way. She considered leaving home. She considered murdering everybody so that nobody would find out about the cranberry sauce.

Christmas can do that to a woman. Fern didn't even like cranberry sauce.

'I bought some yesterday,' said Nora nonchalantly, taking up a tea towel.

Fern staggered, her head light. 'Thank you,' she said, taking Nora's hand and wringing it over and over. 'How can I ever repay you?'

'Somebody,' said Nora, 'needs a little lie down.'

Despite the juiciness of the turkey, the abundance of the cranberry sauce, and the majesty of the roast potatoes, the magic of Christmas was elusive for Fern.

Crowded around the table, all digging in, her family were making daft conversation and/or *nom nom* noises. They were all eating far too much. They would all complain of tummy ache. They would all howl for turkey sandwiches by eight p.m. So far, so good; all was exactly as it should be.

Pushing back her paper hat, Fern refilled Donna's glass

with water and placed Tallulah's red paper napkin on her lap. She risked a wink at Ollie over the centrepiece candle and was rewarded with a wink back, just like the old days.

'Top meal, Mum,' he said, his mouth full.

The gravy *had* needed more salt. Christmas lunch was elevated by Nora's touches. The parsnips were cooked all the way through, with no bullet-hard surprises. The nutmeg in the bread sauce made all the difference. Nora had waved away thanks with prickly annoyance, but had muttered, 'I know what it's like to slave away feeding people who don't appreciate the hard work involved.' A talkative woman, Nana's vocabulary hadn't stretched to 'Thank you.'

It was easy to blame Adam for the lack of magic, so Fern did just that. Watching him covertly as her paper hat slipped over her eye, she saw a man sitting politely, eating his meal gratefully, commenting on the wondrousness of the sprouts, and helping Tallulah cut up her turkey.

He's a guest, thought Fern dismally. Adam was remote, well-mannered, saying and doing all the right things. *He should be saying and doing all the wrong things*.

Every Christmas Adam got in the way, plying Fern with Buck's Fizz when she should be stirring things, and winding the children up to unparalleled levels of overexcitement. He would lean against the cooker, glass in hand, chatting happily as if Fern was throwing together an omelette instead of the most important meal of the year. Washing up with Ollie, he would tell Fern to 'have a sit down', as if the washing up was a personal favour to her. She would rant, he would laugh, and they would kiss in the hall when the kids were otherwise engaged.

But not today. Remembering her manners, Fern turned to the man on her left.

Walter, unguessably old, was guest of honour. His face a wrinkled map of his life, Walter had been coming to Fern for manicures since she'd opened up the Beauty Rooms. He was particular about his hands, which now shook as he cut up his turkey.

'All right, Walter?' whispered Fern, hoping she'd done the right thing in inviting him. Hearing he'd be alone on Christmas Day, she hadn't thought twice, but perhaps she'd misjudged the situation. Walter was silent and withdrawn, the only diner not reciting cracker jokes. Remembering his deafness, she repeated her question, louder this time.

'Yes, thank you.' Walter had his best dentures in, so the smile he gave her was a tad gruesome.

'Tell me if you need anything.'

'Walter,' asked Tallulah, her cutlery held up like cutlasses. 'What was the best present you got today? Mine was a telescope. I'm going to examine the moon later.'

'Why not,' suggested Ollie, 'check out Uranus?'

'My best present,' said Walter in a papery voice, 'is all of you.'

I did the right thing, thought Fern, as Evka raised her glass to Walter, shouting '*Na zdravie!*'

'*Na zdravie!*' they all yelled back as Walter shrank back into his best shirt, which was frayed at the cuffs.

The presents from Evka had been generous and thoughtful; Nora couldn't be parted from her new cardigan, and Tallulah was having a ball with the fake poo she'd unwrapped. The strange fruit cake she'd made for Fern

– 'My muzzer's recipe' – might come in handy as a door-stop. Despite Evka's special way of helping lay the table – 'Best if I stay out of way with pint of liqueur' – she added something indefinable to this strange Christmas.

'I go.' Evka stood up abruptly, hoiking her bra and taking one last mouthful of stuffing.

'Where?' Nora was stricken.

'Booty call,' said Evka, sweeping out. 'Christmas Day rudes are rudest rudes of all.'

'What's a booty call?' Nora looked expectantly around the table.

'Pardon?' said Walter.

'No idea, Auntie. Adam, do you know?' said Fern evilly, standing to clear plates.

'A booty call is when somebody leaves their boots to be mended and they call you to collect them,' said Adam authoritatively, with the merest of eye-widenings for Fern.

Sitting on Adam's lap – she blamed the lack of chairs – Penny said, 'No, silly, a booty call is when a guy—'

Ollie, Donna and Fern coughed heartily until Penny got the message. This took a while; Penny could ignore the most blatant warning, as Fern had discovered when she'd opened the door to her that morning.

'Oh God,' Fern had said, in place of the more usual 'hello'. Adam had arrived just minutes before, been jumped on by Tallie and fist-bumped by Ollie. He hadn't mentioned Penny. 'Penny, isn't it?' asked Fern.

The look on Penny's face said, 'You know who I am,' but her air of bonhomie didn't waver. 'Yes! Merry Christmas, Fern. Thank you for having me.' Pressing a beribboned bottle into Fern's arms, she stepped forward, but Fern stood her ground.

The women were breast to breast, eyeballing each other. '*Am* I having you?'

'I'm Adam's plus one.' Penny's eyes were a make-up masterclass. 'Adam!' She called to him over Fern's shoulder. 'I'm here!'

'So you are,' said Adam, sounding just like a man who knew that whatever he said next would get him in trouble with fifty per cent of his audience. 'Good. Come in.'

Fern stepped out of the way, feeling as crumpled as her apron beside Penny's mannequin neatness. 'I hope there's enough turkey,' she muttered.

'There's enough turkey for the entire street,' said Adam, who had recovered enough to look amused. He could look amused these days; the Botox was wearing off. Given written notice, he could even look surprised. In a lower tone he'd added, 'Is it OK? I can ask her to go.'

'I'm not Scrooge. Of course she can stay. You should have told me she was coming, though.'

Adam had sighed. 'I'm sorry. Can we start again?'

The fresh start hadn't taken. From then on, Adam sat back from the action and Fern worked overtime to conceal her annoyance. The kickback of the magic of Christmas is that Christmas is also very, *very* demanding. Fern was running on empty; usually the celebration could be relied upon to top her up, but not this year.

The *Roomies* special filled the sitting room with colour and noise, as Lincoln Speed ruined Christmas for his physically perfect friends on the small screen. Putting away board games in the conservatory, Fern heard her family's laughter drown the canned variety. Swiping up Quality Street wrappers and empty glasses and Sellotape scraps, she sank onto a chair, looking out at the bare, wintry lawn.

Her reflection, shivery and vague, seemed to squat in the twiggy garden. *You look cold*, said Fern to her image. She rubbed her hands along the raspberry-coloured cashmere sleeves of her Christmas jumper. Soft, consoling, it reminded her of what was missing. *When did I last feel like a woman?* She couldn't remember the last time Adam had taken her in his arms. There'd been a drought of lovemaking long before the moody silences turned them into huffy bed-sharers.

Adam had always found Fern sexy, always longed to touch her. With his retreat, her femininity had curdled. Without the regular feel of his skin on hers, Fern was a husk. It was hard not to blame Adam for this – *all it would have taken to get us back to normal was a sneaked kiss or two* – but that was too easy. Blaming Adam was a habit she must shake.

Penny crept in, her head on one side. 'Look at you, all on your own,' she mewed.

'If you're looking for Adam, he's watching *Roomies*.'

'I'm looking for *you*. To thank you for making me so welcome today.'

Fern checked for obvious signs of sarcasm, but could find

none. 'No problem,' she said as graciously as she was able. Penny wasn't her type – too polished, too self-aware – but that wasn't why Fern disliked her. There was nothing Penny could do to improve Fern's opinion of her except back away from Adam. *But I have no right to demand that.*

Taking a seat, her knees together, on the rattan sofa Fern had long ago 'rescued' from a skip, Penny said, 'It means a lot to be one of the family. Adam and I planned to spend the day together, so when you changed your mind about separate Christmases it was obvious I'd come with him.'

It wasn't obvious to me. 'Like I said, no problem.' Fern felt like an Amazon opposite this bird of a woman. Her new swishy silk trousers, so elegant on the hanger, were pyjamas in the face of Penny's body-con ensemble.

Dead air hung between them, until Fern said, 'So. You and Adam.'

Penny perked up; she'd been waiting for this cue. 'Me and Adam. What do you want to know?'

Everything. Every. Bloody. Thing. 'Is it just work?'

'Ooh, dear.' Penny smoothed out an invisible crease in her lap. 'Is that what he's saying?' She looked Fern in the eye. 'You can tell what's going on, right? Me and Adam, there's a connection. We tried to keep it professional but, well, we're only human.'

'Is it serious?'

'In what way?' Penny looked sweetly confused.

Fern wasn't fooled. 'Is it love?' She was picking at a scab, against all medical advice.

'What?' Penny's guard dropped briefly. 'Whoah, now. That's not for me to tell you, is it?'

'If not you, then who?'

'Adam, of course.'

'We don't discuss such matters. Adam's not with me any more.'

'But he *was*,' said Penny, her composure regained. 'That's why we're having this conversation.' She softened, leaning forward. 'I don't want to hurt you, Fern. I know Adam admires you hugely.'

Looking out again at the garden, Fern swallowed that cobblestone of a word. *Admires*. People admire scenery, or a new bathroom. Fern had been loved and desired; the demotion to admiration was radical, as if she'd tumbled down one of those long ladders on the Snakes and Ladders board on her lap. 'It was pretty *quick*.'

'I can't deny that.' Penny's face was insipidly sympathetic, like a therapist. She had a way of nodding that made Fern want to drop-kick her to the end of the lawn. 'When it's right, it's right. I know the readjustment must be hard but I don't want to fight. We could be friends, Fern.'

Fern collected friends easily. There was always room for one more, always another slice of cake to be cut. At Penny she drew the line. Even so, Fern didn't fight dirty. She couldn't say evil things in a sweet way, which put her at a disadvantage with Penny, who was obviously a pro at hand-to-hand combat.

'The truth is,' said Fern, 'the rot set in a long time before Adam met you.' The truth of this turned Fern's stomach and she felt her face grow hot. 'Even so, I don't think you and I are friendship material.'

There was something triumphant in Penny's demeanour. 'I had to try.'

I've been suckered. Fern watched Penny move away, as stately and gracious as if she was at a state funeral. Now Penny could tell Adam she'd held out the pipe of peace to his ex but she'd been rebuffed. *I'm the bad guy.*

Roomies was over. Adam's voice filled the house.

> *Sometimes stuff just seems to get you down*
> *Feelin' like there's no one else around*
> *You wish you could reach out and find a friend*
> *Who'll be here today, tomorrow, until the bitter end*

'Somebody bring me a Baileys!' yelled Fern, as she rewound the last twenty-four hours in her head. This time yesterday, she'd been watching Penny through a crack in a wardrobe door.

It had been claustrophobic there in the dark, Penny's spike heels around her feet and Penny's cashmere coats crowding her.

Curiosity had got the better of Fern on Christmas Eve as she'd walked Boudi with Hal, among the festive sparkle of the frosted trees in the park. As he'd talked about spending the next few days with his folks, Fern had idly thought *His mother might not be much older than me* as she looked up at Adam's apartment block. It leaned away from the river like a liner, the penthouse dark.

A cunning plan – also a stupid plan, as is often the way – formed in her head. Fern turned to Hal, interrupting him. 'Hal, I have to get back.'

'Weren't you even listening? I was being sad that we won't meet for a while, and you were somewhere else entirely.' Hal didn't look sad. He looked playful. And sexy. Hal always looked sexy; he probably looked sexy picking his nose, or cleaning the lint out of a tumble dryer.

'I'll be sad too!' Fern had mirrored him, tongue firmly in cheek.

'I *will*, though.' Hal's eyes flickered. He brought his voice down a notch. 'I'll miss you, Fern.'

The air was shot through with silver as they stood red-nosed and freezing, staring at each other. Fern wanted to grab his arm, ask *What's happening here?*, but she couldn't. She was only halfway out of Adam's life, one foot stuck in what she must now call the past, yet somewhere on her body was an indelible stamp: *Property of Adam Carlile*.

And so they'd stood, smiling stupidly, until Hal spoke. 'This feels like a kissing moment.'

It did. Fern reached up on her toes, and aimed for his cheek. It wasn't, perhaps, exactly what Hal meant, and her warm lips stayed on his ice-cream-cold face for a fraction too long. 'Merry Christmas.'

'Message received loud and clear.' Hal wasn't bitter; he was resigned. 'See you next year. Same time, same dogs.'

Back at the house, Evka needed little persuasion to collaborate. A connoisseur of revenge, her eyes had flashed at the prospect of adventure. 'You need to know truth of Penny and Adam. You do not believe me that they live together.' She'd reconsidered. 'You do not *want* to believe.'

Adrenalin bounced Fern all the way to Adam's front

door, when it suddenly drained from her body entirely, leaving only doubt in its place. Waiting for Evka to find her keys, Fern said, 'At six o'clock on Christmas Eve I should be wrapping last-minute presents with one eye on an old *Morecambe & Wise*. Not *this*.'

'Is not crime. I have key. You have right.'

Only in Evka's twisted philosophy could that be true. Fern slunk in behind her, hugging the wall, eyes huge. 'Maybe I should just leave,' she'd whispered.

'Why do you whisper?' Evka, perfectly at home, flicked on the lights.

'Blimey,' said Fern, shocked back to her usual volume by the opulence of the flat.

'Tree is fake.' Evka gestured at the giant, dazzling Christmas tree, loaded with colour-coordinated baubles. 'It arrives fully decorated.'

'But decorating the tree's one of the best bits of Christmas.' Adam had always had plenty of input, fussing and tweaking, finally getting out the ladder to plonk the angel on the top. Home-made from cotton reels and an old pair of Fern's white tights, the angel had stared down at Carlile Christmases ever since Ollie made her at primary school. Time spent in the attic had given her a jaded, 'why me?' look, but Fern preferred her to the blingy tart on the top of this tree. 'You're sure they won't come back?'

'I see tickets for Albert Hall carol shit. They are out all evening.' Evka lay on the suede sofa and shooed Fern with her hands. 'Go! See evidence with own eyes!'

Like a cartoon burglar, Fern tiptoed into the master bedroom. It was softly lit, the muted colour scheme saved from blandness by the quality and sheen of the fittings. The bed was unfeasibly wide, a bed made for footballer orgies rather than the comfortable, giggly love Fern and Adam had made beneath their patchwork duvet cover. She ignored it, heading straight for the wardrobes.

Sliding back a mirrored door, Fern had seen only mannish materials hanging up in the wardrobe and a line of shoes on the floor. *Adam's gone all neat.* She was accustomed to tracking him down by following a trail of discarded clothing; once she'd found the pants, her quarry was near.

This escapade was to prove or disprove Penny's presence in the master suite. It had struck Fern – forcibly – that Evka could be wrong. *What if Penny truly is just a guest, not sleeping with Adam?*

The other wardrobe door was sticky. Fern pushed, and it gave onto a view of bright colours, sensual fabrics and a chorus line of stilettos.

Unless Adam's a secret cross-dresser, Penny sleeps in this room. Fern, crushed by the evidence but also strangely energized, looked around her and saw other clues. A chick-lit novel on a bedside table, a pot of hand cream holding it shut. Pushing, as if through deep water, she forced herself to examine the en suite, where her nosiness was rewarded with Crème de la Mer, tampons and what seemed to be an entire Mac counter.

Materializing behind her, Evka had said, 'Now you believe?'

'I believe.'

A rattle at the front door made them both jump.

Fern wanted to push her entire fist into her mouth.

Adam and Penny chatted as they moved across the living area. She heard the clang of keys hitting a bowl.

'I'll probably be fine after a couple of Nurofen,' Penny said.

'Migraines are the worst,' answered Adam.

'You're sure you don't mind? About the concert?' Penny was coochy-coo; Fern imagined her lower lip stuck out.

'I just want you to feel better, Pen.'

Pen. The face Fern saw in the en suite's artfully lit mirror was a peculiar mixture of terror and the desire to smack Adam very hard. She did a small jig as the horror of the situation landed, but Evka was unmoved. Putting her finger to her lips, she guided Fern to the wardrobe.

'Stay.' Closing the door, she shut Fern in.

Fern listened hard to the rumble of voices.

'Evka!'

'Hi. I come back to finish bathroom. I leave shower streaky.'

'I didn't notice.'

'It is my silly pride. I cannot sleep if your shower is streaky.'

'The place was immaculate, as usual.'

In the dark, Fern found time to be irritated; Evka actually cleaned Adam's flat?

Evka's voice rose for Fern's benefit. 'Please come and check spare room, both of you. I must be sure it is up to standard.'

Nipping across the bedroom, Fern crouched, listening hard. As soon as she heard admiring if puzzled noises from the other bedroom, she slipped out and beetled across the apartment. Easing the front door open like a safe-cracker, she was safely in the lift by the time Evka said, 'Please do not feel you have to pay extra. Oh, OK. If you insist.'

The frigid garden swam back into focus. Fern was back in the schmaltzy embrace of Christmas Day. Something had changed when she opened that second wardrobe door. As a present to herself – to go with the enormous bottle of perfume Adam had given her – she unfolded the letter she'd taken from the box earlier.

The past was gone, but relics remained to remind her that the man sitting close to Penny in the next room had once written her a list that made her cry and laugh in equal measure.

THE BITS OF YOUR BODY I MISS THE MOST.

1. This'll make you tut but you know I have to start with your BOOBS I mean come on. They're the best boobs in the UK.

2. In second place is your NOSE. It's small and kind of squashed. I've looked and looked and I'm in a position to confirm that there's no other nose like it.

3. In at number three is your BUM. It's big and it's difficult to ignore. That's why I like it so much. I really like having my hand on your bottom when we walk down the street.

4. There's something about your SHOULDERS. Maybe it's the freckles. Or the way they bunch up around your ears when I make you laugh. They go shiny and gold if you've been

wearing strappy tops in the sun. So they're
excellent in every way.

5. Maybe your EYES should be number one.
They're just brown and a bit round and you
put too much gunge on them but when I look
into them I don't want to look away.

I can't write how I feel, not really. Some things
have to be said in person. When I see you again,
if you let me, I'll say everything.

Where does love go when it runs out? When Adam
wrote those silly, sweet words he'd been crazy about her.
They'd gone on to build a cathedral of love. When Adam
looked at that cathedral he now saw a bungalow.

Fern didn't know how to describe the feelings she had
for Adam. Once so straightforward, they were now
complex, impossible to untangle. There was so much disappointment, and even something related to dislike, as she
watched him blunder through his new life. She'd seen
Tallulah's eyebrows lower when Penny had perched on
Adam's knee; the old Adam, *her* Adam, would have been
too sensitive to allow it, but rock-star Adam only saw as
far as the end of his nose.

And how long before he remodelled that too?

Adam offered to drive Walter home.

'Will you be back?' Fern wondered if that sounded

needy, then didn't care if it did. Adam's place was here, with his children, on Christmas Day.

'Um,' said Adam, a small word that chipped another fissure in Fern's heart. He looked at Penny, who shrugged.

'Of course Daddy's coming back.' Tallulah was wrapping Walter up warm, until only his eyes were visible between his scarf and his hat.

'I guess that answers that,' smiled Adam.

'Who *is* that woman?' asked Nora as soon as the door shut on Adam, Walter and Penny, who'd gone along for the ride. 'What's she doing here?'

It was rare for Fern to clamber up alongside Nora on her aunt's high horse, but tonight she needed the solidarity. Checking that Tallulah had moved out of earshot, she said, 'That's Adam's girlfriend, Auntie.'

She was glad of the support when Nora pulled an eloquently disgusted face.

'Adam should be ashamed of himself, Fern. Yes, she's younger and prettier than you, but that's no excuse.'

Nora's support was always a mixed blessing.

Sandwiches eaten, a comatose Tallulah carried to bed, a burping Nora helped up to the loft, Fern put the sitting room to rights. Punching a cushion here, tweaking tinsel there, she switched the television back on just to have some noise in a room that was suddenly intolerably quiet.

An independent woman, Fern had half expected flying solo to be easy. The dynamic with Adam had been ramshackle; she – more or less – made the decisions and he – more or less – went along with them. It followed, surely, that she was equipped to survive without him.

Only now did Fern realize how vital Adam had been to her decision-making process. His bulk, his humour, the way she could rely on him to disagree with her, all helped.

Even on days that went smoothly, when Fern juggled everything without letting anything clatter to the floor, Fern's new life was a challenge. Christmas evening, that languid, satisfied night, should have been cosy, but all Fern had to look forward to was the embrace of her electric blanket.

Will I ever have sex again? Surely too young to zip up her frou-frou for good, Fern couldn't imagine making love to anybody other than Adam.

Her eyes moved to the cards on the mantelpiece above the fire. Fern had been surprised when Pongo, back from her cruise with a mahogany face, had pressed an envelope into her hand. The card featured, inevitably, a canine nativity scene, and was signed, equally inevitably, with a paw print.

Next to Pongo's card was a drawing on stiff cartridge paper of Boudicca and Tinkerbell in elf costumes. Fern took it down and re-read the looping handwriting on the back. This time around it gave her a jolt.

Some things you have to say in person, so I'll leave New Year greetings until we meet in the park. Hal x

Christmas was doing its magical thing after all. The wording echoed Adam's letter, chosen at random earlier. It felt eerily like a second chance, as if fate had thrown a young Adam into her path and offered her another crack at getting things right with him.

'Mum?'

'Ollie! You frightened the life out of me.'

'Sorry,' laughed Ollie. 'You look guilty, old woman. What are you up to?'

'Me? Nothing.' Fern threw the card into the fire. 'What could I possibly be up to?'

'I dunno. Dad's gone mad, so maybe you have too.' Ollie flopped onto the sofa as if landing from the high jump. 'What's with that stuck-up Penny?'

'If Dad likes her, we should give her a chance.'

'Nice try, Mum. You wanted to strangle her all through lunch.'

'Did it show?' Fern sat beside Ollie, relishing how he let her. Softer, sweeter, today Ollie was more like the boy she'd brought up. The boy she missed, but could never tell him so.

'Just a bit. When she said the roasties were eight out of ten I thought you might push her face into the goose fat.' Ollie budged a little closer. 'Don't know what he sees in her. She's nothing like you.'

'Maybe that's the point.'

They sat, enjoying the fire's light show. The door opened a crack.

'Room for one more on that sofa?' Donna's bump tested the seams of her onesie. 'I can't sleep. This little beastie is partying on my bladder.' She burrowed into Ollie's other side, making a sandwich of her bloke.

'Only four weeks to go,' said Fern. Christmas had

loomed so large, blocking out all the light, that this fact felt new.

'That's another reason I can't sleep.' said Donna. 'Childbirth *hurts*. I thought I'd be cool but now it's four weeks away, I'm not so sure.'

'I did it twice and I'm still here, love.' Fern remembered both births in perfect technicolour detail. How she reached the limits of her endurance and was then asked for more. Somehow she'd found it, and now two strange, wonderful people shared her life as a result. 'Every birth is different, but I can guarantee this. It's worth it.'

'I'd have it for you if I could,' said Ollie, earning an immediate *awww* from both women. 'It's not fair. Guys get the fun part.'

'True,' said Fern, who'd rather not dwell on this aspect of her son's life.

'One thing I can promise. I'll never do to this baby what Dad's doing to me and Tallie.'

'He's not doing it *to* you, sweetheart.' Defending Adam's thoughtlessness was a knee-jerk reaction. Protecting Adam's good name would help her son in the long run; she knew the importance of a healthy relationship with your father. 'Dad's just living his life. You'll always be his number one. When you become a parent your head's wired that way.'

Donna elbowed him. 'I didn't see you turning down that gear he bought you.'

'No, but, well, yeah.' Ollie always capitulated to Donna. 'You got me there, but money's easy, isn't it, when you're as rich as Dad.' He turned to Fern as if something had struck him. 'Does he still give you money, Mum?'

A healthy amount landed – *splat!* – in their joint account every month, an account that only Fern now used. She nodded. Ollie was right. Money – magically, suddenly – wasn't their problem. 'How's the saving going?'

'Well,' said Donna, her dark eyes liquid in the firelight. 'We're up to almost three grand.'

The girl looked chuffed. This wasn't the moment to point out that three thousand pounds, although a meaningful amount of money, wasn't anywhere near enough for a deposit on a flat in their postcode. Fern had four weeks to sit them down for a lesson in cold, hard economics.

'The sooner we get Donna out of her folks' place,' said Adam with feeling, 'the better.' He sounded grim, as if he could say a whole lot more if he chose to.

'I'm staying until the baby comes.' It sounded like this was an old bone, much fought over. 'I want to give Mum and Dad a chance. They love me, Ollie. They'll come round. I'll live with them until you and I have a proper home to offer the baby.' She relented a little. 'It's not so bad there.'

'They barely talk to you,' fumed Ollie. 'When I come to the door they look at me as if I'm an axe murderer. They keep saying the baby's *born out of wedlock*, as if we're living in Victorian times. That doesn't matter any more.'

'It matters to them,' said Donna. 'They really believe it's a sin. They're not saying it to be mean.'

'Nora prefers the term "illegitimate",' said Fern, and they all laughed.

'Nora's all right,' said Ollie.

'But she's always telling you to wipe your feet and comb your hair and she says you dress like a tinker.' Fern didn't like disparaging an old lady, but this universal lurve for her aunt made her feel as if she'd missed something important, some saving grace in the old bat's make-up.

'She's old,' said Ollie, with all the nonchalance of somebody whose skin is as taut as a yacht sail.

A wail sounded from upstairs. Tallie had woken up and was calling out, in a befuddled way, for Fern.

'I'll go.' Ollie jumped up, and Fern smothered her surprise. 'Sounds like she needs a cuddle.'

'He's in a good mood,' said Fern as Ollie's footsteps receded.

'We've been so worried for so long,' said Donna, her hands on her tum. 'Today is a day off from all that shit.' She looked guiltily at Fern.

'I'm aware that you swear,' she smiled. 'I'm sorry, Donna, if I added to the stress at first. I was a bit freaked out back then.' Fern held out her hand, palm up, on the sofa, and was grateful when Donna snatched it.

'God, no, you've been brilliant!' Donna kissed Fern's hand, a gesture that made the older woman teary. 'You've been great, even though we let you down. Ollie knows that.'

'Is that what he thinks? I don't feel let down. It was always about your potential. About your lives, not mine.' Fern squeezed Donna's hand. 'You'll be a mum soon, and you'll realize how keenly you feel everything that happens to your child.'

'He's the one, you know. Your Ollie. He's the one for me.'

'That's lovely.'

'I wanted to say that, because you know . . .' Donna

exhaled loudly. 'My head was turned by Maz. But it didn't mean anything.'

'You don't have to explain yourself to me.' Most of the time Fern forgot about the true father of Donna's baby. Conspicuous by his absence, Maz was a blank.

The baby, when it introduced itself to the world, would have nothing genetically in common with Fern and Adam. Sometimes this small, important truth bit Fern in the bum, making her feel as if she was only pretending to be a grandmother. 'You're a formidable young woman, Donna. I'm just glad you came back. Ollie was a wet weekend the whole time you were apart.'

'I still feel guilty. Ollie would never leave me, not in a million years, but I swanned off with a big idiot.'

'Is this Maz character a big idiot?'

'God, yeah. At least he proved to me how I feel about Ollie. I promise, Fern. We're going to be OK. Your son's the love of my life.'

The door flew open and Tallulah careered in. 'Couldn't sleep!'

'Nor me.' Nora hobbled to an armchair, and looked around the room. 'I suppose you finished the After Eights, Fern?'

'Yes. Every last one.' Fern confessed to a crime she knew was Donna's, and gave her a wink. Despite the challenges awaiting Donna, Fern envied her. The girl believed in 'The One'; she'd even found him. From the vantage point of a twenty-year head start, Fern felt cheated. She'd found her own One at about the same age. *And look at us now.*

Like Santa, The One was a beautiful myth that experience disproved.

Stoking the fire, Ollie said, 'Let's tell ghost stories.'

'Let's not,' said Fern, with a jerk of her head towards Tallulah.

'Once upon a time,' started Ollie.

'Babes,' said Donna. 'What accent is that? Welsh?'

'Transylvanian.' Looking hurt, Ollie started again. 'Once upon a time there was a blood-sucking demon named Penny.'

Nora stifled a laugh, as Tallie insisted, 'Penny's nice!'

'The vampire Penny,' said Ollie, his accent wavering, 'stole husbands and drained the life out of them.'

'What does he mean "stole"?' Tallie swivelled her head from Ollie to Fern. 'Does Daddy love Penny now?' Her face was primed to howl.

'No, nothing like that,' said Fern, in the voice she used to put out fires.

'I thought she was his personal subsistent.'

'That's exactly what she is.'

Nora lifted her nose. 'The child should know the truth.'

'What truth?' Tallulah was sliding into panic, shredding the edge of her nightdress between her fingers. 'Will Daddy run off with Penny?'

'Darling, no.' Fern attempted to put her arms around the wriggling girl.

'Are you having a divorce?' Tallulah asked, urgently.

Shocked into laughter, Fern said, 'Well, we'd have to get married first!' Then, too late, she took in her daughter's expression. 'You know Daddy and I aren't married, darling.'

'You *are* married!' Tallulah stood firm. 'Mummy, you *are*!'

'No, we're really not.' They'd never seen the point. They'd asked each other *Why fix it if it ain't broken?* And neither had had the energy to withstand Adam's mother across a guest list. Perhaps Fern's habit of calling herself Fern Carlile had helped their darling daughter grab the wrong end of the stick; in Tallulah's head, mummies and daddies were automatically married. 'It doesn't matter.'

'I beg to differ.' Nora gestured for Tallulah to come to her, and the girl ran into her arms as if escaping an abductor. 'Here was me thinking you were just rude and hadn't invited me to the wedding. I never imagined in a million years you were actually living in sin.'

'We weren't,' said Fern. 'We were living in this house.'

'That's right, missy. Laugh it up. There's a comfy little pit being prepared in hell for you. You won't be joking then.'

Donna groaned; she'd heard enough about hell at home without it coming up at Homestead House.

'I don't want Mummy to go to hell.' Tallulah began to sob.

'Merry Christmas, everyone!' said Ollie.

'I can't believe this.' Donna shook her head. 'It can't be happening.' She seemed to be overreacting wildly to Nora, struggling to her feet, repeating, 'No no no.' Something in her face, a broken look about the mouth, snapped Fern out of this delusion. 'The baby!' She shot to her feet.

'I'm breaking in two.' Donna staggered, put her hands on Fern's shoulders.

'Jesus, Mary and Joseph.' Nora covered Tallulah's eyes.

'Ambulance, Ollie. Nine nine nine, now!' Fern's order snapped Ollie out of his trance.

His mobile, never far away, was in Ollie's pocket. As he stabbed the numbers he said, 'It's too early, Mum. The baby hasn't finished growing.'

'I'm scared.' Donna looked so young.

'It'll be fine.' Fern had almost worn out that phrase.

CHAPTER SEVEN

New Year's Eve: Salade

Luc chopped vegetables like he did everything else. Neatly, swiftly, with minimum fuss, he was putting together a wintry Gallic salad of red cabbage and carrot. Fern, watching him from the kitchen table, idly wondered if he made love like that. If he removed his underpants and folded them carefully before saying whatever the French was for 'Assume the position, wife.'

'Do you like fennel?' Luc held up a green sprouting bulb. He pronounced it fen-*nel*.

'*Oui*.' The fib exhausted Fern's French. 'Is it just salad for dinner?' she asked, trying to sound nonchalant even though she was voicing her deepest fear.

'Non,' said Luc. He spoke briskly, without frills. 'There is duck.'

Phew. Fern admired the way Luc and Layla cooked in their dark, beamed kitchen that looked out through small wooden windows onto their courtyard. Organic. Local. Seasonal. She aspired to it. *But then I'm tempted by a rosy tomato in November*. Viennetta wasn't seasonal, thank God, and could be enjoyed all year round.

The old stone house in the centre of Saint-Martin-de-Ré had stood for centuries, and withstood all sorts of human crises; its composure had soothed Fern when she'd arrived, a day late and flustered. Sitting by the roaring stove, she'd told Luc and Layla about the white-knuckle drive to the hospital, the dash through pale corridors. 'Donna was screaming like a wild animal. It didn't sound like labour pains. It sounded like she was being murdered.'

Hours had passed in a pastel waiting room as Fern's brain busily concocted catastrophic outcomes. She'd coughed to distract herself, or stood up and sat down, or focused on the anaemic artwork that's always to be found in hospitals.

Perched on the edge of a plastic chair, she watched Adam pace the flesh-coloured lino. Accustomed to grabbing him at times of stress like Tallie grabbed her teddy, Fern wrapped her arms around herself.

Every few minutes Adam's phone buzzed. 'Penny again?' she asked.

'Poor thing's worried to death.'

Hospital waiting rooms aren't the place to air dirty laundry, but Penny's showy anxiety felt faux to Fern: *surely she knows better than to pester us at a time like this?* She suspected that Penny hated the notion of her man and his ex being thrown together at such an emotional time. She closed her ears to the phone, glad when Adam finally turned it off. 'Had enough?'

'Just conserving the battery,' said Adam.

Fern rubbed her eyes. Adam's refusal to acknowledge

Penny's mind games was especially galling in the tense atmosphere. A few feet away new life was kicking its way into the world, but here in the waiting room, thought Fern, things went on as usual.

'It'll be all right, won't it?' asked Adam suddenly, as if the question had been torn out of him.

'Yes.' Fern was adamant. If she was wrong, they could face reality when they had to.

'But it's, what, four weeks early. And Donna seemed so distressed.'

'That's a first-time mum for you,' said Fern, although she shared his fears.

'But what if—'

'Adam.' Fern closed her eyes. 'Please.'

They'd retreated into their own thoughts. *Adam knows I can't predict the future.* Resentment at Adam's need for her to make everything A-OK, as if she was the parent and he the child, clotted deep inside her. A glance at Adam told Fern that he, too, was battling annoyance at her refusal to wade through worst-case scenarios.

Making an effort, they talked of inconsequential things, about Kinky Mimi's rehearsals, about Fern's ambition to buy a heated clothes airer. Every so often the real, the only, topic reared its head and they sat quietly, eyes on the floor, both of them lost in thoughts of the baby, of Donna, of their boy.

Listening to the story later, Layla had said, 'I'm so glad you and Adam were together to help each other. See? You still have that bond.'

Better not tell her about the argument, Fern thought.

The discord had seemed to come out of nowhere, but now Fern saw how their individual grudges had been heated to boiling point in the cauldron of the waiting room.

It had started innocently enough. In fact, they'd both warmed up a little, reminiscing together.

'I wonder how Ollie's bearing up.' Adam plonked himself down on the chair beside Fern's.

'He's probably holding her hand right this minute. He'll be shocked. They don't call it labour for nothing.'

Shuddering, Adam said weakly, 'The blood. And you in such pain. It was a war zone.' He sighed, looked at her with a gentleness that had been absent from his gaze for a long time. 'Everything the doctor did only seemed to hurt you more.'

Memories overwhelmed Fern. Adam the colour of milk; the midwife shouting, 'No fainting, please, Daddy!', the lamb-like cries of a tiny, gory Ollie.

As they leaned back on a shared past, the tension in the waiting room eased.

When Adam said, 'Your dad'd be so proud of Ollie,' Fern loved him, *loved* him, for bringing her father right into the present.

'He would,' she agreed with a tired, soppy laugh. 'Don't know what he'd make of all this DJ-ing though.'

'He'd encourage him.' Adam reminded Fern that his father-in-law had always supported Kinky Mimi. 'He was devastated that we never made it.'

Racking her brains, Fern couldn't recall this devastation. 'Hmm,' she said non-committally. 'Not so sure he'd support the band's midlife crisis incarnation.' Despite thinking this at least once a day, Fern had never described Kinky Mimi's resurgence in those terms to Adam before.

He gaped at her. 'Wow,' he said eventually.

'Oh, Adam!' Fern swatted him, but she'd misjudged the extent of their sudden rapport, and he pulled his arm away as if she meant to harm him.

'Penny's right.' The name lit a firework in Fern's chest. 'Seeing me happy makes you want to spoil it.'

'Please don't quote your lady friend to me, Adam. Penny doesn't know me.'

'*I* know you. I know you want Kinky Mimi to fail just because you're not involved.'

'Are you mad?' Fern snapped, all the rosy glow dissolved. 'Why would I want that?'

'Because you're bitter. You'd like me to collapse without you. You like to be the centre of everything.'

'One thing I'm not,' said Fern, 'is bitter.' *Although I might take it up if you carry on like this.*

'Come on, Fern.' There was a sneer in Adam's voice. 'You even boycotted your own mother's wedding because of bitterness.'

It was Fern's turn to gape. 'That wasn't a boycott. It was a crisis.' Adam knew the pain she'd been in; he'd nursed her through it.

'Your mum needed you there.'

'I bloody went!' yelled Fern. She'd only made it to the registry office because of Adam. He'd listened to her tearful raving as she'd put on, taken off and put on again the chiffon horror of a dress she'd bought for the wedding.

He'd plodded fearlessly through the complex swamp of feeling, refusing to give up.

When Fern's mother moved on so quickly, the scars caused by her father's sudden death had opened up, smarting as though they were fresh. Fern had felt guilty, selfish, but above all, confused. The sensible part of her – the part that ensured there was milk in the fridge and remembered who was allergic to what – had applauded her mum for this life-affirming step. The part that was still a child and needed her parents had wanted to sob and lash out and hide under the covers.

In the maternity unit waiting room, Fern remembered how Adam had cajoled her back into the dress, kissed away her tears and insisted that her eyes didn't look *that* puffy. It was a beautiful memory, one she returned to often. *You stopped me making one of the biggest mistakes of my life.* 'I thought you understood!' yelled Fern.

'I thought *you* understood!'

'Seems we were both wrong.'

Glaring at each other across the room, shivering with indignation and the need to throw something, they didn't at first notice the nurse at the door.

With a coughed *ahem*, the nurse asked, 'Would you like to come and meet your granddaughter?'

Brought back to the here and now by the clatter of shoes on the wooden stairway that wound through the tall house, Fern stood up when Layla appeared.

As tall as ever, hair exploding around her broad, handsome face, physically Layla was unchanged, but her dress sense had evolved since her move to the island. The striped

jumper and linen trousers were so elegant they could only
be French. 'Nice nap?' asked Fern.

'Sorry I wasted some of our time.' Layla looked as grey
as the stone her house was made of. 'But I just felt . . .
urgh.'

'Sit down. I'll make you some tea.' Not *real* tea, strong
enough for a mouse to trot across, with two lovely sugars;
the house speciality was weak, herbal and smelled of
mildew. 'We've got plenty of time to chat tonight, waiting
for midnight and the New Year.'

Luc asked, 'Would you make the vinaigrette, darling?'
and Layla took the requisite ingredients out of the oak
cupboards her husband had built himself.

'This is Luc's recipe,' said Layla, pouring extra virgin
olive oil into an earthenware jug. 'You won't have tasted
better.'

'Never quite understood the concept of extra virgin. You
either are, or you aren't, surely.' Fern, who always meant
to make her own salad dressing but usually grabbed her
trusty bottle of lite mayonnaise, said, 'It's weird seeing you
cook.'

'I always ate at your place,' smiled Layla, expertly
whisking in cider vinegar and a dot of mustard powder.
'The seasoning's key.' She held out a spoon to Fern.

'Bloody hell.' The dressing was a revelation. 'My compliments to the cheffette.' She fumbled for her phone. 'Some
new photos arrived while you were lying down.' There
was abundant cheese and fruity red wine in this harbour
village, but the internet connection was patchy. The only
images Fern had been able to share so far were of an

indistinct blob, a piece of liver in a bobble hat. 'Look, Amelie's out of the incubator.'

'Thank God,' said Layla, with feeling.

'Aw look, she's fast asleep.' Fern held up the screen. 'I was relieved when they told me her name. Youngsters have odd ideas about baby names. Look at those tiny hands!'

'I'll have a good look later.' Layla moved away, reaching up for bowls and cutlery. 'Could you lay the table?'

'Um, yeah.' Fern, not so much quashed as puzzled, put away her phone. She and Layla shared a brain when it came to celebrating each other's joys and setbacks; they giggled and cried together. She tried to catch Luc's eye, to throw a look of *what's up with Layla?* at him, but he was diligently head down, arranging slices of duck on a platter. 'Amelie goes home to Donna's parents' house tomorrow,' she said. This was important news; the baby was doing better than anybody had dared to expect.

'That's good,' said Layla.

'Yup,' said Fern. Something was amiss. The naps. The pallor. The lack of interest. Layla was limp, like a T-shirt washed too many times. Fern's heart lurched behind her ribs as she watched the couple go methodically about their business.

Luc, his jet hair standing up like a cliff above his fore-head, gave nothing away. His reserve wasn't useful at a time like this; if, God forbid, something was wrong with Layla, she'd need warmth and support and a pair of strong arms around her.

'I'll go and see what my daughter's up to.' Fern had to

get away, file her thoughts tidily before they ran away with her.

'Probably next door with Simone,' said Layla, laying a baguette on a wooden board. 'That was love at first sight, wasn't it?'

Popping out into a misty chill that carried the tang of the sea, Fern changed her mind and turned her feet towards the harbour. Drawn by the lighthouse, she thought of Tallulah as she passed shuttered houses on the quiet, blue-grey street.

The girl had blossomed like a Christmas poinsettia, the moment she'd touched down on French soil. The heavy load that had settled on her shoulders in England had been shrugged off as she got her mitts on the local salted caramel and the little girl who lived next door to Layla. The language barrier was no hurdle when there was running and jumping and tormenting Simone's older brother to be done.

It's deserted. Islanders stayed indoors at night, by their fires, munching their fennel. There was no corner shop for emergency purchases of milk or bread or horrible tights, no garish pub buzzing with tipsy talk and the clamour of fruit machines. Fern could have been alone in Saint-Martin-de-Ré at this tail end of the old year, just her and the fog and the lighthouse rearing up before her like a giant willy. A giant willy with a flashing light on top of it – quite a landmark to have at the end of the street. At the end of Fern's street there was only a dry cleaner's.

Tucking herself into a niche at the foot of the lighthouse, Fern ignored the frosty stone beneath her bottom and lost herself in the view of the sea. It was a satin blanket, softly churning in the dark. Every few seconds the lighthouse bit a white slice out of the blackout; it was reassuring the way it kept coming around. Fern could rely on that light.

In her pocket was the letter she'd snatched from the ribboned box as she packed. It was a goodbye. In 1993, Adam had given up.

Dear Fern
You win.
I've poured my heart out to you and written two songs and bugged your friends and mooned about like an idiot. I can't do any more.
I still love you. I will always love you. Even when you're with somebody else and I'm with somebody else my feelings won't change. Fern will always be my first and best love. But I can't force you to be with me.
A x

The ruse had worked. Fern was on Adam's doorstep before the ink was dry. They'd sped to his bed as if there was a pot of gold under his rarely changed duvet. Tangled together afterwards, sweaty and happy, they'd vowed never to split up again. Not ever ever *ever*.

Teenagers haven't seen enough of life to know how the years change people. Fern was Adam's first, but maybe the best was yet to come for him. She made an unhappy noise as tears slid down her cheeks; *I'm the bitter woman he left behind*.

The feeling of the year slowing, coming to an end, should

have straightened out her thinking, but when Fern examined her feelings about Adam, she couldn't dig past the dismay and, yes, she had to admit it – the bitterness. She was bitter that he didn't appreciate their life, that he wanted to rub it out and start again, this time in better trousers.

If there was love left, Fern couldn't find it, no matter how she scrabbled about. She missed loving him, missed the soft cushion it provided. Did that negate the time they'd spent together, when love painted their walls and provided the carpet under their feet?

The sea had no answer.

Tallulah lay along the low sofa by the stove, entwined around the great shaggy bear of a dog named, appropriately, Bear. She'd been keen to stay up for the chimes, but her adventures with Simone had worn her out, and she snored gently into Bear's fur.

'Duck,' said Fern, 'is where it's at.' She put her knife and fork together on her empty plate. Her tummy was full of waterfowl and her brain was pleasantly muggy with the blood-coloured wine that cost the same as a Mars Bar. *The French have got their priorities right.* 'Luc, you're a genius.'

'*C'est mon plaisir,*' murmured Luc. He'd said little throughout the meal, leaving it to Fern and Layla to supply the conversation.

Or just to me. Fern had done most of the talking. Layla had sputtered out halfway through the starter, as if somebody had pulled her plug. She'd given one-word answers to the questions Fern had saved up. There'd been little or no curiosity about Amelie, about Donna, about recent goings-on at Homestead House.

'One hour to go till midnight!' Fern was toothy, trying to amp up the atmosphere.

'I think I'll turn in.' Layla stood, her chair scraping on the stone floor. Her yawn was an amateurish attempt at feigning tiredness. 'Sorry to be a wet blanket, Fern. You and Luc stay up. Open the good brandy. See you in the morning.'

She was gone, her shadow faded on the stairs before Fern could protest.

The candle flickered over Luc's face, a guarded face until suddenly he sighed and made a noise Fern thought of as typically French. More specifically, typically French male. It was like 'Bah!' but might have been 'Bleurgh!' – difficult to reproduce, but she understood him perfectly.

'Brandy?' she said.

'Brandy,' he said.

Fern seemed to be made of fumes. The cognac had suffused her soul. She was groggy and warm, even though she felt as if she had very little in the way of legs; anything seemed possible.

Outdrinking her by two shots to one, Luc was still buttoned-up, erect. They hadn't mentioned Layla as the clock inched towards twelve. Instead they'd put the world to rights; Fern was particularly pleased with how she'd solved the problem of famine in Africa. She couldn't quite remember her idea now, but she knew it was a corker. Something to do with airlifting Ready Brek to Somalia?

'To you, Fern.' Luc lifted his glass.

'To you, Luc.' Fern lifted hers, and they clinked. '*Salut!*'

'Your French is improving.'

'If I ask you a straight question, will you answer it?' The brandy had rolled up its sleeves and booted out Fern's inhibitions.

'I can guess the question.' Luc glanced over at Tallulah, as if to check she was still asleep. 'You want to know what's wrong with my wife.'

What Luc told Fern, in his almost perfect but idiosyncratic English, sobered her up.

'We married very fast, yes? It was a surprise to you, and to Layla's family. Although you *are* her family, she says. I knew she was a special woman when we met, when she brought that poor dog she found into my surgery. She cried over this mongrel as I put him down. She was tender. And she was pretty. Very pretty.'

'She's gorge,' agreed Fern quietly, not wanting to break his rhythm. Her heart was full of love for Layla, two floors above them. And fear.

'We become serious very fast. Because we are not so young, you know, and we have wasted enough time already. My first wife was wrong for me but this time I knew Layla would make me happy. She told me I would make *her* happy. We enjoy the same things. We cook, we sail, we take Bear to the lighthouse and back. Our life is simple.'

'It sounds beautiful,' said Fern, whose own life was a bag of frogs by comparison.

'Do you know why we really bonded? What really brought us together?' When Fern shook her head, Luc said, leaning forward into the candlelight, 'We wanted to be parents.'

'No,' said Fern automatically.

'*Oui.*' Luc was emphatic. 'It was a dream we had both put away. Locked up, *comme ça.*' Luc mimed turning a key. 'I admitted it, then she admitted it, and we cried together. After, we dry our tears and we feel full of courage. We ask why not?'

'I had no idea.' Fern had taken Layla's acceptance at face value. She'd believed her friend was satisfied with being an ersatz aunt, an 'other mother' to Ollie and Tallulah. Other mutual friends were happily child-free, enjoying the freedoms it brought. Fern hadn't scratched beneath the surface. *Because it suited me?*

'So, doctors.' Luc made another French noise, more of a *pffft!* this time, throwing up his hands. 'They push her and prod her and they say no, no babies for you.'

'There are lots of options now.' Fern got up and splashed her face with water from the big old sink. 'You could try IVF. I know it's invasive but—'

'We have tried IVF.'

Fern stared at Luc, hard.

He understood the question on her face. 'Layla didn't want to, what's the word, burden you. The first IVF was about the time Adam made all that money, and she kept it to herself because she knew you were having problems.'

'Hmm. Poor me. Not.' Fern was possibly the only

woman in history who needed support because she had too much money. 'The IVF didn't work, I take it.'

'No. Layla found the drugs they gave her to prepare her body almost impossible to bear. The next one also failed.'

'You've tried twice?' Fern could only imagine the terrible optimism and the crashing collapse of hope.

'Four times.' Luc swallowed. 'We discovered the latest one has not worked when Layla woke up this morning.'

No wonder the poor woman hadn't wanted to 'ooh' and 'aah' over pictures of Amelie. Fern cringed; she'd clucked over the new baby as Layla's body told her, once again, a firm *non*. 'Can you bear to try again?'

'My wife would climb the Eiffel Tower nude to have a child,' said Luc. 'We can't, though. There's nothing left. We've mortgaged the house. Our savings have gone. We must face the truth.' He hung his head, suddenly no longer in charge of himself. 'I fear that she'll leave me, go to London. When we look at each other we are reminded of what we can't have.' Luc rubbed his eyes roughly with his knuckles. 'I can't easily do without her now.'

'You won't have to.' Fern came close to Luc, hugged him, her head on his shoulder. 'Layla loves you. She's not a quitter.'

'Like Adam?' Luc grabbed Fern's hand as she pulled away. 'Love isn't always enough.'

'You aren't me, and Layla's not Adam.' Fern glanced at the clock. 'I need you to shut up and listen and then I need you to say "yes" to everything I suggest.'

When fireworks silhouetted the lighthouse and the village streets filled with the sound of bells, a champagne cork popped in Layla's kitchen.

'To us!' Fern yelled.

'To us!' laughed Layla.

'To downtrodden women everywhere!' shouted Tallulah, who'd woken up as the adults were hugging each other and crying and apologizing and thanking each other. She had low expectations of grown-ups, and this bunch were living down to them. Tallulah couldn't work out what all the tears were for.

'What a year.' Fern felt worn out and exhilarated, as if she'd just run a marathon. 'What a bloody terrible, wonderful year.' Any year that had produced Amelie couldn't be all bad.

Barefoot in pyjamas, Layla was giddy, a high colour in her cheeks. It had taken some very determined convincing/bullying to get her to agree to Fern's proposition. The midnight deadline had helped; Fern insisted they would celebrate something truly special as the clocks struck twelve.

It had been an obvious solution. Fern had too much money; Layla had too little money. It didn't take a genius to see what should happen.

'I can't,' Layla had said. 'It's too much and it'll be a waste because it won't work.'

When Fern had asked Layla to visualize the tables being turned, she knew she'd broken through. 'Let me do this,' she'd begged. 'Please.'

Layla's nod had kick-started the chimes.

'Adam suggested the very same thing,' said Layla, wiping champagne from her chin.

'Adam?' Fern was nonplussed. 'Hang on, you told Adam?'

'Yeah.' Layla winced. 'Are you annoyed?'

'There's no reason why you shouldn't tell him, I guess.' Fern felt uncomfortable, something she rarely felt around her friend.

'I should have told you first.' Layla chopped the air with one hand, making her point. 'But Adam caught me at a low point. He wanted to talk about, you know, you and him, and my head was full of my own problems. He could tell something was up, and I just cracked and told him.' She smiled. 'He's a good guy, Fern. He's just not as expert at twisting my arm as you are. I said no to his offer.'

'You're too proud for your own good, you goose.' So what if Layla had told Adam? They weren't schoolgirls, fighting over besties. Fern knew the two talked; earlier Layla had said something about Fern looking daggers at Adam all Christmas Day, and Fern had defended herself.

Tallulah, tired of trying to get Bear to take a sip of her half glass of champers, said, 'Is Luc in a trance?'

Standing stock still, Luc looked past them all, tears rolling down his hewn rock of a face.

'Oh, Luc,' breathed Fern. The man's depth touched her. He was the old-fashioned type, strong and silent; that didn't mean he was cold. Never again would she ask why Layla had married him. 'It'll work this time. I feel it in my bones.' The couple had agreed only to accept sufficient money for one round of IVF. Privately, Fern knew she'd pay for as many as they needed. As many as they could bear; Fern would ask Layla at some point about the rigours of the procedures, but not tonight. 'You two are going to be parents.'

Layla wiped Luc's tears, and slipped her arm through his. 'We used to talk like that.'

Out in the courtyard, allowing Bear a last leisurely widdle, Fern saw Layla and Luc's light go out on the top floor. She imagined them holding each other tight, wishing and fearful, making tentative plans. There's nothing as warm as two people close together in a bed, faces close, hair mingling.

The urban cackle of a text arriving spoiled the calm. Hal was wishing her a 'hippy new year'. On a whim, before she could examine the impulse, Fern dialled his number. The patchy coverage cooperated. She'd never called him before, and he sounded surprised when he picked up.

'You're in France!' he said.

'And you're pissed.'

'Yes. Yes I am.' Hal burped and then apologized profusely, before tapering off. 'Remind me, what am I apologizing for?'

Music played in the background. It was moody music, not a party anthem. 'Where are you?'

'In bed. But I'm not alone.'

Bear was scratching at the back door, but Fern didn't see him. She saw instead a bedroom in London. A messy bed, containing a naked Hal and a just-as-naked girl of his own age. An unlined girl whose breasts were cheerful and whose bottom was polite. 'Sorry. I'll leave you to it. Happy new thingummybob.'

'I *was* alone but now you're here.'

'Oh. I see.' Fern let Bear into the house and strolled around the courtyard, head down. 'I feel good about this year, Hal.' *I do*, she insisted to herself. *I really do.* Her relationship with Adam wasn't the be-all and end-all; Fern was determined to lift her eyes and notice the other people in her life. Really notice them. 'I hope this year brings great things to you.'

'That's sweet,' said Hal. 'You too, babes.' He'd never called her that before, and Fern pulled a face. *Nobody* had ever called her that. It wasn't an Adam word. 'Listen,' said Hal, his voice more intimate. Fern imagined him delving deeper beneath the covers. She wondered what he was wearing, and then decided not to wonder that because it made it impossible to concentrate on what he was saying.

'Fern, what's happening with us?'

That was the question she'd wanted to ask, but hadn't dared. Wrong-footed, she took the easy option and pretended to misunderstand. 'In what way? We're on the phone right now. Sometimes we walk dogs or drink coffee.'

'Don't do that. You know what I'm asking.' There was a scritchy sound, and Fern imagined him scratching his head the way he did. 'Is something happening?'

Her stomach melting, Fern closed her eyes. One of them had to be realistic. Hal would be sober in the morning; she mustn't compromise herself by saying something she'd regret. He might not even remember this conversation; *I must protect myself.* 'You're a nutter, Hal. Get to sleep.

Drink some water, or that head of yours will be sore in the morning.'

'Goodnight.' Hal didn't press her. Perhaps he'd forgotten already.

The goodbyes were hard. Layla kept returning for one more hug, one more tearful thank-you. Fern had never left Tallulah behind before, but as she waved from the tiny airport's one departure gate her daughter was already involved in some intense plot with Simone.

Climbing into the clouds, Fern already missed the soft colours of the Île de Ré and the mellifluous language of the French. During the short flight she toyed with a newspaper, resigned to seeing Lincoln Speed's self-absorbed smile in the TV guide. The Christmas episode of *Roomies* had pulled in the largest audience of the festive season; the great man had celebrated by visiting a children's hospice in the afternoon and dining with a transsexual porn star at Nobu in the evening.

The money would continue to flood Adam's bank account, until it washed his whole life clean. Fern felt like one of the stains it was working hard to dislodge.

London's sky was milky white and the air was a cold slap in the face. As soon as she switched on her phone it vibrated bossily.

The first thing Nora had done with the mobile Fern bought her for Christmas was to send her a text saying, *Central heating playing up typical are you trying to freeze me to death you'd like that wouldn't you yours sincerely Nora.*

Tempted to reply that yes, she would quite like that, instead Fern set down succinct instructions for dealing with the temperamental boiler. As she finished, a cacophony of alerts announced a flood of texts from Ollie. She read them rapidly, one after the other; the incoherent snatches added up to a crisis Fern had dreaded.

'Ollie?' Fern called her son. He was flapping, out of breath. 'Am I getting this right? Donna's parents won't let you see Amelie?' The other grandparents were under the impression that Ollie was the baby's natural father; Donna had been adamant on that point.

'They won't let me near the house, Mum. They're blanking Donna as if she's a ghost and they call Amelie "it". It! My little girl and they're calling her *it*!' Ollie was running out of breath, traffic blaring in the background. 'Donna talked to the council. They might give her emergency housing, but it's in a really shitty block, Mum. I'll move in with her if she gets it.'

'No.' Fern was in Mother Knows Best mode; one of her favourites. 'Turn round and get Donna. She has a home and so do you, and so does Amelie. Take them back to Homestead House.' Fern admired the girl's gumption, but she couldn't stand by and watch Donna drop through the cracks. 'You won't all fit in your room, so take mine.'

'You're amazing, Mum.'

'Remember that next time I'm shouting at you to get up. Give your ladies my love, and see you later.'

The queue for the taxi rank was long and cranky as the

reality of British weather hit returning holidaymakers. Fern thought about Hal. Or rather, she let thoughts of him back in. He'd been battering at her mind throughout the flight.

He's brave, she said to herself. Not many men his age would contemplate any sort of relationship with a woman zooming through her forties. She'd been wrong: he was no young version of Adam; in his twenties Adam had thought of middle-aged women as mother figures. Homely ladies, good for tea-making and hot dinners, but whose sexuality was a no-go area.

Hal is Hal. This has to be about him or I'm not being fair. So much of life wasn't fair – men left their wives and moved in with bitches; women who longed for babies couldn't conceive; youngsters were forced to grow up because of one slip of a condom – that Fern was keen to be as just as possible in her dealings with other people. Hal's bravery deserved to be matched by her own courage.

'Hal, hi,' she said as he picked up, sleepy-sounding. 'Do you want to know the answer to the question you asked last night?'

'Yes,' said Hal, abruptly wide awake.

Forty minutes later a motorbike pulled up in the airport car park. Hal held out a helmet and patted the pillion seat.

This'll ruin my hair, thought Fern as she swung a leg – with only a slight *oof!* – over the bike. She'd thought he'd collect her in a car and was glad she hadn't had fore-warning, because motorbikes scared the bejaysus out of her.

'Arms round my middle,' ordered Hal.

He was snug to hold in his leathers. Fern squeezed and he laughed, 'Ready?'

Not really. 'Yes!'

The speed was exhilarating. Like sliding down an endless banister. Fern yelped in Hal's ear as they curved round corners, the bike leaning to one side, before straightening up to eat the road.

They couldn't communicate, a detail which added to the anticipation. Between her legs the machine pulsed with dynamic male energy as they soared forward. Fern was making progress, speeding up, getting on with it.

Fern was leaving Adam behind.

I can't keep waiting for him to change back into the man he was before. Money had changed her lover; their arguments had changed them both. Fern hadn't been emotionally available for her friends while she churned about in her own troubles. She'd dropped the ball with her children.

Today would mark an end to that. She'd start living again. Not just for others, but for herself. Yes, she was a slightly shop-soiled edition of the Fern who'd first fallen in love, but she wasn't yet ready for a wipe-clean, high-backed chair with a view of the garden. If she was being scrupulously fair, Fern had to admit that she was due a little sexy fun.

The ride to the chi-chi boutique hotel she'd booked while waiting for Hal to arrive was the most extended foreplay Fern had ever known.

CHAPTER EIGHT

February: Légumes

Another postcard landed with a soft *whack* on the doormat, its colours a welcome contrast to the bills. 'Dad's in Ebeltoft!' called Fern as her offspring bustled about upstairs, preparing for their day.

'Where's Ebel-thingy?' asked Tallulah, limping down the stairs with one shoe on, one shoe off, and both of them covered in mud.

'Denmark.' Fern read out the card as she poured cereal and wrote CLEAN T'S SHOES!!! on the kitchen black-board. '"Watch out Ebeltoft! Here comes Kinky Mimi! We tore up the stage last night! We're HOT! Xxx"' She pinned it to the noticeboard, along with all the others. 'Dad'll run out of exclamation marks if he carries on like this.'

The small European tour had been set up by Penny, who'd also had the T-shirts printed. Tallulah wore hers to bed, proclaiming 'KINKY MIMI RIP UP EUROPE!' among her soft toys. When she lay a certain way it read 'KINKY MIMI RIP', which made Fern snigger, and felt more appropriate.

'How did Dad sound on the phone last night?' Adam called every evening before going on stage, telling Ollie and Tallulah all about the new town he found himself in. Never Fern. That was how things were between them now. To Fern it felt like a quiet war, a subtle re-drawing of boundaries. 'Still moaning about his back?' The conversations were nothing like the gung-ho cards.

'Keith's feet are playing up,' said Tallulah, picking out chocolate loops from her bowl. 'What does playing up mean?'

'Dad's got a cold sore.' Ollie laughed, a short *hur hur*. 'He was whingeing about room service sending him Lapsang Souchong instead of English Breakfast tea.'

'Very rock'n'roll,' murmured Fern, hoping Tallulah wouldn't hear.

But Tallulah, defender of her father's rock-god delusions, did hear. Funny, thought Fern, how she heard that but I can stand at the bottom of the stairs calling her name for ten whole minutes.

'Daddy's going to be as famous as Elvis. Stop being mean, Mummy.'

'Yeah,' said Ollie, enjoying himself. 'You're so *mean*, mommie dearest.'

Swatting him with the gas bill, Fern was delighted by the teasing. He hadn't called her 'mommie dearest' for years. Despite the treadmill of casual jobs that had Ollie coming and going all day and night, with barely time to take a bite of toast in between, he'd relaxed enough to allow some of the old playfulness back in. 'You watch it,' she laughed. 'You're not too old to put over my knee.'

'You've never put him over your knee.' Tallulah, as ever, was a stickler for the truth.

A wail started above their heads.

'Madam's awake,' said Fern.

'I wish I could breastfeed her,' said Tallulah. 'Donna's so lucky.'

'Shut up.' Ollie pulled a face. 'Jesus.'

'I love Amelie,' said Tallulah. She said it a thousand times a day, sometimes to the baby herself, sometimes to thin air. It would be hard not to love Amelie, who seemed designed to be adored.

Amelie was, as Fern told all her clients, a nicely *finished* baby. Not one of those raw red little creatures, like her own two. Tallulah had been stubbornly bald until she was nearly a year old and Ollie had looked like a prawn wearing a nappy for months. At five weeks old, Amelie was, according to Nora, a 'bobby dazzler', with skin the colour of coffee, a head of dark hair, and lashes that curled like a beauty queen's.

Another department had opened in Fern's heart the moment she met the tiny girl. She couldn't quite remember life before her. It must have been a strange life, with no soundtrack of baby noises to nudge them all into feeding or changing or cuddling. *What did I do all day?* Fern was involved in all aspects of Amelie's care, dispensing her hard-won wisdom to the new parents, always giving Amelie a thorough once-over before she went out in the grand pushchair Adam had bought.

Holding her was therapy. Fern could gaze at the baby's soft features indefinitely. There was a lot of competition for Amelie; she was the pet of everybody in Homestead House. And there were a lot of people within those four walls. Sandwiched between the generations, Fern was the cog that kept it all whirring.

Up in the loft, Nora bumped into things, complained about being too cold or too warm, spilled things on the carpet and then denied spilling things on the carpet. A floor below, Evka took up the spare room with her extensive collection of very small items of clothing, resolutely not cleaning anything and having loud phone conversations with various conquests. Next door to her, the new trinity of Ollie, Donna and Amelie had commandeered the master bedroom with all the kit necessary to keep one small human dry, warm and fed. Along the corridor, Fern was getting used to a single bed again and vowing each day to repaint the black and purple walls still studded with gobbets of Blu-Tack from Ollie's posters. Tallulah's room, defiantly non-pink, was the child's refuge. She spent more time there than she had before; Tallulah's reversion to carefree giddiness in France had been short-lived.

'Amelie sounds a bit colicky.' Fern cocked her head, listening to the baby's cries like Sherlock Holmes considering a clue. 'She might need to be picked up. Gentle movement can help.'

'She sounds fine to me.' Standing up, Ollie wiped his mouth. 'I'll go and check.'

'Remember!' shouted Fern as he went up the stairs at the only speed he ever went up the stairs – far too fast. 'Date night tomorrow!' Once a week, without fail, the young couple were released into the wild, with instructions to eat, drink and be merry, while Fern babysat, fending off offers of help from her various dependants. On those evenings it was just her and Amelie, in a cocoon of talc and Babygros.

'Where are you going, Mummy?' Tallulah looked anxious.

'Just out, darling.' Fern cupped her daughter's face and kissed the furrowed forehead. Tallulah was clingy of late, demanding details from Fern whenever she left the house and jumping from foot to foot if her mum was a minute or two late. 'To see a friend.'

'Who?'

'A nice lady. You don't know her, Detective Inspector Carlile.' It was half true. Hal *was* nice, but he was no lady. 'I'll be home before dark.'

'Good.' Tallulah brightened. 'Maybe me and Nora'll have cheese toasties for lunch. She makes them just right.'

Evka was in the hall when the doorbell went. 'I'll get it!'

Peeking past Evka, who evidently considered over-the-knee woollen socks and leather shorts ideal cold-weather wear, Fern saw a couple in the porch. He was tall, imposing, with an Easter Island face; she held her handbag like a shield.

Oh no. Fern's heart dropped. 'I'll deal with this, Evka.' The couple gawped at the Slovak as if she was naked. 'Hello, come in.' Fern smiled, knowing it wouldn't be reciprocated.

The woman looked up at the man, enquiringly, as if uncertain whether or not to take Fern up on her offer. He nodded down at her, and they entered the house, eyes darting to either side, as if entering a high-security prison. When Binkie slithered towards them, they flattened themselves against the wall. The cat farted nonchalantly as she passed.

'Sorry about . . .' Fern glared at Binkie, who consistently lowered the tone. 'I'll fetch your daughter.'

Donna was already on the stairs, Amelie in her arms, bundled up in a trailing lacy shawl that Nora had crocheted. More hole than anything else, the wispy garment was nonetheless one of Donna's favourites. 'At last,' said Donna, her voice barely there.

Eyes suddenly wet, Fern showed Mr and Mrs Palmer into the sitting room, where they sat stiffly on the sofa, knees together like debutantes. 'I'll leave you alone,' she said, as Donna and Ollie entered with little Amelie.

'No.' Donna's father put up his hand, as if stopping traffic. He was a man used to being heard. 'It's best you hear what we have to say.'

Sitting down gingerly, Fern groaned inwardly at the state of the sitting room. She had a *live-in cleaner* and yet there were books opened out on the rug, sweet wrappers papering the hearth, and a mug on every surface. She read disgust in Mrs Palmer's eyes and wanted to defend herself. *I'm doing my best!*

'Mum, Dad.' Donna was almost shy, holding out the baby. 'Do you want to hold her? She's changed so much since you saw her.'

'Oh,' said her mother, and Fern read a lot into the short syllable. She heard longing. She heard love. But she also heard a form of disgust.

'You've named her?' asked Mr Palmer.

'She's Amelie.' Donna was cowed, hesitant, nothing like the dominatrix who policed Ollie's every waking moment. 'You know, like . . .'

'My mother,' said Donna's father. He chewed his lip for a moment, lost in some place in his head. His eyes were just like Donna's, dark and deep, but they had none of her vivacity. Their glitter was hard. 'We've come here in a spirit of openness to work out what's to be done. About . . .' He waved a large hand in the baby's general direction. 'About this.'

Fern saw his wife flinch as Donna retreated with Amelie, the tiny offering that had been rejected. *You big bully*, she thought.

'How'd you mean?' Ollie sat on the arm of Donna's chair, his arm across the back of it.

'Young man,' said Donna's father, looking at him with self-righteous scorn, 'I'm sorry to be blunt, but what has this baby's future to do with you?'

'Dad . . .' Donna shrank as if her father had hit her.

'She's my daughter,' said Ollie. His voice shook. 'I'm taking care—'

'She's not your daughter,' said Mr Palmer. 'We've discovered a thing or two since you ran away, Donna.' He turned his cold wrath on Fern. 'You're not her grandmother, Mrs Carlile. We're here to collect our daughter and our grand-daughter.'

That was a short-lived spirit of openness, thought Fern.

'Hang on, mate.' Ollie stood up. He was red in the face, his limbs twitching like a rag doll's.

The signs were all there. Fern knew Ollie was close to blowing his top. She'd seen that expression on his face when an older boy stole his Tonka Toys, or when Adam had told him off for something he didn't do. She reached over, put a hand on his arm. 'Ssh, love,' she said. 'Let Donna have her say.'

Donna had the loose look of the new mum. As if her body had been given back to her and she wasn't sure what to do with it. The baby, unaware of the battle raging above her head, made spitty noises as she nuzzled the striped cotton at Donna's breast, impatient, entirely secure. 'If I come with you,' said Donna, and Ollie looked as if his heart had stopped, 'what's the plan?'

'You'll go back to your studies,' said Mr Palmer. 'You'll graduate, go into the law. The baby . . .' He paused.

'The baby?' prompted Donna.

Her mother spoke, stumbling, with none of her husband's gravitas. 'This house is no place for a baby,' she said. 'It's full of waifs and strays. Who was that who opened the door? What influence are these people having on you?'

As one of 'these people', Fern felt racy. Insulted, but racy all the same.

'The woman who opened the door helps me out when I'm tired. She sings your granddaughter to sleep.' Donna sounded hurt on Evka's behalf. 'And by the way, she's a true lady.'

'Too fucking right!' came an accented shout from the other side of the closed door.

'You see!' Mr Palmer poked a finger in the air. 'Is that the language you want around a baby?'

'It's preferable,' said Ollie, 'to what you say.'

'Like I said, boy, this is none of your concern.'

Boy? Fern sat forward. 'My son has a name.' For Donna's

sake she wanted to keep things polite; for Ollie's sake she wanted to bop this egomaniac on the nose.

Finding her voice again, Mrs Palmer said, in a pleading way, 'Donna, what can you offer this child? Really? A spare bed in this madhouse? Her parents living in sin? Why not let some other couple, good people who can't have children of their own, have the blessing of a baby in their lives?'

It took a moment to sink in. Fern and Ollie were silent, exchanging blank glances that were beyond puzzlement.

Donna spoke. 'Adoption? How can you even . . . ? Why would you say that, Mum?' She was incoherent with rage. Beneath the rage, Fern knew, lay a strata of blistering pain. 'Don't you love Amelie just a little bit?'

'We can love the sinner,' said Mr Palmer, 'while we hate the sin.'

'We do love her!' His wife was crying. 'That's why we want a good life for her.'

'Her place is with me. I can give her the best possible life.' Donna bared her teeth and slammed her fist against her chest. 'Me. Her mother. Me.'

The door swung open, rattling its hinges. Evka stood, hands on hips, oddly superhero-like in her leather shorts. 'Come on. Out. You are bad flippin' pair,' she snapped at Donna's parents.

'We'll go when we're ready,' said Mr Palmer, all dignity.

'You're ready.' Ollie jumped up.

Sobbing, Tallulah barrelled towards Fern, pushing her face into her shoulder. 'Don't let them give Amelie away!' she howled.

'Nobody's giving anybody away.' Nora, black glasses on,

cardigan done up all wrong, wobbled in the doorway. 'I never heard such nonsense in me life.'

Donna's father towered over them all when he stood up. 'One last chance, child.' He shook his head sorrowfully when his daughter wouldn't look at him. 'You know where we are when you change your mind,' he said, putting his hand on his wife's back, ushering her out. 'When you come crawling home, we'll be waiting.'

'She has a home,' said Fern, heartily sick of this man. 'And for your information, I *am* Amelie's grandmother.'

'And I'm her dad,' said Ollie, tailing the pair as they made for the front door.

'And I'm her great-great-aunt!' shouted Nora, as they reached the front gate.

'And I'm her unbelievably sexy friend!' screamed Evka as they clambered into their car.

'They sound like monsters.' Layla wore a soft hand-knit, the neck pulled up to her chin as she listened to Fern's dramatic recreation of the visit. 'Poor Donna. How is she?'

'Sad. But she's proud, you know? She holds it all in. Bit like you.'

'I can see you're dying to ask. Yes, all's well.'

'Thank God! Are you taking it easy?'

'Not really. I'm pregnant, not ill.'

'Don't be clever, miss. Luc worries. And so do I.'

'Look, Fern, I've been here before. I can't think about it

too much. I can't invest too much of myself. Otherwise it'll tear me apart when . . .'

'I have such a good feeling about this. I really do. This time'll be different.'

'Please don't say that, Fernie. It's reckless to hope.'

'I'll do the hoping for both of us.'

'You don't have to call every day. I'm a big girl now.'

'I like calling. You like me calling, too.'

'I do! You look nice, by the way. Off on a hot date?'

'Ha ha ha ha ha ha ha!'

'Crikey, that touched a nerve. Where are you going?'

'Nowhere. Well, only round to see Hal's studio. To look at his work.'

'Of course. You've always been so interested in pottery.'

'Shut up! I *am* interested. He's so crazy about what he does. I'm sure he's talented.'

'*Very* talented. You're blushing! Like a Jane Austen character. Are you being careful, like we said? You're vulnerable at the moment, Fern.'

'And lonely. Even with all these bodies in the house. Allow me a bit of fun, Layla.'

'Fun, yes. Heartache, no. I sound like Nora, but I'm right. Take it easy.'

'Everything's easy with Hal. There's no baggage. He never takes what I say the wrong way. I don't expect anything from him, except to be around. It's easy and I need one part of my life to be easy.'

'Is that Amelie I can hear?'

'Yeah. She's a cry-y baby. Like Ollie was. Oh. Look, we don't have to talk babies, not until you, you know . . .'

'I love Amelie already, even though I've only seen her on Skype. I want to talk about her.'

'Sure?'

'Sure.'

'Do I really look all right?'

'The make-up's discreet. The hair is tamed. That blue jumper does great things for your colouring. Those are the jeans that work. So yes, you look more than all right. You look great.'

'For my age.'

'You look great full stop. Easy rider Hal's a lucky chap.'

'Thanks for fitting me in, you angel.' Pongo stretched out on the treatment bed, naked as the day she leapt from her mother's womb. Spry and bendy, and disconcertingly that strange varnished colour all over, Pongo was out of context in the treatment room and Fern, accustomed to seeing her fully clothed in the park, covered her new client's torso with a towel.

'I couldn't let you suffer with a sore shoulder, could I now?' Fern still didn't know how Pongo had found her address. She looked at the clock as she kneaded her client's back, and hoped her carefully applied maquillage hadn't sweated off. She'd be a tiny bit late for Hal, but he wouldn't snipe or point at his watch. He'd simply be glad to see her.

'Mmm! Aah! Yess!'

Mortified, Fern blocked out Pongo's disturbingly orgasmic reactions. Shutting her eyes, she was back in the hotel room on New Year's Day. An intimate, low-lit room, it was designed for seduction with glinting gilt accents and a bed smothered with blood red throws.

It was golden in her memory; a perfect evening captured forever in amber. Hal had been lusty, tender. Fern's response to his touch had surprised her. She'd come alive beneath his hands; big strong hands that were capable and gentle.

'Are you all right, dear?' asked Pongo groggily.

'Oh. Yes. Sorry!' Fern's hands had paused. She set to once more, teasing the knots in Pongo's shoulder. It was satisfying, but it wasn't enough to keep her thoughts in the room.

There had been Dutch courage first: champagne delivered on a silver tray. The cost of it made Fern nauseous until she reminded herself it was a drop in the *Roomies* ocean. Another bottle was needed before she reached out and drew him to her and their lips met. Delicate at first, then happily, greedy.

They'd rolled around in the velvet, wound up together. Falling off the bed had prised their mouths apart, but they were too impatient to clamber back up. Once they'd stopped giggling, once she'd seen the intent in Hal's eyes, Fern had sat astride him, peeling off her top, bending to kiss his mouth. His lips were soft, determined.

They were new.

So accustomed to Adam's body, to Adam's touch, his mouth, Fern was a traveller in a strange new land. It hadn't felt forbidden, as she'd feared. The very existence of Penny gave her permission. She sank onto Hal and they were glued together, murmuring.

When Hal pulled his shirt off, buttons flying everywhere,

Fern felt as if her heart must surely be jumping out through her skin. He was so . . . young. That was the only word for the expanse of Hal's chest. Hal's body was discreetly worked on; younger people were all gym nuts, Fern suspected.

Her own body was not worked on. It had been left to its own devices while Fern got on with eating eclairs. Her sudden shyness, a change in pace, didn't go unnoticed.

'It's OK,' Hal had whispered. 'We don't have to.'

'I do want to. I do. I really do.'

'I know. Sssh.' He'd kissed her forehead; a loving gesture free of desire, it had calmed Fern, and excited her.

'Kiss me,' she said. And he did. Over and over.

It had been better than sex.

Almost.

'I think my half-hour's up.' Pongo twisted to look at Fern. 'You really put your back into it, don't you? Why don't you have a little lie down, dear?'

'I might just do that,' said Fern.

Heading for the door, Fern barked instructions left and right. 'Donna, don't forget the health visitor's coming in half an hour. Have Amelie bathed. Nora, could you turn the oven on at six? One hundred and eighty. Boudi, bad dog, off the sofa.'

In the sitting room, Tallulah was on the rug with Evka, both of them embroiled in an intense game of dolls. Tallulah could lose herself in the miniature lives of her countless Barbies and Kens; Evka was the only adult who entered their universe with her. *I suppose it beats cleaning*, thought Fern, who seemed to be paying Evka to play with her daughter. 'Tallie, finish that project for school tomorrow, love.'

'After I finish this game, Mum, pleeeeease.'

'What's happening with the dolls?' Fern loved hearing about their bizarre lives.

'This Barbie is rejecting male domination.' Tallulah held up a doll in a ball gown which she'd slashed and daubed with red paint. 'That's her boyfriend.'

Evka held up a surfer dude. 'Ken is bastard just like my boyfriend,' she drawled. 'Is cruel. Soon Barbie will flee country just like me.'

'Um, OK.' Fern was sorry she'd asked.

Bowling in, Ollie gave them all a perfunctory 'Hi' and bounded up the stairs.

'Oi! Did you remember to pick up nappies on your way home?' called Fern.

For an answer, Ollie shook a Mothercare carrier bag. When Fern carried on, he said, 'Can't stop, Mum. My shift at the White Horse starts in half an hour.'

At the mirror by the door, Fern applied some lipstick: a bolder colour than usual. She scrutinized it, withstanding the impulse to wipe it off. This was a red lippie day.

Remembering, she shouted up the stairs, 'Oh and Donna, use the new hypoallergenic baby bubble bath!' She turned to leave but came up hard against Nora. 'Christ!' she exclaimed without thinking.

'Scarlet lips?' Nora peered at Fern's mouth.

'For a change.' Fern noticed that one of Nora's eyes was

off kilter, the iris skittering to the right. *Was it like that before?*

'There's only one reason a woman puts on scarlet lipstick. To see a fancy man.'

Hal *was* rather fancy, but she didn't share that with her aunt. 'I'm just off to see a friend.'

'Hmm. I know the manner of *friend* you're seeing.' Nora folded her arms; Phase Two of her usual process. Next would be a look to the heavens and a 'God save us'. 'A fine example you're setting with a new baby in the house.'

'I've checked with Amelie and she doesn't mind.' Fern reached for her jacket on the coat stand. Laden with raincoats and school coats and puffas and Barbours, the coat stand was perpetually on the cusp of collapse, but somehow managed to stay upright. Fern felt it to be a kindred spirit.

'What about Tallulah? She sees her father hounded out of his own home and then her mother takes up with some gigolo.'

'I don't think they make gigolos any more, Auntie.' Buttoning up the oversized buttons of her on-trend pink jacket (another impulse buy), Fern refused to rise to Nora's goading. It wasn't easy; Nora was a virtuoso goader. 'Must dash.'

Nora didn't budge. Firmly in Fern's way, she said, 'No wonder Tallulah's taken to stealing and lying about it.'

That got through. Fern was no match for Nora's long apprenticeship at Nana's knobbly knee. 'She hasn't *taken to* stealing, Auntie. Tallie did it once and then confessed, for God's sake. My daughter's not a liar.'

'You're too busy painting your face to notice there's more to it than meets the eye.'

'Auntie, sometimes you go too far. Way, way too far.' Fern was shaking. It didn't feel right to talk to an elderly relative this way, but a nerve had been touched. 'It's one thing to land in my house like a cuckoo and expect me to run around after you, but it's quite another to interfere between me and Tallulah.'

'I know you don't want me here,' said Nora, switching seamlessly from bully to victim. 'I'm just an old broken-down old—'

'I don't have time for that speech again,' said Fern, reaching around Nora to tackle the latch. 'Save it for later.'

'Charming,' said Nora.

The studio was a high-ceilinged industrial space in a warehouse complex, atmospheric and dusty with tall iron-framed windows along one side which filled the room with the watery but insistent February sun.

'This here's my latest batch.' Hal, his hand in Fern's, the tickling of his fingers on her palm making it difficult to concentrate, showed her wooden shelves of bowls. 'They haven't been for their last firing yet so the glazes will change. The heat brings out their personality. D'you like them?' He sounded as though the answer was important.

'I love them.' Fern traced the rim of a dish. It was sensuous, but solid. Just like Hal, who was much improved by his clay-spattered overalls and the dust that clogged his hair and made it stand on end. 'You're an artist, Hal. A real artist.'

'I'm lucky to do something I love. Just wish I could make a decent living at it. Sharing a house isn't much fun.'

'I dunno. Always somebody to talk to.' Fern let go of his hand and drifted around the room, picking up a plate here, a mug there. 'Always something going on.'

'No privacy. I daren't buy fancy cheese 'cos it gets nicked out of the fridge.' Hal laughed. 'Now I've said that out loud, it doesn't sound like the worst problem in the world. I just want somewhere that's mine. If I moved out of London I might be able to afford it.'

Fern felt something stab her.

'But I love it here.'

Phew. 'There's a lovely atmosphere in this studio.'

'Creative spaces are like that, don't you think?' Hal rubbed at a mark on a jug the colour of the pale sky outside. 'Places where people make things. Pottery. Paintings. Music.'

That set off unwelcome associations. There was no room for exes in Fern's head today. She'd promised her libido it would be in charge. Hal was in the here and now, solid in his work clothes, wandering about his domain. Fern's need reached for him, like a flower stretching towards the sun. He turned his back, fiddling with the dial of a bulky metal kiln. 'Almost hot enough. Then I can start firing.'

Fern worked fast. In this bright room she found the courage that had failed her in the flattering light of the hotel. Stepping noiselessly out of her jeans she slipped down her pants. Silky nothings with lace edges, they were nothing like her customary John Lewis pack of three cotton midi briefs. Pulling the blue jumper over her head, Fern tossed her hair, undoing all the careful styling. *Bra. Quickly. Before he turns around.*

'Shall I put the kettle on?' Hal turned. His eyes widened and his lips parted as his eyes travelled the length and breadth of Fern.

Sideways on, one leg bent, shoulders back, she let him look. She kept her nerve. *This is what a woman of my age looks like.* Fern was neither a lingerie model nor a pensioner. She was what she was.

And she was, according to Hal's whisper, 'Beautiful.'

Hal strode to her and pressed her to him, her soft parts meeting buttons and zips. It was a matter of moments to undo them all and soon they were both naked, both trembling, both eager.

Pushing a tray of paints and brushes off a low table, Hal ignored the clatter they made on the concrete floor. *The mess . . .* thought Fern, who apparently couldn't switch off the housewife side of her brain even when about to make longed-for love.

The kisses, harder, full of purpose, brought her mind back to the matter at hand. Hal was like warm marble, a statue come to life as he laid her on the table.

'Sure?' he said, his voice so close to her ear it could have sprung from inside her own head.

'Sure sure,' gasped Fern, who felt as though her body had been wound tight and might explode if he didn't make his move.

Like all first times, it wasn't epic. They laughed about

the speed of it, but they were both satisfied. Until the kissing started up again, when their appetites were renewed.

Definitely one benefit of a younger man, thought Fern as Hal grabbed her hips and pressed her against a wooden dresser, the crockery rattling to the rhythm of his thrusts and her cries.

'Is everything—' A girl's voice from the doorway died away. '. . . all right?' The blonde, skinny thing in a stained apron ducked her head and retreated. 'God sorry sorry Christ sorry.'

'Uh oh,' said Hal. 'I'm going to be the talk of the complex.'

'Then let's give them something to talk about.' Fern barely recognized the woman she'd become since stepping into the studio. 'What do you want from this, Hal?' she asked, her mouth against him.

'You.'

Fern had only ever had meaningful sex with two men in her life – she didn't count the pre-Adam fumbles with sixth-form idiots – and she'd left one an hour earlier, and was now sitting in the dark with the other.

Since *that* day in the studio, Fern and Hal hadn't had a chance to renew their acquaintance with each other's underwear. Fern was too shamefaced to return to the warehouse – there'd been applause as she left – and Homestead House was out of the question.

Her time with Hal and her family life were entirely separate, as if she was two women in one body. There was Fern the mum, the cook, the nanny, the chauffeur, the storyteller, the tucker-in. And there was Fern the lover. When she imagined the two lives mingling, it seemed impossible. Introducing Hal to her family was such an absurd idea it almost made her laugh.

Ollie would *die*. Tallulah might vomit. Nora would reach for her Bible. Adam . . . he might be pleased for her. They were chums now. They were pleasant. A line had been drawn under the old niggles, all IOU's torn up.

She sneaked a look at him in the dark of the school hall. He was intent on the harp solo, shrinking in his seat each time the hesitant Year Eight pupil plucked the wrong string. They'd already sat through the Year Seven jazz band, a clarinettist who'd burst into tears before playing a note, and their own daughter at the back of the choir belting out an unrecognizable 'Hey Jude'.

Sitting together, shoulder to shoulder, on the familiar uncomfortable chairs, felt solidly parent-like. In public they were still a unit, able to look as if they were enjoying themselves and then able to make it to the double doors without speaking to the deputy head (bad breath) or the head of the PTA (bad attitude). They still fitted together.

'Funny way to spend Valentine's night,' whispered Fern.

'I've had worse,' said Adam. Leaning in, he mouthed, 'Paris.'

Fern smirked. Paris, where the bed had broken and not because of any hot action, but because they were in the sort of cheap and nasty hotel that gives cheap and nasty hotels a bad name. 'Don't forget the London Eye.'

Adam had been sick on the London Eye. All over the roses he'd bought.

He sighed. 'We were never much cop at the romantic bits, were we?'

'We did OK.' Fern didn't much care for that past tense, even though she knew it was appropriate, even though she'd spent the whole of the clarinet solo daydreaming about that bit of Hal where his lower back met his bottom. 'Tallulah wants you to come back to ours for dinner,' she said brusquely as the lights went up, careful not to sound as if she wanted it too. Because she didn't. *For all the chumminess, being with Adam just reminds me of everything we've lost.*

'Nut roast!' said Adam, in the pseudo-jolly tone of a man who's spotted a corpse in the river but is determined not to let it spoil his day.

Tallulah sprawled back in her seat, pretending to die. 'It's 'cos Donna's a vegetarian,' she said, taking care with the word. 'Mum's been experimenting.'

'Oh good,' said Adam flatly.

'It's highly nutritious.' Fern put the lumpen roast on the table.

'She always says that when it's disgusting,' said Tallulah.

As the table filled up, as faces fell at the sight of their dinner, Fern took Amelie from Donna's grasp. 'Sit, love, and eat. I'll hold her. You should be on your way by now.'

'On her way where?' Adam poured gravy over his slab of nut roast. A lot of gravy.

'It's date night.' Fern answered before Donna could, excited for the lovebirds.

Tallulah was studying Donna, whose heavy make-up covered the eye bags doled out to all new mothers. 'Eyeliner is against my beliefs,' she said. 'But yours does look completely stunning.'

'I just hope I can stay awake on the bus.' Donna, who was honour bound to enjoy the roast, did her best with the sticky mass on her fork.

'Did you put that new cream on madam's bumbum?' Fern jiggled the baby in her arms. 'Is the rash clearing up?'

'Yes and yes,' said Donna, stifling a yawn.

'Can I have a go?' Adam held out his arms. Sitting back from the table, he stared at Amelie as if trying to memorize her. 'I'm besotted with you,' he said. 'Completely besotted.'

Ollie said, 'She's not like other babies. Their cries go right through you. Amelie cries like a little lamb.'

'A little lamb in a horror film,' said Tallulah.

Nora, who'd given up with the nut roast and was ostentatiously buttering bread, said, 'Has the real father not seen Amelie yet? What's his name? Moss or something.'

'Maz,' said Fern. She glanced at Ollie and Donna, whose heads were down. Adam was looking up to heaven and probably counting to ten. Or a hundred, maybe; Nora had that effect on people. 'Amelie's biological father has decided not to be involved. As for *real*, well, Ollie's her real dad in the true sense of the word.'

'Hmm,' said Nora. Then, in case anybody had missed it, she said it again. '*Hmm.*'

'Hey chaps,' said Adam, changing the subject and passing Amelie to his other arm, 'Penny's arranged for us all to be in the audience when they film the London episode of *Roomies.*'

The mood picked up. 'Can we go backstage?' Ollie looked more like an excitable teenager than a family man.

'Can we meet Lincoln Speed?' Tallulah's darkest secret was her deep love for the star. Everybody knew about it.

'Don't see why not.' If Adam was trying not to look smug, it wasn't working. 'Might bring my guitar. Give 'em a song.'

'Perhaps he'll name his new baby after you!' Tallulah was nothing if not ambitious.

'He's already named it,' said Adam. Lincoln Speed's latest chip off the old block had been conceived with a make-up artist. In a cupboard, apparently, which seemed less than romantic to Fern, who had higher expectations from a date. 'Harrington.'

'Why does he call all his children surnames?' Fern reeled off the list, a dark-side Waltons. 'Winwood. Ford. Drummond. Hamilton. Boyd. Reilly. Griffin. Benton.'

'They're gorgeous names.' Tallulah defended her idol. 'If you have another baby, Mum, let's call it Carruthers.'

'Mum's far too old to have a baby.' Ollie found the idea comical.

Fern less so.

Nora prodded Adam. 'What number are you in the hit parade?' Even she'd been impressed when Kinky Mimi released a track on iTunes. 'Melt My Panther' had been reviewed by an online magazine: 'sneakily funky with a banging underbelly'. Fern had no idea whether that was praise or not.

'One hundred and twenty three,' mumbled Adam, kissing Amelie extravagantly on her flossy hair. 'We're building our audience,' he added.

'How's Keith's hernia?' asked Fern, all innocence.

'He's recovering, thank you.' Adam knew what she was doing, and was tart when he added, 'Even rock stars get hernias, Fern.'

'Cannot imagine Justin Timberlake with hernia,' said Evka.

Other families might talk about the big things, about life and death, around the table but at Fern's house it always came down to trivia. She was glad; hernias were a lot more entertaining than philosophy. She asked Evka how her latest typically English pastime had gone. 'Harrods, wasn't it?'

'Yes. Is just big shop.' Evka curled her lip. 'I thought it sells tigers or has gold walls. Very disappointing. Like man I meet in Harrods lift.' She shook her head and sighed. 'So bad at sex.'

Fern coughed but Tallie's giggle meant she hadn't got there in time. As ever, Nora made no comment; her brain filtered out Evka's vulgarities.

Tallulah asked, 'What did your boyfriend in Bratislava do that was so cruel, Evka? Did he oppress you?'

'Or suggest that you wear, like, actual clothes?' added Fern.

'Worse than all these. It is unspeakable. I do not speak of it.' Evka clenched her teeth. 'I never go back.'

'Not ever?' Fern was alarmed; she might need the spare bed back at some point.

'Good!' Tallulah clapped. Not yet old enough to see past the end of her dainty nose, she judged everything by how it affected her. 'You can be my big sister forever.'

Nora leaned into Evka's side. 'You have a home here for as long as you want one, dear,' she said.

A look passed between Fern and Adam. She appreciated his empathy, even if he was now officially living elsewhere.

Waving off Ollie and Donna, smothering their concerns about leaving Amelie with reiterations that she was in the best hands possible – 'I'm her grandmother, after all!' – Fern was proud of herself for being able to say that contentious word with barely a gulp.

'A grandmother in my early forties,' she said to Adam as they stood at the foot of Amelie's white cot, another of his extravagant gifts. 'It's not how I saw my life panning out.'

'Life has a habit of taking you by surprise.' The sleeping baby softened their voices, made their conversation intimate. 'Fern . . . is there anything you want to tell me?'

'Like what?' Fern closed the door softly behind them. *Has he seen me with Hal?* They held hands in the park these days. It felt erotic and illicit; far naughtier than the sum of its parts.

'Like, are there any developments I should know about?'

This was classic Adam. 'Not really.' That was true; *it's not like Hal is my boyfriend*. Fern was unable to name what was going on with Hal, even though it was important to her, even though anticipating the feel of him was what got her through the days when Tallie was surly and Ollie was exhausted and Amelie was restless and Donna was drooping and, and, and . . .

Yet there was no Valentine's card propped up anywhere, no bouquet in a vase. Hal wasn't Adam's business. After all, Adam had never come entirely clean about Penny. Evka's ongoing espionage kept Fern up to date; the happy couple had installed a Jacuzzi on their balcony and Penny had a new selection of red underwear. Fern knew all about Adam and red underwear; it had been her secret weapon when he wasn't in the mood. One flash of red suspender and they were up the stairs before you could say 'stereotypical bloke'.

'OK. I just wondered.' Adam looked thwarted, and part of Fern – the newly discovered evil part that could spy on him – was pleased. It was so hard to have any effect on him these days that she took what she could get. 'Any chance of a coffee?'

'That ridiculous machine you bought is still taking up half the kitchen, so yes.' Fern couldn't just seem to say 'yes'; every interaction between them came with a side order of sass.

On a stool, Adam watched her do battle with levers and buttons. There was a lot of steam and some bad words, but eventually a cappuccino was put in front of him.

'You know Italians only drink cappuccino at breakfast time?' said Fern, leaning against the worktop with a nice simple mug of tea.

'I do. But I'm not and never have been remotely Italian.' He took a sip. 'Lovely,' he smiled, and he was old Adam again, no posing, no best behaviour. She'd almost forgotten how much he relied on coffee. *Better than sex*, he used to say with a wink, before adding *not sex with* you, *obviously*. They were neutered now, as asexual in each other's company as Tallulah's Barbies and Kens.

'Anything *you* want to tell *me*?' There was a challenge in Fern's eyes.

Adam held her gaze. He seemed to be turning something over in his mind before he said, 'No.'

We're quits.

'I've written some new songs. Europe was inspiring.' As Adam chit-chatted about the tour, he reached out to fiddle with the lid of a cardboard box, tracing the roses on it with a forefinger.

'Yes. Europe is, um, very, um . . .' Fern folded her arms around her middle to stop herself snatching away the box. If Adam opened it he'd find the letters he'd written during the Great Rift, and he'd know she pored over them. And she would die of embarrassment.

I can't die, she thought. *I'm too busy to die and nobody else can do Tallulah's plait the way she likes it.*

Ding dong!

Saved by the bell, Fern said, 'Could you get that, Adam?' and swept the box into a drawer when he meandered out to the hall.

'Happy Valentine's Day!'

Penny.

In she came in her inevitable heels. All in red – Fern let out a tiny growl – Penny was clutching roses and choco-lates and champagne. 'Happy Valentine's, Fern!'

A kiss happened; there was no way out of it. Penny's

cheek was cool. 'I'm not really celebrating this year,' said Fern, impressed by her visitor's insensitivity. *What with the father of my children leaving me, and all.*

'But it's the most romantic day of the year,' cooed Penny, who seemed to have ingested a book of clichés on her way over. 'Hey, Kinky boy, the table's booked for nine so get your skates on!'

This seemed like news to Adam. 'Table?'

'Don't say you've forgotten?' Penny lowered the flowers and stage-whispered comically at Fern. 'Men! What are they like?'

Well, that one's just like the one who used to LIVE WITH ME. 'Off you trot,' Fern said to Adam, knowing how the nut roast squatted in his stomach like a boulder. 'Hope you can do justice to the set menu.'

The side-eye Adam gave her was one of the best he'd ever done.

'Waaaaaaah!' Amelie's theme tune erupted out of the baby monitor.

'Already?' Fern had foreseen an hour of peace before Amelie started her nightly concert. 'Coming, sweetheart,' she muttered, setting down her tea.

'Let me,' said Penny. She was a-jitter, excited. 'I love babies. I'm good with them. I'm the baby whisperer.' She had one foot on the bottom stair.

'Yes, but . . .' Fern couldn't stop her. 'Oh, OK. Second door on the left.' If this was how Penny sold Kinky Mimi, no wonder Adam believed in her. It was a strange sensation, knowing your ex's mistress was tending to your granddaughter; Fern was next door to disgruntled.

'You're very territorial about Amelie, aren't you?'

It wasn't unkind the way Adam said it, but Fern heard something she couldn't entirely like in his tone. 'I wouldn't call it territorial. I adore her. I look after her.'

'She's not yours, though, love.'

He chooses this moment to call me 'love' for the first time in a long time. 'What's your point, Adam?'

'Just that you have a lot to say about how Donna and Ollie should bring her up.'

'That's hardly surprising. One, I'm her grandmother, and two, I've done this twice over already. Donna needs support. She's still a teenager.'

'Don't get all up in the air about it.'

'Who's getting all up in the air about it?' said Fern, all up in the air about it. 'Are you saying I'm interfering?'

Adam thought for a moment. 'Yup, Fern. Sorry but that's exactly what I'm saying. They have to find their own way. Nature kicks in. Amelie won't starve, will she? Maybe you should hold back a bit.'

'Am I allowed to hold her? Or should I get written permission?'

'You're doing a great job. Just give the kids a bit of space, yeah?'

'As much space as you give them? Should I move out and leave them to it? Adam, you sleep soundly every night up in your penthouse.' *With the baby whisperer.* 'I get up at two a.m. to soothe that child. I'm there when she ruins her clean clothes, when she has a temperature, when her poo is the colour of nothing on Earth. I don't need a lecture from you and your credit card, thanks very much.

If you did more than buy stuff I might listen to you, but for now, save it.'

Adam held his tongue. Fern remembered this from their old arguments, the ones that had ended with making up. Adam would go quiet, not retaliate, and eventually she would crumble and apologize and he'd apologize and they'd go on as before.

Or maybe not. Each of those spats had added one more hairline fracture to their foundations.

'Tell Pen I'm waiting in the car.' Adam drained his cup and left.

'Wah, wah, wah!' said Amelie.

'Me too, darling.' Fern put her face in her hands. Another fail at post-split relations. *I'm so bad at this.* Where was the manual for dealing with a man who'd broken your heart yet still turned up for dinner?

Plus, he's right. Fern was so keen to make things OK, to make it up to her children, that she was overdoing it. *I've turned into the classic overbearing mother.* The trouble was, it felt so good sorting out Amelie's everyday needs. It was something she could do with confidence, without second-guessing herself every step of the way. Curing Amelie's wind was a breeze compared with negotiating the minefield of her emotional life.

Pulling herself together, Fern made a date with herself to think about this later. For now, she needed to get upstairs and calm Amelie.

The keening stopped abruptly. Fern rattled the baby monitor.

'Clever girl!' Penny was cooing. 'That's it. Back to sleep, poppet.'

Fern gave Penny her due; Amelie, who could howl for hours, was appeased. Fern, slightly ashamed of her ill will, decided to thank her warmly when she came down.

'Can I tell you a secret, Amelie?'

Fern, intrigued, held the baby monitor to her ear. She could just about make out Penny's words.

'Your grandfather's a wonderful man. A special man. You're a lucky little girl to be surrounded by all this love.'

Fern blinked hard.

'Your grandmother will always put you first. I see in her face how she adores you. And your grandfather will protect you. Did you know he cried when he told me you'd been born? He's your biggest fan.'

Fern wiped her eyes. Adam *was* all those things. *I'd forgotten.* Or maybe she'd blotted it out; it was harder to lose a fine man than a silly little shit in stack heels.

'He's going through hard times, your granddad. His wildest dreams are coming through but at a terrible cost, Amelie. I promise I'll help him. Because I love him. I've never known anybody like him. When he walks into a room I don't see anyone else. I hope one day you love somebody like that, Amelie.'

Fern switched off the monitor. 'Adam's in the car,' she said when Penny reappeared. 'Thanks. For getting the baby back to sleep.'

'My pleasure.' Penny was all bustle again, pulling on gloves, snatching up the flowers.

'Have a nice time.'

Penny stared at her, one foot out of the door. She seemed to be weighing up Fern's meaning. 'Thanks,' she smiled, eventually.

Later, with Evka out doing things Fern would rather not know about to a man she'd met at the Tower of London, and Tallulah and Nora both safely in bed, Fern swiped through the latest pictures of Amelie on her mobile.

The most photographed human on earth – unless you counted every other new baby – Amelie looked, Fern had to admit, more or less the same in every shot. Even so, Fern could pore over each snap, enjoying the gentle burnish of Amelie's skin, the curled waxy fingers, the exuberant hair that escaped from her knitted hats.

The hats were gifts from Nora, who was knitting like one possessed. Jackets, bootees, hats all sprang to life on her blurred needles, all of them in the cheapest acrylic wool, all of them fluorescent pink. Donna thanked her and used them all, quite a sacrifice for a girl who used to spend all her Saturday job money in French Connection.

Choosing an image of Amelie in Ollie's arms, Fern attached it to a text, and started to type.

Hi Mum!

She was stuck. She erased the two words.

Hello Mum.

Bit formal. She went back to 'Hi Mum!' and then thought hard.

Here's your first great granddaughter! It's about time I

sent you a pic, isn't it? She's healthy and happy and the light of our lives.

Kisses? Or not?

Such hesitation with her own mother. It was a poor state of affairs. Although only in her sixties, and by no means *old* old, Fern's mum wouldn't be around for ever. There were a thousand good reasons to get in touch, but if Fern didn't reach out, she couldn't be rebuffed; she wasn't sure how she'd cope if her mother didn't reply. Or, worse still, replied in a way that hurt. Even now, it singed Fern's feelings to hear her mother putting Dave first in a way she never had with Fern's dad.

Impatient with herself, Fern added a row of x's and sent the message. The period drama she'd taped did little to distract her from her thoughts as she glanced continually at the small screen of her phone.

A tiny burp from the baby monitor made her smile. Amelie had slept soundly since Penny left, only an occasional mew escaping her cherub lips.

Ping! A text arrived.

What a pretty baby. x

Just one line.

Fern thought of Tallulah, asleep upstairs in her cosy room. She couldn't imagine a future where she and her daughter relinquished the unique mother/daughter understanding. They would always have it to call on; always have a safe place they could go which shut out the rest of the world while they really *talked*.

It was time to call on that bond. Fern stole into Tallulah's room and sat on the wrought-iron bed. 'Tallie?' She stroked the dark, damp hair back from the girl's forehead and smiled as her daughter swam up towards her from a dream.

'Mummy?' Tallulah was drowsy, puzzled.

'We need to talk.' Extracting Tallulah from the covers and folding her up on her knee felt like old times. Tallulah swooned into her mother, her head tucked beneath Fern's chin. 'Nora's right, isn't she? You'd never shoplift.' Fern felt the child tense. 'And even if you did, you wouldn't take yukky old liquorice laces.'

Tallulah began to cry, and Fern let her.

To: adamcarlile@gmail.com
From: fernsbeautyroom@gmail.com
22.17
Re: Tallie

Hi Adam

I know you're out at dinner so I'm sending this instead of calling while it's fresh in my mind.

I had a long talk with Tallie tonight. As you know, she hasn't been the same since the shoplifting/suspension incident. The whole story came out with lots of tears. She's been protecting somebody all along.

So, it goes like this.

There's a girl in Tallie's class called Carey. Nobody likes her. She's rude, a bully, knows all the worst words, smokes. Our basic nightmare. I've heard about her from other mums. But Tallie noticed that Carey likes animals and, in her words,

'nobody's all bad if they like animals.' She made an effort to
be friendly. At first Carey was 'mean' but after a while she
softened and soon they were seeking out cats to stroke
together and daydreaming about how many dogs they'd
own when they grew up. Tallie's friends all thought she was
crazy, but Tallie felt she'd found a soulmate.

Carey opened up about her home life. Grim, grim, grim.
Borderline abuse I'd say – lots of drinking and slapping
about. No wonder the girl misbehaves. One day Tallie
noticed a change in Carey. She was snappy and quiet.
Presumably, something terrible had happened at home,
but Tallie was upset and thought Carey didn't like her any
more. Trying to make friends again, she offered to buy
Carey some sweets – you know how generous she is – and
they went to the newsagents together.

That's when it happened. Carey reached out for a whole
box of liquorice laces, and scarpered. The owner noticed the
empty space and raised the roof. Tallie said 'It was me.' The
school was called and, well, we know what happened next.

Tallie took the blame because the headmistress had made
it clear to Carey that she'd used up her last chance. If she
broke the rules again, she was out. Tallie knew what would
happen at home if Carey was expelled.

It gets worse.

Carey hasn't spoken to Tallie since. She doesn't even look
her in the eye, which upsets Tallie terribly. And now her old
friends make jokes about Tallie being a thief and a 'crim'.
She was crying by the time she got to this part and as you
can imagine so was I!

We should have trusted her, shouldn't we? Nora kept

niggling at the subject, saying there was more to it. She was right. We might never have got to the bottom of it if Auntie hadn't nagged me.

How can we help Tallie through this? What do we do next? Goodnight. Let's talk about this tomorrow.

Fern

'But I don't need a Valentine's card.' The phone close to her ear as she chopped fruit for Donna, mixed pancakes for Ollie, and stirred brown sugar into yoghurt for Tallulah, Fern felt as if Hal was there with her in the kitchen. The sky was still dark; Fern was always the first up.

Hal's voice warm in her ear, he said, 'I'll make it up to you.'

'Interesting. How, exactly?' Fern bit her lip as she put the kettle on. She turned and Nora was suddenly there, like a genie. 'Oh God!' Fern reared back.

'Good morning,' said Nora, pointedly.

'Look, I'll ring you back.' Fern ended the call. 'Auntie. You're up early.'

Nora belted her dressing gown even tighter, as if to protect herself from vice. 'That was him, I assume. Your bit on the side.'

'It was a friend,' said Fern, laying out a cup and saucer for Nora.

'You were giggling like a schoolgirl.' Nora sat down, almost missing the chair. The clumsiness was getting worse. 'A fine example to set your daughter.'

'Talking of Tallulah . . .' Fern pushed her aunt's sniping aside. This was a time for gratitude. 'You were right. About the shoplifting.'

'Of course I was right.' Nora managed to be offended by the compliment.

Fern told the tale. 'So, you see,' she ended, 'I should have probed more at the time. I took my eye off the ball. With your help, I'll put that right, and help poor Tallie deal with the fallout of what was a kind impulse.'

'Your children run riot,' said Nora, face set like a snooty bulldog. 'One's a schoolboy father, the other's mixed up with a bad crowd.'

'Tallulah was trying to help her friend. Nobody's just *bad*, Auntie. The child has problems at home.'

'And Tallulah hasn't?' snorted Nora. 'This home is as broken as any you'll see in them documentaries.'

'How can you say that?' Fern's pledge to be nicey-nice forgotten, she reacted shrilly. 'Our children are loved and cared for and—'

'And and and.' Nora's head wobbled. 'And you gallivant around town with some *man*.' She spat the word as if it was an insult. 'You're no spring chicken, Fern. You're making a fool of yourself.'

Perhaps that barb landed too close to Fern's deepest fear, but she heard herself say, in a voice full of repressed anger, 'It's you who's making a fool of me! I do everything I can for you but nothing's ever good enough.'

'Everything you can? Where were you when Mother was dying?'

'Eh?' Taken aback, Fern scowled.

'Did you visit? Did you help?'

'Auntie, I was fifteen.' Fern's memories of her grand-mother's death were vague compared to classroom romances and youth club discos. 'I know it must have been hard for you.' Fern rewound, ratcheted down the volume, got a hold of herself. *You're dealing with an old lady.*

'Hard?' The word didn't hit the spot for Nora, who unleashed a *harrumph* the like of which Fern had never heard. 'All I ask is a place to lay my head for a while.'

The 'while' had stretched to eight months so far. Fern held this behind gritted teeth.

'You've stuffed me in the attic with the rest of the rubbish.'

'It's a loft, Auntie. A refurbished loft with spotlights and underfloor heating and a new bed.'

'You make me use a bathroom that makes no sense.'

'It's a state-of-the-art wet room.'

'You talk over Alan Titchmarsh.'

That should have made Fern laugh. It didn't. She was beyond laughter. 'Maybe we should leave it there,' she said.

'No wonder Adam got away from you. This other chap will disappear, too, mark my words. You're just like your father. Not a bit of use. He never visited me and Mother, you know.'

Everybody has their tipping point. Expert practitioners like Nora found them with ease. Fern's tipping point was hearing her dad criticized when he wasn't there to defend himself. The volume rose again, right up to eleven. 'Are you surprised? Why would anybody visit you? You're mean and you're cruel and you think the worst of everybody! No wonder you're on your own.'

Nora's usual battle expression, a smug mask, fell away to leave a broken, crumbling look.

Immediately regretting what she'd said, Fern gulped. *It's the truth*, she thought, knowing that didn't excuse her. Perhaps it had to come to this. Perhaps this was how Nora managed her affairs. *I'll help her all I can with the practicalities but this poisonous woman has to* go!

Turning, her head in the air, Nora was sanctimonious. 'I know when I'm not wanted. I'll go. This minute.' She put one slippered foot in front of the other.

'If only,' said Fern, who didn't believe a word of it.

'Oh dear,' said Nora. 'Oh dear, oh dear.' She fell awkwardly, slumping to one side before landing full length on the floor.

'Auntie!' Fern dashed round the table and knelt beside her.

A scream from the doorway. Tallulah and Evka gazed down, mouths agape.

'Mummy, you've killed Nora!' shrieked Tallulah.

'She died of broken heart,' said Evka.

Fern nodded, taking it all in.

The doctor, peachily young but tired-looking, did his best to be kind despite his weariness. 'It was coincidence. Your aunt's collapse was always going to happen. It's pointless blaming yourself.'

Drained, a pulse drumming in her temple, Fern peeped through the glass slit in the door. She saw a sliver of Nora, her eyes closed, her white hair mussed on the pillow.

When Fern approached the bed, Nora's eyes flicked open. 'What'd he say? Bad news, no doubt. Typical doctor.' She fussed with her sling. 'This is going to get in me way at home.'

'You're not coming home just yet.' Fern pulled the hard chair with the plastic upholstery closer to the bed. 'You haven't been completely honest with me, Auntie.'

'Don't tell me yet, Fern.' Nora looked every second of her years, her pale face apprehensive. 'Have you seen what's on the telly?' She gestured weakly to the set clamped to the wall.

'There's no escaping *Roomies*,' said Fern, fussing with Nora's covers.

Although turned right down, a small ghostly Adam sang: You wish you could reach out and find a friend Who'll be here today, tomorrow, until the bitter end.

'Let's keep chatting, Fern, and then tell me later.'

'That's fine by me. Where were we up to? I think you'd just left school.' The hours that needed filling at the hospital had been the first opportunity the two women had ever had to really talk. Nora's life story, once begun, poured out. Fern had the distinct impression that Nora had never talked about herself at this length, or in such detail. *Nobody's ever been interested enough to ask.*

'That's right. I was sixteen and quite a looker, although you'd never think it to look at me now.' Nora fingered her flossy white hair. 'This was gold, then, and I wore it piled up on me head.'

'What did you want to be?'

'I had one big ambition. I wanted to be a librarian.'

As dreams go, that sounded do-able.

'But,' said Nora, on a sigh, 'Mother fell ill, so that was that. My brothers had left home and I was the only close family she had. I looked after her.'

'Nana didn't die until thirty years later, though.'

'She recovered, but she was prone to relapses.'

'What was actually wrong with her?'

'Bad nerves,' said Nora. 'She suffered terribly.'

Hmm. Fern's dad, the kindest of men, had grown impatient with Nana's malingering. Every time one of her offspring went against her – proposing to the wrong girl, moving away – Mother would have 'one of her turns'. No doctor ever found a reason for these turns; all pronounced her to be in perfect health. 'Did you never have a job, Auntie?'

'Mother liked to have me near her. Nobody knew her funny little ways like me. I didn't have time for a job Mother didn't believe in paid help, so I kept the house clean, and I cooked all our meals. Mother was most particular. She had standards.'

As long as somebody else did the work. 'You loved her very much, didn't you?'

'Yes.' Nora pursed her lips and nodded. 'Yes, I did.' She shut her eyes. 'Mother never once said thank you.'

'Not for anything?'

'I didn't want thanking, don't get me wrong. I knew me duty. But just once would have been nice. A little appreciation.' Nora opened her eyes and stared fearfully at Fern. 'God forgive me for speaking ill of the dead!'

'If it's the truth, there's no harm,' said Fern, sensing the old lady needed permission to unburden herself. 'It's only me, Nora. You can tell me.'

And so it all came out. How Nora realized she'd been chosen from childhood, as the only girl, to be the one who walled herself up alive with mother. 'There was a deal, of sorts,' said Nora. 'If I remained at home then eventually I'd get the house.' She cupped her hand around her mouth and whispered, 'I hated that house, Fern!'

'Tell me about the good times.'

The good times seemed to consist of a snail's-pace constitutional every Sunday, when Mother would comment on the state of the neighbours' gardens, plus the occasional foray to a Julie Andrews film at the local cinema. 'We rarely had visitors; Mother chased them away, didn't she?' Nora asked, guiltily.

''Fraid so, Auntie. She was chilly. I was scared of her.'

'She was always right, though.' Like a rescued cult member, Nora couldn't quite shake off the brainwashing. 'She lived by the Bible, and she made sure I did too.'

Fern couldn't recall anything in the Bible about being an old cow. 'What about romance?'

'Mother was very careful to protect me from the lusts of men.' Nora raised an eyebrow as if daring Fern to comment. 'I'm as pure as the day I was born, and that's the way I like it.'

Just as well, thought Fern. *It's unlikely to change.* 'Was she protecting you, or keeping you for herself?'

'A little of both,' conceded Nora. 'She warned me about . . .' Nora looked both ways and mouthed 'sexual relations'. She narrowed her eyes. 'The pain. The horror. The endless laundry.'

'That sounds more like war than sexual relations.'

'Keep your voice down!'

A picture built. It wasn't that Fern had formed the wrong impression of Nora – all her faults and failings were present and correct – but now she understood her.

'You and Nana,' said Fern. 'You lived in a bubble, didn't you? Home. Church. Early to bed.'

'We did.' Nora was tired, her eyelids fluttered. 'I don't understand the outside world, Fern. I don't like it.' Her head sank. The tablets were working.

'And you're afraid of it,' said Fern gently, putting her snoozing aunt's good hand beneath the covers.

Nana had taught her daughter well. Nora had swallowed it all whole: the world is full of sin; men are dangerous; trust nobody. *No wonder she can't show love*, thought Fern, pausing to look back at her aunt. *Nobody's ever shown her how.*

A text landed. Fern scrabbled for the phone before it could wake the patient.

A wavery voice came from the bed. 'Is that your fancy man?'

'Sleep, Auntie!'

You. Me. A dirty weekend in a 5 star hotel. Yes?

Fern gulped.

YES.

CHAPTER NINE

March: Entremet

'Fern? Make it quick.'

'Is that the new way to say *Hello, what can I do for you*, Adam?'

'I'm being interviewed. I've had to leave the journalist in my club.'

'You own a club?'

'I'm a member of a club, in Soho.'

'You used to say those places were pretentious ghettos full of arsewipes.'

'I used to say a lot of things, Fern. I'm not being rude, honest, but what's up?'

'You're having Tallulah to stay for the weekend.'

'Am I? I can't.'

'Well, you can. Be warned; she's just found out what castration means and she's very pro it.'

'Why can't she just stay at home with you? I'll come over as usual.'

'I'm going away for two nights.'

'Oh.'

'So I'll drop her off on Friday, about five.'

'No, hang on, you can't just land this on me.'

'*This* is your daughter, Adam. Evka's going to be out much of the time, juggling her lovers and visiting Nora. Ollie and Donna have too much on their plate with his jobs and the baby to have energy to spare for Tallie. She'll love staying with you. Penny can spoil her rotten.'

'But, no, hang on, there's a band meeting in the diary this Friday.'

'Have it at your place. Adam, you have responsibilities. This weekend I'm not there to take the strain for us both. You'll enjoy it.'

'I know I will – it's not that. I loved evenings when it was just me and Tallulah in the house. But—'

'See you Friday.'

'Where the hell are you going anyway?'

'Sorry. You're breaking up. Bad line.'

The foot in Fern's hand was unlovely. It was at the end of an equally unsightly leg belonging to Mr Gibbs, who was blissed out as Fern ran her hands over his hairy toes.

It helped to think of something else when Mr G was in. His feet smelled like the bits of cheese Fern would find forgotten at the back of her fridge. *Hal*, she thought, and instantly felt better.

And nervous. Even a rusty dater knows that a mini-break in a swanky hotel takes a couple to the next level.

Adam intruded on the daydream, barging in the way he used to do when she was having a dreamy bubble bath

Claire Sandy

and he wanted to talk about wiring. He'd been on her mind since their phone conversation, his image hovering in a way it hadn't for a while. Fern no longer woke up every morning to the raw shock of missing him. It was easing. She was recovering. Fern remembered when she hadn't wanted to recover; when she'd clung to the pain because it was *something*.

She'd never compared the two men in her life. To keep the competition fair, she imagined them side by side at the same stage of their lives, as she worked her way up Mr Gibbs' ankle with sure, steady strokes.

At Hal's age, Adam had been thin enough to satisfy Penny with no need to diet. His face had been Fern's favourite face, composed but witty. A different design to Hal, but every bit as sexy; *I'm a sucker for good looks*. That surprised Fern. If asked, she'd have said that a sense of humour, or kindness, or the ability to cook a sausage without burning down the house was more important in a partner than beauty.

Now Adam was a badly drawn sketch of himself. Everything was a touch farther south than before. Those big, beautiful pansy eyes were smaller, as if they'd seen too much and needed a rest. There are physical results to ageing that surgery and exercise can't erase. *I should know.* Fern gently put down the foot and stood in front of the full-length mirror, appraising herself with neither false modesty nor over-confidence.

Unbidden, a girl came to mind. The girl who'd interrupted her and Hal mid-naughtiness in the studio. She'd had all the litheness of youth, all the benefits that young

246

women don't even know they're enjoying, with their clear eyes and their plump skin and their moustache-less upper lips.

'Are we done?' Mr Gibbs sounded disappointed. 'Sorry about me bunion, lovie.'

'Stop asking. I'm not giving you any details, Fern. You'll have a whole weekend without making any decisions, without *doing* anything. And I'll have you to myself for forty-eight hours. With a lock on the door.'

'But the expense, Hal!'

'Don't spoil the romance.'

'I find it hard to log out of being in charge.'

'For once, you'll be massaged and pampered, instead of doing it for others.'

'Are you sure, Hal? I can't help feeling you should be taking some sweet young thing, like that girl at your studio.'

'Her? She's a bitch. Steals my Cup-a-Soups. What's a *should*, anyway? If I did what I should, I'd be working for the family firm, doling out financial advice, with stupid letters after my name. Until the day I killed myself with the office stapler. Look, Fern, if I can withstand my mum's disappointment I can certainly choose which woman I see.'

'Be nice to your mum, Hal. I bet she's lovely.'

'I am nice to her! My family aren't close like yours. The emotions run in straight lines. We don't talk. I mean, really *talk*.'

'Shame. Mind you, I barely ever talk to my own mother.'

'Take your own advice then, and be nice to *her*. Ring her as soon as we stop talking.'

'It's complicated. There are old wounds that haven't healed. Every time we talk we manage to hurt one another.'

'Then visit. Talk it out.'

'She lives in Corfu.'

'Book a plane ticket. Say your toyboy sent you.'

'Don't call yourself that!'

'I like it. It's daft. It doesn't describe me, I know. So where's the harm?'

'If you're a toyboy, then I'm a cougar.'

'And the problem with that is? Seriously, Fern, jump on a plane. *After* the weekend.'

It was so simple to an onlooker. To a younger onlooker. Hal couldn't imagine the gut-wrenching poignancy of being at the beginning of some kind of an end, however distant that may be. He'd find out, when he caught up, that life wasn't so simple.

Commenting on the plushness of Adam's apartment, Fern took care to look as if this was her first sight of its splendour. 'Cor,' she said. 'This is a bit spesh.'

'Thank you,' said Penny, before Adam could.

A cheer went up from the sunken seating, and Tallulah stood behind her mum.

'Don't be shy,' wheedled Fern. 'That's only Kinky Mimi.' She accepted the hugs and the kisses as the boys of yesteryear bore down on her.

'You haven't changed a bit.' Lemmy's new teeth flashed like neon lighting fitted into a tired old room.

'It must be, what, eighteen years?' Keith was still attractive, in a man-next-door way. He walked carefully, as befitted a man with his problems.

Tears suddenly in her carefully-made-up eyes, Fern was moved to see the old gang back together. 'They were great days, weren't they?' she said.

Penny pushed through the throng of beer guts. 'And they'll be great again,' she said, tapping her notepad with a pen. 'If we can get on with the meeting.'

Setting Tallulah up in a corner with her homework, Fern hugged her tightly. 'You'll be OK?'

'I'll be with Daddy.' Tallulah found the question silly. 'Will you be OK?'

'Yes, darling. You're very kind to ask.' Fern waved at the band. 'See you!'

'Hang on.' Adam scooted across. 'When are you picking up Miss T?'

'Lunchtime Sunday. About two. If that's cool.'

'Or Tallie and I could go for a roast in the pub and I'll drop her home after that.'

'Please please,' squealed Tallulah, who considered pubs awfully grown up.

'Good plan.' Fern turned to go.

'You look nice.' Adam spoke low, like a spy passing information.

Penny, watching them like a meerkat sentry over Kinky Mimi's heads, ordered 'Mind the rug!'

Fern stepped back hastily. The rug, a vile leopardskin

number, was a sacred relic, sent to Adam by the mighty Lincoln Speed himself, in celebration of the *Roomies* platinum disc. Everybody – except, predictably, Fern – had decided to find the rug 'beautiful' rather than the 'smelly' it so obviously was. Tallulah had made it clear that Adam must leave it to her when he died, although she added, 'You're not allowed to die, Daddy.'

Adam and Fern stood either side of the heirloom. 'Going somewhere glam, Fern?'

'Adam,' said Fern. 'Could we have a word? It won't take long.'

'Well, I—'

Penny speed-walked towards them. 'Adam, we're all waiting.'

'Guys, can I have a minute?' Adam's question was greeted with genial approval.

'I need to talk to Adam,' said Fern.

'Uh-huh.' Penny stayed where she was, as Adam looked at the rug.

'It's private.'

'I know all Adam's affairs,' said Penny, with what seemed to Fern an unfortunate turn of phrase.

'It's a family matter.' Fern pulled down an iron shutter and Penny trotted back to the sofa, one eye on them at all times.

'Adam, it's Nora. She's ill.'

'You said it was just a sprained wrist.'

'That's the short story. The long story is, well, longer.'

They sat on a grey sofa by the door.

'She has something called . . .' Fern hadn't said it enough times yet to be sure of it. 'Late-onset cerebellar ataxia.'

'Is it . . .' Adam didn't want to say it.

'Fatal? No. Although it does shorten life expectancy. The sad thing is what it does to your life before it ends it.'

'This sounds bad.'

'It really is, Adam. She has a tough few years ahead. She'll deteriorate physically. It affects, well, everything. Her ability to walk, to coordinate movement. Her eyesight will suffer. That's started already.'

'The black glasses!'

'Exactly. Her poor iris wanders all over the place. And the clumsiness wasn't gin. It was this bloody degenerative disease. It causes depression.'

'Which explains the crabbiness.'

'Although she was always crabby. The worst bit is dementia. When it starts it'll be rapid.'

'Fern. You're crying.'

Adam's arms went out but fell back.

'I'm fine. It just hits me sometimes. The list of problems is so long. Fatigue. Bladder control.'

They pulled a joint face.

'Then, later, her speech will go. She already slurs. It won't happen all at once. I keep reminding myself of that. Nora might have years left. Or it might be months.' Fern ended on a squeak.

'What about treatment?' Adam was pinching the bridge of his nose, taking it in.

'There's tons of it, but no cure. All the docs can do is help with the symptoms. The cerebellar ataxia just gallops on, shutting down Nora as it goes. Miraculously, there's a space in a nursing home attached to the hospital where they have the right sort of expertise to care for her.'

Adam was gentle. 'It's for the best.'

'I hate that expression,' said Fern with a wan smile. 'But you're right, of course.'

'No way could you cope with all that.'

'I know. I can visit. We'll all visit, won't we?'

'We won't let her be lonely.'

'Right.' Fern slapped her thighs and stood, snatching up the pretty new holdall she'd treated herself to. 'Gotta fly.'

The hospital wasn't really on the way to where Fern had arranged to meet Hal, but she allowed extra time. Hal had been disgruntled that he couldn't pick her up at home.

'Am I a dirty secret?'

'You're a sexy secret.' *For now*. Secrets have a way of forcing their way into the light.

The room was as cosy as Fern could make it, given the underlying smell of Dettol and the clatter of hospital life. Daffodils sat on the windowsill and Nora's favourite cushion was at her back. A silk scarf patterned with poppies covered her sling.

Sitting up in bed in a pristine new nightdress buttoned to the neck, Nora looked small. Fern wondered why people looked smaller in hospital, as if the beds were oversized.

'You should have seen me dinner. Slop. No wonder folk come in here and never get out again.'

Setting out fruit and chocolates, Fern was grateful for Nora's curmudgeonliness. It showed spirit, and Nora would need buckets of spirit to withstand the onslaught of her condition. Without her dark energy to keep her going Nora might already be dead. The thought sliced through Fern; now that her empathy gland was engaged, there was no going back. She was on Team Nora.

'I brought you the *Reader's Digest* like you asked.' *Demanded.*

'That's a fat lot of use. Me eye's wonky today.'

'So it is.' The blue iris jitterbugged. Fern didn't flinch, even though it was gruesome to see. 'How about a nice audiobook instead?'

'No pornography, thank you very much.'

'Jill Mansell, Auntie? Or is that too risqué?'

'No. I like her.' Nora took a chocolate. 'I've got me first MFI on Monday.'

'MRI, Auntie.' Nora's dance card was full. A multi-disciplinary team was working on her case: a neurologist, a physiotherapist, a specialist nurse.

'I suppose you'll be too busy to come with me.'

'I've cancelled all my Monday clients. I'm sitting in on the session with the speech therapist as well.' Fern needed to hear information from the horse's mouth; Nora tended to paraphrase, grumbling that the doctors all looked like schoolboys and what did they know, anyway.

'I won't be able to pop in tomorrow, Auntie.'

The brief look of panic was hastily replaced with disdain. 'Gadding about, I suppose?'

'Yup. Even though I'm not exactly sure what gadding

about entails. I'll be with my fancy man, but Evka's going to pop in, keep an eye on you.'

'That Evka's a good girl.'

And I'm not? Fern kept her amusement to herself as she took one last look around. 'I'll be off.' Hospital farewells are always poignant, even when the patient isn't in immediate danger. It felt appropriate to kiss the lady in the bed, but Nora would recoil, claim she was giving her syphilis. 'Ta-ra, then.'

Slurring only slightly, Nora spoke fast. 'That lady's coming back tomorrow, she said. The one with the papers for me to sign.' She looked out of the window, a black rectangle on the wall. 'For the nursing home. They can have me straight away, which is handy.' She looked back at Fern, her face naked, with no melodrama. 'Will you visit me, Fern? Will you bring my Tallie?'

'No, Auntie,' said Fern. 'We won't visit because there's no way you're going to a nursing home. You're coming home to your family.'

Nora took Fern's hand and gripped it very tightly for a woman so diminished.

'I love you, Auntie,' said Fern.

'That coat does nothing for you,' said Nora.

When Fern had imagined her middle age, she'd seen dull repetition, all the fun and drama long gone. Like a mum in a Kellogg's ad, she'd be upstanding, warm, mature. *Yet here I am, waiting at the park gates for my toyboy, having*

just made a life-changing promise to a woman I couldn't stand two weeks ago.

The filling in a generational sandwich, Fern was still caring for the younger ones while taking responsibility for the age group above her. All while finding the time to buy a flattering bra online. *Which will shortly be removed in a plush hotel room.*

A black cab growled to a halt at the kerb. Fern bounced into the back seat beside Hal, and was soundly kissed.

'Where are we going?' The taxi's wheels turned in the direction of the station. 'Into the city? Or out to the country?' Either option was divine. A Georgian townhouse with a hip bar in the basement, or a four-poster in an ancient manor house.

'You'll see.' Hal was nervous, giggly, unable to sit back. 'Christ, I hope you like it.'

'I'm going to love it.' Hal wasn't to know that any working woman weeps with gratitude if she's handed so much as a biscuit she hasn't had to buy, store and fetch herself.

'Just here, mate.' The taxi stopped just a few streets away. Hal stepped out ahead of her, taking Fern's hand as if she was a Regency heroine alighting from a carriage.

Terraced houses, three storeys high, marched down a long, typically London street. Midway through gentrification, every other house had a Farrow & Ball painted front door with an olive tree either side of it. Other front gardens boasted bins lolling on their sides among forests of thistle. A dog barked. Somewhere glass shattered.

Taking Fern up the path of a sooty house, its curtains

half pulled and a black bag full of empty bottles in the porch, Hal produced a key.

'Welcome,' he said, 'to your hotel.' He was watching her intently.

Carefully non-committal, Fern said, 'I see.'

'The porter will take your luggage to your suite.'

Fern handed over her new luggage to Hal.

'I'm a bit skint, Fern,' he said, leading her up the stairs. 'I couldn't afford a real five-star break but this'll be even better, I promise.'

'Mmm,' said Fern, reaching the landing and pixilating the seatless toilet beyond an open door.

'It was a lot funnier and more charming in my head.' Hal turned back, tilted Fern's chin and kissed her. The smell of burning mince receded as Hal's signature scents of clay dust and soap enveloped her. Holding her tight, his lips moved to her hair. 'I wanted you all to myself. I want to wake up with you.'

'This hotel,' said Fern, as the nylon carpet squeaked beneath her feet, 'is the best I've ever stayed in.'

The top floor was a long way in new heels. Fern passed posters tacked to woodchip walls, and doors with hand-written *KEEP OUT* signs. A noisy bath was taking place beyond a crackle-glazed door.

The room at the top was large, with a generous bay window.

'This is lovely!'

'Don't sound so surprised.'

In contrast to the fluff-covered stairs, the room was

virginal and clean. Floorboards, walls, blinds were all white and a snowy duvet ballooned on the wide bed.

'I spent all last weekend painting.' Hal watched Fern the way Boudi did whenever she opened the fridge. 'There's all the little touches you'd expect from a hotel. Complimentary dressing gown.' An obviously new towelling robe hung on the back of the door. 'Million-thread-count cotton bedding. Tea and coffee making facilities.' Hal pointed at a mini kettle and two mugs on a low table. 'I even bought those shortbread biccies in cellophane. Free wi-fi. Hot and cold running snogs.'

Crossing the distance between them, Hal bent Fern backwards. The kiss was hard, hot, resolute. He lifted her palm, pressing it to his lips, his eyes on hers. 'En suite facilities,' he said seductively, sliding a corrugated plastic door to show off the avocado bath and orange carpet tiles. 'The design is intriguingly retro, but there's posh toiletries and a new Orla Kiely towel.'

Fingering the vase of tulips by the bed, Fern smiled at the Ferrero Rocher laid on each pillow. 'You've gone to so much trouble. It's so *you*. Much better than any bland old hotel.'

'Phew.' Hal wiped his brow with an exaggerated gesture. 'There was a chance you'd turn and run.'

Fern hadn't been wealthy for so long that she'd forgotten it's possible to have fun on nought pence. Instead of flexing his credit card, Hal had spent days preparing. It was all for her and she was touched. 'Call room service, would you? See if they can send up a guy, about yay high.' She touched the top of Hal's head. 'He has to be funny and thoughtful and gorgeous.'

'And horny as hell?'

Fern blushed like a virgin. 'I wouldn't put it like that.' She peeked at him from beneath her eyelashes. 'But yeah, OK.'

'I'll see what I can do.' Hal began to undo his belt and something stirred deep inside of Fern.

'Come here, you,' she said.

'We smell of each other.' Hal nuzzled Fern's neck like a pony, before slipping out of bed and shimmying into his jeans. 'Christ, it's getting on for midnight, Fern.'

'No!' The hours had passed in a blur of limbs and mouths and exquisite pleasure. Fern had arched her back, cried out, begged; like her Pilates class, but more fun. 'I'm starving. You've made me hungry.'

'I'll whistle up room service and then there's a massage booked.' Hal shot down the stairs, calling out to somebody as he went. The house was alive with noise, Fern only noticing it now that she was alone in the 'suite'. Doors slammed. Feet slapped on floors. Reggae boomed above laughter on the storey below.

At least two of the things Fern had done since checking in were new to her. Hal treated sex as a playground; his enthusiasm was infectious but Fern would need to catch her breath before she got back on the swings.

As somebody in the street yelled 'Josh, you're a wanker!' Fern realized she hadn't made her daily call to Layla.

Sifting through the useless debris that weighed down her handbag – *Why is there a set square in here?* – Fern's fingers encountered some folded paper.

'Bad timing,' she muttered, taking out the old letter that had migrated from its box to her bag. The Zara holdall was a portable black hole, sucking in random objects from the atmosphere.

Or is it perfect *timing?* Adam's heading on this letter was '7 Things a New Boyfriend Would Do that Would Definitely Annoy You'. Between the rumpled new sheets of Hal's bed might be the ideal place to read it. Hal wouldn't have committed any of the transgressions Adam had dreamed up back in '93.

Something struck Fern. She and Adam had been younger than Hal at the time of the Great Rift. Fern was so used to being the older woman that it seemed easier to believe she'd *never* been as young as Hal. That she'd been born with cellulite.

7 THINGS A NEW BOYFRIEND WOULD DO THAT
WOULD DEFINITELY ANNOY YOU

You seem to be getting over me. Perhaps you're sitting there choosing who to go out with next. (DO NOT sleep with the bloke from Holland and Barrett. The one with the swoofy hair. I will react VERY BADLY if you sleep with him.) Whoever you go out with will annoy you. You're easily annoyed. Here are some of the mistakes this new guy will make.

1. They won't pay attention while you tell the hour-long story about how you chose the top you're wearing. They'll nod all the way through and by the time you finish they'll have forgotten what you were talking about in the first place and say something like 'what top?' (Yes, I know, I did this ONCE. Never again.)

2. He'll refer to conversations with his mates as 'banter'.

3. He won't ring when he says he will. If he rings he won't leave a message.

4. If you put on a few pounds he'll say, 'Somebody needs to keep away from the pork pies.'

5. He'll blame your 'time of the month' if you threaten to punch him. (You've threatened to punch me many times but I know it's nothing to do with periods. You're just violent.)

6. He'll try to wheedle out of nights out with your friends. (He might have a point, actually.)

7. He won't love you. Not like I do.

'What you reading?' Hal hovered above her with a tray, looking for somewhere to set it down.

'Nothing. Just an old . . . nothing.' Fern swallowed, bemused by the sudden time travel from the nineties to now, from Adam's jokey heartbreak to Hal's muscled shoulders. She patted the bed. 'Put it here. We'll be careful.'

'The bastards have eaten all the nice bits and pieces I bought.' Hal was sheepish. 'It's only toast and jam.'

'Toast is just right.' Fern took the knife out of the margarine tub. The sweating yellow surface was pebble-dashed with crumbs of various colours. 'Blackberry jam! My favourite.' Beneath the lid, a random pattern of green mould livened up the dark surface.

They fed each other fingers of dripping toast. The mould didn't matter. Only Hal's lips mattered as they slid down Fern's neck and did their thing on her breast. With a hungry groan, he laid her back among the bedclothes.

The tray jumped in the air.

'Shit shit shit!' Hal leapt up, his head in his hands at the sight of the tea tidal wave lapping over his new duvet cover. The jam was like bloodstains.

'It'll wash out.' Fern laughed until Hal saw the funny side.

'I wanted everything to be swish.' He pulled a crestfallen face.

Deep in her bag, Fern's mobile chirped.

'Leave it.' Hal grabbed Fern's wrist, pulled her to him over the crockery graveyard. 'It's just us this weekend.'

Disengaging his fingers, kissing them as they curled back, Fern shook her head. How could a carefree singleton, without even a cat to feed, understand? Fern was accountable for a newborn, a bed-ridden pensioner and a Tallulah.

Call me asap

'Is something up?' Hal registered Fern's expression.

'My friend. The pregnant one. I should have called.' Fern pushed her arms through the uncooperative sleeves of the dressing gown. 'I'll call her outside, in case it's . . .' Fern couldn't finish the thought, couldn't say *bad news.*

The oversized robe flapped around her, its cuffs over her fingertips, as Fern bolted down the stairs, swerving to avoid a man meandering along in his underpants.

'Evening!' he said genially, scratching his balls.

Finding the sitting room, an empty oasis of psychedelic carpet and fake leather, Fern perched and dialled.

'Tell me,' she squealed when Layla picked up.

'It's you, thank God.' The line crackled like a forest fire as Layla moved the handset. 'Right. How'd you spell Amelie?'

When Fern didn't answer, Layla added, 'I've put together some little presents for her and I didn't want to misspell it. I feel bad that I didn't congratulate Ollie at the time. Fern? Are you there?'

After spelling out the name, Fern asked, 'Why the "ASAP"?'

'I want to get to bed.'

The baby was hanging on in there. Layla mentioned this in passing, and Fern responded with a neutral 'Good, good.' Eight weeks was longer than any of Layla's other implanted eggs had survived. Fern didn't counsel optimism or positive thinking; she would simply be there while Layla and Luc waited it out.

The house rose late on Sunday morning. Fern luxuriated in her lie-in. Nobody needed help with their nappy, or their homework, or their false teeth. Already, she was used to the leisurely schedule at Hal's.

Everything revolved around sex. Fern hadn't tuned into a news broadcast or made a shopping list. It was the first weekend in years she hadn't nosed around Sainsbury's with a trolley. *But I have had some rather splendid orgasms.*

Venturing downstairs for fresh supplies – it wasn't fair to leave all the room service to her host – Fern left Hal sleeping, his mouth slightly open. She crossed her fingers that the kitchen would be empty, but it was already populated with folk standing around eating cereal from bowls held under their chins.

None of the people making space for Fern would remember flares from the first time around, and half of them were in their underwear.

'You must be Fern.' A tubby Chinese girl bucked the trend by wearing an actual sweatshirt over actual jeggings.

Foraging in cupboards, Fern smiled.

A boy in striped budgie smugglers said, 'Man, we've heard a lot about you. What have you done to our Hal?'

They all *hur-hurred* good-naturedly.

A girl in a sports bra and skater skirt said, 'Shut up, Josh.' She rolled her eyes at Fern. 'Ignore them. They're arseholes. Nice to meet you at last.'

Realizing she thought of Hal's housemates as 'girls' and 'boys', Fern was introduced to the cornflake eaters. She wondered how she could feel so connected to Hal yet poles apart from these jolly, welcoming people?

Because Hal's special.

The crew in the kitchen, teasing each other and running cold water over greasy plates, were oversized, happy children. They helped Fern scrape together an approximation of breakfast. Another day of this and she'd start to fantasize about vegetables.

Unpeeling a cheese string, one of the underpant boys said, 'Actually, Fern, I think you might know my mum.'

Her eyes on the godforsaken margarine tub, Fern shrank into herself as if a shaft of light had illuminated every wrinkle, as if her birth certificate was taped to her forehead. Looking up, she saw an absence of malice in the boy's eyes. *He's not mocking me about the age difference.* He really did just think she might know his mum.

What's more, Fern *did* know his mum. 'Say hi to her for me!' she called as she schlepped back up to the penthouse suite.

'Sex please!' shouted Hal from the bed as she staggered in with the tray.

'Are you bionic?' Fern remembered a bank holiday when Adam had made a victory lap of the bedroom because they'd 'done it' twice in a row.

'We're running out of time. You'll disappear soon,' said Hal. 'When I call you, you'll talk to me in your spy voice.'

'Do I do that?' That didn't sound very nice to Fern.

'I know you're busy and I know you have people who rely on you. Just make a little space for me, yeah?'

'I do make space.' Didn't Hal realize how much planning it took to get away? 'If it were up to me we'd spend every weekend together.' *Although maybe not here*, she added silently.

'It *is* up to you.' Hal sat up, arms resting on his knees, glowing flesh all on show.

A timid knock sounded. Hal stepped outside, a pillow

over his equipment, and had a whispered conversation, before returning with a towering wedge of chocolate fudge cake. 'Seems they didn't eat *everything* after all.'

Fern almost had another orgasm at the sight of the cake. They shared it, one fork between them, not caring if they smeared it on the bedclothes. The only clean bedding available after the tray disaster was a Liverpool FC duvet cover. It smelled of Wotsits, somewhat marring the Claridges vibe.

So what? What happened beneath the covers was what really mattered. When Fern and Hal's skin touched it sizzled. Natural dance partners, they were always in step, the rhythm never faltering.

Generous, soppy, suddenly thrillingly butch, Hal communicated his feelings through sex. Neither of them mentioned love; Fern respected the word too much to flirt with it. At another stage in her life, Fern would have needed to hear it before she dived into the sexual deep end, but now she was in charge of her desires, and didn't need promises. She only needed what she saw in his eyes; *I make him happy*.

He made Fern happy, too; it was enough.

A shaggy male head appeared around the door. 'Got a screwdriver I can borrow, Hal?'

'Mate!' Hal gestured, appalled, at Fern. 'I've got company!'

The curls disappeared.

'Sorry about him.' Hal stopped the fork en route to Fern's mouth. She whimpered; that cake was *good*. 'Sorry about a lot of things.'

'Like what?' Fern took the fork out of his hands.

'The flush not working. The mouse that ran across the

265

floorboards. The midnight burping competition out on the landing. I live in a dump, don't I?'

'I once shared a flat where we got into a stand-off about whose turn it was to buy toilet paper, so we all carried a personal roll in our handbags. You won't always live like this.'

'You'll never come back here, will you?' Hal was rueful, as if he wouldn't blame her.

'Overnight stays are tricky, Hal.' Fern saw his face fall. 'If you want a woman who's always available, you gotta go fishing in your own age group.'

'Not listening not listening!' Hal jumped up and bounded over to the en suite. The shower sputtered into life.

There was cake left. And then there wasn't. Licking her fingers, Fern lay back against Liverpool Football Club's red and white stripes. The silly indignities of Hal's home weren't a problem. What bothered her was how they highlighted the ravine between them. It wasn't just about age; if anything, being with Hal made Fern feel younger. Blood pounded in her veins. She felt strong and powerful. *I feel like a woman.*

The gap that really counted was the difference in experience. Fern was way in front, a few stops ahead on the journey. Hal was a beginner.

When he hurtled, still damp, from the shower and rolled her over, tickling her, kissing her, that gap didn't seem to matter half as much as the simple, sparkling euphoria she felt.

'Mum? You look different.'

Fern twisted this way and that, away from Ollie's scrutiny and the half-smile on his lips.

'Where have you been? Mum? What're you up to?'

'Let me get my coat off before you interrogate me.'

Evka, in rubber gloves and a micro-mini, shooed him out of the kitchen before turning to Fern. 'You been sexing it up good, yes?'

'Yes. I mean no.' Fern changed the subject, saying, 'Rubber gloves? Are you . . . I can't believe I'm saying this but are you doing housework, Evka?'

'I clean loft.'

'Did somebody hold a gun to your head?'

'For Nora.' Evka peeled off the gloves.

'She won't be home until Wednesday.'

'No. She is on sofa watching *Cash in Stupid Attic*.'

The hospital had discharged Nora early; something about overcrowding. Fern felt panicked. *I should have been here.* 'Is she OK? Christ, her medication. Did the baby disturb her? How did she manage the stairs?'

'We all help,' said Evka, following Fern. 'We manage.'

'Auntie!' Fern fell to her knees beside the armchair.

'There you are!' Nora, in a twinset and Crimplene skirt, looked more healthy in her natural habitat. 'Did you have a nice time?'

'Yes.' Fern braced herself for an acerbic comment that didn't come. 'Are you warm enough? Did you take your tablets?'

'Do not fuss.' Evka was stern. 'I have grandmother back

in Slovakia and I take care of her. I know what to do. Don't I, Nora?'

'She's an angel,' twinkled Nora.

Fern was silent for a while. She'd never witnessed a twinkle from Nora before.

Up. Down. Up. Down. Up. Halfway down, then up again.

Nora went to bed to rest, as instructed, but she was a demanding patient. *I'll have legs like a racehorse if this carries on*, thought Fern, pounding up to the loft for the umpteenth time with a *Woman's Weekly* and a Hobnob. She found Ollie there, sitting on the side of his great-aunt's bed, both of them peering at the screen of his laptop.

'And then you press *that* button.' Ollie waited while the wizened finger dithered.

'This one?'

'Yup. See?'

'This is miraculous,' squeaked Nora. 'This Internet lark will catch on, mark my words.' She pecked at keys, exclaiming and giggling.

'Do you want me to do your hair later, Auntie?' Nora was dishevelled. With no real cure, it was important that Nora stay plugged into the world, not become the invalid at the top of the house.

'I was wondering when you'd offer.' This was Nora-speak for 'yes, please.'

'Switch *off*,' Fern told her mind. It took no notice. *Dryer needs emptying*, it reminded her. *Check Tallulah's homework diary*. As she wiped the work surface, her mind grumbled *Not that cloth!*

Housework bled into every corner of her consciousness if Fern let it. It was a full-time job masquerading as a sideline. Everywhere she looked, dumb objects found a mouth and screamed for her attention. The broken egg cup on the shelf beside the cooker had been awaiting a good glueing for weeks on end. A scribbled note commanding 'Molly! urgent!' had been pinned to the corkboard for so long that Fern no longer knew who Molly was. (She hoped this Molly wasn't hog-tied in a disused lock-up waiting for rescue.)

Shut up, Fern told the kitchen sternly, switching off the lights. Today she'd been chauffeur, hairdresser, agony aunt, cleaner, chef, nanny, good cop/bad cop/cuddly cop as well as a beauty therapist. For now, she was just Fern. Not a mother. Not a niece. Not a grandmother.

I'm a lover. She was Hal's lover. Fern said it aloud. 'I have a lover.' Not too loud, even though only Binkie, blowing off surreptitiously into a cushion, was around to hear. Fern liked being a lover; it beat being a partner hands down.

The ties that bound her and Hal were gossamer, as opposed to steel. They dipped in and out of each other's lives, always welcome but never staying too long. Fern knew he was out there somewhere, possibly thinking about her, possibly thinking about the Spice Girls or his feet. Who could say? Tomorrow she would meet him and the other dog walkers at the park gates and his mouth would twist into a skewed smile because Pongo and Maggie had no idea what Tinkerbell and Boudicca got up to in between rambles.

They'd keep fastidiously apart. There'd be surreptitious winks. It was *fun* having a lover.

Whereas Adam was no fun any more. *Correction*, thought Fern: *Adam and me are no fun any more.* He seemed to be laughing it up with Kinky Mimi. And Penny. Fern and Adam had lost their fun mojo. Adam was half the man he used to be in her company, as if he'd been warned not to engage with her, not to be interesting or interested. He was impatient to get away; only half his attention was on Fern.

There were many ironies to splitting up, including the fact that it was only now that Fern appreciated how much Adam had done around the house. Accustomed to feeling like the martyred workhorse of the family, Fern had reminded Adam about pulling his weight every day of their life together.

He didn't think of it as 'reminding'; 'Stop bloody nagging me, woman!' he'd yell, when she shouted something about the bins/the MOT paperwork/the cellar. 'Don't help or anything, Adam,' she'd say, baby in one hand, saucepan in the other, the washing machine sashaying across the kitchen floor in a trail of suds.

'I do have a career, you know,' Adam would grumble, up a ladder, hanging a framed alphabet in Tallie's room.

'Me too. I have two, in fact. One that brings in money and one that doesn't. You lot are a full-time job.'

Now that there was only Fern to be Mummy, Daddy and chief exec of Homestead House, she saw the invisible stuff Adam had taken care of. He'd cleared the horror-film gunk from the pipes under the sink. He'd parked the car nose out, so she could exit the driveway without killing a neighbour. He'd known which recycling container was which. He'd read a Malory Towers to Tallulah every evening. He'd listened to and commented on Ollie's play-lists. He'd deflected half the insane requests Tallulah made. He'd shouldered half the telling-off duties.

Sure, he'd never notice that they had no milk. He'd expect a home-made cake for everybody's birthday, but hand him an egg and some flour and he'd probably cry. Adam had never typed an Ocado order while de-nitting a child's hair, nor did he know which temperature to wash knickers at, but his absence taught Fern that for every petty chore Adam shirked there was another petty chore he'd done without fanfare.

Settling down on the sofa, remote control close to hand, large glass of wine *in* hand, Fern wondered if they'd ever be able to talk to each other about how they felt right now. Splitting up with a man was as intimate as living with him, if you were bound by children and property and general *blah*.

We used to talk about everything. Until they talked about very little. Later still, all they talked about was *it*. The problem. Their inability to keep the Carlile show on the road.

For now, Fern had a couple of hours of quiet. Ollie and Donna were larging it (if that was what the yoof still called it) in a club; Amelie was snuffling in her cot; Tallulah was asleep with a book fallen over her face; Nora was, incredibly, surfing the net.

And Evka was out there somewhere, in the rainy metropolis, seducing another Englishman to add to her collection. Fern burrowed beneath the blanket Tallulah kept on the sofa, grateful to be indoors on such a damp, inky night. Evka wouldn't permit any worrying about her, but lately Fern had started to fret when it got late and there'd been no jangle of buckled boots on the stair.

I have enough people to worry about without adding to my assortment. Evka held herself so haughtily high that it had taken a while for her to get under Fern's skin. Since Nora fell ill, Evka had come into focus, sharpened up until now she was solidly 3D. The selfishness had fallen away; she'd do anything to make the old lady comfortable. More than once, Evka had compared Nora to her grandmother in Bratislava.

Fern hadn't exactly been eavesdropping as Evka told Tallulah about her family, but she hadn't exactly walked away, either. In fact, she'd glued her greedy ear to the door as Evka described the full house on Dargovska Street.

'Grandmother, mother, father, uncle, four cousins, three brothers and me all live together,' Evka had said, in her brittle accent. 'All in close. Like birds in nest.'

'Do you miss them?' Fern had saluted: *that's my Tallie, getting to the heart of things as usual.*

'No.' Evka had been so firm, it could only be a lie.

Zapping through the channels, disregarding the ruby rings discounted from lots of money to hardly any money, the made-for-TV films about a beautiful woman in danger from a very bad actor, and the endless squabbles of *EastEnders*, Fern settled for an old episode of *Who Wants to Be a Millionaire?*

Shouting 'B: a form of nut' or 'C, you fool, C!' at the screen, Fern wondered if Evka had been drawn to Homestead House not because it was cheap, but because it was full of people. Doctor Fern diagnosed homesickness. *The flinty exterior is armour; deep down she's sad.*

If Adam were here, he wouldn't let Fern watch *Millionaire* and he'd warn her against reading people's minds. *Not another lame duck!* he'd plead, but Fern liked her ducks lame. True, Evka didn't seem all that sad when she staggered home covered in love bites, but melancholy takes many forms.

The walls juddered. Far above Fern's head, an elderly lady was banging a shoe on the floor and hollering her niece's name.

Hurtling up the stairs, grateful to Amelie for snoring through the outcry, Fern burst into the loft. 'What? Are you OK?' She had visions of another stroke; she'd almost had one herself.

'Fern!' Nora sat up straight, her face bright as if she'd seen a vision. 'I've had one of them epiphany things!'

Slumping with relief, Fern sank to the bed. 'That's nice.'

'I want people to be sorry when I die, Fern, not relieved!'

'Nobody would—' Fern was cut off, as Nora carried on, shouting like an old-style preacher.

'I want to know love! I want to inspire love! I want to feel it! I want to mean something! I want to know people!'

'Oh Auntie!' Fern was on the verge of tears. 'That's so sweet.'

'I want an orgasm!' bellowed Nora.

'Yes, well, that too,' said Fern, no longer needing to cry.

'Is it too late, Fern?' Nora reached out and clasped Fern's hands.

'It's never too late.' Fern wanted to believe this.

'Do you forgive me?'

'What for?' Fern knew what for, but was keen to absolve her aunt. The sad biography she'd heard at her hospital bedside had explained the woman's quirks.

'I've been a right . . .' Nora mouthed the word 'bitch'.

Pretending to be scandalized, Fern assured her that she hadn't.

'You lie as badly as you make moussaka,' said Nora, who had some way to go before she was reformed. 'You're a good girl, Fern.'

'It's nice to be a girl.'

'Help me with this website form, will you?' Nora swivelled the laptop. 'How do I send it?'

Fern scanned the page. 'Um, are you sure this is what you want?'

'I've never been so sure of anything in me life.'

'In that case, press that little arrow there.'

Nora clapped at the *swoosh* sound effect, as her dating profile went off to twilightdating.co.uk.

Downstairs once more, Fern paced, the glass of wine swapped for a bigger glass of wine. Amelie was tucked into the crook of her arm, her face placid. Only minutes ago the baby had been squirming and screaming, but a little cooing and a little rocking had calmed her down.

Amelie had a habit, however, which made her parents despair. However gently they put her back into the cot, the moment her bum met the mattress she began to grizzle again. Fern had no option but to keep the baby up, in the hopes that prolonged jiggling would send her off to sleep.

'You're a naughty girl,' she said in sugared tones, kissing Amelie's nose. 'You made me a granny in my early forties. I needed a few more years to train for the part. I should be in a windcheater with a handbag full of Werther's Originals and half-used tissues. Where are my tartan slippers and my bifocals on a chain? Eh?' She tickled Amelie's cheek and the baby made one of the nicest noises Fern had ever heard, and her heart ballooned with tenderness for the dependent, tyrannical little scrap. 'Let's have a look at your great-great-Auntie's profile, shall we?' Fern bent over her iPad, jumping back when a picture of Nora filled the screen.

Fern would have brandished a crucifix if she'd had one. Nobody could accuse Nora of photoshopping herself; at a funeral, all in black, Nora scowled as if there was a wasp under her strange, enormous hat.

'*Interesting* username.'

Nora had plumped for 'oldgalfullaspunk'. Fern briefly considered telling her aunt that the meaning of 'spunk' had changed from 'vitality' to something quite different, but she didn't feel up to it. Oldgalfullaspunk's age was filled in honestly, as were her height and weight. No gilding the lily for conscientious Nora. Fern read out the 'About Me' section to Amelie.

'I am a straightforward, reliable virgin, making up for lost time. Are you willing to fall in love before the curtain falls? I make no claims to beauty, although I do match my shoes to my bag. I don't think I have a sense of humour. WLTM a clean man who wears a suit. No gold diggers.'

The doorbell rang, and Amelie's face screwed up.

'Nonono,' begged Fern, pressing her lips to the baby's forehead. She scooted to the front door, ready to reprimand Ollie and Donna for coming home so early; she'd insisted they stay out until midnight. Instead she said, 'Oh.'

On the step stood a tall, lean young man, with powerful shoulders tamed by a well-cut jacket. Launching into a speech, he left Fern no time to say anything. 'Hello. You must be Fern. I was wondering if I could . . .' The stranger tailed off, staring at Amelie so hard that Fern held her a touch tighter.

'If you could what?' Fern kept one hand on the latch, disgruntled by the man's hypnotized expression.

'Is that her?' He spoke softly, in awe, as if Amelie was an apparition.

Fern joined the dots. As he shifted and the porch light found his goatee, she saw that Maz was younger than she'd assumed, only about twenty or so. 'Yes, this is her,' she said uncertainly, still keeping the half-closed door between them. 'This is Amelie.'

Handsome, with regal features and haughty, hooded eyes, Maz repeated 'Amelie,' wonderingly.

The newcomer was too far away for Amelie's newish eyes to focus on. Fern saw how much the child resembled her biological father. The same tawny palette for skin and eyes. The same exquisite eyebrows.

'Donna's out,' said Fern. 'So's Ollie. I'll tell them you came round.' Maz springing to unexpected, vivid life on her doorstep had thrown her. This man, who'd hurt her precious Donna, allegedly claimed he wanted nothing to do with his daughter; but now he looked overcome to meet Amelie face to face.

'She won't let me see her.'

'That really is between you and Donna.'

'Please don't.' Maz put a hand out to meet the closing door. 'She's so beautiful. Is she, like, healthy and everything?' He had a south London street accent, at odds with the tailored clothes.

'She's perfect.' Fern couldn't help smiling. It occurred to her that Amelie had another grandmother, one who never saw her, would never get to touch her warm skin.

'Can I hold her?' Maz held out long arms. 'Please.'

His eyes were enormous, wet-looking in this light. 'Donna wouldn't like it,' said Fern apologetically.

'Just for a minute. Please.' The begging was low-key, but all the more persuasive because of it.

Reluctantly, Fern held out the bundle of baby. At no point did she feel she was doing the right thing; he could turn and walk away, be at the gate in three strides. Something compelled her; the right of a father to hold his own daughter. She corrected Maz's hands so he supported Amelie properly.

'She's heavy.' Max was dazed, like a man who'd just stepped out of a plane wreck.

'They might look like little flowers, but they're tough.' Fern held her hands together to stop herself snatching Amelie back. 'She looks like you.'

'Does she?' Maz was pathetically grateful for her comment. 'I've never held a baby before.'

'It's not hard, is it?'

'Nah. It's great.'

'May I . . . It's cold out here.' Fern accepted the baby into her arms, relieved to have her back. 'She should be in bed really.'

'You're looking after her dead well.'

'That's Donna's doing,' said Fern. She had to add, 'And Ollie, of course,' out of loyalty to her son, who was working himself into the ground for this guy's daughter.

'I'd better go, I s'pose.' Maz couldn't quite turn away, as if Amelie was a cuddly magnet and he was a pile of iron filings. 'Goodnight, Amelie.' He wiggled his fingers at the child.

Amelie sneezed.

'Goodnight, Maz.' Fern leaned against the closed door, wondering what she'd just done.

CHAPTER TEN

April: Savoureux

'If I was thirty years younger,' murmured Pongo, as Hal bounded towards them in his vintage sheepskin jacket.

'Or he was thirty years older,' suggested Fern.

'God, no, darling.' Pongo winked one bloodshot eye. 'He'd be in his fifties and no use to me!' As Hal joined them she asked archly, 'Just got out of bed, Tinkerbell?'

Hal smiled a hello at the others. Only Fern would have noticed the microscopic raise of an eyebrow he gave her.

'Did you leave some lucky girl lying in it?' Pongo's laugh rattled like a spoon down a waste disposal unit. She nudged Fern. 'We think you've got some sweet young thing tucked away, don't we, Boudicca?'

'Do you now?' Hal looked at Fern, his dimples dancing. 'You could be right, ladies.'

Maggie defended his fellow male. 'Leave him alone.'

'I don't mind,' said Hal, hands in pockets, falling into step. 'I could tell you her name.' He seemed to enjoy Fern's stumble. 'But then I'd have to kill you.'

'Are you crazy about her?' Beneath her fleece, Pongo was a romantic.

'Yeah.' Hal looked at Fern. 'I am.'

'Is it reciprocated?' Pongo seemed to enjoy living vicariously through Hal and his Miss X.

'I have no idea.' Hal was trying so hard not to laugh, the whole lower half of his face was caught up in a pout. 'I hope so.'

'I'm sure she's crazy about you too,' said Fern, in a squeaky voice that made Boudi glance at her, confused.

Pongo gushed, 'Of course she is. Lucky girl.'

'I'll introduce you some time.'

'Bring her walking with us,' said Maggie, his bald patch gleaming in the spring light.

'Great idea,' said Hal. 'I don't know when I'm seeing her again, though. Could be tonight. About eight.'

'That might be a bit short notice for her,' said Fern helpfully.

'Yeah. True.' Hal scratched his chin. 'I'll see if she can do tomorrow evening. She has commitments, you see. She's a very responsible girlie.'

'That might be better for her.' Fern knitted her brows. 'Seven-thirty's a nice time for a date, isn't it?'

'Yes. I've always liked seven-thirty,' said Hal.

'What *are* you two on about?' Pongo had lost interest and was stooping to scoop up the complicated poo her Chihuahua had gifted to the public.

'Does she like wine bars?' asked Fern. 'Does she like that one in the old fire station?'

'She *loves* that one. I'll suggest we meet there, tomorrow, at seven-thirty.'

'Good luck,' said Fern heartily.

'FETCH!' yelled Pongo, throwing a stick.

'Up already, Auntie?' Fern hung up Boudi's lead and pulled off her gloves in the warm kitchen. All was bright and warm and clean; Evka had whisked through with her Marigolds after Fern took Tallulah to school. 'How'd you feel?'

'Fine, fine.' This was Nora's stock answer. If she'd been standing there with her own severed leg in a shopping bag, she'd have said the same.

Giving Nora a discreet once-over, Fern ran through her mental checklist as she assembled an eggy breakfast for them both. No signs of eye wobble. Not particularly slow or clumsy. 'Auntie, count for me.'

Without hesitation, Nora chanted, 'Twenty, nineteen, eighteen.' Counting backwards from twenty was one of a checklist of six questions designed to screen for dementia. Fern rotated the questions, which included 'What month is it?' and 'Without looking at the clock, what time is it to the nearest hour?'

'Lovely.' No signs of slurring. 'How did your date go?'

'So-so.'

The evening before, Fern and Evka had delivered Nora to a small bistro. Hair freshly set in concrete, wearing a new and horrible nylon dress, Nora had been adamant that they leave her at the door, but her chaperones had other ideas.

Once inside, it was obvious who was waiting for Nora.

He brought the average age of the place up by a couple of decades, and wore the most hamster-like wig Fern had ever seen.

Striding across, Evka bent over the table. 'Good evening, sir,' she said. 'We are this lady's friends. We wish you pleasant evening and we warn you that if you disrespect her I find you and break neck like matchstick.'

'He seemed friendly.' *And gaga.* Fern doubted if the old chap could count backwards from twenty, or even find his own face with his hands.

'Sure, he was a looker, but the man lied to me, Fern.'

Recovering from the notion that hamster-head was 'a looker', Fern asked 'How?'

'He took five years off his age. He claimed to be a mere seventy-eight, but the lying toad was eighty-three.'

'Isn't that just a little white lie, Auntie?' Fern felt sorry for Nora's beau, kicked to the kerb in his baggy suit.

'I live honestly now. I pray to God every night to forgive the lies I told you.'

'What lies?' Fern stepped back in theatrical horror. 'You mean . . . you're not my Auntie?'

'Cheeky,' said Nora. 'You know the lie I'm referring to. I should have been straight with you about my symptoms, but I was scared you'd turn me away if you knew I was sick.'

Life had taught Nora to distrust people, that there was no bright side. 'We all tell lies, Auntie.' Fern's secrets were lies by another name. Hal was classified information; it was common sense not to tell her children – not yet, anyway – but Fern couldn't explain why she kept it from

Adam. *After all, how can I be unfaithful to a man who's left me for a new lover?*

A lot had changed since Fern had reluctantly let Nora come to stay. *Would I have turned her away if I'd known she was sick?* Fern hoped the answer was 'no'; the crotchety old hen who'd almost pecked her to death had become more human since giving up her secrets. Nora could sympathize – to a point – with others, and was now a fully paid-up member of the family.

'Have you given any more thought to sleeping down here?'

'I like me loft.'

'The same loft you were going to write to the Pope about? You said there were mice and draughts and a funny smell.'

'That was then. This is now. If you don't want to climb the stairs, don't bother, missy.'

Pride kept Nora hostage in the loft. She knew they all watched her. From Fern right down to Tallulah, the family was a network of loving spies. Donna had suspected a tumble in the bathroom; Ollie reported his great-aunt's eye doing its dance. Tallulah was the most vigilant; she counted four slurred words in Nora's rant about sex scenes in BBC costume dramas.

'Besides,' said Nora, 'there's nowhere for me to sleep down here. The downstairs loo isn't big enough for me to use as a bathroom. It wouldn't work.'

'What if I make it work?'

'No, madam,' said Nora, with an air of finality.

'This ain't over, old woman.'

'I saw one last night,' said Nora, looking up at the ceiling.

'One what?' Fern checked the *Great British Bake Off* wall calendar. 'Don't forget we have a meeting with your MDT later. They'll assess you to see if we can start you on amitriptyline for your nerve pain.'

'A willy,' said Nora.

'Sorry, what?'

'I saw a willy. My first one.' Nora sighed. 'Not very well designed, are they?' She frowned to herself. 'Certainly not a colour I'd choose for walls.'

'When, where?' was all Fern managed to say.

'In his car. I asked. He was happy to oblige.'

'I bet he was.'

'I couldn't stop laughing at first.'

Poor man, thought Fern. *Poor, poor man.*

'But then I popped on my glasses, and now I know my way around one.'

Fern went pale. *Later I'll Google 'how to rinse your brain'.*

As Nora ambled off, presumably to ponder penises, Fern dialled Adam's number. The God that Nora was so chummy with presumably accepted her new hobby; He was more easy-going than Nora made out. 'Adam, hi, do you have a minute?' Fern started all their phone conversations this way, as if she was intruding.

'Sure.'

'About the shed. Your studio.'

'Yes?'

In the background, a shouted 'Who is it?'; Penny marking her territory.

'Only Fern,' said Adam.

Only. 'I was wondering, will you use it again?'

Adam paused. 'That's like saying – well, it's putting me on the spot.'

Fern knew what he meant; *That's like saying, am I ever coming home again*. Was 'home' the right word? It was one of Fern's favourite words.

Adam was puzzled. 'Why now, all of a sudden?'

'We have to face facts. Nora won't be able to tackle the stairs much longer. It was fine when she was a visitor, but now she'll be with us until, well, the end . . .' That was one of Fern's least favourite words. 'The shed could be converted into an annexe. I wouldn't ask if I didn't have to.'

'It makes sense.' Adam sighed. 'I'll get a man in to move my desk and my gear. Penny can find me a studio somewhere local.'

Drumming her fingers, Fern endured a conversation between Adam and Penny she could only half hear, which ended with Adam returning to say, 'Pen's heard of this brilliant warehouse space on Manor Road. Creative. Lively. She'll get me in there.'

'No,' said Fern, far too quickly. 'That place is full of, um, bats. And spiders.'

'Bats?'

'Poisonous bats. Dry rot. It's haunted.' *By my toyboy.*

'Er . . . OK. Maybe not there.'

Feeling odd about evicting Adam – *have I pushed him out of the nest for a second time?* – Fern found herself rooting out the box of letters as they both thrashed out the practicalities of converting the shed. 'Adam, listen to this,' she said impulsively. The letter on the top of the pile was strangely appropriate.

MYSTIC ADAM LOOKS INTO THE FUTURE

I've been studying my tarot cards. I made them myself so I'm not sure how accurate they are. CUE SPOOKY MUSIC. Here is how your future pans out.

* You'll get back with Adam who isn't all that great but is frankly your best bet. He loves you. A lot. More than he could love anybody else.
* Adam will become a famous singer-songwriter. He will ignore the crazed fans who jump on his limo. He will only have eyes (and all other bits) for you.
* You will marry Adam.
* You and Adam will buy a big house.
* You will have a chain of beauty salons called 'Spotz Begone'.
* Babies will happen. Just one, or enough for a football team and no I'm not being sexist, girls play football too. So! Ha! YOU'RE being sexist.
* I will love you forever.
* You will live happily ever after.

'Your tarot cards were right about some of it,' said Fern. 'But 'Spotz Begone'?'

'It's catchy.' Adam's laugh was wistful. 'Listening to that is like meeting your younger self. I was determined to get you back, wasn't I?'

'It worked. Up to a point. The last two prophecies didn't really pan out.'

Adam's voice was quiet; Fern imagined Penny loitering just within earshot, pretending to do something. 'I've never said I don't love you, Fern. You've never said that to me.' He hesitated. 'Or have you?'

'Love didn't seem to be enough,' said Fern.

They were silent until Adam said, 'I'll get back to you about the shed.'

Banging around the house like the ball in a pinball machine, Tallulah finally located Fern out in the recording studio. 'Guess what?' She threw down her school bag.

'You're getting married.' Fern was gathering the last of her daughter's forgotten patients, all now ex-insects, into a black bin bag.

'I'm going to make sure a million more girls have an education.'

'Single-handedly?'

Tallulah looked pityingly at her stupid mother. 'My class is raising money for a charity in Tanzania. They build schools for girls. Just girls. Because girls have a terrible time of it, Mum.'

As Fern tidied and sorted the airless, underused room, Tallulah reeled off the challenges facing her counterparts abroad. 'If they go to school they're less likely to die of AIDS and they can get jobs and they can be independent. Like me. Have we got any Cheese Strings?'

Glad to see Tallulah so animated, Fern asked, 'Who's involved?'

'Oh, Maya and Georgia and Lily and Millie and Bronwyn and Eva and Yasmin and Tess and Lauren.'

The old crowd. So there'd been a thaw in playground relations. Fern breathed a sigh of relief; eight-year-old girls were harder to handle than the EU when it came to policy change. 'How about Carey?'

'It's not her thing.' Tallulah was evasive, turning on the spot, her arms out aeroplane-style.

'Shame.' Fern could have drawn her initials in the dust on Adam's keyboard.

'Why does Carey hate me?' Tallulah still twirled.

'I'm sure she doesn't.' Fern trod carefully; it could be hard to distil complex emotions into a form her daughter could digest.

'Carey should like me. I got in trouble for her.' Tallulah stopped twirling abruptly and staggered. 'I love being dizzy.'

'Me too. Maybe Carey feels guilty because her rash behaviour made so much trouble for you. Do you think Carey's family say "sorry" to each other?'

'No!' laughed Tallulah. 'She gets the blame for everything.'

'She's not used to people being kind to her, doing things for her.' Fern felt for the confused kid living in a home of hard edges, at a loss for how to cope with Tallulah's warmth.

'I miss her. Carey's loads more fun than anyone else.'

'We can't always have what we want, honeybun.' Mums have to lay bare the hard facts. Fern was ready to follow it up with a hug, but Tallulah displayed that incredible resilience all children can call on when they need it.

'Yeah,' she shrugged. 'I want you and Daddy to get back but that won't happen either, so . . .'

The certainty was a punch; the acceptance was another. Fern didn't show she was on the ropes. Glad that Tallie had moved on from mourning, Fern also felt pain for the girl's acceptance of a life she hadn't asked for. 'We both—'

'I *know*, Mum. You both still love me, I know, I know,' said Tallulah. 'So. Cheese Strings?'

Fern wasn't good at knitting or smoking or working out celebrities' ages. It turned out that she was also crap at sexting.

oh god I want you.

She erased that, tutting furiously.

I'm imagining you right now.

That's OK. Fern sent that one, and fanned her face at Hal's (very speedy) reply.

wish U were here. Nakd. What would U do 2 me?

Correct your spelling, for a start. Fern cringed, shrinking down into her armchair, sending frantic glances at the door. This house was full of people, and any of them could walk in to find her in her jaded trackies, getting down and virtually dirty.

I would put your

Nope. She tried again.

First I'd touch my

God no. Growling with annoyance, she rang Hal. 'I can't,' she said as he picked up. 'I'm a rubbish sexter. I give up.'

Hal's laugh was deep and rumbly, like a Tube train slowing in a tunnel beneath her feet. 'It doesn't matter.'

'It does. Everybody sexts these days.' No doubt Penny had a diploma. 'You'll think I'm uptight.'

'How could I think that when yesterday we . . . Look, I'm with a customer right now, but you get my drift, don't you?'

'I do.' Fern was pathetically grateful. Perhaps twenty-first-century adults could carry on a relationship without sexting.

'I'll see you tomorrow night, yeah? Love you.'

Fern drifted to answer the Beauty Room door in a haze. 'Hi Walter,' she said mechanically, seating him at the manicure table. She looked at all her familiar bits and bobs. The base coat, the files, the buffing tool all meant nothing to her.

Love you.

Was it throwaway? Everybody said it. Donna said it to all her friends. But if Hal was in the habit of saying it, why hadn't he said it before? Did Hal, sexy, funny Hal, love Fern, abandoned mother of two?

'I need a right good manicure today, Fern.' Walter spread his hands on the white towel.

'Where are you off to?' roared Fern, back in the room.

'No need to shout, dear.' Walter pointed to one of his sticky-out ears. 'New hearing aid. It's a belter. I can hear a fly cough.'

'Brilliant!' Fern liked this cheeky new Walter; his deafness had alienated him. 'Are you off somewhere special?'

'The cemetery.'

'Oh.' Fern dipped Walter's fingers into a bowl of tepid water.

'It's my fiftieth wedding anniversary today, so I'll take my dear wife some flowers and have a bit of a tidy-up. We had thirty-one of those years together before she went.'

Nineteen years alone, and still observing their wedding date; Walter had depths Fern hadn't guessed at. She recalled the Boite Rouge menu she'd kept from her posh meal with Adam on their anniversary, never suspecting it would be their last.

A pounding on the door made them both jump. Nora, in dark glasses the size of TV screens, said, 'It's your mum, Fern. On the phone. It's urgent.'

Unaccustomed to worrying about her mother – Mum was a self-contained unit who asked for nothing – Fern was frightened. Wiping Walter's fingers, she said, 'Auntie, you remember Walter from Christmas Day? Keep him company, will you?'

'I remember him.' Nora didn't sound impressed.

The kitchen landline was by the fridge. 'Mum? What's happened?'

'You tell me, Fern.'

'No, no, what's up?'

'Nora said you needed to speak to me. You sound frazzled, love.'

'Nora called you?'

'Yes. What's going on?'

'Nothing. I did want to chat.' Fern scoured her brain for a topic. 'How's Dave?' Any other subject felt too complex and, Fern realized, too intimate. *I should want to speak to my own mother about my life.* Bracing herself, Fern said, 'Amelie's doing great. Four months old now, and a little tooth coming through.'

'Aw. Bless. So you think of her as your granddaughter, do you?'

'Don't you?'

The sound of swallowing came over the long distance line. 'If you say so, love.'

'I do, Mum. I do say so.' Amelie hadn't asked to be born. The least they could give her was an unqualified welcome.

'I didn't mean to speak out of turn.'

We relate as if one of us is returning a faulty skirt to Marks and Spencer. Fern spotted a message on the chalkboard in Nora's shaky handwriting.

Invite her over to see Amelie!!!

A long anecdote about Dave's heroic struggle to build a barbecue area had begun. Fern wiped at the board with her sleeve. As she waited for a moment to jump in, Fern wanted to say *I'm happy you're happy, but I need a mum!* Realizing she'd left her client alone for too long, instead she butted in with 'Mum, gotta run.'

Nora wouldn't let Fern hug her, brushed aside the thanks, but she had a wide smile on her face as she barged into the hall table.

'Look at my tummy!'

'Stand sideways so I can see. Oh Layla, you're a proper pregnant lady.'

'I never thought I'd be so pleased about my jeans not fitting.'

'Any sickness? Any wooziness?'

'No, Doc, nothing like that.'

'I lay on the floor whining for the whole of my first trimester with Tallie.'

'I wouldn't mind a bit of sickness. It would feel like there's something really there. That this isn't all a dream.'

'The scans tell you that, you idiot. Your baby's in there, twiddling its thumbs.'

'We almost talked about names the other night. We stopped ourselves. Tempting fate and all that.'

'Fate owes you, Layla.'

'You know that, and I know that, but nobody's told fate.'

'You say *love you* sometimes, don't you, when you end a phone conversation?'

'Yeah. Only with people I love. Like you. Why?'

'Nothing.'

'Fern?'

'Listen, I should shoot off. It's Ollie and Donna's date night and I want to have a shower before they slope off.'

'Give them all a kiss from me. Especially that Amelie.'

'Bye!'

'Bye. Oh, and . . . I like Antoinette for a girl.'

'So do I. I really do. Bye, Layla.'

'Love you.'

Fern shamed Ollie and Donna into keeping up the date night tradition. 'Did you really just say you'd rather have a baked potato than go out?' She was determined that they wouldn't lose their rights to be teenagers at least once a week; as she said to Evka over the family tub of ice cream they were shovelling their way through, 'Sure, they're tired, but they'll perk up when they go out.'

'But Ollie DJs two nights of week.' Evka encroached on Fern's side of the mint choc swirl. 'He is always in club.'

'Donna needs a break. New babies are slave-drivers. Get *off*.' Fern rapped Evka's knuckles with her spoon. 'Keep to your own half.'

A text arrived from Hal. Not exactly a sext, it still made Fern's temperature rise.

An expert in all things filthy, Evka said, 'Ah, that's from *him*. Does he like your new lacy underwears?'

'How do you know about . . . actually, no, don't tell me.'

'I try on, but panties are too big and bra is too small.' Evka looked with sympathy at Fern's chest. '*Much* too small. Do not blush. I approve of lover,' said Evka grandly. 'Do not get serious with him, Fern. No-strings bonking is fun. I should thank beast of boyfriend who did unspeakable thing to me. Before him I was like you and Adam. In coma. Same man every day, same penis every night. Marriage is sex prison, Fern. You escaped.'

'It wasn't marriage.'

'It was same as.'

That was true. 'I felt married. It was a personal marriage, without a priest or a registrar or a horrible sit-down meal with third cousins. Which made it *more* binding, not less.'

'Now you are like me. In charge of self. Queen!'

'It does have its upside.' Fern felt able to confide in Evka about Hal. A little. 'My *friend* makes me happy. He's a good thing to come out of all the mess.'

'You are type to fall for him. Stupid love ruins everything.'

'What's so wrong with love, Evka? It makes the world go round.'

'Not my world.'

Fern didn't dare ask what made Evka's world go round. 'Finding somebody to love is everybody's ambition. Commitment is beautiful, not restricting. It sets you free when you have a rock to rely on, when there's something muscular to make you feel safe.'

'Your rock ran away.'

'Any news from the rock's flat, by the way?'

'Penny has over-the-knee boots at back of wardrobe. PVC.'

'PVC?' Adam had made noises over the years about PVC, but Fern had just laughed. *Imagine the chafing*, she'd said.

'And whip.'

'Jesus.' He'd kept quiet about wanting a whip. *Is Adam the whipper or the whippee?*

'Those rats in Penny's flat stay for long time . . .' Evka checked her make-up in a small mirror. 'I have date. I met him in queue.'

'A queue for what?' Fern was half listening, still assimilating Adam's new toys.

'I did not know. I want to queue like English, so I stand behind him and we snog and we never get to front of queue.'

Fern was still thinking *PVC* . . . when Maz rang the doorbell, minutes after Evka left the house.

'Me again,' he said, with doleful eyes.

'You can't keep doing this, Maz.' Fern shook her head, sad for him and sad for herself, put in this sticky position again.

'Are they here? We could talk right now.'

'It's date night again.' She smiled. 'Are you watching the house?'

He seemed to take her seriously, putting his hand over his heart. 'No, no, I swear. I pass this way every Thursday and I just can't resist.'

'This has to be done properly. For Amelie's sake.'

'The feelings,' he said, as if he hadn't heard her. 'The feelings were unexpected.'

'It's a rush, isn't it?' Fern couldn't help smiling. The young guy in front of her was probably experiencing his first brush with unselfish love. 'Oh, come in, then. Just for a minute or two.'

Checking that Tallie was asleep – Fern didn't want anybody to see what she was doing, which rang an alarm bell, but one faint enough to ignore – Fern brought Amelie downstairs, bundled up in trailing crocheted blankets.

'Hello, little girl.' Maz took her tenderly. 'Do you really think she looks like me?'

It couldn't be denied. 'Something about her brow. And the shape of her eyes.' Fern stood awkwardly, hands together, watching father and child work each other out. She could see that Maz was near tears; she felt like an intruder. Eventually, she said gently, 'Time to get her back to bed, Maz.'

'How about I put her to bed?' Maz was pleading with his whole body.

'I don't know, Maz . . . Sorry. No.' Maz was nudging Fern, inch by inch, to a place she didn't want to be. *It's my fault for opening the door.* 'Donna would hate that.'

'It's not that much to ask. A minute alone with my own flesh and blood. Go on, Fern. Please. I'll be careful. I'll tuck her in. I just want a moment with her.'

It felt shabby, leaning over the baby monitor as Maz cautiously climbed the stairs with his gurgling armful. Penny's overheard monologue had taught her this underhand trick.

There were murmurs, muttered endearments, interspersed with splutters from Amelie, then, 'You're mine,' said Maz, loudly, clearly. 'Got that? I'm your daddy, Amelie. You're mine.'

Fern listened hard, but after that there was only the soft hum of the monitor. She heard a squeak on the stairs and dashed out to see Maz in the hall. He held Amelie out to her. He spoke immediately, as if to stop Fern protesting.

'She won't stop wriggling. Nappy needs changing, probs.'

As Fern wound her arms around Amelie, she was conscious of their proximity to the front door. 'Maz, I can't let you in again. Speak to Donna.'

'We both know what that one'll say.' Maz blew a kiss to the baby and was gone.

Spring had sprung behind Fern's back.

The park was a carpet of daffodils as she and Hal passed it. Hal had relinquished his scarf. Fern's nose wasn't red.

'This is the plan for the evening.' Hal held up a finger. 'One. We drink wine. Two. We eat pasta in that funny restaurant. Three. You kiss me to death.'

'Beats yesterday. I cleared a U-bend.'

'Hardly any U-bend clearing tonight, I promise.' Hal was jaunty, his arm tight around her shoulders as he marched her along. 'Come on, before the wine runs out.'

Luckily there was plenty of wine left. As Hal put down the glasses on their usual corner table he apologized for her house white. 'It looks like a sample. We need to find another boozer.'

'This is fine.'

Hal supped and snaffled a crisp and crunched it and looked around him and pointed at a sweet dog that had just come in, and Fern said, 'I'm sorry, Hal, but I can't do this any more.'

'The pub's not that bad!' Hal laughed a shower of crisp shards.

'Not the pub. You and me. *This*.' Fern pushed her wine away.

Hal stared, a crisp in his hand. 'I don't get it,' he said

eventually. 'Everything's fine, better than fine. I'm not pushing. We're having fun.'

'That's the point. I'm having fun, yes, but it's just fun. I'm not explaining myself very well.' She sighed, crushed by Hal's expression. 'Don't take it personally, please.'

'How else can I take it?' Hal sat back, chin out. 'What's wrong?'

'Me. Nothing's wrong with you.'

'The old "it's not me, it's you".'

'Yes, exactly that. It's true this time. You're lovely, Hal, kind and gorgeous and I can't wait to see you, but when I do see you it's just not *enough*.' Fern pulled her chair closer to his, stricken by the feeling of loss even while she was still trying to shake him off. 'I'm not ready for fun. Not this sort of fun.'

'Everybody's ready for fun.' When Hal grumbled like that, his chin down, he sounded like Ollie.

'I was a partner, a half, for so many years. You were a baby when I got together with Adam. While you were learning how to suck your thumb I was already in a committed relationship. I'm unlearning the habits of a lifetime. It's too much to do that *and* give you what you deserve.'

'Don't make out you're doing me a favour.' Hal was sullen, leaning to one side, avoiding her eye.

'I'm still stumbling about in the ruins of my relationship, Hal.'

'Very poetic.'

Fern bridled. 'Do you want to talk about it or just snipe? This isn't easy.'

'Oh, it isn't easy?' Hal sat forward, all sarcastic

sympathy. 'You poor love. It's ever so easy for me, listening to why I'm not good enough.'

'I'm not saying that.' Fern could practically taste his hurt. 'I need to heal before I embark on something else. If you weren't so lovely I wouldn't have been tempted. I wasn't looking for anything to happen, but there you were.'

'And the rest is pisstory,' said Hal.

'Please be nice, be *you*.'

'This is me,' snarled Hal. 'I'm not a toy you pick up and put down. Some warning might have been nice.'

'Can we stay friends?'

'Of course! I really need somebody to go shoe shopping with! No, Fern, we can't be bloody friends. I don't like you enough to be your friend.' Hal stood so abruptly he tipped over his drink. 'Shit,' he snapped, looking down at his ruined jeans. 'You were right, Fern. I don't have to be with an old woman. I should be with somebody my own age. They might not be such selfish bitches.'

Everybody watched as he stalked out of the pub like a gunfighter. Fern put her face in her hands and wept, and everybody looked away again.

Still in her jacket, Fern sat on the end of her single bed in what had been Ollie's room and gazed at the rocket-ship light fitting. She'd used up all the energy at her disposal acting normal for Nora, who'd asked suspiciously, 'You're back early. Everything all right?'

A bath, she thought. A long bath, and a good cry. The

urge to call Hal, to shout 'Gotcha!' was strong. She resisted it, just as she resisted the urge to check her phone for texts. It was the right decision. It was for the best. She'd mishandled it spectacularly, but there you go.

The anger had surprised her. Hal's equilibrium was hard to dent. Perhaps he wasn't used to being 'let go'. *He's a golden boy.* But no longer *her* golden boy.

Outside, voices were raised. 'Shut up, Ollie,' Donna was saying. She stormed in, displaying her iPhone like a warrant card. 'Can you explain this, please?' she said, eyes sparking.

Focusing, Fern saw a Facebook page. 'me'n'my lil darlin' was the caption beneath a selfie of Maz and Amelie, shot by the baby's cot. Fern's mouth twitched; she felt like a pinned butterfly. Something gave her the feeling that Donna was about to pull off her wings.

'Did you let this joker in? When we were out at that stupid club?'

'Maz is so sad, Donna.'

'Oh my days,' howled Donna, throwing back her head. 'Are you for real? Maz is a player. He's worming his way in. He wants Amelie for himself.'

'That would never happen.' Fern tried to bring down the temperature.

'Yeah? Well, if he can get into *my own bedroom*, who knows what he can do?' Donna was shaking; Fern's second casualty of the day.

Perhaps, if I do my best, I can infuriate Tallie as well before I turn in. 'Donna, it was wrong and I'm sorry.'

'Bit late for sorries!' Donna shook off Ollie's restraining hand.

'What can I do but promise it won't happen again?'

'She's my baby.' Donna was crying now, her anger dissolving into tears as anger so often does. She beat her chest. 'Mine!'

'Actually, she's Maz's too.' Fern had to say it; to stay schtum would be to do her sort-of daughter-in-law a disservice. 'At some point you have to face that.'

'His name's not on the birth certificate, Fern. He has no rights.'

Fern was baffled. 'Whose name is on it?'

'His.' Donna gestured at Ollie, lurking by the door, wearing the *who, me?* expression of men when their womenfolk fight. 'Ollie's the father. End of.' She pushed past her boyfriend and disappeared.

'That's not fair, Oliver.' Fern wearily peeled off her jacket. Even a bath felt like too much effort now; she needed to be in bed. 'You can't lie to Amelie about something so fundamental.'

'I wasn't thinking straight. It's done now.'

'Sorry, love. Not good enough.' Fern had never demanded high exam grades or virtuoso piano playing, but she expected decency from both her kids. 'I'm truly sorry about Maz. I was soft. I told him to go through the proper channels, but he was so moved by seeing Amelie I let him hold her.'

'Mum, you do so much for us.' This had the air of a prepared speech. 'But back off, please. Let us do it our way.' Ollie ran his fingers through his towering hair. 'Donna makes out Maz is the big bad wolf, but he's only a cocky sod. She feels guilty. About her fling. So she, um, what's that word you use?'

'Projects?'

'Yeah. She projects so he's the enemy.'

'But I should back off.' Fern felt small.

'Yeah.' Ollie looked as if he was putting a sickly old guinea pig to sleep. 'Just a bit,' he said.

Row A had been in their seats for what felt like hours. Because it *was* hours. Fern hadn't realized how long it took to record half an hour of television comedy. She'd been cowed by the size of the studio, by the banks of lights overhead, by the purposeful crew members beetling about and barking into headmikes.

'Front row?' Tallulah had been impressed, but now their prized seats were a penance. So close to the performers, they felt duty bound not to fidget or yawn. Laughing like drains at every joke, even when they heard it for the eighth time, clapping until their hands were raw, they'd begun to wilt.

The whole clan was assembled, except for the oldest and the youngest. Nora was babysitting; today was a good day, with no eye trouble, no slurring, no knocking over vases.

At the end of the row, Penny laughed harder than anybody else. She sounded as if she had a chicken down her bra. Squeezing Adam's hand excitedly, as if they were tweenies at a Justin Bieber concert, Penny was wringing every ounce of excitement out of the evening.

Seeing the actors this close was a buzz. Watching them

between takes, Fern and Tallulah swapped notes on who was most like their character. The flighty teenaged girl was a dreary mope when the camera wasn't on her, and the grumpy granddad was a sweetheart. Lincoln Speed was touched with gold dust, stealing every scene. He looked just like he did on the screen, bursting with sex appeal despite his somewhat battered face. Fern could discern some subtle scalpel work, but she turned to goo along with every other female in the studio when his eyes crinkled and he threw out some gag in his cheese-grater voice.

He's won me over! Lincoln Speed was a true star; his charisma was so heady, it eclipsed his many and varied failings. Tonight he held the evening together, turned the air into wine, won over every doubter.

If it wasn't for Lincoln and his leather trousers – Fern couldn't think of anybody else who could carry them off over forty – Fern would have drifted away altogether. The lumber in the attic of her mind clamoured for attention.

A week since she'd performed the Grand Slam and pissed off three people dear to her. Hal hadn't been in touch; not so much as a late-night drunken insult/endearment. Ollie kept his distance. Donna stood guard over Amelie as if Fern was a stalker, cold-shouldering her out of all the little tasks Fern had used to do, had loved doing.

The clumsy set piece in the pub spooled endlessly in her head. *It came out wrong.* She should have started by telling Hal how much he meant to her, the confidence he'd given her at a low point in her life, what an incredible person he was. None of that got said. His surly response made her forget the script.

Fern had expected Hal to be a little hurt, but philosophical. She'd expected surprise, then dismay, then, perhaps, maybe, a little resistance. She'd thought he'd fight for them, give her reasons why they should stick together.

I would have stood my ground. Fern didn't doubt the common sense of her decision. *That doesn't stop me feeling as if I've lost something precious.* She remembered the time she'd lost her dad's signet ring on holiday. *It's irreplaceable*, she'd sniffled; so was Hal.

The insult – 'old woman' – had amazed her. With hindsight, she should have known that the gentlest of people lash out when they're upset. Hal wasn't perfect. He was just another human with needs of his own, and she'd humiliated him.

Her failure to exit gracefully, to treat Hal with respect, was a wound that refreshed itself every day.

'Quiet, please.'

The lighting rig blazed onto the New York apartment just feet from Fern. Lincoln Speed sprawled on a sofa, hands behind his head, and drawled his catchphrase:

'What ya gonna do about it?'

Fern obediently whooped along with everybody else. She turned, catching Donna's eye, and Donna stopped mid-whoop.

The glare again. If Donna's eyes were lasers, Fern would be as full of holes as a Swiss cheese. Fern had always admired Donna's righteous fury, smiling to herself at the way the girl kept her son in check. Being on the receiving end was different; she sympathized with Ollie now, and understood why he sometimes hid in the conservatory. *I might join him there.*

Allowed out for a fifteen-minute break, the audience – Fern favoured the term 'hostages' – milled about the foyer.

'So,' said Adam to Fern, bouncing on his heels as if they were vague associates meeting at a cheese and wine do.

'So,' said Fern. She remembered something. 'Tallie! Come here and tell Daddy about Carey.'

Listening to his daughter spill her woes, Adam's brows knitted.

The Botox must have worn off, thought Fern, taking in his excruciatingly tight trousers and ankle boots so pointy they could have filleted a salmon.

'You know the magic cure for this?' Adam waited for Tallulah to answer.

'Does it involve hitting?' she said hopefully.

Sometimes Fern worried about Tallie.

'No,' said Adam patiently. 'It involves talking. Instead of lying in your bed going over and over it in your mind, *ask* Carey why she ignores you.'

'She'll run away,' said Tallulah. 'You don't know what it's like, Daddy. She'll push me. Everyone will see.'

'Keep asking. People behave badly when they don't know what to do with their emotions. If you tell her you forgive her, she'll open up.'

'I don't know if I do forgive her.' Tallulah's lower lip stuck out. 'She's being really mean.'

'Do you miss her? Do you want her back? Do you believe she could be a good friend to you?'

'Yeah.'

'Then talk to her, sweetie. Talking always helps.'

Does it? You and I talked ourselves out of a relationship, thought Fern. It was good advice, all the same. Glad that their rickety family set-up still worked, Fern used the window of two minutes or so before Penny returned from the vending machine she was currently kicking into submission to thank Adam. 'You've taken a weight off Tallie's shoulders.'

'She's a resilient kid. She can handle this.'

'I guess if she can handle a separation, she can deal with a classmate.'

'Perhaps it's a helpful lesson. Ironically, she might benefit from discovering early on that her parents are just fallible people who make mistakes like everybody else.'

'Mistakes?' Missing a layer of skin this evening, Fern was easily singed. 'We were a mistake, were we?' She said it lightly, but it didn't land that way.

'There you go again. Twisting things. It was just a turn of phrase.'

'OK, keep your hair plugs on.'

Adam touched the back of his head. 'You noticed?'

'Of course I noticed.' Fern had been fond of Adam's small bald patch. Most mornings it had been the only part of him visible above the duvet. On Valentine's Day she liked to draw a heart on it.

'Penny's idea,' said Adam, his eyes cast down. 'Go ahead. Laugh.'

'Why would I laugh?' Fern needed closeness tonight, not more acrimony.

A bell rang. Penny cantered over. 'Back to the studio! Chop chop!'

Fern remembered the eulogy she'd recited to Evka about long relationships, and added a postscript: *Once it's over, you'll find you can't even chat any more without suddenly taking a detour into brambles.*

Time passed. Fern wasn't sure how much. She felt as if she'd been born in that uncomfortable studio seat and might well die there. Finally, the floor manager shouted, 'That's a wrap, folks!' and led the cast in a round of applause for the audience.

'Thank the sweet Lord baby Jesus,' muttered Adam, massaging his calf.

A tremor of anticipation went round the room as Lincoln Speed strode to the front and said, 'Hi London!'

'Hi Lincoln!' They were in the palm of his hand.

'We have a special guest tonight, a Londoner, one of your own.'

Fern and Tallulah locked eyes, their mouths open.

'Daddy!' whispered Tallulah.

'He wrote the song you hear at the top of each episode. He's a huge part of *Roomies*' success and he's my good friend. Adam, dude, take a bow.'

Penny reacted as if this was the single most exciting thing that had happened to any *homo sapiens*, ever. 'Up! Up!' she cried, like a stage mother encouraging a tap-dancing tot.

Rising awkwardly, Adam turned and waved to the crowd, who were adoring him, just like Lincoln had told them to.

'Lookee here,' said Lincoln, as a techie scuttled in to hand him a guitar. 'If only we knew somebody who could play this. Come on, Adam! Get up here, you old dog!'

The front row all turned to one another, sick with excitement, pulling faces. Adam jogged up to Lincoln and was smothered in a manly hug. Everything Lincoln did was exaggerated, as if he was ten per cent more real than everybody else.

'Take it away, bro!' Lincoln kissed a startled Adam. Nobody would guess they'd never met before that moment.

Sometimes stuff just seems to get you down
Feelin' like there's no one else around

Accompanied only by Adam's guitar, the song was sweet, melodic, with none of the bombast of the telly version.

How long is it since I heard Adam sing? He'd sung all the time when they first moved to Homestead House. His voice was delicate, full of feeling. Around Fern people turned to one another, held hands. In her peripheral vision she saw Penny dab her eyes.

You wish you could reach out and find a friend
Who'll be here today, tomorrow, until the bitter end

This performance was nothing like the camp excesses of Kinky Mimi. Caught up in his moment, Adam sang the song as if the words had just occurred to him. He was in his element. For the three minutes that the song lasted, Fern wasn't his ex; she was a fan. *Did I ever appreciate how much his music meant to him?* She couldn't, hand on heart, answer 'Yes.'

> *Your mates are here to stay*
> *And your life's a holiday*
> *With Roomies!*

Wild applause broke out. Exhausted hands found the energy to clap some more.

'That's my daddy!' shouted Tallie, to general 'Aww!'s.

But that's not my Adam. The man on stage, sexily thin and styled to perfection, was a new Adam, possibly an improved one. *Certainly a happier one.* Fern wanted to weep. Not to cry, not to blub, but to lie down and weep until this realization lost its poison.

The audience stood and shook itself, like Boudi getting up from a long snooze by the fire. As Fern switched her phone back on to check on Nora, a text bounced onto the screen.

'Guys,' said Adam, eyes bright, giving into their hugs and congratulations. 'Lincoln's asked us all to the after-party!'

'Yay!' Donna was wired.

'What ya gonna do about it!' hollered Ollie, who only pretended to be unimpressed by celebrity.

'I can't.' Fern tucked her phone away. 'See you at home, kids. Adam, can you—'

'You don't have to ask me to drop my own children home.' Obviously Adam was still smarting from their snappy exchange.

Darting away before anybody could protest, Fern

pushed through the crowds and went out into the darkness, obeying the text.

At night the park was different. The trees stood about like muggers, and each rustle in the bushes made Fern jump. With her way lit only by the moon, she had trouble keeping to the path. Her heels kept encountering squishy grass, unbalancing her.

'Hal?' she called. The park was *their* place, the only possible venue for . . . *what is this we're doing?* Fern wasn't sure. She'd merely answered his summons. The thought of touching him again was exciting. *But I mustn't backtrack.* She repeated that to herself as she saw a dark figure rise at the bandstand. It was either Hal or a serial killer; either way, she sped up to meet him.

'Hi.' It wasn't a serial killer. Hal's hands were in his pockets, his mouth a thin line. He sat back down on a bench placed awkwardly in the middle of the bandstand, an ornate Edwardian structure now peeling and covered with graffiti.

'Lori is a slag,' read Fern, taking a seat beside him. 'Nice to know.'

Hal didn't laugh. 'I need to apologize.'

'You don't,' began Fern, but Hal shushed her.

'Let me say it. You're not a selfish bitch. And you're not old. You're you, you're just you, not old, not young, just Fern. I was way out of order.'

This wasn't joyous or light; Fern's excitement crawled

into a corner and died. 'Are you here to fight for us?' she asked.

'No.'

'OK.' Fern nodded. Relieved, in a way, that life wasn't giving her the option to backtrack, she was also disappointed. Romantic ideals are immune to logic.

'You were right, Fern. There's no future for us, and we're both people who like a future. The ingredients are there. I fancy you. I like you. I like you a lot,' he said, as if dancing around that other L-word. 'I'll always remember you, Fern.'

'Me too. You, I mean. It goes without saying I'll remember myself.' *Shut up.* Fern tended to over-talk at moments like these. She imagined herself as a wrinkled old dear in Tallulah's spare room, reliving her glory days when she was Hal's Older Woman.

'The thing I most want to do at this moment is kiss you.'

'You won't, though, will you?'

'No.' Hal clasped his hands together and looked down at them.

It would have been wonderful if Hal had fought for her. If he'd beat his chest like a silverback gorilla and taken her there and then in the bandstand. But that was fantasy, and this was real life. When there's much at stake, common sense trumps romance. Yet another unpalatable factoid women pick up by their forties. 'Thank you, Hal. For waking me up. And for letting me go.' Fern thought of his hands on her, and her eyes fluttered shut. 'You made me feel whole and female at a time when I felt out of step and finished.'

Hal stood up suddenly. 'This is horrible. I'm going, Fern.'

He did just that. Fern stayed on the bench, idly looking

up into the rafters of the bandstand. With her head in that position, the tears rolled right back into her eyes, as if they'd never been shed. She wanted to shout that she'd miss him; she wanted to know if he would miss her. She didn't allow herself either indulgence.

An uninvited thought muscled in.

Donna and Ollie don't always have their date night on Thursdays.

Tearing through the dark, Fern punched redial over and over, only to hear her own voice say maddeningly, 'Hi! You're through to Fern and Adam.' She imagined Nora, collapsed, lifeless. She imagined Amelie in a passenger seat, being driven God knows where.

Explosive with adrenalin, Fern took off her shoes to sprint the last couple of streets. Letting herself in, she yelled, 'Nora!'

'Yes, dear?' Nora emerged, small, fat, Mrs Tiggywinkle-like, from the sitting room. 'Did you have a nice time?'

'Oh. God.' Fern slumped and suddenly she felt where the pavement had damaged her feet. 'I thought Maz would be here. He *is* watching the house, Nora. He lied, you see, about passing by each Thursday because Donna and Ollie don't only go out on Thursdays, so—'

'Calm down, Fern.' Nora unwrapped a Fisherman's Friend. 'I've locked Maz in the utility room.'

That's when Fern heard the thumping. And a weedy 'Let me out!'

'Tea?' asked Nora, making for the kettle as the utility room door juddered.

'This is false imprisonment!' whined Maz through two inches of wood.

'How long has he been in there?' Fern took Nora by the shoulders.

'An hour or so.' Nora stroked Binkie, who was oiling about her legs. 'He's been ever so nice and quiet. Hearing your voice set him off again.'

'Nora, shouldn't we let him out?'

'I think *not*. That boy has some apologizing to do. He turns up, all big eyes, saying you told him he could see Amelie any time.' Nora opened a new packet of cat treats as Maz hollered and thumped. 'I give him one of me looks. I was suspicious, see, 'cos you'd only just driven off. All a little too coincidental for my liking.'

'He's been watching the house. That's how he knows when Ollie and Donna are out.'

'I says to him, I says, I'm not Fern. You run along, sonny Jim. Well, he didn't like that.' Nora groaned as she bent to fill Binkie's dish. 'Fancies himself a charmer. Kept this big smile on his face the whole time.'

Fern remembered the doe eyes and the hand on his heart. 'I can imagine.'

'He talks and talks, thinking he's winning me round. All about *Oh, I love Donna* and *Donna used me to have a baby* and how he wants to be a proper father, and all this flim-flam. I says to him, your smile doesn't reach your eyes, young man. That's when he pushes me out of the way!'

Fern had brought this on her infirm aunt. 'Did you fall?'

'I did not.' Nora seemed insulted. 'I grabbed the little sod's arm as he pushed past me. We wrestled for a bit.'

Not exactly a fair fight. 'Are you hurt?'

'Did me the world of good. Made a nice change from doctors prodding me and shaking their heads. There's life in the old girl yet!'

Fern could only agree.

'So, anyway, he rushes up the stairs.'

Fern thought of Amelie, soft and vulnerable in her cot, and put her hands to her face.

'But I think quick. I shout, "Tyson, quick! Put the baby in the utility room!"'

'Who the hell's Tyson?'

'Tyson doesn't exist, Fern,' said Nora patiently. 'But Maz isn't to know that, is he? Tyson's a scary name. Maz comes running down and crosses the kitchen in two strides, looking around for the utility room. In he goes and bang!' Nora clapped her hands. 'I slam the door and lock him in. I wanted to ring you, but of course I'd left the phone in there when I was getting a choc-ice from the freezer.'

Fern drew a veil over Nora's doctor's-orders low-fat diet. 'You, Auntie Nora, are a heroine.'

Voices in the hall and feet-stamping and mickey being taken announced the arrival of everybody else, high on the after-show party.

'Mum!' Tallulah was first in, bursting with news. 'It was fabulous! There were little umbrellas in the drinks! Lincoln Speed fell over! He smelled of tramps!' The thumping redoubled. 'Who's in there? Is it a werewolf?'

'It's Maz.' Fern put up her hands as the outrage started. 'Listen! We have to decide what to do with him.'

'He was going to take Amelie,' said Nora, never slow to throw petrol on a fire.

'We don't know that,' said Fern.

'Who's Maz?' said Penny.

'Maz?' Donna was still taking it in. She turned and dashed upstairs to see her daughter. 'This is all your fault, Fern!' she yelled. 'You encouraged that bastard.'

'Now, Donna,' began Adam, but Fern put a restraining hand on his arm.

'Let her. She's right.' Fern pointed her thumb at the door. 'Police?'

'Let me at him,' said Ollie, face screwed up with fury.

Fern knew her son was a lover, not a fighter. 'We won't fix this with fists, darling.'

'Daddy said you fix things with talking,' said Tallulah. 'Can we get him out quickly? The freezer's in there, and I want Viennetta.'

'The kid's right,' said Fern. 'Donna won't like it but if we're going to resolve this, we need to talk. Maz is obviously an arrogant so-and-so who's not used to hearing "no", but if he and Donna can behave like adults they can lay down some ground rules.' She turned to Ollie, pulled him to her. 'The first rule is that he respects *you*, as the man who's bringing up Amelie. As Amelie's daddy.'

Ollie nodded, his face tight with emotion.

Promises were made on both sides, through the door, and Maz emerged. 'I couldn't find the light switch,' he said gruffly, looking shaken, as Tallulah barged past to get at the Viennetta.

Aware he had nowhere to hide, Maz took Adam's lecture

meekly. Adam was grave but measured; Penny looked up at him adoringly the whole time, like a First Lady staring up at the President of the United States. 'No turning up unannounced,' he ended. 'Agreed?'

'Agreed.'

Tallulah leaned against her dad and trained sad eyes on Maz. 'You can't help being a man, but try to be a nice man.'

Donna refused to come down. Fern could imagine the atmosphere upstairs. She walked Maz to the gate and asked him, in a low tone, 'Would you have taken Amelie, Maz?'

He didn't reply, just looked at her for a long time with those ladykiller eyes. 'If I had,' he said eventually, 'it would have been the biggest mistake of my life.'

'Show's over.' Fern shooed out the mob in the kitchen. 'Ollster, go up and see to your little family. Tell Donna I'm sorry, and she can yell at me all she likes in the morning.' Fern sounded jaunty but inside she churned with regret, hoping against hope that her intimacy with Donna wasn't ruptured for good. 'You, young lady. Bed.' Tallulah made a disgusted noise. 'And you too, not-so-young lady.' She smiled at Nora. 'We have so much to thank you for. You cleared up my mess tonight, Auntie, and you saved little Amelie from a foolish boy.'

'I'm not quite ready for bed,' said Nora.

'Your energy levels—' began Fern, nurse-like.

'Twenty, nineteen, eighteen, seventeen . . .' Nora's counting was interrupted when a voice at the kitchen door made them all turn. 'Are we going to finish our game of Scrabble, Nora love?' asked Walter.

'Walter,' said Fern stupidly. She turned to Nora. 'Nora.'

'Yes, they're our names,' said Nora, stomping haughtily by.

'But . . .' said Adam, who, like Fern, had noticed that although Walter was immaculately turned out as usual, he was also a little tossed. Tie askew. Top button undone. Dear God – lipstick on his papery white cheek.

Ollie had the decency to wait until the sitting room door had closed before gagging. 'Old people. Doing it. Gah!'

'I'm sure they're not doing it,' said Fern, putting her hands over Tallulah's ears. 'Maybe a bit of kissing.'

'That's bad enough.' Ollie was still young enough to believe that love had an age limit.

'I hope she's on the pill,' said Adam, and Fern thwacked him, forgetting they'd fallen out earlier.

'Ooh, careful,' said Penny. 'He bruises like a peach.'

'This time I mean it,' said Fern sternly to Tallulah. 'Bed.'

'I want to cuddle Amelie.'

'She's asleep.'

'No. She's there.'

Donna had stolen down in novelty slippers. 'Amelie won't settle,' she said, holding out the baby. 'Here, Fern. You're the only one who can get her to sleep when she's like this.' She smiled. 'She needs her grandma.'

'Get in,' said Nora, turning back the covers.

Fern clambered in beside her, enjoying the old-lady smell of talc and eau de toilette. 'This is cosy.' She remembered how she used to peer in, afraid of the battleaxe in the bed.

A tray balanced on the hillocks of the duvet. The two women munched buttered toast thoughtfully. The loft was tranquil, its angled ceiling throwing soft shadows in the lamplight. Fern considered confiding in Nora about Hal, but thought better of it. A leopard couldn't change every one of its spots and she couldn't bear to be preached at. She inched closer to Nora, wondering which shops still sold the winceyette monstrosity her aunt was wearing and realizing that the mum-shaped hole in her life was partly filled by this odd, endearing woman.

'He's the one, you know,' said Nora, brushing crumbs off the covers. 'Walter. He's the one for me.'

CHAPTER ELEVEN

May: Fromage

French hospitals smell much the same as English hospitals: disinfectant, cabbage. Moreover, Fern felt much the same in the small Hôpital Saint Honoré as she felt in English hospitals. Worried. Helpless. Impatient to see a doctor, fearful of what he might say.

Plus he'll be saying it in French. Her grasp of the language didn't extend beyond asking where the station was.

Looking down at her feet, Fern was surprised to see the decrepit trainers she kept for around the house. Tucking them under her, she fidgeted on the chair. When Luc had answered Fern's daily Skype call, telling her he'd just come home to a scrawled note from Layla to say she'd dialled 15 and called an ambulance, Fern reacted like a cat reacts to a bucket of water. She'd jumped a foot in the air and booked an air ticket online; cats, obviously, leave out the second part.

I let Layla down before. Fern had learned her lesson. Layla now lived under a microscope of love. As she riffled through flimsy gossip magazines in the waiting room, probably picking up thousands of French germs on her nervous fingers, Fern dredged up all she knew about pre-eclampsia.

Not good on detail, she could remember only lurid headlines. Bed rest until birth! Possible premature birth!

A mumble of voices in the fluorescent-lit corridor, and there was Layla, being wheeled along by an orderly. Stately in her wheelchair, she was like a pregnant queen, both hands clasped over her stomach.

The sight of the much-talked-about bump moved Fern to tears, but she wiped them away and jumped up as the orderly spoke in French and left his patient there.

'Is it pre-eclampsia?' No need for a hello; with old friends, the nitty-gritty is got down to immediately.

'No.' Layla fluttered her eyelids, as if irritated with herself. 'Just high blood pressure. I felt faint. I panicked.'

'So no bed rest?' Fern knew that bed rest sounds lovely, just what every working mother would prescribe for herself, but in reality it was lying on your back for weeks, even months. The allure of endless *Judge Judy*s would soon wear off. 'Phew.'

'I can't believe you're here.' Layla was ashen, her face gaunt for somebody in their fifth month of pregnancy. 'You nutter.'

'What's in the envelope?' Fern gestured to the large, stiff brown envelope on what was left of Layla's lap.

'Ah, yeah.' Layla swallowed and tapped the envelope. 'This is my eighteen-week scan.' Her voice was stretched wafer-thin. 'It's not good, Fern.'

'How not good?' Fern's grammar fell out of her brain. 'Not good how?'

'The image shows a possible problem with the nose bone. It's not developing like it should.'

'Oh.' Fern absorbed this. 'But a nose . . .' she said, 'that's not so bad, is it? They can do amazing surgery now.'

'That's not the point,' said Layla, closing her eyes. 'A lack of nose bone can signify serious problems.'

'Are they sure?' Fern spoke low and soft in the harshly lit room.

'No. The baby's in an awkward position. Not cooperating.'

'Wonder where it gets that from?' Fern was kneeling now, looking up at Layla's face, which drooped like a flower after rain.

'How very dare you,' said Layla gamely, trying not to cry. 'Unfortunately, the pregnancy's too far along for a nuchal fold test.'

'Is that the one that measures the fluid at the base of the baby's neck?' Fern remembered the tense sojourn waiting for Tallie's nuchal fold results. There'd been talk of 'possible abnormalities' which had been forgotten with sprightly relief the moment they were ruled out.

'Instead they've offered me something called a quadruple blood test. That doesn't rule out or confirm the problem, just calculates the risk.' Layla sighed. 'As you can probably tell, I'm an expert at this stuff by now.'

'So there's no way of knowing for sure?'

'Yes. An amniocentesis. They offer that if the blood test gives you a high-risk outcome.'

'Right, right.' Fern absorbed this unwanted information. 'Let's hope it doesn't come to that, eh?'

'They gave me a stack of leaflets to take away.' Layla paraphrased starchily: 'Mothers must be aware that there's a risk of the baby miscarrying.' Layla ended the sentence on a dry sob, looking down at her body. 'Not *the* baby,' she said, her mouth turned down. '*My* baby, Fern.'

'I know, I know.' There didn't seem to be any words available to Fern. 'I know, Layla.'

Luc appeared, his dark features set. '*Mon trésor*, Layla, *mon ange*.' He bent and took one of her hands, kissing it passionately, as if it was all that kept him alive. Fern looked away, feeling like an intruder, but Layla held on tight to her with her other hand.

'Oh, Luc,' said Layla, and all pretence at self-possession disappeared. She was talking and sobbing and drumming her heels on the wheelchair footrests. 'I don't want these tests. I won't let them put a needle near my baby. Don't let them, Luc.'

Full of sadness, Luc managed to be firm. 'We need to be prepared,' he said.

'Why?' Layla's hair had escaped its elastic band and was floating around her head in wild, coiled curls. 'We made a baby at last. It's growing inside me. I don't want to know if something's wrong.'

'But I do, Layla.' Luc was sad as he pressed his point.

'They mentioned termination.' Layla's voice rose to a screech.

'No such thing will happen.' Luc shook his head. 'This is our child and we'll look after it and love it, him or her, but we should do that the best we can. We must be strong for the child. If we're prepared it will be easier. We owe that to *le bébé*, non?'

This was love in action. Fern felt privileged to be so close to the white heat of it. Love takes on the big topics, and renders them down into bite-sized pieces.

Eventually, Layla said 'OK,' and let out a huge breath of air as if expelling something.

They all said nothing for a long while as the hospital bustled around them.

The traveller next to Fern on the hard plastic airport bench was scrolling through gossip sites. Fern envied her state of mind; how lovely it would be to flit across silly stories of reality stars' wardrobe malfunctions. Fern's mind was alive with statistics and facts and fear.

The colourful screen paused for a second before moving on, but not before Fern had recognized the distinctive foxy features of Lincoln Speed.

What's he done now? Fern knew that Adam lived in fear of Lincoln endangering *Roomies'* success by falling off the wagon, as the star had done so many times before. Hell, he not only fell off the wagon, Lincoln usually set fire to the wagon beforehand.

Accessing the gossip portal on her iPhone, Fern found the piece. There was Lincoln Speed, his slash of a mouth smug as he posed in the midst of a gaggle of schoolgirls. His leather jacket, bristling with zips and flaps, was out of place among the navy blazers and ponytails. The girls' uniforms looked very like Tallie's uniform. *Hang on!* It *was* Tallie's uniform. *And that's Tallie!*

Blushing, thrilled, Tallie was in the crook of Lincoln Speed's arm as her schoolmates crowded around, fit to burst at being so close to a real live celebrity.

> St Garvan's School for Girls in Kingston-upon-Thames had a very special visitor today. Superstar bad boy Lincoln Speed (49) dropped by to say howdy. A source close to the star tells us that Lincoln is a family friend of lucky pupil Tallulah Carlile (8).
>
> The charismatic soft-hearted playboy chatted with the girls and signed autographs before school head Sister Mary Augustus remonstrated with him for smoking on school property and asked him to moderate his language.
>
> As the heart-throb was driven away in a blacked-out limo, the girls shouted, 'We love you, Lincoln!'

The high street looked very English after Fern's twenty-four hours in France. It was a relief to readily comprehend signs and posters, even if they were only offering her ten sunbed sessions for the price of eight, or telling her not to leave donations outside the charity shop overnight. She'd left Layla and Luc promising she'd stay positive; Fern tried to stay positive that Layla and Luc would stay positive, but that was proving a big ask.

The guy in the estate agent's, his blingy suit making him look even younger than he was, half rose as Fern entered. His expression clearly said *I'm supposed to be on my tea break*, but he managed to say, with professional good will, 'How can I help you?'

Fern took in the pictures of house fronts all around the walls, their prices and dimensions underlined, as if they were hopefuls who'd joined a property dating agency. 'Actually . . . you can't help me,' she said, and turned around.

I mustn't interfere. I must not interfere.

Stepping out into the street, Fern dodged back into the estate agent's, crouching a little as she peered out of the window over a rack of property brochures.

Across the road, in overalls, Hal ate a Twix and stared in at a chemist's window.

Hal! was Fern's first electric thought. Then, *When did he become so interested in multivitamins?*

'Did you want to enquire about a house?'

The estate agent man-child sounded sarky as Fern scuttled to the other window to keep track of Hal. 'No, um, I just . . .' she said.

Hal stopped to sling a coin in a cup, bending to share a word with the lady begging by the Pound Store. Fern studied him. Hal didn't look happy or unhappy. He looked calm, a little bored; he looked like himself. Fern was gripped with envy, an unusual emotion for her. She generally took care not to compare her inside with other people's outsides. Hal's ease, his obvious peace of mind, shook her.

Such a prize, such a beauty, *yet I kept him in the shadows*. Hal had accepted the secrecy without a murmur. He'd been a gent. Fern, however, was only now able to face the real reason for the secrecy. *I didn't want to scupper any tiny chance I had of getting back with Adam.* Hal deserved more than keeping somebody's seat warm.

'Thank you, bye,' gabbled Fern, darting out of the shop, watching Hal's retreating back. She wanted to run up to him, wanted to kiss him. *Do I still have that right?*

The answer to that could only be 'no', so Fern turned sharply on her heel, slapping straight into a man who turned out to be Adam.

'I wasn't doing anything,' said Fern compulsively.

'OK,' said Adam, puzzled. He took her arm. 'Here. Come and help me choose a book.' He steered her into the independent bookshop that served excellent coffee and displayed handwritten staff reviews. It was sunny but cool in there, and Fern drifted towards the 'just published' table as Adam gravitated to the thriller section. A gentle man, he nonetheless loved a paperback with a bloodied knife on the cover. As if reading her mind, Adam held up a book called *Death is my Friend*, featuring a severed hand lying in the snow.

Fern held up a ghosted autobiography of somebody who'd been kicked off *Hollyoaks* for being drunk on set. They both giggled.

There'd been another sea change; the receding tide had taken with it the recent animosity. There were no snipes, jibes, sudden huffs. Fern and her ex were cordial, chummy even. Back in harness, they did their best for their extended family. Both had modified their behaviour: Adam no longer chucked money at the children or undermined Fern; Fern no longer misconstrued every second word Adam said.

The agreement not to discuss Penny was unspoken. Fern heeded the old saying; she couldn't find anything nice to say, so she said nothing at all. In his turn, Adam was sensitive about family gatherings, only bringing Penny now and then. She never turned up unannounced any more; words had evidently been had.

Working in well-oiled harmony, Fern and Adam were excellent co-parents. She was proud of this and saw it as a real achievement. Sidling over to the thriller section, Fern brought him up to date on the studio's refurbishment to granny/mad aunt annexe. 'The little bathroom's just been tiled. The oven for the kitchenette arrives tomorrow.' Money truly did talk when it came to building work; it said 'hurry up'. The job would be done and dusted in a matter of days. 'Nora will have somewhere to entertain Walter.'

'That's still going strong?' said Adam, amused, adding a Patricia Cornwell to his pile.

'Auntie's resigned from her dating sites. Three weeks in and everything's peachy. They're off to his wife's grave this afternoon.'

'And I thought *I* knew how to show a girl a good time.'

'Where'll you get the time to read all those?' Fern only ever snatched a few pages of her current book at bedtime. It was always the same few pages; she fell asleep and couldn't remember what she'd read. At this rate, she'd finish it just in time for her telegram from the Queen.

'I've got all the time in the world.' Adam coughed, as if making an important statement. 'Kinky Mimi is no more.' When he saw Fern's face go very stupid, he clarified, 'The band's broken up. Again.'

'Aw, no. Why?'

'It's been on the cards for a while. Keith's heart was never in it, and now that he's got gout . . .'

'I thought only Tudor monarchs got gout?'

'So did I. With that, and Lemmy transitioning to a woman, there didn't seem much point carrying on.'

Fern did her *scuse me?* face. Lemmy as a woman was a worse thought than, well, Lemmy as a man. 'Blimey.'

'Blimey indeed. So I'm at a bit of a loose end. Might nip over to L.A. for the *Roomies* live episode.'

'Nip over? Get you,' smiled Fern. 'That'll be a blast. Lincoln Speed – you know, your bestie – is a hell of a risk for a live episode, don't you think? He's bound to swear or something. Be prepared for Tallie to beg to come with you.'

'It's term time,' said Adam, no longer the flash, spoiling daddy. 'I'll make it up to her. Here, let me get that for you.' He took a cookery book out of her hands as they joined the queue for the till. 'Fondue?' he smiled. 'Bit Seventies, isn't it?'

'It's a way of getting more cheese into your system, so I'm all for it.' Fern hesitated. 'Sorry about the Mimis, Adam. You gave it your best shot.'

'And failed again. No *accidental* pregnancy to blame this time.'

It was a throwaway comment, but it hit Fern hard.

'Ancient history. Sorry,' said Adam as she dipped her head.

Recently, life had ganged up on Fern, breaking through her careful defences and holding a mirror to her folly. She'd been carefully avoiding the legitimacy of Adam's anger about Ollie's conception, but now it sank its teeth into her. 'I'm sorry, Adam. I shouldn't have done it,' she said, a hint of sob in her voice.

'Hey, listen, shush, stop,' garbled Adam.

'No, you were right. Nobody should foist parenthood onto somebody else.'

'But I wasn't just somebody. I was your partner.'

Confusingly, Fern and Adam seemed to have swapped sides. 'I'm trying to apologize. Stop making excuses for me.'

'Sorry,' said Adam again.

'I was blinded back then. Young people always feel that they're running out of time when really they have acres of it. We could've waited.' This alternative universe wouldn't have Ollie in it; that didn't sound like a universe Fern wanted to live in. 'I should have consulted you. We should have discussed it.'

'Yeah, but . . .' Adam shrugged. 'I would've said no and I would've been an idiot and we wouldn't have Ollie, which means we wouldn't have Amelie, and it all works out in the end.'

'So I don't need to be sorry?'

'I wouldn't go that far. I was quite enjoying it.'

Fern wiped her scarlet nose. She'd never perfected pretty crying. *Is Adam truly forgiving me for one of the main reasons we split?* Where, then, did that leave them? 'I interrupted you. About Kinky Mimi.'

'Nothing much left to say. It leaves a sour taste in your mouth, Fern, when you do your best and it's not good enough. Nobody to blame except myself this time around.'

'This isn't like you.'

'It is. It's just like me. What does my life amount to?' Adam's mood had performed a faultless handbrake turn.

'Adam, watching Nora has taught me something. And it's not just that after seventy you need a damn good bra. It's taught me that all we leave behind us is love. You have tons of that, Adam.'

'I do, don't I?' Adam brightened. 'That's a lovely way to put it.' He reached out and they embraced warmly, naturally, with minimal body contact, like fond friends. Not at all like ex-lovers who'd broken sundry promises.

As they pulled apart, Adam pushed Fern's hair out of her eyes. It was an old gesture, one she'd thought he'd never make again, and they both smiled goofily at it.

Grateful for the new rapport, Fern knew it was only possible because they'd sucked all the romance out of their connection. Looked at that way, this warm and sunny friendship was a horribly sad thing.

Raising his hand in farewell, Adam turned away as he smiled, 'Good thing we never got married, eh? No divorce to negotiate!'

'So,' began Tallulah, smug at having her mother's full attention. 'I've written it all down for my biography.'

Passing by as Tallulah opened a lined pad, Ollie said, 'Autobiography, idiot.'

'Whatever.' In her best reading voice, Tallulah began, 'That morning I woke up at seven as usual. Or maybe seven-oh-four. I got out of bed and—'

'Could we cut to the bit about Lincoln, darling?' Fern, stirring a risotto, could feel herself ageing; Tallulah's anecdotes were dreaded for their length.

'OK. Umm . . .' Tallulah traced a few lines with her finger, then started again. 'I was a bit upset at break time because I'd lost my Quavers. I wandered about on my own a bit. Carey was on her own too, but she wouldn't look at me. I really wanted to play with her. And I missed my Quavers. Suddenly somebody shouted "It is Lincoln Speed!" We all ran over to the fence. On the other side was my brother Ollie and the huge massive star Lincoln Speed.'

'Ollie was there?' interrupted Fern, as the arborio rice plumped up in the pan.

'Yes, Mum, Ollie, please shush,' said Tallulah severely, as if she was reading out a will. 'Girls were screaming and I almost did a wee when Lincoln shouted "Where is Tallulah Carlile?" Everybody screamed even harder. I said "Here I am" and stuck my hand through the fence but Lincoln said . . .' Tallulah looked up. 'Do I have permission to say a swear?'

'No.'

Sighing, Tallie carried on. 'Lincoln said eff that and climbed over the fence. Ollie was saying not to but then he laughed and climbed over as well. Lincoln Speed gave me a huge hug and even kissed me on the cheek and one girl fainted and a prefect was sick. He said really loudly in his fantabuloso accent, "I hear you and your friend aren't hanging out any more. Where's Carey?" And Carey said "Here" and put her hand up as if she was in Maths, and Lincoln pulled her into the hug and said "You two are pals, so behave like it, dodos. Carey, do you dig Tallie?" Carey said she did. Everybody was laughing and shouting. I said I digged Carey so Lincoln Speed made us shake hands and he said "I don't want to hear no more of this, umm . . ."' Tallulah eyed her mother. '"*Male cow poo*. From this moment on you girls are blood sisters, got it?" And then Sister Mary Augustus came out and she was all red and she was going on about smoking and she made Lincoln go away. Ollie winked at me and then he ran because Sister Mary Augustus is much bigger than him. She's much bigger than most people. Me and Carey were like celebrities after that. All the girls followed us around. We promised never to not talk again.' Tallulah slapped her book shut. 'By the way, Mum, Carey's coming over later. Is that OK?'

'Yup.' Fern stared into the risotto as her daughter flew out of the room. 'Hey, mister,' she called as Ollie passed, out to a bar job or a DJ job or maybe a supermarket job. 'Thank you.'

'Shut *up*, Mum.'

'You're getting kissed whether you like it or not.' Spoon aloft, Fern chased her son to the front door, where she pulled down his beanie and kissed his nose. 'I thought it was all Adam's doing. How on earth did you convince Lincoln Speed to go to Tallie's school?'

'I got chatting to him at the after-party. He's into the same bands as me. He's cool.' Ollie shrugged. 'Guess he was bored, waiting around until he flew back to the States, so I asked him if he'd play fairy godfather and he said yes.'

'That was a very special thing to do for your sister.'

Fern laughed at Ollie's discomfort. 'Can't you be mushy with your poor old muvver for once?'

Ollie's arms went round her, very tight, for a split second and then he was gone, but Fern was left with a radioactive stripe where he'd touched her.

'Make them sexy.'

'They're eyebrows, Evka. How can I make them sexy?' Poised with her tweezers, Fern looked down at Evka's brows, two swooping, malevolent bats. Each time there was a cancellation at the Beauty Room Evka seemed to sense it on the wind, and in she'd dash to throw herself on the treatment couch.

'I clean penthouse today,' said Evka, as Fern got down to business. 'Why Penny still there? What is job now that Kinky Mimi is dead? I tell you,' said Evka, who liked to answer her own questions. 'She wants job of Mrs Carlile.'

'Hold still.'

'Thank baby Jesus that you have revenge sex with stud.'

'He wasn't a stud, it wasn't revenge—' Fern gave up. Evka never listened. 'That's all over, anyway.'

Pushing the tweezers away, Evka sat up, trembling with annoyance. 'Why? Are you super-crazy? You are heroine of own story, Fern, but book of your life is more dull than bus timetable.'

Pressing Evka back down, Fern muttered, 'Whereas yours'd be on the top shelf.'

'I live for adventure.'

'Really?' Fern had noticed that Evka went out less these days and showcased fewer love bites. 'Nothing adventurous about ensuring Nora takes her dysphagia meds or helping her into the shower, or building a cardboard castle with Tallulah.'

'I enjoy these things.' Evka was defensive.

'It shows. That's when you look happiest.' Fern had noticed that Evka's tales of her sexual exploits were lobbed like grenades, but when she described what she'd been up to with Amelie and Tallie and Nora, the girl's face shone with an ordinary happiness that subverted the hard glamour of her make-up. 'Do you miss your own grandmother? Your little sisters?'

'I leave it all behind.' Evka was brusque. 'I am new me.'

Having tried becoming 'new', Fern wasn't sure she believed in the notion. 'And what happened to the old you?' Laying a hot flannel over the pink and punished skin of Evka's eyebrow, she dared, at last, to ask, 'Evka, what did your boyfriend actually *do* that was so terrible?'

'He asked me to . . .' Evka pressed the flannel into her eyes. 'To . . .'

To what? *Bugger him?* Fern romped through various possibilities. *Rob a bank? Give up sugar?*

'Patrik asked me to marry him.' Evka was as still as a stone martyr on a tomb.

'That's all? That made you flee the country and start shagging the entire UK in alphabetical order?'

'He want me to be downtrodden housebitch,' said Evka, adding, 'Like you,' because she was unable to leave a sentence without a sting in its tail, even when visibly upset.

'So you didn't love this Patrik?'

'Love is cobblers,' spat Evka.

You loved him all right.

'It does not matter to me. I do not talk of him.' Evka sprang to her feet. 'We are done.'

'But I've only finished one eyebrow,' protested Fern. 'You only look half sexy!' She followed her lodger out into the hall, where Nora and Walter stood, taking off their jackets, beaming from ear to wrinkled ear.

'Hang about, love,' said Nora, her dark glasses almost tumbling off her nose as Evka whistled past her. 'Me and Walter have an announcement.'

All the inhabitants of Homestead House were winkled from their hidey-holes: Donna in a onesie, Ollie half asleep, Tallulah in a *This is what a feminist looks like* T-shirt, Amelie mewling, Evka scowling. They all waited to hear the proclamation.

'We're getting married!' said Nora.

It took a second to sink in, then Nora was mobbed by her family, who took care to mob Walter as well.

There was only milk to toast the happy couple, and soon they all had matching white moustaches around the kitchen table.

'Where did you pop the question, Walter?' asked Donna.

'At the grave of my beloved first wife,' said Walter, somewhat pooping the party until Nora trilled, 'She gave us her permission!'

'Sweet,' said Donna.

'And creepy,' growled Evka.

Nora didn't think so. 'Walter really loved his Fanny,'

she said with feeling. 'Today she handed him over to me so I can look after him.'

Everybody knew who'd actually need looking after as they toasted generous, dead Fanny. Nora had been frank with Walter, laying out her prognosis in all its ugly glory. It had made no difference to his feelings.

'It's never too late to find happiness,' Nora was saying. Her dark glasses were still firmly on; *today must be a wobbly eye day*, thought Fern tenderly. 'Walter's the love of my life. He's Heathcliff and Terry Wogan rolled into one.'

'That good, eh?' said Ollie.

'What's more,' said Nora proudly, 'he's the best kisser in the south-east of England.'

The house was festive, filled with a dancing light that seemed to shine out of Nora and Walter and their excitement.

'What sort of wedding will you have, Auntie?' asked Tallulah.

'White, of course!' said Nora.

'But of course,' smiled Fern.

'I want bridesmaids, doves, a Rolls-Royce, a marquee, a veil, a band, vol-au-vents, confetti, temporary toilets. All the bells and whistles.'

'Are you sure, Auntie?' Fern knew how much energy it took for Nora to accomplish an ordinary day; the stress of the most wedding-y wedding ever might kill her.

'I'm only doing this once,' said Nora, pulling a sniffy face. 'Don't fuss, Fern. I'll cope.' She began ostentatiously to count. 'Twenty, nineteen, fifteen, umm, twelveteen . . .'

Fern put down her milk.

'Twenty, nineteen, eighteen, seventeen, sixteen, fifteen!' Nora threw back her head. 'Your face, Fern!'

'She's a minx,' guffawed Walter. 'I can't wait to carry my Nora over the threshold.'

A man designed for matrimony, Walter warmed Fern's heart with his old-fashioned gallantry, his talk of 'my' Nora, although she seriously doubted his knees would stand up to carting her aunt over his threshold. Fern thought of the refurbished annexe, almost completed; it would stand empty now. As would the spot in Fern's heart that Nora had hollowed out and furnished.

Evka spoke in Nora's ear. 'Why you leave us? You don't need man for security.'

'Bless you, Evka, I'm not looking for security,' said Nora. 'This is the last great adventure of my life. Well, to be frank, it's my first great adventure.'

'Marriage is prison cell, not adventure,' said Evka, her one sexy eyebrow arching while the other, less sexy one flatlined.

'Adventures come in all shapes and sizes,' said Fern. For Nora, they involved fried-egg sarnies, early nights and round trips to the hospital for MRI scans. Under her breath, she said to Evka, 'See, *love's* the only true adventure.'

'I miss Patrik,' said Evka vehemently. She looked at Fern, astonished, as if it was Fern who'd said something outrageous.

'Do something about it, then.' Fern took Evka's seat when the girl slipped out of the room.

'For obvious reasons,' said Nora, enjoying holding court, 'we want to move quickly. Maybe a month or so.'

Fern knew who'd have to organize Nora's extravaganza. 'Hold on a darn tooting minute, Auntie. A month?' She didn't have the first idea where to source doves.

Ollie had an idea. 'Get married on Midsummer Day. We always have a party then anyway.'

Yesses all round. *Kids are so resilient*, thought Fern. Midsummer was an anniversary she'd rather forget. 'I'd better get cooking,' she said, opening the fridge to see what ingredients she could bully into a semblance of dinner. As she began to peel things, chop things and suspiciously sniff other things, normality returned to the kitchen. Tallulah wandered away. Donna took Amelie on a tour of the garden. Binkie yowled a protest about his empty dish.

'Auntie,' said Ollie. 'I think we've found a flat. One-bedder, opposite the library. It's dinky but there's a shared garden for madam to sit out in.' He threw a glance Fern's way. 'Not too far from Grandma.'

It's hard to look over somebody's shoulder when you're pretending not to interfere, so Fern was relieved when Ollie said, 'Oh, just take it, Mum,' and handed her the estate agent particulars. She gasped at the asking price of the flat, which was little more than a series of interconnecting cupboards.

It was Nora who'd noticed that the young parents didn't want to leave the house on their date nights. She'd brought it up with Fern, pulling rank as an elder. 'You know why Ollie and Donna don't want to go out, don't you?'

'Maz,' Fern had sighed.

The conference with Maz's parents, an elderly Bengali couple who were mystified by their son's behaviour, had gone well. Despite Donna's ongoing cynicism, Maz was promised limited access if, and only if, he played by the rules. 'After what happened with Nora, you need to win our trust,' Adam had said, and Maz had nodded, tears in those liquid eyes, before continuing to behave just as he wanted.

It was Fern's belief that Maz's feelings for Amelie were real; the immature fool just couldn't resist using the baby as a stick to beat Donna with. He turned up at the door unannounced, 'bumped into' Donna at the mall, and texted late at night that he'd apply for full custody.

It was all immature bravado, but Adam and Fern fought fire with fire, taking out a restraining order. Only temporary, the order would give them breathing space. The security camera fixed to the porch should have made them feel safer, but had the opposite effect. When Donna had put her foot down and declared an end to date night, Nora had said to Fern, as she poked her hard in the shoulder, 'They fall asleep on those nights out. Donna fell face-first into her spaghetti at that snazzy Italian restaurant last week. Ollie told me they shout over the music in the discotheque, talking about Amelie. Don't you see, Fern? They don't want or need a break from their baby.'

Fern had to abandon her preconceived take on Donna's unplanned motherhood; far from being a burden, Amelie was the young couple's adventure.

'They're naturals,' said Nora. 'Amelie's the making of your son. You don't have to look over their shoulders and test the bath water and tell them over and over what Ollie did at Amelie's age. They'll figure it out as they go along.'

Fern had heard echoes of Adam's warning to stop

meddling all those months ago. Somehow it had been easier to take it from her aunt.

Then Nora had owned up about her own, colossal meddling. 'Don't shout. I'm sick and it might kill me if you raise your voice in anger. Fern . . . I've offered them the deposit for a place of their own.'

Fern hadn't shouted. She'd merely gasped.

'Ollie's a proud one, but I said if it'd make him happy, he could look on it as a loan.'

The women had shared a thought. The loan would be an inheritance before too long.

Unable to condemn Nora, Fern saw parallels with her own youth, when another aunt had conjured up a home for her to live in with her own baby. Fern hadn't been able to resist asking, 'So, Auntie, you're not broke, after all?'

'I reckoned you wouldn't let me stay unless you had to. You always were a soft touch, Fern, and there was nobody who loved me enough to take me in. I was terrified.'

'You were terrify*ing*.'

'I'm sorry I lied, dear.'

'I'm not!' There'd been room for one more in Fern's heart; it seemed to be made of elastic.

Back in the kitchen, tossing vegetables into a wok, Fern faced up to a disagreeable fact: by the end of Nora's Big Day, she'd have lost a second mum. To Walter.

It was hard to cast the prospective groom as a wicked seducer; he was whistling tunelessly as he helped Nora out of her chair, both of them almost but not quite toppling over. They went upstairs for a lie down before dinner. Fern suspected it was a euphemism.

Jogging past the kitchen, Ollie retraced his steps, re-appearing. 'Mum,' he said. 'Sorry for suggesting Midsummer. I forgot, you know, Dad leaving and everything.'

'Doesn't matter,' said Fern. 'It's a lovely idea.' After Midsummer Night, she and Adam would be onto their second everything since the split. Time galloped heartlessly on.

'You OK?' Ollie looked frightened, as he always did when his mother was out of sorts.

He still needs me to be stable, thought Fern, with a poignant burst of love. 'I'll be OK if you give me a hug.'

A hug was delivered. It smelled of Sudafed and burritos. 'Hugging gets easier when you've had a baby,' said Ollie.

Staring and staring, Boudicca bored a hole in her mistress's head. Fern was ironing the whole gamut of human clothing, from tiny frilly pants to ripped jeans. She'd cleared out the fridge, ruthlessly sending half-eaten yoghurts to their death in the pedal bin. She'd lined up Nora's bedtime tablets. All the while, she'd ignored the whippet's beady eye.

'OK, OK, I give in.' Fern attached Boudicca's lead and allowed herself to be dragged out into the lavender dusk.

'Fern!' Donna, in sweats, Amelie on her hip, called from the step. 'Do you fancy a passenger?'

Boudicca stood stock still, the picture of heroic patience, as the little human they were all so bloody keen on was strapped into a pushchair. Didn't they know there were squirrels to chase, and poo to inspect?

'This'll give me a chance to have a bath.' Donna said 'bath' with a disbelieving groan, as if she'd won the lottery. She held up her arm and sniffed the fabric of her hoodie. 'Yew. Nobody warns you that babies have something against their mummies achieving basic hygiene.'

'Use the fancy bath gloop.' Fern knew the restorative power of a long, hot bath; often it was all that stood between her and a jail term for murdering her entire family with a whisk.

'Before you go, there's something I need to get off my chest.' Donna tucked Amelie in, primped her hat, tickled her soft brown cheek. She straightened up. 'About you and Maz. The way you encouraged him.'

Boudicca went from paw to paw. Humans were so *slow*. Especially her humans.

'If I'd thought for one minute that he was going to—'

'I'm not angling for another apology.' Donna was so sure, so firm. Fern was dealing with another woman, not a girl. 'I go too far, Fern, and sometimes I need to say sorry. You let us live here and you sat up all night with Amelie just to let me sleep. You're the last person I should get angry with.'

'I went behind your back.' Fern had looked hard at her own behaviour and didn't like it much. 'I thought I knew best. But you did, Donna.'

'You wanted to believe we could all get along. I want to see the good in people, too, but there's a lot of my parents in me and I only see the shadows.'

'Any sign of your mum and dad defrosting?'

'Not gonna happen.' Donna let out a pretty sigh. 'You can't fix everything, Fern.'

To Boudicca's relief, that seemed to be the end of this bout of yada-yada-yada. His mistress, deep in thought, walked far too slowly for the dog's liking as they made their way to the park.

Pointing out birdies and bow-wows to the uninterested, snoring baby, Fern took a different route to the rut worn in the grass by Pongo and Maggie and Tinkerbell. She'd been avoiding them.

'Butterfly!' cooed Fern, like a kids' TV presenter.

Amelie wiggled in her sleep.

Hal had been Fern's long, hot bath. He'd been her reward, her haven. The speed of change in Fern's life had been dizzy-making since last Midsummer. In a year when nothing stood still, Hal had been a constant, a calm centre.

'Squirrel!' Fern had been thinking so hard about Hal that the chap strolling through the park gates seemed just like him. It took a second for her to realize it *was* Hal.

It's fate. Fern stood stock still, her knuckles white around the buggy handle. *I brought him to me.* She let out a hybrid cry/laugh and regretted her decision to leave the house without mascara. *Perhaps I deserve another bath . . .*

Pausing, Hal looked just like himself, right down to the last Hal-ish detail. This shouldn't have been a surprise, but it cheered her enormously. Jeans. Creased white shirt. Deck shoes. Buoyant hair that she used to grab when he was inside her. Hal swept a look around the park and Fern grinned, rehearsing what she'd say, hoping she didn't look embarrassingly overexcited. Starting towards him, Fern picked up speed and the buggy bounced on the grass.

Looking over his shoulder, Hal held out an arm to a girl who ran to catch up with him. Neatly glueing herself to his side, she let Hal wrap the arm around her.

Fern made a sharp right, as if the pushchair were an offroad vehicle, and plunged into the trees.

'Boudi!' Fern brought the dog to heel as she squatted behind a tree, peeking out at the couple.

They were talking. Not laughing, which pleased Fern. This new, mad Fern. Fern wanted to believe that only she could make Hal titter. *He'll certainly bloody laugh if he spots me hiding here.* She crouched, inching the pushchair around the tree so as to keep its bulky trunk between her and the meandering couple at all times.

Didn't take him long to replace me. It was a teen thought, unworthy of a woman pushing her grandchild, but Fern was smarting as if somebody had just pulled a plaster off a scratch on her heart. Forcing herself to look straight at the girl, one detail leapt out at Fern; the swishy-haired, boy-hipped lovely was about Hal's age. No stretch marks under that sundress. Her nipples probably pointed to the heavens when released from her bra.

Putting a hand over her eyes, Fern let out a long breath, pushing out all this dumb nonsense. Whether or not the girl had cellulite was beside the point – although it would be nice if she did, if her nickname was something like, say, Satsuma Bum.

The connection between Fern and Hal had been what made them, *it*, happen. Perhaps he had a connection with

345

this infuriatingly slender young person. Perhaps he didn't. *Either way, it's none of my business.* Fern had been the one to pull down the circus tent; no point complaining when Hal found somebody new to play with.

Homestead House shuddered with activity. Televisions blared. Radios stuttered. Boudicca barked and Binkie hissed, as Amelie, who'd slept like a doll since her walk in the park, began to bawl.

'Mummee!' yelled Tallulah down the stairs.

'Can't hear you. Come down,' said Fern, which she always said when somebody she'd given birth to insisted on shouting at her from the other end of the house.

Tallulah ignored her, which she always did. 'I'm throwing you down a letter.'

A soft toy, Pluto – or was it Goofy? Fern always mixed them up – landed in the hall with a piece of pink notepaper tied around his waist.

Dear Mummy, read Fern, flattening out the note on the worktop. *I refuse to be a bridesmaid. You can't make me. I'm allergic to big dresses. I'll run away and tell the newspapers. Signed your loving dorter T xxxxxxxxxxxxxxxxxx*

Composing a reply – something diplomatic along the lines of *you don't have to do anything you don't want to, but it would make Nora so happy*; she could resort to threats later – Fern noticed something missing.

Guilt. That vague air of guilt that had dogged her, like a personal weather front, since she'd started seeing Hal.

She thanked fate for stepping in and stopping her approaching him at the park.

Secrecy was said to be titillating, but Fern had felt seedy. Even though she was a free agent, even though Adam had 'moved on', as they say.

Fern rotated her shoulders, let her head drop back. Tension she'd been carrying around had simply dissolved. Hal was a comet in her sky; the light had been bright and fabulous, but temporary.

I behaved better than Adam. Unlike her ex, she'd waited a decent amount of time. Unlike her ex, she hadn't introduced Hal to the children under false pretences.

A world without Penny might look very different. Fern felt her neck, rubbing at the tender part. Penny's presence made the separation take hold. By now, Fern would have broken and called Adam in the middle of the night; they might have talked out their differences. The thought of Penny beside him in bed, listening in, had made a sweet, tearful, conciliatory call impossible.

A text showed up on her phone. Fern, avid for news from France, snatched up the mobile.

Quadruple test shows high risk. Am considering amniocentesis. Let's not Skype tonight. Just want to sleep. L xxxxxxxx

High risk. The two words seemed bolder than the rest of the text. Fern longed to speak to Layla, but she respected her friend's request and looked around for something else to do. The best response to impotent turmoil was physical activity.

Heaving the recycling bag out to the bins, Fern saw

Evka smoking in the dark garden, dragging on the cigarette ferociously as if trying to teach it a lesson.

Evka turned at the rustle of household waste. 'You give worst advice.' Her voice was dense with tears. 'I call Patrik. I say "you are my adventure". He say "ha!" He say "too late." He is in love with Veronika.'

'Oh. Oh no.' From the way Evka said it, this mention of Veronika merited a response.

'Veronika is slag. Veronika is stupid. Veronika eats with stupid slaggy mouth open.'

'I have a vivid mental image of her now.'

'Patrik says "I do not love you any more." So I say I never love him, he is bad in bed, like making love to sock puppet. I cut off call. Patrik rings back so *he* can cut off call. And now I want to die under wheels of iconic red London bus.'

'You can't die, Evka, you're taking Tallulah to school in the morning.' When there wasn't even the ghost of a giggle in response, Fern told Evka she knew how she felt. 'The end of things is hard. But we'll prop each other up.'

'I am limping duck now.'

'Yes,' smiled Fern. 'You'll fit right in here.'

'Men are bastard sods,' said Evka, with none of her usual vehemence. You'd almost think she secretly liked bastard sods. Unusually nervous, she chewed at her lip as she said, 'Fern, I must tell you . . . there is something you must see. In penthouse.'

'Really?' Fern, troubled by Evka's expression, said light-heartedly, 'Is it worse than PVC boots?'

'Much, much worse than horny boot.' Evka reached out and grabbed Fern's hand, hard. 'It changes everything.'

'This is like old times,' said Adam.

'Not that old,' said Fern.

'No, well,' Adam shrugged apologetically. 'What I mean is, it's great to have everybody together, doing what the Carliles do best; stuffing their faces.'

All the main players were on stage, milling around the marble island in Adam's penthouse, picking at the delicacies that had been laid out with a finesse Fern aspired to but never achieved. The scene was Instagram-worthy, everybody in their best duds to celebrate the happy couple's engagement, gathered around a feast in a bang-on-trend kitchen.

'This spread looks delicious,' said Fern to Penny, proud of her selflessness, hearing Evka's Slavic tut. Evka didn't believe in 'everybody getting along'; she believed in burying love rivals in unmarked graves.

'I have this brilliant A-list caterer,' said Penny, as if knowing phone numbers was a skill. 'Madonna has his mini quiches flown to her in Los Angeles.'

'No crisps?' asked Nora, forlorn despite her new dress and the blue eyeshadow she'd aimed at her eyelids.

'No Twiglets?' Tallulah wavered between shock and unhappiness.

'Well, no,' faltered Penny. 'But why not try an aged Parmesan beignet?'

Tallulah looked sad for Penny and her strange ideas. 'There'd better be Arctic Roll for afters.'

Fern, who'd seen the croquembouche in the fridge, said, 'Manners, Tallie. Eat what you're given.' *Even if what you're given is unpronounceable and completely inappropriate for a tiddler like you.* She fussed with the neckline on her blouse. It felt wrong, as if her whole outfit had gone completely out of fashion as soon as she set foot in the penthouse. A desire to run made her toes tap in her one decent pair of heels. Evka's dispatches from the front line had scored a thick black line under the vague daydreams she sometimes indulged in. The ones where a switch was flicked and all was 'back to normal'. *This,* Fern told herself, *is normal now.*

'Adam is crazy for the avocado mousse,' said Penny, whose summer plumage was as showy as her winter gear. Her floral dress was boned, pulling in her waist and supporting what Fern was pretty certain were bigger boobs than this time last year.

Fern wondered fleetingly if Adam had suggested the enhancement – he'd always been partial to her own bumps – but decided that she'd trained him too well; if Adam had ever suggested plastic surgery to Fern, she'd have throttled him with her bra.

There I go again. Fern introduced some avocado mousse into her mouth to interrupt the chain of wrong-headed thoughts. *Adam is different now.* She coughed; the avocado mousse tasted of dead things.

'Daddy's mean.' Tallulah browsed the offerings. 'He won't take me to Hollywood with him.'

'He won't take me either,' said Penny.

'It's just a quick trip,' said Adam, beleaguered. 'A couple of days.'

'I want to meet the men who make films,' said Tallulah, 'and tell them to stop putting ladies' chests in them for no reason.'

'I'll take you in the summer hols,' said Adam. 'We'll do Disneyland as well.'

The promise was made so blithely; pre-*Roomies*, they'd saved all year for their annual fortnight in the caravan. Two weeks of Adam constantly expostulating how expensive everything was, finally erupting in a Llandudno mini-mart that he wasn't 'made of Cornettos'.

Tallulah tried to look as if she was above Disneyland, but nobody was convinced. 'Remember, Mummy, when I wanted to be a Disney princess?' She giggled. 'Imagine waiting around for a stupid prince to save you! I can save myself.'

You clever girl. Tallie had already worked it all out. Fern would have to learn from her own child, and start saving herself: Adam was no Prince Charming.

'May I say, Fern –' Walter leaned over the island, his new tie trailing in the soft-shell crab – 'you look especially delightful today.'

'Do I?' Fern, grateful for Walter's olde-worlde gallantry – he *noticed* women – shrugged, playing down the careful blow-dry, the new top from Whistles, the smoky eye she'd achieved with the help of a YouTube tutorial.

'Yes, you do look well,' said Penny, evidently not able to stretch to 'pretty'. 'When you make the effort. Doesn't she, Adam?'

'Suppose she scrubs up nicely.' Adam was newe-worlde; he took the piss out of women.

'Mummy's beautiful,' said Tallulah, with the same certainty she quoted statistics. According to her, 104 per cent of people like meringue.

'What about me, Tallie?' asked Adam, woebegone.

'You're too thin,' said Tallulah. 'But I have to think you're handsome 'cos you're my dad.'

'Well, that's something,' said Adam.

Covertly sneaking peeks at his midriff, Fern saw that Adam's love handles were reasserting themselves. Was he smuggling calorific contraband into the apartment? A bag of Frazzles here, an iced bun there? He'd regressed to more comfortable clothing now that Kinky Mimi had been pronounced dead for the second time, looking more approachable in his Motörhead tee and his favourite jeans, which were easily as aged as the Parmesan.

That morning, while putting on and wiping off her make-up – there's a knack to Adele eyeliner, and it took a while for Fern to perfect it – Fern had treated herself to another letter from the box. *Or was it a punishment?* After Evka's revelation, Fern couldn't be sure. Some clear water had to be put between her and Adam; *but not yet*, she'd begged, opening the letter to remind herself of happy if obsolete truths.

Dear Fern
    You think you're fooling me by not responding to my letters or my phone calls and stepping over my body when you leave your house. You're not fooling anybody!!! You're obviously

DESPERATE to go out with me, so I have graciously decided to take you back.

There are CONDITIONS you must agree to before I take back your sorry ass.

1. Never ask me if you look fat
2. Never ask me what I'm thinking
3. Put a strict limit on the time you spend getting ready to go out (14 hours or so)
4. Never talk to my mum about me. You and my mum must not stop talking suddenly when I enter the room. You and my mum must not roar with laughter when I then leave the room.
5. Just ignore all this shit and come back please because I'm unravelling and I'm eating too many takeaways and I want to kiss you and I can't watch films because suddenly every actress in the bloody world reminds me of you.

There was one, only one, un-chic detail in the penthouse. The primary-coloured plastic alphabet magnets on the fridge clashed merrily with the subdued colour scheme.

'Are those your doing?' Fern asked her daughter.

'How'd you know?' giggled Tallulah.

'Because you've spelled "patriarchy" wrong.' Fern could *taste* Penny's desire to get rid of the gaudy letters.

'How about,' said Penny, '*this?*' She pushed her hand through *smAsh thE paytriarchY* and rearranged the magnets to spell *Congratulations*.

Penny's ability to get everything so perfectly right and yet so arse-throbbingly *wrong* confused Fern. Didn't the woman notice Tallie's expression as she demolished the child's favourite slogan? So keen on detail, Penny missed the big picture.

'Have you found new job yet?' Evka, encouraged by the flagons of Prosecco she was downing, was blunt. 'Because no Kinky Mimi, no manager.'

'I already have a job.' Penny managed – just – to avoid sounding defensive. 'I manage Adam's life.'

Fern and Evka would go over that and enjoy it later; for now, they carefully ignored each other and relished the thought of Adam's life needing 'managing'.

'What exactly do you manage?' When Evka sounded that friendly, she was at her most dangerous. 'His socks?'

'I've set up a number of meetings with big cheeses in L.A.'

'Cheeses?' queried Evka.

'Important industry people. I'm making sure he capitalizes on *Roomies*. He'll score films, collaborate with the greats. Adam's going to be a colossus. He could be world-famous.'

Adam rocked on his heels, staring into the depths of his beignet.

A phone was passed round so everybody could examine shots of the flat that Ollie and Donna were in the process of buying.

'Blooming screen's so small,' grumbled Nora, bringing the phone right up to her nose.

'The pictures are actual size,' said Ollie. 'Seriously! We can't swing a kitten, never mind a cat.'

'I don't care,' said Donna with relish. 'Our own four walls!' She turned to Fern. 'No offence,' she said quickly, her hands to her lips.

'None taken.' Fern wasn't offended, but she couldn't turn off the part of her brain that emitted a fug of wistful nostalgia whenever the new flat was mentioned. It was right, it was proper that children grow up, become independent and move out. *But this feels too quick.* She'd only just got used to Ollie catching a bus on his own. 'There's no feeling in the world like having your own house. Do you remember, Adam?' She turned to him. 'When we got the keys to Homestead House?' *When we got the keys to the house that ultimately came between us.*

'It feels like a thousand years ago,' said Adam. 'And it feels like yesterday.' He clinked glasses with Fern.

The crystal rims pealed like tiny bells. Fern buried her face in her drink. When Adam spoke that way, invoking their past with an intimate edge to his voice, she felt his power, a power over her that couldn't fade, no matter how much she judged him and found him wanting. No matter how many other women sidled in between them.

Wanting to say something, desperate to express herself but unable to capture the words, Fern opened her mouth, hoping providence would provide, just as Ollie tapped on her arm.

'Any chance,' he said, holding out the baby, 'of changing Amelie? She's done something truly impressive in her nappy.'

'Oh *God!*' Adam bent double. 'What are you feeding that child?'

'I'm suffocating.' Tallulah feigned a faint.

Holding her nose, Fern took the toxic child, who was gurgling happily, unaware she'd just become a major factor in climate change.

'Use the master en suite,' said Adam, backing away. 'You'll have loads of room in there.'

Again, a frisson from Penny as Fern passed her. *I'm encroaching on her territory.*

'Don't get too accustomed to this level of luxury, Amelie,' said Fern as she changed the baby's nappy – somewhat recklessly – on a white satin chaise longue. 'You'll soon be back to Homestead House.' She picked her up, holding Amelie's warm body close, smelling the back of her neck, feeling the baby's wholesome strength; this was a girl built on adoration and milk. 'I love you, beautiful.' Babies have the power to squeeze feeling out of their servants. As Fern drank Amelie in, her mind hopped to Layla and she held the baby even tighter, forcing a little burp out of her.

The offending nappy neatly bagged, Fern looked around for the bin, all the while studying the bathroom the way forensic officers examine a psychopath's lair. Each costly tub of face cream was noted, each quirkily shaped bottle of perfume, all the Mac/Bobbi Brown/Chanel eyeshadows and foundation and primers and under-eye lighteners and mascaras and BB creams and pore minimizers. Fern checked out the back of the door and felt the fabric of the silk robe between her fingers. Everything seemed new; even the towelling slippers were pristine.

And the smell! The room was a medley of feminine scents, a pink and gold gossamer wrap of jasmine and rose and vanilla.

It bore no relation to Fern's bathroom, which smelled of Head & Shoulders and usually featured a pair of Tallie's knickers on the (warped) floor. This room confirmed something for her. Something about Penny.

It wasn't right to peer through the concealed door into the master bedroom. 'Don't judge me, Amelie,' whispered Fern as she gently toed open the door.

There it was. The immense master bed. A crime scene, according to Fern's feverish imaginings and Evka's reportage.

A desire to hurt herself, a rabid sadomasochism, made Fern savour each detail slowly, almost lovingly. *It must be faced*. Adam was Penny's now.

Her stinging eyes found the bedside table. And stopped there. She looked for an age, taking in what she'd found there, weighing it up. Just a small object, it punched above its weight. It changed everything. The voice that Fern had lost when Adam had clinked glasses with her had a lot to say.

'Amelie,' she said. 'I need to talk to your grandpa.'

The search for the bin revealed it hiding behind a mirrored cupboard door. Its lid snapped open to reveal, lying atop discarded cotton-wool balls, a small white plastic wand with a story of its own to tell.

Just as Evka had said.

Fern stared at it and was certain, full of purpose as she rejoined her family, catching the tail end of Walter's anecdote, which ended, as his stories tended to, with 'and then, oh, hang on, what was I saying?'

In a chef's hat, Adam ferried more goodies to the island.

Swaying on a stool (it had taken three people to get her up there), Nora groused, 'Why aren't we using the dining table instead of standing about like beggars?'

'This is casual dining,' said Penny. 'It suits our vibe.'

'I don't have a vibe,' grumbled Nora. 'But I do have a sore bottom from this stupid stool.'

'Dining tables are so out,' said Penny, with a shake of the head for anybody who might labour under the misconception that they were in. 'The buzzword is informality.'

Swamped by his family, Adam was in his element, slapping Tallulah's greedy mitts away from the plate of sausage rolls (surely not supplied by the A-list caterer?) and challenging Ollie to eat a whole chili. His light burned brighter; he was at one with himself when the children were around. *When I'm around?* Fern wasn't sure, but her resolve redoubled.

Offloading Amelie onto Penny, Fern whispered to Adam, 'I need a word with you.' No time like the present. She felt carbonated, like a shaken can of lemonade.

'In a sec. I'm on duty.' Adam pointed to his chef's hat.

'I need to speak to you, Adam.' Fern leaned in.

Adam leaned out. 'It can wait until we've all eaten. Here.' He shoved the cheeseboard her way. 'Get stuck into that.'

The wooden platter was a work of cheesy art. A runny one. A hard one. A goaty one. Grapes and crackers. A knoll of pickle. Even a woman on a mission must eat.

Fern scooped up the almost liquid Brie with a poppyseed biscuit.

'Ye Gods, that's good!'

'But so fattening,' said Penny, holding Amelie away from her as if the baby might explode.

'If Mummy wants to be fat,' said Tallulah sternly, 'that's her preroga-thingy.'

'Thank you, darling. I think.' When Fern compared the delights of cheese and the delights of abs, cheese always won. Cheese didn't play fair, lying wantonly on the board, flashing its fat content at her. 'Excellent selection, Adam, as usual.'

Buying the cheese had always been his job. Adam used to love sitting back, watching his wife lay waste to his masterpieces. Fern could remember being massively pregnant with Tallulah, and Adam saying in wonder, 'I've never known anybody who ate Stilton in bed before.' At least, she hoped it was wonder.

I need to say my piece. Fern felt like a clean sheet of paper; she wanted Adam to scribble on her. With her new clarity, Fern saw Hal for what he was; a diversion. A lovely, exciting diversion with added orgasm, but a diversion all the same. The age gap was a red herring; Fern had the imagination and the courage to make it work with Hal, but she hadn't wanted to make it work, because what Fern wanted was Adam.

Pride and hurt and anger had ganged up together, creating enough noise to obscure the love. A love that had sputtered and wavered, like a candle in a draught, but had never gone out.

I can forgive him. He can forgive me. It can still be all right.

Describing her wedding dress, Nora sketched it on her body with her hands. 'I want frills here,' she said. 'Straps here. A bit of embroidery. Buttons all down the back. Chiffon-y sleeves. Pearls on the hem. A detachable capelet.'

'You'll be a right bobby dazzler,' said Walter.

'I'm not so sure,' mused Penny, looking as if she'd heard a sick joke. 'Why not pop along to Sarah Burton at Alexander McQueen? She made Kate Middleton's wedding dress and her signature silhouette is simple and chic.'

As Nora's signature silhouette was lumpy and bumpy, Fern took another scoop of Brie to stifle her impulse to make a stinging retort to Penny. Whatever Nora wanted on her big day, Nora would get; she didn't have to live up to Penny's narrow notion of good taste.

'I'm making the dress meself,' said Nora complacently, and Fern died a little inside, knowing her house would be knee deep in 100 per cent viscose white fabric for the next few weeks.

Champing at the bit to say her piece, Fern plotted where to begin as she cosied up to the cheddar. She and Adam had ventured further and further into the maze. It was time to start following the trail of breadcrumbs back out into the open air.

'Adam . . .'

'Hold on, love.' Adam was riveted by Ollie's re-enactment of a dance-floor fight during his last DJing stint. Adam was embedded in the party, wrapped up in the hubbub as drinks were poured, plates passed around, stories swapped. *If only I could talk secretly with him.*

Leaning against the fridge, Fern squirmed as the plastic letters dug into her back. She turned and rearranged them. Rooting through the red and blue and green magnets, she found an exclamation mark.

adAm!

Positioning herself carefully – and awkwardly – so that nobody except Adam would be able to see the fridge, she poked him in the ribs.

Wheeling round, Adam saw his name and cottoned on. Swiftly, taking advantage of the fact that everybody else was engrossed in Ollie's mimed punches and kicks, Adam pushed three letters together and borrowed Fern's exclamation mark.

Wot!

Like a magician's assistant, Fern moved her fingers deftly. Some letters were missing, and for some reason there were four 'x's. It was tricky to encapsulate what she wanted to say but she hoped he'd catch on.

i no aBouT PeNi

Enjoying the game while still pretending to hang on Ollie's every word, Adam screwed up his face, unable to fathom her meaning until she enlarged with more magnets.

U & PeNni

Adam swiped all the letters to the floor, where they clattered around Fern's feet.

Interrupted at the climax of his story – the bit where one hipster threw an organic beer in another hipster's face – Ollie said, 'Dad?'

'Mum and I need to step out onto the terrace for a second.' Adam took Fern by the arm, as if making a citizen's arrest.

Nora called after them. 'It's raining. You'll catch your deaths.' Despite her recent reincarnation as a smokin' hot bee-atch, she retained her spinsterish preoccupation with colds.

Pulling the glass doors shut, Adam asked, 'Are they all staring?' without looking back at the party.

'Yes.' Fern huddled over in the spitting rain. 'Act normal.'

'I am,' said Adam. 'Take your own advice. Penny was right next to you.'

'She couldn't see. I made sure.'

'What did you mean, "I know"?' Adam made sarky quotation marks in the air. 'What do you know?'

'I know that you and Penny—'

'Would you like to hear what I know?' Again with the air quotation marks. 'About you? Or *u*.' He drew the letter in the air.

'You know a lot about me, Adam.' The conversation was unfolding all wrong. Fern blamed herself for barging into such a delicate subject; this was not the poignant turning point she'd envisaged. *I should have planned this, got him on his own.* 'None of it matters. What matters is the here and now.'

'Pardon me for daring to have an opinion,' said Adam, his face neutral for the benefit of their audience, 'but I'd say that your affair with a guy half your age matters a great deal.'

Fern's flabber had rarely been so gasted. 'How'd you know about that?'

The lack of response was telling.

'Penny,' sighed Fern. 'Did she have me followed?' Her voice rose to a disbelieving squawk.

'She has her ways.'

'Are we in a B-movie? Did she dust my knickers for fingerprints? Why are you so interested?' Fern took a step closer, her fringe dripping into her eyes. 'Are you jealous, Adam?'

'I didn't want the mother of my children making a fool of herself.'

Fern's nostrils flared. That was a slap to the face; *as if it's delusional to believe a younger man like Hal could find me desirable.* 'That's just mean, Adam. Nobody made a fool of anybody. I was careful not to involve the kids.'

'How old was he?'

Ignoring him, Fern said, 'This isn't how I saw this going. What I was trying to say, what I still mean, is that the last eleven months don't matter, Adam.' She almost said 'Ads'; the endearment felt denied to her still. 'What I mean is . . .' *What do I bloody mean?* This version of Adam was the one she couldn't talk to, the spiky one, the one she'd asked to leave. *I'm not keen on this version of me, either.* She marshalled her thoughts as Adam looked out over the modest skyline of their suburb. Best to just come out with it. Best not factor in how much depended on the next couple of minutes. She thought of the 'evidence' in the master suite and found the courage to say it. 'We still love each other, Adam.'

That skyline must have been fascinating, because Adam stared at it for some time. 'This is so you,' he said at last. He was quiet, thoughtful.

'Good me or bad me?' Fern was fearful, her voice as small as Tallie's when she asked to come into their bed during a storm.

'You accuse me. You belittle *my* accusation. Then you say you love me. Same old Fern, expecting me to fall into step and follow you around like a puppy dog. Like Boudi.'

'Yes, Adam,' said Fern, refusing to mirror his stony tone. 'Same old Fern. Same old Adam. Same old kids. Don't you see? That's the beauty of it.'

'If it were that simple . . .' Adam made a growl deep in his throat and shot a look at the others, who'd found the croquembouche and lost interest in the terrace. All except Penny, who turned away, white-faced, when caught staring. 'All our problems would still be there, Fern. Along with some new ones, just for fun. We don't work, Fern. We fell apart. I refuse to be glued into place just because your boyband chum let you down.'

'He didn't!' Fern was indignant. 'I finished it.'

'So your bed's empty. That's not my concern.'

'This isn't about bed. Well, it sort of is. But . . .' Fern was choked by weeds. Adam had thrown her love back in her face. Her red, agitated face. 'I'm going to cry now and it's not fair because I can't think when I cry and . . .' She was off.

They both turned away from the windows. Fern saw a blurry row of chimneys, a church spire piercing the rain clouds a few streets away.

'Don't cry,' said Adam. He sounded as if he wanted to be fonder but couldn't manage it. 'I'm sorry.'

'Don't say sorry,' hiccupped Fern, hating the way tears overwhelmed her at times of stress. She'd cried all the way through her dad's eulogy; there'd been snot all over the Order of Mass. 'You'll only think I made you say it.' She wanted to ask Adam if he'd meant the word picture he drew of her as some ogress who pulled him and posed him like Tallulah did with her Ken doll. She scrubbed at her face with her fingers.

'Go easy,' said Adam. 'You'll rub your features off.'

No point being sweet and funny now! Fern was haughty – *apres*-quarrel haughtiness was a habit she'd learned from her mother, one that had never done either of them an ounce of good – and she went back inside ahead of him.

I have my answer.

Like an octopus, her family had wrapped its tentacles around Fern, urging her to stay for the movie, to squash up alongside them on the L-shaped sofa and watch Doris Day flirt with Rock Hudson. Ollie had been suspicious; 'Why are you going home on your own? What's wrong?'

'I'm fine, sweetheart.' Fern had kissed him on his forehead, held her lips there for a second. 'Bit of a headache.'

Adam had barely raised his hand to say goodbye. Penny had seen Fern to the door, proprietorial and over-polite. 'So lovely having you over to ours,' she'd said.

Fern bent down and shook the man by the shoulder. He woke, looked up at her, startled, his eyes wide.

'You're on my doorstep,' said Fern.

'*Kde je? Musím s ňou hovorit!*'

'English?' asked Fern hopefully.

'A leetle.' The man unfolded long legs to tower over her. 'Please. I am Patrik.'

'You've been crying, Patrik.' Fern shook her head as he struggled to translate. 'Never mind.' It looked as if Evka was going to get her happy ending. 'Let's get you indoors. One more inmate can't hurt.'

She heard the walls wheeze as she closed the front door. Homestead House would be full tonight, but there'd be an Adam-shaped gap where her ex should be.

My ex. That had always felt clunky in her mouth. The last eleven months had rewound; Fern was as raw as the day he left.

CHAPTER TWELVE

June: Café

Confetti was trodden into the mud where the lawn used to be. The lanterns, dusted off from last year, shone down on a Midsummer wedding considerably more rowdy than the small family dinner of a year ago.

Tables dotted all over the garden were littered with the debris of a good time had by all: smeared plates and streamers and overturned glasses. The wedding had reached the raucous stage, after the vows and the poems and the toasts and the grub, when ties are loosened along with inhibitions.

Young, old and in-between were getting on down to Kinky Mimi, reformed for one night only. Adam squeezed his eyes shut, meaning every word he sang, as behind him Lemmy bashed out the rhythm in a sequinned maxi.

Once again, Homestead House had embraced all comers, the garden swelling to accommodate everyone: the band; the dancers; the I-never-dancers; the makeshift bar; the cake on its special platter.

This house loves a party. Fern had switched on every light indoors, so that radiant rectangles glowed in the warm evening of the longest day of the year.

367

In time-honoured tradition, tiny bridesmaids were being twirled by the best man. Tallulah and Carey screamed as Ollie swung them round and round. Identically dressed, the two girls were now a BOGOF deal.

Fern, keen to start serving coffee, began to push the rubble of the banquet onto a tray, glad that Tallulah had compromised about being a bridesmaid. *It took forever to find that camouflage satin.*

A waltzing couple knocked into Fern.

'Oopsh! Excoosh me.' Nora's speech was noticeably more slurred. It didn't stop her bossing Walter about; luckily he spoke fluent Wife. They'd been dancing since the band struck up, Nora leaning on her Zimmer frame and on her husband, who was wearing a tuxedo several sizes too large for him.

A warm breeze tickled the lanterns and ruffled Fern's updo. She could sniff new beginnings in the air. And endings. The to-and-fro of life.

Weddings always get me. Fern blinked away soppy tears and leaned her knuckles on the table, facing away from the dancing and singing. *Get a grip.*

'Woo-hoo!' Penny threw her hair around. 'Wahey!' She was practically mobbing the stage, if a corner of the decking constituted a stage, and if one woman in a fascinator constituted a mob.

The Mimis' number one fan, thought Fern, skirting Penny with a loaded tray, her expression carefully neutral as Adam socked it to the crowd, head back, knock-kneed, eyes squeezed shut.

Every inch the suburban rock god. The offer to play at

Nora's wedding had been an olive branch, one Fern had gratefully grabbed when Adam had appeared two days after the humiliations of the engagement party.

Sheepish, he'd waited to be invited in; if he'd had a cap in his hands, he'd have wrung it. Instead he had flowers, Fern's favourites. 'To say, not sorry, I know you don't want sorry, but to say please, from now on, let's be nice to each other.'

She'd wanted to kiss him, but she hadn't. So much of her life was about restraint, it seemed. 'Yes, let's be nice.' She'd pushed the word out, a stone in her mouth. 'Friends.'

'Friends,' he'd repeated, and they'd stared at each other until he'd handed over the peonies.

Since then they'd spoken most days; her new friend was eager to do his bit for the wedding. Adam had lugged hired tables through the house, repeated directions over the phone to half-witted guests, calmed down Tallulah when she'd panicked that marriage might be 'a male chauvinist pig plot'. He was around more, less apologetic about his presence, with time to chat about this, about that, about nothing.

But when people who have loved each other talk about nothing, they're having a very important conversation. Fern forgot to be bitter; it was exhausting.

'Sexy!' Patrik's English was patchy, but he'd picked up the essentials. Splay-legged on a garden chair, he seemed to be enjoying the lap dance Evka was performing for him. 'Shake that booty, hot mama!'

'I love you!' howled Evka, a born-again romantic who'd forsaken all others for her old love. She straddled Patrik and gave him a kiss that reminded Fern she had to Hoover the car.

'Mind your backs! Coming through!' Fern negotiated her way through the heaving, jiving throng. She was tipsy on atmosphere only; she'd been too busy hosting to take more than a sip of champers. *But what champers!* Fizz was one area where you got what you paid for; Fern could get used to Dom Perignon.

On Donna's shoulders, Amelie, now a bonny six months, chuckled like a Buddha in her ruffles and lace.

She looks like Ollie! Fern paused, watching the little boho family of three jigging about in their best clothes. Perhaps love could transform features; perhaps Ollie's fierce protectiveness and devotion had reached into Amelie on a cellular level.

Untidy, disorganized, with no doorbell, the micro-flat two streets away made Fern's fingers itch when she visited, which was often. She'd come to terms with the fact that they didn't need her; the main thing was that they *wanted* her, so she sat on those itchy hands and didn't wipe any surfaces or empty any overflowing bins or comment on their diet of Coke and sandwiches.

'More!' shrieked Penny, clapping like an electrocuted sea lion.

'As you asked so nicely . . . !' Adam was high on the buzz of performance. 'This one's the title track of our latest album, which also happens to be our last album.' He detached the mike from the stand and lashed the lead à la Frank Sinatra. 'We sold eight whole copies of that

CD.' As his audience clucked sympathetically, he added, 'Even my mum refused to buy one.'

'True!' shouted Adam's mother, who seemed to have drunk Fern's share as well as her own, her matronly new frock tucked into the back of her control pants.

In the centre of the action, Nora flagged. Ever vigilant, Walter shepherded his new wife off the dance floor.

Dumping the tray, Fern grabbed a chair and set it down for Nora in a quiet corner where Binkie and Boudicca had retreated. They were united for once, avoiding the invading army of humans on their turf.

'Here, Auntie.' Fern plumped the cushion.

'Don't fush, Fern.' Nora squeezed into the canvas chair along with her ruffles and bows and pleats. Her trailing veil was trimmed with mud. Evka had made up Nora's face with a heavy hand. With the false eyelashes and the fake tan, it had been touch and go whether Walter would recognize his betrothed.

'Best day of your life?' Fern was confident of the answer.

'It would be if you'd hurry up and therve the coffee.' Nora slumped forward a little, putting her hand to her head, and Walter produced two tablets from his waistcoat pocket. 'I can't take them without water.'

Happy to be needed, Walter tottered off in search of a tap.

'I feel thorry for the me who didn't know Walter,' said Nora, watching his back recede into the crowd. 'He's changed my life.'

'You've changed his, too.' Fern carried out her usual

371

covert checks on her aunt's condition. The pressure of such a momentous day must surely be having an impact.

'Thop eyeballing me!' Nora was on to her. 'I'm fine. Twenty nineteen eighteen. Seven o'clock.'

'You'd tell me if you weren't, wouldn't you?'

'I tell you everything.'

'Yeah, you do,' smiled Fern, hoping this rule would be relaxed regarding the wedding night. She already knew too much; Nora had sent her to the chemist with a prescription for Viagra. 'Slip away if you need to. The annexe is all ready.'

Nora's inability to climb stairs – 'Like a Dalek!' Tallie had said – ruled out Walter's two up, two down. The newlyweds would live in the garden, within nagging distance of Fern. 'Tallie and Carey have made a banner of red felt hearts and they've strewn the bed with what look like weeds.'

'It's the thought that counts,' said Nora unconvincingly, jamming on dark glasses as her left iris began to ricochet in time to Kinky Mimi. She'd been up half the night glueing diamanté onto the frames. 'I don't mind going, Fern, I really don't.'

'Going where?'

'Up there.' Nora pointed at the sky, still resolutely blue on the longest day of the year.

'Oh shush, Auntie.' A skeletal hand gripped Fern's heart.

'Let me talk about dying, dear. If I went tonight, I'd die happy. I never dreamed of such happiness during the years I was walled up with Mother. Walter and I agree; everything from this moment on is a bonus.' Nora took off her glasses and fixed Fern with her one good eye. 'What I can't bear is . . .' She reached for a hanky secreted in her corset. 'Is leaving you.'

'You're not going anywhere just yet.' Fern waggled her finger. 'D'you hear me, old woman? I couldn't easily do without you now.'

Bearing a jug of water, Walter reappeared. 'Now, now, ladies. No tears today.'

'Shorry, hubby,' simpered Nora, swallowing her tablet like an eager-to-please child.

As Walter dabbed at his wife's eyes – one of her false eyelashes had come adrift – Fern saw more evidence of love's powers. Walter had willingly, *ecstatically*, bound himself to a woman with little time left, and none of it pretty.

He truly is The One.

'Look at our Adam!' said Nora, as the guests cheered the leaping, falsetto finale, Kinky Mimi giving it their absolute all. 'He's like a youngster.' She wrinkled her nose at Walter. 'Reminds me of you. Being in love has taken years off Adam.'

'Hmm,' said Fern, taking up the dirty plates again and adding some more for luck. 'If you say so.' Nora, along with the rest of the family, had surprised her by taking readily to the new status quo.

In the relative calm of the kitchen, Fern popped an apron over her finery. Water ran. Steam billowed. She needed respite from the high emotions of the garden. 'Who's that?'

Fern untied her apron at the command of the doorbell. 'Ah. Maz.'

'I know! I know!' Maz put out his hand to stop her closing the door. 'I'm not invited, I know, and that's cool. I just want to hand over a present.'

Taking the wrapped box, Fern said cagily, 'Thanks, Maz, but as you know, I can't let you in.'

'God's honest truth, I'm not asking to come in.' Maz stepped back, put his head on one side. He looked thin and young. 'I just want to, like, let you see I'm doing my best.'

That's all any of us can do. 'We're getting there, Maz. Don't do anything to derail the process.'

When Donna had shown Fern Amelie's birth certificate, with 'Masud Sikdar' named as the baby's father, both women had cried. It was no denial of Ollie, as Donna had feared. It was the right thing to do, the righteous thing to do. As is so often the case, it was also the hardest.

'The second my name was put on that birth certificate, everything changed.' The way Maz underlined his statements with splayed palms and wide eyes made them less believable, not more so. 'That restraining order was over the top, man. I'd never hurt my own flesh and blood.'

The restraining order was entirely necessary; Adam's lawyer had wondered why they left it so long. No need to blot this day by arguing with Maz. Once bitten, twice shy was Fern's mantra for dealing with him. *I want to trust him, but . . .*

'Maz, I've got fifty people waiting for coffee.'

'Let me help you!'

374

'Maz, you're seeing Amelie next Tuesday, with Donna and me. That's the arrangement. Let's stick to it.'

'Will that Nora be here?'

'No. *That Nora* will be on honeymoon.' In Bognor Regis, or 'the Vegas of the South Coast,' as Nora had taken to calling it.

'Good.' Maz's relief was understandable; like any red-blooded young man, he didn't want to meet the doddery old dear who'd held him hostage. 'Say hello to Donna and Amelie for me.'

'And Ollie?' Maz's attempts to Tippex out the man looking after his daughter irked Fern. 'One day, Maz, you and Ollie are going to shake hands and make your peace. For Amelie's sake.'

'Yeah. Well. Dunno about that.'

Funny, that's what Ollie always says.

'Coffee!' With Evka's help, Fern ferried specially-bought cafetières to each knot of guests. 'Cups are on the buffet table,' she recited over and over. 'Help yourselves to milk and sugar.'

Everything was tickety-boo; Fern's wedding list had been ticked to death. 'Spoons?' She pre-empted a question from Luc. 'By the cups.'

A little tiddly, Luc grabbed Fern and planted a kiss on each of her cheeks. 'Bravo, Fern. What a 'appy day!'

Reeling a little from the grab and the kisses, Fern mimed exhaustion. 'This wedding has taken over my *life*.'

'Your son is verree talented.'

DJ Dirty Tequila had warmed up the crowd for his father.

'Yeah,' said Fern, proud but baffled by what Ollie did. 'He's sick.' She bit her lip. 'Is that right? Sometimes I can't make out a word Ollie says. I'm always half an hour behind with the jargon.'

As Layla boogied towards them, Fern took advantage of her BFF privileges to rub the bump that ruined the line of Layla's cerise dress.

'Junior likes Adam's singing. She was leaping about for that last number.' Layla looked down at where her unborn daughter hid inside her; since the amniocentesis had revealed the gender, Layla had been impatient for the birth, anxious to meet their little girl.

'A Kinky Mimi fan in the womb!' Fern lifted her head to see Adam over the heads of the adoring/pissed crowd. She saw him wink at Penny, who was singing along in the ostentatious way Nora sang the hymns at mass. As if to say, *I know ALL the words and am going STRAIGHT to Heaven/the after-party.* 'Honestly, Layla, you wait ages for one baby, then a load come along at once!'

'Are you OK?' Layla slipped her arm through Fern's. 'You've put so much into today. Don't spread yourself too thin.' She lowered her voice, following Fern's line of sight to where Adam was talking to Penny, their faces close together. 'After all you've been through in the past year, I wouldn't be surprised if this wedding created chaos in there.' She tapped the side of Fern's head.

'More here, actually.' Fern laid her hand over her heart.

The friends shared a shimmering moment the way friends can, when the mutual understanding and acceptance is total.

Luc, scrolling through a news website on his phone, said 'Hey! They've found your monsieur Speed.'

'Lincoln Speed?' Fern looked over his shoulder. 'Is he OK?'

'He went feral in the Hollywood Hills,' laughed Luc. 'What a freak. It says here he kept himself alive by stealing picnics. He's not 'andsome any more.'

'Ooh-er.' Fern recoiled from the mad-eyed, filthy face on the screen. 'He looks like a museum model of Neanderthal man.'

Monsieur Speed had disproved the theory that all publicity is good publicity. The world had watched the live *Roomies* episode, shocked but unable to look away as a coked-up, blind-drunk Speed punched a co-star, groped an eighty-year-old audience member and sprayed the camera with urine. By the time he'd broken out through a fire escape and stolen a police car with a baby in the back, lawsuits were flying and networks of all nations had pulled the plug on *Roomies*.

Briefly, Adam had been on camera, rubbing widdle off his sleeve and wearing the expression of a man watching his royalty payments disappear down the plughole.

Now, in the garden, Fern bobbed up and down, peering through the crush to see Adam as he yelled, 'That song was for an incredible woman. Penny, I couldn't have done it without you!' Penny's upturned face shone; love spilled out of her. Adam was her One, all right.

This wedding was stuffed with Ones, it seemed.

Pulling a gossamer-fine pashmina around her shoulders, Fern enjoyed its embrace as she dipped like a swan over the tables, chit-chatting, checking all was fine, agreeing that yes, Nora did look very, um, *bridal*.

'This is definitely the last number, and one you'll all know.' Adam strummed the first chord of the *Roomies* theme to a huge cheer of recognition. He shaded his eyes with his hand. 'Anybody seen Fern?'

Fingers pointed. Tallulah shouted, 'Over there Daddy! In the horrible wrap thing!'

Fern shrank. She lived in fear of hearing her name called from a stage. She couldn't even watch audience participation shows on television; she had to leave the room in case the presenters somehow reached through the screen and roped her in. 'Hel-lo!' She waved awkwardly as all eyes turned towards her.

Including Penny's eyes, which were shining with tears only just held back. Nodding encouragingly at Fern, Penny forced her mouth to arc; a poignant smile, there was nothing malicious in it.

'This one's for you, Fern.' Adam found her face as he bent sideways, hand on hip like a Poundland Jagger. 'I've taken a few liberties with the lyric.'

Feet began to tap. Bridesmaids were swung. Walter jigged a little.

Sometimes stuff just seems to get you down
Feelin' like there's no one else around

Everybody sang along. It was the end of an era; *Roomies* had died a sudden, very modern death on live TV.

But even in endings there are beginnings
I wish I could reach out and find my Fern
I want her today, tomorrow, until the bitter end

The singalong petered out as everybody listened to the fresh lyrics. Fern let out a gasp, as if she'd been holding her breath for a year. Which, in a way, she had.

Fernie – can I come home?
Fernie – can I come home?
Throw your cares away
I am here to stay
And our life's a holiday
With Fernie!

The band stopped dead.

'Come on, Fern!' shouted Layla. 'Can he come home?'

'Yes!' yelled Fern, jumping up and down in her pinchy new shoes. 'Yes, Adam, yes!'

Adam threw his microphone in the air and leapt off the improvised stage. The crowd willingly parted as he raced towards Fern.

'I love you.' Fern was breathless as he closed in on her, as the whole glorious day and velvet night shrank to just them. 'I love you stupidly and insanely and cosily and sexily and—'

He kissed her. 'To shut you up,' he told her later, but

the kiss said different. The kiss was full of hunger, sad and celebratory at the same time. Despite the excitement it sparked, Fern relaxed for the first time in a year.

I'm safe, she thought.

Leaning against him, head buried in his shoulder, Fern enjoyed the sensation of being led as the crowd parted once again, clapping and cheering, to let Adam take her indoors.

At the kitchen table, hunched over, leaning in, her fingers plaited in his, Fern bent forward and kissed Adam again. Kissing Adam was permissible now. It was *mandatory*.

'Are you really, truly, seriously back?' Fern was afraid she'd fallen asleep; this dream, although better than her usual ones about being chased by a giant moth, would nonetheless break her heart when she woke up.

'I'm really truly back. Cross my heart. Do you really truly want me back?'

'Yes.' Tears, springing from nowhere, meandered down Fern's face. This was too much. She was overloaded.

'I'm never leaving again, not even to go to the post office.' Adam's broad face was creased into a smile so wide he looked unhinged. 'I'll handcuff myself to you.'

The tears had a mind of their own. No man had ever said to her, 'You're so pretty when you cry'; they usually backed away into a taxi. 'I'll stop in a minute,' she promised. 'I'm just so . . . happy,' she bawled.

'While you're crying, I'll say my piece,' said Adam. 'The fridge magnets were wrong. I've never slept with Penny. Never even kissed her. Got that?'

'I know you haven't.' Fern took one of her hands away

to wipe her running nose before replacing it in Adam's grasp; he pulled a face, but gamely kept hold of her slimy fingers.

'But at Nora's engagement party you and the fridge magnets accused me of having an affair.'

'The magnets said I knew about you and Penny,' said Fern, blinking as the deluge slowed. 'I meant I knew that you *weren't* having an affair, that Evka was wrong.'

'Evka?' Adam looked confused, as if he'd come in halfway through an episode of a complex political thriller.

'She's been spying for me while dusting your crevices.' Fern tried to look remorseful but found she couldn't. *All's fair in love and separation.* 'Evka carried home clues, like Binkie bringing in dead birds. She had my best interests at heart, but each one reinforced my suspicions.'

'So, hang on, I'm confused, you *did* think me and poor old Penny were at it?'

'At first. Mainly because poor old Penny went out of her way to make it look as if you were lovers. I swallowed all her PR spin.'

'When did you discover the truth?'

'I had an epiphany.' Fern felt almost shy explaining it. It was so delicate, a breath of intuition that had landed without warning, like a butterfly. 'It was the way you looked at her at Nora's party, when we were all eating and chatting. It's not how you look when you're in love.'

'I see.' Adam's face softened. 'You mean, not the way I look at you?'

'The way you *used* to look at me, to be precise.'

'Fernie, how am I looking at you now?'

'Like you love me. But it's been a while.'

They savoured the beauty of the new order (which was actually the old order), before Adam said, 'Why'd you trust Evka? She's a man-hater.'

With the benefit of hindsight, Fern could only agree; the trouble with hindsight is, it always turns up too damn late. 'While I was changing Amelie, I poked around the master bedroom. Just like Evka said, it was full of Penny's face creams and her robe and whatnot.'

'Pretty damning evidence.'

'Except . . . where was your shaving kit? Your Aqua di Parma aftershave? Your nose-hair clipper?'

'You're a right little Poirot. They were all in the spare room, where I slept. Alone.'

'Then I saw something that clinched it.' Fern wasn't referring to the pregnancy test; the plastic stick played a central role in another love story, not Fern and Adam's.

The life it changed was Evka's; she'd taken the test while cleaning Adam's flat, but was too fearful to read the result. 'Please, Fern, you check, yes?' she'd begged. Fern had been able to whisper 'negative' into Evka's ear, just an hour or so before finding Patrik on the doorstep. His exquisitely timed arrival had saved Evka once and for all from a crazed promiscuity that had stopped being fun.

'More accurately, I *didn't* see something that clinched it.' There had been no book by the right-hand side of the bed. 'No way could you nod off without a few pages of a bedtime story about a hatchet-wielding reanimated Nazi. No book in master bed, no Adam in master bed. Case closed.'

'You know me so well,' said Adam, grave now, wondering at the importance of it.

'Were you aware of Penny's red underwear, by the way? And the PVC boots?'

'Christ, no.' After thinking for a moment, Adam looked hopefully at his reinstated partner and said, with a raised eyebrow, 'Although . . .'

'Not a chance, mate.'

'Worth a try,' said Adam with a wink.

'It really wasn't.'

'So . . .' Adam brought them back to the narrative of Fern's epiphany. 'Out you came, bursting to tell me you knew there's nothing going between me and Penny.'

'Or "Peni", as I had to spell it.'

'Unfortunately, Einstein, I had *no idea* that you suspected me of sleeping with her in the first place. So when you said that you knew about us—'

'You thought I was accusing you?' Fern let out a mock scream. 'What are we like?'

'We're like fucking idiots,' said Adam happily.

'Tell me about Penny,' said Fern. 'I need to know. How far it went. How you felt. The lot, Adam.'

'Right. So. Um. Well.'

'In your own time,' said Fern.

'Look, after you chucked me out, or I left you, or whatever the hell happened, I was lonely. No, I was *alone*. I can't find a word to do it justice. I'd always shared everything with you, and suddenly there was nobody to talk to.'

Me too, thought Fern with strenuous empathy.

'When you and I *did* talk it was strained and catty. I

was so proud of Kinky Mimi but you rolled your eyes about it. Penny was *there*. She was interested. She believed in the band.'

'True. But Penny's also one of the reasons we split up.' Seeing Adam's puzzlement, she said, gently, certainly, 'How would you have felt if I'd fibbed about a new male friend? If I gave them a new, feminine name and lied about how often we met?'

'I'd feel bad,' conceded Adam. He sighed. 'Very bad. It was dumb to keep her a secret. That made it look seedy, when in fact it was just business.' Adam's lips twisted the way they did when he was preparing to say something he'd rather leave unsaid. 'It was exciting, Fern, to have, well, a *fan*.' Adam winced. 'I should've told you about the lunches and the coffees. Now I can see why you flipped when she moved in. I didn't see it through your eyes.'

'And I didn't see it through *yours*.' After all those months of blaming each other, Fern and Adam were rushing to claim all the blame for themselves. 'I stopped listening.' It was the biggest single regret of her life. 'I stopped cheerleading. Kinky Mimi are bloody *ace*, Adam.'

'We can come up with reasons why we fell apart, but for now I'm only interested in reasons why we should get back together, Fernie. Let's clear up the whole Penny saga. At the time, I needed her. She was a fairy godmother. When Penny's on your side, it feels like you can do anything, plus, sorry, but I liked her company. No, present tense – I *like* ol' Pen. But sleeping with her . . . come on, Fern. Do you think I'm mad? There'd be a ton of small print to read the minute you got each other's knickers off. If I'd known you were jumping to conclusions—'

'There was no jumping involved,' interrupted Fern. 'Penny took me by the hand and led me to the conclusions. But, listen –' she said, noting the slump of Adam's shoulders – 'I'm not out for vengeance.' Fern had the imagination to put herself in Penny's (considerably more expensive) shoes, and was compassionate enough to forgive her. *Almost* forgive her.

Adam looked uncomfortable. 'At first I didn't notice anything odd about Penny. I just thought we got on great, that we worked well together, that I had a friend I sorely needed. Now I see there was no rat problem at her flat, that when she moved into the master suite she expected me to share it with her, but it took ages for me to realize that she, well, *liked* me.'

'You needn't look so bloody pleased with yourself. Penny doesn't *like* you, Adam. The woman's in love with you.'

'Is it love when it's not reciprocated?'

'Yes,' said Fern emphatically. No love goes to waste; no love should be insulted by being told it's something else. Especially not today, with love dripping from the midsummer trees and cocooning Homestead House in its non-judgemental, non-denominational embrace. 'So, we've established that the woman loves you. Now tell me . . . does she know she can't have you?'

'I told her about my cunning plan to change the lyrics and throw myself at your feet. She was the only one who knew.'

Not quite. Fern remembered Nora's comment about Adam being in love. *She meant with me!* 'Were you gentle?'

'I think so.'

'You only *think* so?' Fern hoped Adam had broken the news softly, with no faux naivety about the effect it would have. Apparently Penny had been gracious, supportive, even managing to listen when he rehearsed the updated lyrics. Penny could chew up anything – nails, barbed wire – if it meant pleasing Adam. 'She smiled at me when you sang.' It had been a flash of pure communication between the women; Penny had handed Adam over, all the fight gone from her. 'I'll be kind to her in future. Penny's in pain.'

For now, Adam said, Penny would live in the apartment rent-free until a buyer was found. After that, she'd be released into the wild. Fern suspected that Penny's history was littered with Adams; in all likelihood her future would be the same.

Tonight, though, was no time to dwell on Percy Waddingsworthington. 'Sorry for spying on you, Adam.'

'S'all right. It's nice to know you care enough to be disgustingly underhand.'

'I never stopped caring, Ads.' Fern felt able to call him that now. 'Not for one second. It was all front. I had to protect myself while you flitted around, being a pop star, living the high life . . .'

'I really, really miss Baked Potato Fridays,' said Adam sorrowfully.

As Adam opened up, Fern was shocked at the turmoil beneath the surface. Adam had been jolted to his foundations, first by the unexpected success and wealth, then by the collapse of their relationship.

'Not having to earn a living is liberating, yeah, but when you can do anything, what do you do?' Head back, eyes closed, he said, 'Without you and Ollie and Tallie, I was just a waster with loads of time on his hands.'

'Yet you looked so cocky,' said Fern. 'I should have seen through it.'

'How? Even I half believed my own hype. The only way was forward; going back seemed impossible. Even so, moving on – with Penny, with A. N. Other – was out of the question.' Adam put his head to one side. 'Unlike some people I could mention.'

'Hal,' said Fern heavily. It was inevitable that conversation had to turn in that direction sooner or later. 'In a nutshell, I moved on because you'd moved on.'

'Except I hadn't.'

'I know that *now*. I'm not saying it was revenge, or tit for tat.' Fern wanted to do justice to Hal without upsetting her back-from-the-dead partner. 'But, God, it helped.'

'Didn't help me much.'

'I'm sorry. For hurting you.' Fern couldn't regret anything so lovely as Hal, but she could wish it hadn't happened. 'Will it be a stain, a blot on our copybook?' She swallowed hard.

'I won't let it,' said Adam. 'I just won't let it.'

'Thank you.' Love was up to its old tricks, doing the heavy lifting, working a minor miracle in a suburban kitchen.

'Fern, let's say Penny did mislead you—'

'No, let's not just say it. She *did*.' This was an important point, one that had to be agreed upon before they moved forward.

'OK, OK, but it didn't work, did it, Fern? She couldn't drive a wedge between us, however hard she tried. Because here we are.'

'Where's here, Adam? Is this really it? Should we talk things out, or make a deal, or take it slowly, or—'

'Let's take it extremely fast,' said Adam. 'I'm home and I want to stay. This old house, with all its rotting windows and its uneven floors and its horrific tiles in the downstairs loo, is where I want to be. With you. And our children. And Amelie. And Nora. And Evka. And Patrik. How come everybody wants to live here?'

'Because it's bloody fabulous here. Even the tiles in the downstairs loo. They're *fashionably retro*, Adam, not horrific. And you and me,' she leaned in for a kiss just because she could, 'we're fashionably retro, too.'

DJ Dirty Tequila's chill-out playlist suited the mood as weary dancers flopped into chairs, coffee was drained, minicabs called by tipsy people trying to sound sober as they recited their addresses.

Penny made unsteadily for the bar, which by now was running low.

Hope she likes Cointreau and Tizer, thought Fern, making a mental note to assign Ollie to walking-Penny-home duty when he'd finished his set. *If that's the right word*. Surveying the embers of the wedding from a bench at the dark end of the garden, beyond the lanterns' reach, Fern and Adam sat side by side on a bench, sharing a half-full bottle of Dom Perignon. 'Makes you think, doesn't it, a night like tonight?'

'Yup.' Adam tipped the bottle into his mouth. 'Think what, exactly?'

'About life. Love. Longevity.'

'And other things beginning with L. All in all,' said Adam, 'we were good at splitting up.'

'Not *that* good, thankfully.'

'I didn't get any cake.' Adam pouted as he realized. 'Is it all gone?'

'Every last mouthful.' Fern had been up half the night icing. Only at the last moment had she realized she didn't have a plate big enough to hold the chocolate/vanilla colossus. Setting off grumpily to panic-buy a dish, she'd almost tripped over a brown-wrapped package on the front step.

Curvaceous, pearly, the hand-made platter was enormous; a truly celebratory piece. She'd recognized the style. It was a sweet touch from Hal. A lasting memento.

'What's the sigh for?' asked Adam.

'Nothing. Everything. Oh God, I'm off again.' Fern reached for the hanky in Adam's pocket as a light went on up in the eaves. 'Looks like Evka and Patrik have retired for the night.' Fern dabbed her eyes. 'Do you think they'll ever move out?'

'People don't move out of Homestead House,' said Adam, wryly.

'You did.'

'Not for long.'

Fitting her cheek into the spot where it was meant to be, against Adam's chest, Fern murmured, 'If we just sit here perhaps the guests will let themselves out and the dishes will wash themselves.'

A long, joyful note of laughter penetrated all the way to their hidey-hole at the end of the garden.

'Layla!' they smiled together.

'She looks so *well*,' said Adam. 'Women are so cute when they're pregnant.'

'Don't know about cute,' said Fern. 'We're warriors when we've got a baby inside us. Especially when . . .'

They both fell silent.

'They're *strong*,' said Adam. 'God knows what I'd do in their shoes.'

The ground had tilted beneath Fern when Layla had Skyped to share the results of the amniocentesis. Fern had kept repeating, 'They're *sure*? They're absolutely certain?' until Layla had almost snapped, 'Fern, they're sure. It's a girl and she's tested positive for Down's syndrome.'

Furious with the uncaring universe, Fern had said, 'What now?'

'What else?' Layla had shrugged. 'We wait for our daughter to come out and say hello.'

Fern had been struck dumb. By the courage and the love and, if she was honest, fear.

'Will you be godmother?' Layla had asked. There was defiance in her voice, and the tiniest hint of a tear.

'Hell, yeah.'

'You're the perfect godmother,' Layla had said, 'for our perfect daughter.' Then they'd both cried, but the tears hadn't been desperate ones. They'd laughed too. 'No wringing of hands, OK?' Layla had warned. 'Luc and I have longed for a baby, and now it's happening. We're going to love her.'

'No, you're going to lurve her!'

'We're going to la-la-la-LURVE her!'

A simple plan, but a foolproof one.

Looking up at Adam, Fern said, 'Let's be really biased godparents. Let's side with our goddaughter on everything, and give her sweets and let her stay up late.'

'Good idea.' Adam kissed her nose. His lips strayed down her face, then stopped short of her mouth. 'Did Nora seem all right to you today? She kept yammering on about giving us a wedding present, as if it was us getting married.'

'Kiss me!' Fern was greedy about Adam's kisses since she'd regained access to his erogenous zones. 'Mmm. I think you've got better at kissing. To answer your question, Nora's definitely OK, but for some reason she bought us a present. She'll give it to us later, she said.'

Another noise bit through the night: a reedy wail that could only be one member of the family.

'Poor Amelie. It's way past her bedtime.'

'Spoken like a true grandma.'

'Of all your pet names for me, that's my least favourite.' Something struck Fern and she said happily, 'I never think of myself as a step-granny. She really is *ours*, isn't she?'

'In all the ways that matter, yes. DNA's meaningless, I've decided. I think she's going to be musical.'

'Maz was at the door earlier.'

'What?' Adam sat up. 'Why didn't you say?'

'Because I knew you'd react like that.'

'Why can't he stay away like he promised? The little sod abandoned poor Donna when she needed him.'

'He's young.'

'We've all been young. It doesn't excuse him.'

'Better learn to tolerate him, Ads. He'll be around forever. The kids bring people into our lives and we have to go with the flow. A few years from now we'll be exchanging worried glances about Tallie's boyfriends.'

'Don't say that. I've only just got used to her having teeth and forming whole sentences.'

'What's going on?' Fern sat up, peered down the lawn to the house. 'The music's stopped.'

The guests were chattering like monkeys, and Fern heard Ollie say, 'She's down there, I think, at the end of the garden.'

Fern stood up as a figure stole through the blackness, its outline firming up as it drew nearer.

Stock still, Fern could only gape.

'This must be Nora's present,' said Adam. 'The clever old bat.'

Fern's mother, a little crumpled from her long journey, stood a little way away from her daughter. 'Am I welcome, love?'

Fern ran to her mum, and they were both sorry and they were both happy, and Adam left them to it.

Homestead House was full once more.

Up in the loft, Evka and Patrik were having audibly

athletic sex: Fern insisted they were playing 'indoor football' to Tallulah and Carey, who were sleeping head-to-toe in Tallie's bed.

In the spare room, Fern's mum was making herself comfortable, texting pictures of Amelie to Dave, and holding a framed photo of her deceased first husband to her heart while she had the good long cry she so sorely needed.

Out in the garden, the lights had gone off in the annexe.

A couple of streets away, still the Homestead empire, Ollie and Donna were crashed out with Amelie, who took up the lion's share of the new Ikea bed.

At the window of their bedroom, Fern and Adam drew the curtains and turned to each other.

'It looks like a bomb site out there,' murmured Fern against Adam's lips.

'I love it when you talk dirty.'

'How did I let you talk me into clearing up tomorrow?' Fern cuffed him around the head, lovingly.

'Everybody'll help. We've got all day.'

'I should just steep that lasagne dish.' Fern turned away, but was twirled neatly back into Adam's arms.

'No,' he said sternly, as if shooing Boudicca away from a delicious cowpat. 'I don't want to let you out of my sight.' It felt a little like an affair, but with zero guilt.

Like newlyweds themselves, they were being thoughtful, careful with each other. Secretly, Fern looked forward to when they'd be an old pair of slippers once more; she craved normality. There was a future to-do list already writing itself in her head.

More lovemaking.
Less criticism.
More fun.
Less time spent as CEO of Homestead Enterprises.
More good old-fashioned togetherness.

Adam's kisses were intense, as if the months apart had scooped out a void that only Fern's body could fill. As he led her to the bed – their bed – she remembered how he'd wordlessly handed her a letter out in the garden, as goodbyes were said and good luck wishes rained down on them from the departing guests. Now the note sat with its comrades in the faded box, but she could quote it already.

Dear Fern

Two Great Rifts are enough for any couple. Let's keep talking to each other, and snogging each other, and being each other's best friend. We almost threw a diamond in the trash but now we can spend the rest of our lives making up for it.

I want to empty your bins forever, mum of my kids, maker of my cuppas, sexiest thing ever.

A xxx

Lying together on the rumpled bed, messily entwined and perfectly comfortable, Fern listened to the house ticking and shifting in the dark. All the people she loved – and that figure had expanded in the past year – were within cuddling range.

'How poor are we?' whispered Fern, hoping Adam wouldn't move.

'Not really poor. The same as we were before *Roomies* with a bit extra. We're fine.'

'But we're not wealthy any more, thanks to Lincoln Speed's offensive meltdown?'

'Nope. Sorry, Fernie.'

No doubt Lincoln Speed would go on to star in his own rehab reality programme, but *Roomies* was dead in the water.

'For richer, for poorer, remember?' Fern played with Adam's chest hair. He had just the right amount; not enough to remind her of the filter in the dryer; not so little that her thoughts turned to raw chicken.

'The money just complicated everything. Now it's just you and me and, well, the fifty other people in this house. We can have the perfect marriage.'

'Perfect?' Fern curled her lip. 'I've gone off that word.' The wedding had gone to plan, yet had been only a blurred copy of the image in her head, an image placed there by the countless magazine articles and TV programmes and Instagram images she'd gulped down unthinkingly over the years.

The pristine cloths on each table were spotted with Ribena smears and red wine. The delicate flower arrangements wilted. Binkie had thrown up a furball on the cake. Tallie had mangled her divine but simple head dress. Nora had proudly told the congregation she wasn't a virgin.

'Today was perfect,' said Adam.

'Actually, yes, it was.' Fern might have to redefine the word.

'I've had an offer for the penthouse, or, as you prefer to call it, my mid-life crisis den.'

'Good.' The sooner that flat was off their hands, the better. Fern had plans to spend the profit on Homestead House. The roof needed attention, and the gutters were full of moss. Now, more than ever, the house represented Adam and Fern; she'd give it some TLC, tidy the roof, paint the shed. 'You are . . .' She blinked hard. 'You are *glad* to be back in this house, aren't you?'

'What?' Adam sounded as upset as he was surprised. 'Are you seriously asking me that?' He squeezed her hard. 'This place is the centre of the universe.'

THE END

Acknowledgements

This book wouldn't be in your hands right now if it wasn't for my brilliant editor Caroline Hogg, and the rest of the team at Pan Macmillan. Thank you for your insight, dedication and breezy professionalism.

Thank you also, Matthew and Niamh, for allowing me to lock myself away and write.

Dinner Party Recipes and Tips

by Claire Sandy

The first tip about having a dinner party is don't, under any circumstances, call it a dinner party. 'Come round for a bite to eat!' is the best way to phrase it. Lower expectations, and then surpass them. You needn't produce a towering pyramid of profiteroles, just feed them well, treat them kindly, and get them a wee bit squiffy. Below are my rules. This is hard-won advice, people: I suffered so you don't have to.

1. *Choose your guests with care.* Invite people you like. Sounds simple, but I've often deviated from this cardinal rule and I've lived to regret it. If the people you like are also chatty, greedy and appreciative, so much the better. They'll forgive your little mistakes. Never throw a grudge dinner; cooking an elaborate meal in order to impress (and thereby somehow *demolish*) a love/ work rival, your horrible ma-in-law, or that couple across the road who cast sniffy looks at your window boxes does. Not. Work.
2. *Don't overdo it.* Three courses? Are you kidding? When every plate, spoon and pot in the house is already in

use? I've never offered a proper starter and I've had no complaints. A meal, especially with coffee and all the lovely chocolatey treats the guests bring (if you've abided by rule one, above), entails long hours sitting on one's bum, so stand your guests up for nibbles, and let them roam.

3. *Let your guests serve themselves.* Personally, I eat like Henry VIII whenever I go out for dinner, but it's kinder to let your friends pace themselves, and discreetly leave out the element of the meal they secretly loathe. Lay out the food in your prettiest (which doesn't mean poshest) dishes, add serving spoons and let them graze. (And if you invite my husband, ensure he goes last or nobody else will have anything to eat.)

4. *Keep calm.* This is a cliché, I know, but your visitors really are here to see you. The food is a bonus. If something goes wrong, look hard at it, swear to yourself (this helps) and think how it can be rescued. I once made a pavlova that looked like . . . well, let's not go into that, but I smashed it up and laid it out with strawberries and cream and presented it as a do-it-yourself Eton Mess. I've had to stick slices of beef Wellington under the grill while diners sat salivating, knives and forks in their hands. If you overcook the carrots because you've been dousing yourself with Aperol spritzers, throw out the little buggers and declare that carrots are off the menu. Go with it.

Below are three of my tried and trusted recipes. Like the magazines say, these are triple-tested. Dammit, they're tested into double figures. With these in your repertoire, you can build a meal around them with confidence. So what are you waiting for? Look up 'Nice People' in your contacts, set a date, and get planning.

A KILLER NIBBLE: Marinated Parmesan

Yes, at first sight this looks like a heart attack-inducing bowl of cheese but oh, the taste. It's divinely subtle and moreish, salty and spicy, and it will all disappear; there may even be fist fights at your kitchen island.

Roughly chop your (rather pricey, sorry) 250g chunk of parmesan until it looks like rubble (not dust – this is a rubble situation, please). In a bowl, combine the cheese with one crushed clove of garlic, two finely chopped spring onions, one teaspoon of chilli flakes and 125ml of your favourite extra virgin olive oil (the one you're a bit scared to use because it cost so much). Give it a stir, and leave the whole thing to its own devices for a couple of hours. Decant into another bowl and stir in finely chopped oregano. Guests just dip in with their fingers, invariably muttering about 'dairy' and 'cholesterol', and just as invariably eating it *all*.

A KILLER SIDE: Baked Rice

This bulks up a plate, looks delicate and tastes delicious. It has a delicate but definite savouriness, and is the recipe

I'm most asked for when I 'entertain'. This serves four normal people, or just me and my husband.

Whack on your oven to 190°C (170°C fan). In an oven-proof pan with a lid, melt some oil and butter and sauté six chopped shallots (I cheat and use frozen ones). When the shallots are soft, chuck in (over your shoulder, if you like) two teaspoons of cumin seeds. Add 250g basmati rice and 50g toasted almonds, and stir until the rice is coated with the lovely buttery sludge. Season well at this point. Pour in 550ml hot vegetable stock, add two lime leaves and bring to the boil. Lid on, and into the oven it goes for twenty minutes. This will keep warm-ish for a while, so no need to time it too carefully. It tastes just as good at room temperature, although remember to tease it a little with a fork before setting it out.

KILLER DESSERT: Bark

Yes, bark. I suppose it's called that because it looks a little like the bark from a tree. Your dinner needs a swan-song to send your guests out into the cold feeling full and cared for; this indulgent, chocolatey, unthinkably calorific treat will do the trick. Combine with ice cream, or hand out with the coffee and those stupid fruit teas everybody's so mad about these days.

Line a baking tray with baking paper. In a medium saucepan, melt a generous knob of butter (generous knob! Made myself laugh!) and heat up 100g of unsalted cashews, a pinch of allspice and 1 tablespoon of maple syrup. Let this gooey mess cool.

Separately, melt 200g milk chocolate and 200g dark chocolate. Pour them on to the baking tray and swirl them together in a carefree, arty way until you have a blobby chocolate shape. Roughly chop your cooled buttery nuts and scatter them over the chocolate. More melting – this time it's 25g white chocolate, which you drizzle over the whole slab. If you like, use a toothpick to tease the white chocolate into feathery patterns. If you like the taste of chilli with chocolate, now's the time to scatter a few flakes.

Let it set, and then ease the whole abstract creation off the baking paper and on to a large platter. Allow your guests to break pieces off for themselves and expect conversation to slow down into a series of orgasmic grunts.

What Would Mary Berry Do?

The perfect bake is no piece of cake

Marie Dunwoody doesn't want for much in life. She has a lovely husband, three wonderful children, and a business of her own. But her cupcakes are crap. Her meringues are runny and her biscuits rock-hard. She cannot bake for toffee. Or, for that matter, make toffee.

Marie can't ignore the disappointed looks anymore, nor continue to be shamed by her neighbour and nemesis, Lucy Gray. Lucy whips up perfect profiteroles with one hand while ironing her bed sheets with the other. Marie's had enough: this is the year it all changes. She vows to follow – to the letter – recipes from the Queen of Baking, and at all times ask, 'What would Mary Berry do?'

Husband Robert has noticed that his boss takes crumb structure as seriously as budget cuts, and with redundancies on the horizon he too puts on a pinny. Twins Rose and Iris are happy to eat all the half-baked mistakes that come their way, but big brother Angus is more distant than usual, as if something is troubling him. And there is no one as nosy as a matching pair of nine-year-old girls . . .

Marie starts to realize that the wise words of Mary Berry can help her with more than just a Victoria sponge. But can Robert save the wobbling soufflé that is his career? And is Lucy's sweet demeanour hiding something secretly sour?

A Very Big House in the Country

One house. Three families.
What could possibly go wrong?

For one long, hot summer in Devon, three families share one very big house in the country. The Herreras are two tired parents, three grumbling children and one promiscuous dog. The Littles: she's gorgeous, he's loaded – but maybe the equation for a truly happy marriage is a bit more complicated than that? As for the Browns, they seem oddly jumpy – especially around each other.

By the pool new friendships blossom, but at the kitchen door resentments simmer. Summer crushes form, secrets are swapped and when the adults loosen their inhibitions with litres of white wine they start to get a little too honest . . .

Mother hen to all, Evie Herrera has a life-changing announcement to make, one that could shatter the summer holiday and rock the foundations of her family. But will someone else beat her to it?

Snowed in for Christmas

Everybody wants it to snow at Christmas . . .
Don't they?

Asta's plane touches down in Ireland as the first flakes of snow begin to settle. As the weather worsens, it turns what should be a flying visit into a snowed-in Yuletide with her chaotic family.

Asta fled her childhood village years ago, with a secret hidden deep within her. That secret is now a feisty sixteen-year-old, Kitty, who's keen to meet her long-lost relatives. It seems there are many family mysteries waiting to be unwrapped, along with the presents under the tree . . .

Missing the man she left behind in London, yet drawn to a man she meets in Ireland, Asta is caught in an emotional snowstorm.

Maybe this Christmas Asta will find a cure for her long-broken heart?

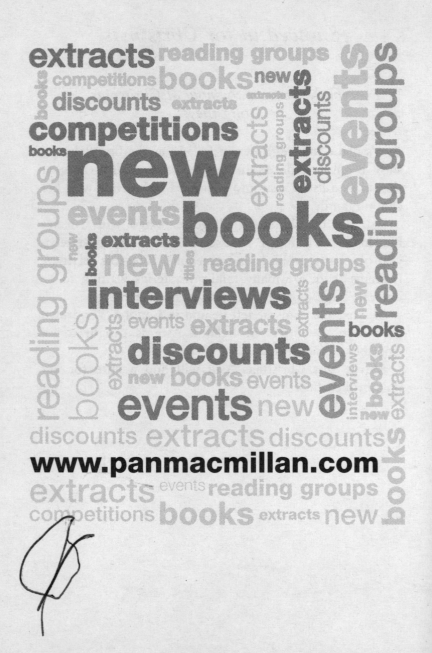

extracts reading groups
competitions books new
discounts extracts extracts
competitions new events
books extracts discounts events
new reading groups
events books
extracts new titles reading groups
interviews events
events extracts discounts
discounts new books events books
events new interviews
discounts extracts discounts
www.panmacmillan.com
extracts events reading groups
competitions books extracts new